CHASE MARTIN

A Song of Triumph

The Scorching Fields

Raimund

Flames licked the night sky. They danced and swirled red and yellow and blue, creating a show for the gods.

Raimund's face seemed to melt away into the snow. He fell to the ground, waiting for it to be over. For the dragon to burn him alive. For death to take over. He wondered whether he would see his mother and father again. They too were taken by fire.

But the darkness of death never came. Instead, the darkness became eye level with him. The puffs of breath blew his hair and cloak. He peeled his eyes open and saw the beast's snout only a foot from his own nose. *This cannot happen. Not to me. Why have the gods cursed me?* He had never shaken so much as he stood. His footing was unstable; any gust could've knocked him to the ground, but the storm that was wailing had stopped. It seemed the snowflakes had frozen in the air.

Raimund could finally see his sword near a tuft of rocks. *I can get it and cut this beast's throat. Bring the head with me to Viguran.* But something stopped him. He had frozen like the snow and ice. The beast's yellow eyes stared into his soul. Were the gods judging him? Was the monster debating eating him?

His foot trembled as he took a slow step back. Then another. A thicket of trees was behind him. He could get to the forest and disappear, unless the blue flames had burned it down. His feet carried him back. The beast never moved. As Raimund reached the trees, he saw the size of the monster. A long black neck held a head larger than any manor in Viguran. Long shadows stretched from either side like arms. Claws bigger than ten swords combined curled from scaly legs. *This is not true. I died in the flames. Potter was the only one to live.*

But it all felt real. He was standing across from a dragon.

His hand found a tree and a broken branch. That would be his sword for the time being. Never taking his eyes off the beast, he disappeared into the forest. It was darker than the dragon's shadows. His branch vanished from view. Once his hands went dark, he knew he had to go back or get lost for the wolves to find him. He slunk back toward the edge of the forest and hid behind a fallen tree. The dragon huffed smoke while it stood like a statue. He wondered how far Potter, the large boy, had raced. It hadn't been but a few minutes. The dragon could eat him after devouring Raimund. Were the flames visible to him? *Stay away.* He hoped Potter could hear his thoughts.

The night lasted for what seemed like days. Raimund never slept. His eyes were stuck on the beast and the yellow eyes that looked back. *Once morning comes, I can escape through the trees.* But the sun never rose. He thought he was dead again. How the light never came above the peaks, he couldn't know. But it would, and he would rejoice when it did.

The beast that killed Sile for some unknown reason couldn't stop staring either. Her charred body and burning home haunted Raimund. The smell of her skin as it cooked, and the horrid sight of her melted flesh and eyes. *As long as I keep its attention, Potter will survive. He'll make it south. Then it's up to me.* He had to see Tundavik and Devro and Mar and Yvanne and everyone else he left behind. He had to show them he had survived. Had to make sure they survived. Raimund grabbed a branch as tears filled his eyes. The only way he could get away was if he killed this dragon, stopped it from harming the mountain, and got revenge for poor Sile.

He wrested his branch free from the snowy ground and stepped out of hiding. A low hiss filled the air as the dragon's yellow eyes pierced him. That didn't stop him. His feet carried him, and soon he was running at the beast. He screamed out with his branch ready to kill. The dragon didn't move. "Die beast!" Raimund yelled as he threw the branch at the great snout. The dragon followed with its eyes of summer as Raimund dove under its wing, leapt to the rocks, and found his sword.

"For Sile, you bastard! You killed her!" The dragon's scales were like armor, and the sword did nothing, but Raimund didn't stop cutting at the beast. "How dare you! She was kind! She wished to see her daughter one more time! You killed her! You killed her! You killed her!" He drove the metal point into the dragon's leg, but it was no use. The dragon swatted him away like a bug and ripped the sword out, which fell into a thousand pieces.

"Die." Raimund cried with his face in the snow. "Die." His eyes screamed for sleep, his stomach for hunger, himself for death.

In the great shadow cast on the mountain, Raimund shivered. It was cold even under a beast that breathed fire. He crawled away, tears frozen on his cheeks. *Kill me.* He wanted to shout, but couldn't muster the strength. *Burn me.* But the beast had its opportunity. Raimund didn't know how he was still alive.

He stood as he got away from the dragon and faced its snout. His body melted as the scaly beast huffed on him. It was like he was in a warm wool bed. "What do you want?" His breathing was heavy, but the dragon listened. The dragon's head came closer, doubling in size. He let out a low hiss. Then his legs went. It felt as if an avalanche could come at any moment. His long black scales for fore and hind legs came forward. Raimund took a step back to keep from being crushed. The beast moved past him, its gape large, snow and wind spiraling about the mountaintop. Raimund's hair whipped at his face. Large, leathery wings were flapping and flinging trees from the forest toward the ground.

Then, the dragon lifted off and flew into the night sky.

His eyes grew as the shadow overtook the mountain, making the snow look like ash. He stood with the help of a tree limb and felt the rush of freezing air on his face and arms. It penetrated his clothes like knives. The beast roared and soared. The flapping of the wings was louder than anything Raimund had ever heard. Orange flames licked from its lips, and a trail of smoke showed the path. The dragon dove below the clouds of snow.

Where are you going? Raimund thought to himself. Maybe the dragon wasn't all that bad. Maybe Sile's death was an accident, and Raimund should just let it be. *Unless the beast is going after Potter now,* the thought made him sweat in the freezing cold.

"The dragon wishes for you to follow," a familiar voice said from beyond the trees. It was a woman's voice, and it echoed. A smattering of crows cawed and flew overhead. Sile emerged from the trees. Her red hair was as bright as fire — no — actually on fire. The flames danced on her head, wisped with the wind. "The dragon calls for you to follow, yet you do not answer."

Raimund kicked snow halfheartedly. "You're not real," he whispered.

"I am very real," she said as her footsteps brought her closer. Bare in the winter snow. Her clothes were tattered, like she had fought off a bear, but her skin had no cuts or bruises.

"You're like that monster I saw with Potter," he yelled over the wind. "You wish to lure me. Kill me." Raimund backed up, but he hit some rocks. His black trousers turned white from the snow, his face hard as ice. "Stay away."

"I do not wish to kill you," Sile's voice echoed as if it weren't actually coming from her mouth. "I am here to help. Just like I helped before when we rescued Potter from the prison." Her body seemed to twinkle like a star, her hair always fire, her footsteps leaving a trail of smoke.

Sile reached out her hand and waited, but Raimund shook his head. He wouldn't touch her. *She isn't real.* He repeated to himself.

"Come," Sile said, "come with me and the dragon and see what's in store for you."

"The dragon will kill me if you don't first." Raimund used

the small rocks to hold himself up as the wind and snow and ice beat at him. "Leave me be. Let me leave this mountain. Let me live."

Sile wrested her hand back. Her nostrils flared in anger for a split second before going back to a smile. "There is only one way off this mountain. We both know it. I was killed. Potter will be next. Either you go with the dragon or you follow our fate." Raimund closed his eyes as the fire on her head grew brighter than the sun.

When he opened them, she was gone.

The snowstorm died down again as Raimund clung to the rocks. He gripped his cloak as tight as he could, his knuckles aching. The sun rose in the east. Strips of light flooded through the gaps in the mountain peaks. Raimund could barely keep his eyes open. He knew if he fell asleep, he would freeze to death. He would never see if Potter made it. If Devro took Vigur. If Mar stayed safe.

The sound of wings filled the air. *Flap, flap, flap.* He braced for the ground to shake as the dragon slammed onto the mountain. The beast missed Raimund by a foot. Its head was red and breath warm. The occasional flame escaped teeth. The beast's head, larger than a house, lay at Raimund's feet. "What do you want now?"

The dragon didn't move. The giant head and long neck bent low enough for Raimund to do the unthinkable. *Stupid,* he told himself. *Whatever that thing was, it wasn't Sile. You're just a crazed fool.* The dragon moved its head closer. Air from the gaping nostrils warmed Raimund. He had no idea what he was thinking when he climbed atop the dragon as if it were a horse.

Then he flew into the sunrise.

Tundavik

The air was thick with smoke. Tundavik could barely even see the fire that caused it, but in the distance was a brilliant light. He made his way toward it, over the bodies of the dead, charred and smoking; down a rough hill made of rocks … or bones; up a great mountain, jumping to reach the peak. And below the mountain, he saw a million men in armor. Swords and spears raised in battle. Ships from the ocean beyond launched boulders from trebuchets.

Then Tundavik's face melted as a black dragon, larger than the mountain he stood on, flew overhead. Thick flames shot from the beast's maw. Everyone below caught fire. Screams filled the air, and he had to cover his ears as they bled. Entire forests burned as the dragon flew past. Every town crumbled to ash. A small rider on its back commanded the monster to lay waste to the entire world.

A woman appeared in front of him, her body a work of art of tiny bumps in slithering patterns. "You must go to Ritaeum. You must find the orb. Nhamcaryn is coming, and you must stop it." She spoke without moving her mouth as the smoke bellowed all around them, twisting and snarling and grasping at Tundavik. Pulling him down into the ground. It was like a million hands all tugging at him. "You must find the orb," the woman said again. "You must stop the coming of the dragon."

***

Then he woke.

He grabbed his face to make sure it hadn't melted. Sweat dripped down his body, cooling him even more than the rain outside. Glem sat in the bed next to his. "You mutter a lot in your sleep," the young boy said.

Tundavik's heart was racing, his chest feeling like it was going to burst, his head spinning. The young boy jumped out of bed and went to the other side of the small house, where the cookfire was burning with a pot of stew over it. "Just roots," Glem said. "Father couldn't find much with all the flooding." The house was smaller than most stables. A fire used for cooking as much as heating, took up the center of the home. There was one bed, large enough for Glem and his parents to share. Tundavik slept on a cot just below the family bed. It wasn't anything great, but he was glad to be invited into a home all the same.

A middle-aged man, younger than Tundavik, named Gordo, nodded with his son. "It's hard out there. Haven't seen so much flooding in years. 'Tis a bad omen." He shook his head and *tsked*. "I worry what your army being here means for me and mine."

Tundavik wiped sweat from his brow. Sticky from sleep, not the fire. "We'll be on our way soon enough. If they had built a bridge over the river, we wouldn't have this problem."

9

"Pa says that's the lord's duty. We don't have no money for that," Glem said. The boy was nearly a teenager, older than a few of the boys who had joined the march from Storyah. Glem had attached himself to Tundavik ever since he saw him ride into their village on horseback.

"But now there's a war," Gordo said and pursed his lips toward Tundavik.

Tundavik got out of bed and found his clothes. It wasn't very soft, but it was better than sleeping on the ground, and he was thanking the gods every day he finally had a sturdy roof over his head. Not all men were as lucky. Others pitched tents or slept under trees that leaked water onto them. Glem found a plate for the stew and handed it to Tundavik. It tasted like the earth.

"I still thank you," he told the father. "Any idea when the flooding will stop?"

"When the mountains stop crying," Gordo said as he sharpened a knife. "Swallow's season is always full of water. The peach trees love it. Us? Not so much."

"So you stay on the north bank and never go south?" Tundavik asked as he finished the stew. The River Samosay was just to the south. It had been engulfed with snowmelt from the Asara and the rain that seemed never to end. The downpour had made it harder to travel down the coast from Storyah, but not impossible. They crossed the rivers Arner and Midlock easily enough. They had stone bridges built. But the Samosay River had nothing until the wooden bridges near Riverton. Considering he had seen wooden debris in the floods, Tundavik doubted they were even still standing.

"Meret cries her season is over," Glem said. "At least that's what Ma told me. Where is she anyhow?"

Gordo sniffled. "She went to find some clean water. Not sure we're gonna find it out there, what with all the pissing and shitting and flooding."

"I told my men to go downstream," Tundavik laced his boots. "The swell may bring it back though. When the war is won, I'll remember your hospitality. I promise that."

"But will the captured king?" Gordo said and went back to sharpening his knife.

When the letter had arrived from Whitehall that Devro was missing, Tundavik had sweated from nerves. But when the letter from Vigur arrived, it was like a punch to the gut. The usurper, Ultiir, had Devro. At any chance uncle could kill nephew. *Hopefully Ultiir has a shred of dignity,* he thought, but he was still worried. He hadn't seen the boy in months. They had crossed the Asara and into Whitehall, then Tundavik left with Sir Mar for Storyah. Landing in Gereduss and finding Mar seemed a lifetime ago now.

"Well," he stood, "I best be tending to the army. I'll see you for bed." Gordo shook his head slowly, like he was disappointed, and Glem nodded.

Tundavik didn't want to step outside, but he had to see what trouble the men were getting into. He had already admonished a few for looting. Others visited the camp followers too many times. Tundavik threatened to cut their cocks off if they slept with a whore again. It was different this time. Not like the Bezir campaign at all. Back then, the men wanted to fight, to win, to kill. But those were the mites. His men now were going against their brethren, potentially distant family. Tundavik had to keep them focused so they wouldn't think of that.

Tundavik's boots were filled with water as he hopped off the step to the house. The banks disappeared as the river bloated. Many of his men had tried to build a crossing over the River Samosay, but failed each time. The river surged and touched everything in its path. Fields flooded. Houses floated down the currents. Even some people and animals got caught up in the flood. Their bodies lined the bluffs.

He could barely see the small village through the thick fog that came with the morning sun. The army from the Flewthlands had been making camp down the coast of Viguran. This was the last stop near the ocean. If only they could get over the river, then they would head inland toward the capital.

"… and your mother's a whore," he heard a soldier shout at another. Through the fog, he could just make out a circle of men with two in the middle throwing punches at each other. He wondered what the fight could even be about. *Boredom makes boys of us all.*

"What's the meaning of this?" Tundavik yelled as best he could after stalking over to them, his boots sinking with every step. The circle of men who jeered and cheered began to murmur and watch the ground. The two in the middle threw softer punches, but Tundavik distracted them. "Where are your lords?"

"Lord Furrow is …" a young man said before trailing off. "He's inspecting the baggage train."

He's with the camp followers, Tundavik thought as he shook his head. "Well, go find him. I want," he lifted his leg to stop from sinking further into the mud, "him to show you what happens when you fight each other." The young man ran off. The two in the middle had stopped now that no one was cheering. "What are you two doing? Should be training with dummies, fake ones at least. What are your names?"

"Fallan," one man said. He wore only his trousers, his body covered in water and mud and now some blood. "This is Torza. He stole from me, my lord."

"I'm no lord," Tundavik said as he got closer to Torza and Fallan. "What did he steal?"

Torza kicked his feet. He at least was smart enough to wear boots. He had a fresh scar on his black eye that bulged. Fallan wiped his brow and said, "Nothing important, my lord."

"Important enough to fight instead of train."

"He stole his whore," a man from the circle shouted, and laughter followed from the rest.

Torza wiped water from his hair, but the icy rain just soaked it more. "Tis true, my lord. Fallan don't know how to pleasure a woman, so I decided it was best for me to do it."

The young man and Lord Furrow of Nye emerged from the fog. Furrow was about the age of Tundavik, his hair and beard graying just as much. He was wrapped in a hooded red cloak to shield himself from the pouring rain, with a seahorse embossed on the front. "My lord," he bowed.

Tundavik rolled his eyes, not wanting to correct anyone anymore. "Lord Furrow," he said as cold pellets of rain dropped harder and faster, "are these your men?" The lord nodded. "Well, take care of them. They're embarrassing the entire army when they do things like this. And be sure to keep them away from the whores. As I said before, I don't want to cut any cocks off." He glared at Furrow, whose hand went to cover his groin. "Is this clear?"

"Clear as the mud," someone shouted before Furrow could say. "As clear as the summer sky."

Tundavik rubbed the bridge of his nose as he walked away. He could hear Furrow yelling at his men. The roads had all been washed away, so his path was blinded, but Tundavik knew where he was going. He journeyed through the small town touched only by the war nature waged. He wanted to see bright flowers and gardens of food that lined the river, to watch as the animals grazed the land, laugh as the children enjoyed their young lives. The rain put a stop to those wishes.

The baggage train was just outside the village. Wagons and carts full of weapons and armor and tents and axes and whatever food they could find. Most of it was hardtack, though the bakers did their best to find wheat and flour for bread. The rain would've molded it by now anyhow. Lords and their men stood guard. Most of them were from the Flewthlands, though some, very few, Eastlanders joined them. Lord Furrow being one. Lord Toware of Riverend was from the Flewthlands. He had been the first lord to vote for the Flewthlands to join Tundavik. He was thankful for that. No matter how much Lord Barnet Lovell tried, Lord Toware still went with Devro.

"Trouble?" The lord asked Tundavik. He was wearing mail armor and a thin cloak atop his head. He stood straight as a pillar, as if the cold rain didn't bother him at all. Tundavik's hair was soaked through, and he had to stop his teeth from chattering.

"I'm tired of the camp followers, is all."

"Those Eastlanders," Toware spat, and his men in blue

armor around him muttered in agreement, "they know nothing but fucking and drinking. I knew we should've left them to their hamlets and marched forward."

"Do you know where most of them are?" Tundavik couldn't see much through the fog and rain. The gray overcast hid the sun.

"The whores?" Toware pointed. "A little farther down that … road."

"Why don't you bring your men with me?" Tundavik asked, and Toware couldn't hide the large smile that grew on his face.

Whatever road there had been was gone like all the others. He couldn't imagine it was made of stone, probably just a dirt path where travelers and merchants and farmers all killed the grass. He didn't need exact directions anyway. As he got closer to the end of the baggage train, he could hear moans and laughter. Small tents had been erected on small hills. Water created brooks and creeks in the minuscule valleys. As he climbed a hill, he was happy not to be sinking, though the hillside was as slick as anywhere else.

Tundavik gave a nod, and Toware's blue men went into the tents and pulled out any man they found, most of them naked. Their trousers around their ankles. Screaming curses as the chilly rain hit their bodies and that their fun had been taken. "Walk back to camp," Tundavik said, and Toware kept his hand on the hilt of his sword.

"My clothes, m'lord," a shivering naked man said.

"There are more in camp," Tundavik answered. They sent the naked men away. All with goosebumps as they made their shameful walk back into town for everyone to laugh at them.

"I believe I saw Lord Hedric," Toware whispered. "His wife back in Lyeland will surely be pleased," he chuckled. "Want us to take care of the whores as well? They won't be no trouble for my men. I'll make sure no raping occurs too."

"Thank you, but no. You may take your men back to camp. Make sure no one else stumbles out here," Tundavik said as the whores crawled out of their tents. A young girl stumbled from the tent in front of Tundavik, wrapped as best she could in a shawl. Tundavik helped her stand properly on the mud. "What's your name?"

"Seena, m'lord," she said meekly.

"Well, Seena, what are you doing here?"

"Making money, m'lord." She didn't look him in the eye. Instead, she kept her head down with her black hair. She was a plump girl, and far too young to be out in the cold servicing men for coin.

"Where are your parents? Why are you out here?"

"Gone, m'lord. They died a long time ago from a sickness. Think they caught it from some mites traveling through." She brushed her hair away as the rain stuck it to her face. Other women and men were emerging from tents and dressing with looks of confusion about where their customers had gone. "And the war has been hard on us all. I hadn't eaten in days in Raior before going to a brothel. No ships'd come to the city in fear of being ransacked. We'd even had pirates come and steal away folks. The whorehouse made me feel rich."

"I don't want my men distracted. I need them focused on taking Vigur, not on our following."

"Forgive me, m'lord," the girl bowed her head. "We've in

need of coin and they're in need of relieving frustrations. What else are we supposed to do?"

Tundavik boots were sliding down the hill before he caught himself. Rain got in his eyes. "I don't know. The war will be over soon when we take Vigur. There will be celebrations galore across the kingdom. I'm sure you'll make enough to last a lifetime." He looked the girl up and down and saw a few sores near her mouth and on her chest. *No need to tell her the syphilis will make that lifetime short.* "We'll feed you until we're over the river. But once we cross, I need you all to stay here. That lord," he pointed to the back of Toware's head as he smacked the backs of naked men, "is brutal. I don't want you to be hacked to pieces by him." Seena's eyes widened. Tundavik nodded at her new fear. "My men can take out their frustrations on Vigur."

Yvanne

Her baby kicked, and Lady Marla Mae squealed in excitement. "How wonderful," Marla clapped her hands. "I remember when I was pregnant with my little soldiers. The number of kicks and turns was enough to shake a house." Yvanne smiled as the lady placed a hand on her bare stomach again. "Oh, did I tell you how I almost didn't survive the pregnancy? Three boys and the gods seem ready to take you, but my husband and the doma prayed and prayed and here I am today. Just as lucky to be alive now as I was then."

Yvanne clasped Marla's hand. *Just what I want to hear about while pregnant. The chance of dying.* "I'm glad we found you and rescued you. Whitefork is important to the Lands of Asara just as much as any other town or village."

Lord Roul Straiver had attacked and looted Whitefork with the combined forces of the Byway and Goldfield. Lord Oda Mae, his wife, and closest advisers were all imprisoned. Yvanne led the great host of men that had gathered in Whitehall and marched through the Duke's Pass, destroying any semblance of power Ultiir had in the region. The forces of the Byway were stopped at the Yellow Tower, Lord Tedbalt Gurn of the Tower captured, Lord Roul killed by a

Lodean man. The Goldfield regiments fled back into the Kinglands. She hoped Ultiir, being from Goldfield, would share their cowardice.

Marla grabbed a loaf of seeded bread and shared some with Yvanne. They were in what was left of the lady's solar. Anything of importance was gone. Jewels and dresses and silverware and golden chalices. "I do hope the war is over when you have the babe," Marla said. "Raising a child in this mess cannot be good for their soul."

"I agree. That's why I must march onto Vigur soon."

"In this state?" Marla cocked her head. "Shouldn't you rest?"

Yvanne was tired of everyone worrying about her 'state'. Yes, she was exhausted, and sore, and hungry; her ankles were swelling, and in the morn she would occasionally vomit. But nothing would stop her from taking Vigur. From rescuing Devro, who withered away in the dungeons. The men followed her. Her alone. "I can rest on the journey and after Vigur is won. I hear the palace is a lovely place to give birth. Might even dip my child in the Montla and fill them with Vigura's gift."

"How wonderful that would be." Marla went to her balcony and looked down. Yvanne could barely make out the Whitefork below. It was a milky water. Slowly flowing down the mountains and eventually into the Montla. *If only I could sail there.* But the rocks and waterfalls would be too dangerous. "I hope my boys are alright out there. I haven't heard from them in so long," Marla said. "The last time they wrote, they were nearing Rushton."

Yvanne stood slowly and waddled over to Marla. "I'm sure they are safe. You saw what we did to Lord Roul. The

Asaramen are strong."

Marla Mae wiped away tears. Below them was the army camping in the ruined town. Homes and shops and taverns and barns had been destroyed. Any fields in or near the city burned. The forest was almost burnt too, but some snow seemed to save it. Now, the men were cutting the great spruce and oak trees and readying the trunks to be turned into siege engines. It would slow them some, but having trebuchets and ladders and rams and ballistae when they reached the walls of Vigur was indispensable. The camp was full of infantrymen, cavalrymen, and knights. Purple, red, yellow, green, and blue tents were scattered about, making the desolate land a rainbow.

"I should be thanking you a thousand times for freeing my husband and me," Marla said as Lord Oda Mae inspected some troops on the dirt below. "Did you hear the news from Midmount? A soldier from Hightail raped Lady Rida, and now she's pregnant. Her husband won't even speak to her. It's terrible." Grief overtook Marla as she cried and cried, the tears not stopping. Yvanne pulled her close. She had to comfort a woman old enough to be her mother. "If … that … had happ—happened to me …" Marla sobbed.

"But it didn't. You're alright." Yvanne said as she brushed her fingers through Marla's golden hair. "Only a few scrapes and bruises, but you're okay. And I'm sure your sons are fine too, just like you and your husband. You'll be reunited eventually." There was a knock on the door. "Why don't you rest? I'll have someone watch your door." Marla nodded and went to lie down on the ripped cushions of a chaise.

Little Tiro was at the door along with Sir Loc. "We've

come to retrieve you, my queen." Tiro said with his hands behind his back and his chin held high. "A rider for you."

"You can drop the formalities, my good sir," she mussed Tiro's hair. "Sir Loc won't do anything to you if you don't address me as queen. Isn't that right, sir?"

"Well," Loc started, but Yvanne clicked her tongue, "it's not exactly proper for a knight, and Pollard may have his hide for it, but it doesn't concern me."

Yvanne put her arm on Tiro's back and they walked away from the solar, stepping over damaged armoires and broken glass. Lord Oda's place of power wasn't grand, but it was made of white stone taken from the quarries in the Asara, and it glistened even as the sky was darkening from clouds. They walked down steps that led to the camp below. The village was built just a few miles from the mountains, which rose with jagged edges into the sky. The Whitefork flowed down the slopes. Waterfalls rushed in the distance. The setting sun bathed the entire area in yellows and reds, as if the whole place were on fire again.

By the time they reached the ground made entirely of mud and dirt (the grass and paths destroyed in the rampage) Yvanne wanted to lie down. Her feet and ankles and legs and thighs and torso and chest and everything were sore. But she couldn't show it. There were enough people worried about her, and more worried she wasn't capable of handling the army. She had to prove them wrong.

The reason Tiro, or Sir Tiro, and Sir Loc fetched her became clear when she saw brown banners plastered with the cream-colored face of Anebro, the god of the warm summer winds. When she was younger, she had seen the same banners. Her father had gleefully told the story of all the male heirs to Weathers Edge dying and there only being a daughter left. He married her older brother, Diero, to the surviving girl. Weathers Edge was somewhere in Maertan along the Drewogh coast. Yvanne still had no idea why her father was so giddy about some village in the middle of nowhere.

Diero stood taller than anyone else around. He was lean, his brown head of hair covered his brow, and he wasn't wearing armor, merely a gambeson of white. He had already found their other siblings when Yvanne reached him. "Little sis," he hugged her, lifting her off the ground. "Or should I call you my lady, my duchess, maybe queen? So many titles."

Yvanne giggled and took a deep breath after Diero set her onto the ground. "Just call me Yvanne. Titles aren't important around family."

Pollard, clad in his white armor that had dimmed from the dirt and battles, embraced Diero as well. "Didn't think you'd come all this way. I was sure when father sent out the letters you'd be the one to stay away."

"Stay away?" Diero laughed as he shook arms with their other brother, Ed the Loon. "Haven't you heard? Rowan is in the war now. Who else do you think freed Redington and is now sailing the Nokys? I'm waiting for the queen of Maertan to send her forces to back you as well."

"Weathers Edge is far away though," Yvanne said. "The Rowai were on ships."

"I'm better than the Rowai; I marched all the way here. Ready to beat back any of the usurpers' dogs. I am sorry I missed the death of father though. Weathers Edge was besieged with snow for months."

Yvanne said, "That's alright. I missed it too. The daken said he died peacefully, and I choose to believe her words." Tiro brought over a wooden chair for Yvanne, but she didn't sit in it, just rested her hands as she held up her tiredness. "I'm glad you came. I'm glad any of my brothers and sisters could come."

"Not many of us," Diero said, looking from Yvanne to Pollard to Ed.

"Cada is protecting Whitehall with the Sea Snakes. I heard Lady Lolly and her husband are meeting us in Goldfield," Yvanne said. "Hopefully, they don't run into any trouble. Ed here arrived about a week ago. You should've seen him in the battle."

"The Loon is stronger than any other," Ed said of himself.

"And how is the Town of Sendals?" Diero asked. Gamm Lars in Plajul was known as the Town of Sendals for the ancient women-like creatures that seduced any who visited. Some say the creatures still lived there.

"Perfect as always." Somewhere, Ed the Loon had found a mug of ale. It smelled strong, but he drank it with no problem, some dripping on his chest hair that protruded from his leather tunic. "The prick-of-a-lord doesn't want to die, so I've nothing to do there but sit and wait. The only good things in Plajul are my beautiful wife and the whores," he laughed as he drank more, almost choking. "When I received word of Yvanne's march, I didn't hesitate. Lord Yit ordered me to stay. I told him to fuck himself and his wife's corpse. We'll see how much trouble I get in later, but I brought any man who wanted to join me, and here I am."

"And how much fighting do you get up to?" Diero asked, his hands on his hips. "I know at Weathers Edge we just have to deal with Bahr raids and sometimes a pirate or two. I doubt the Town of Sendals sees much attack."

Ed wiped his mouth and passed the mug to one of his soldiers. "Refill." He ordered. "A few rebellions in the east here and there. That king doesn't know how to control his people. But remember, we fought side by side against the mites. Nothing made my cock grow more than seeing their heads sliced in two," the Loon roared.

Yvanne shook her head. "Why don't we go to my tent and finish this talk? We need to speak about strategy too. I know Gordo is trying to make the perfect plan."

"Gordo's here too?" Diero asked as he followed Yvanne and their brothers and a few guards across the makeshift camp. "He must've traveled the farthest. I assume Lord Albert," he said with a mocking tone about their eldest brother, "didn't come since you are still the duchess?"

"He wants to stay in Canniage for the time being. His new wife just had another child."

"Taking after our father," Pollard muttered. As they passed the soldiers and the lords and the men-at-arms, many of them bowed and said, "My queen," to Yvanne. Some daken were tending to the wounded in their tents, smiths were busy finding any steel to make more weapons, bakers were doing their best to make bread and crackers and she even saw a few with fresh eggs from a hen.

"Don't look down on those who enjoy being inside a woman," Ed howled, "just because you'll never feel the joy." The Loon patted Pollard on his back, his plate armor singing with the clap. "Why anyone would take that shit vow to become a knight I will never understand."

"Honor. Duty." Pollard said.

"I've as much honor as you, little brother," Ed clapped his big, bear-like hands. "It might be a little further down in me though."

"Pollard does a good thing protecting Yvanne and the people of Whitehall." Diero said.

The talk ended when they reached Yvanne's tent. She had been sleeping in the castle with Lady Marla since Whitefork was liberated, but her tent was still used to plan the rest of the war and the attack on Vigur. Her tent was larger than the rest, right in the center of the ruined town. It was a great white cloth plastered with bears. Through the flaps lay her sheepskin-covered bed that she let her handmaid, Jacka, use at the moment; the center of the tent was a desk a mess with maps and letters. Chairs decorated the left side. It was where her council would meet. Now, she had more people. Gordo and Lords Cul and Aimora and Urses de'Marisco were peering over maps, talking of plans. They all bowed when she came in, and Gordo found Diero where they chatted about lost time.

"Sit, sit," Lord Cul of Mount Meret said. His face was always angry, his brow lowered and eyes squinted, but his fighters from the peak were some of the best warriors Yvanne had, so she put up with the old Cul.

"Before we start, I'd like to hear of any issues on your trek from Whitehall," Diero said as he and everyone else found a chair. Yvanne stood with Cul, Aimora, and Gordo by the desk. Tiro was off to the side. *Probably waiting to catch me if I fall.*

Pollard stepped forward. "Not much in the Duke's Pass, just a few skirmishes. Lord Pilly of Rockforge thought he could besiege the Crossing, but Lord Osbern Lot wouldn't fall so easily. We were able to help fortify and rout Pilly's men. Then we came across a host of traitors in the lowlands. Lords Edward Tall, Tedbalt Gurn, and Tyro Widl all declared for Ultiir."

"We made sure your gods took them as the traitors they were," Aimora finished. "Then we saved the Brownfork and the Whitefork. It was all too easy."

"We still lost men," Yvanne said as she looked over a map of her duchy. The Lands of Asara was covered in mountains and valleys. Rivers and glaciers. Forests and meadows. It was all hers. But war divided it.

Urses was standing close to Yvanne. She had released him from the prison in Whitehall, and now she trusted him, maybe too much. When he didn't want to come on the march to Vigur, she had to force him. Her sister, Cada, didn't trust him at all, so it made more sense to keep Urses close instead of letting him have free rein over Whitehall. "We will win a thousand more once we reach Vigur," Urses said in a low voice. "They will see our host and switch sides, I'm sure of it."

"We just can't forget the ones we lost," Yvanne said.

"Of course," the old Lord Cul said. "Let's not lose anymore on the march south."

"So, what's the plan?" Ed asked. "My men and I are itching to leave this milky water and scour the Montla. They've been training all day and night."

"We don't need to rush into things," Gordo cautioned. He took off his helm to show his balding head. "We need to be cautious about Vigur. Ultiir has surely seen to its defenses."

"When was the last time the city fell?" Pollard asked.

"The mites besieged the city," Diero said, "but it never fell.

So not since Valor the Betrayer lost the city to the Vlylahl Forces."

"Just a couple of centuries," Ed swatted it away like a bug. "We'll break the walls down in a day's time and this war will be over."

"I like the optimism," Aimora said. Lord Aimora Dore and his men had gotten strange looks in very town and village they went through, even looks of fear. The Lodean people weren't welcome this far in the lowlands. Yvanne made sure it wasn't an issue. The swords and shields they carried didn't hurt either. "But I don't think it will be so easy. We've been trying to come up with a plan. Lord de'Marisco is the only one who's seen the city of recent years."

"They have stone walls and watchtowers," Yvanne said. "What more is there?"

Urses scratched his chin. His baby-face scrunched with thought. "Ultiir wasn't able to do much to bolster the defenses when I was there. Of course, it's been months now, so I've no idea what's changed. Lord Geary's death would've certainly done a number on the city guard though. Whoever replaced him was surely not as competent."

"So just spikes and stakes and traps?" Gordo said and tapped his finger on the map of Vigur. "Lord de'Marisco has proposed Lord Cul and his warriors lead the vanguard. I haven't seen them fight in battle, but from what I've been told, they'll do just fine."

"And Lord Cul," Cul spoke of himself, "doesn't agree."

"Like I've said," Urses began, "you have the best chance of breaking through the walls. I'm sorry to say, but without you, we'll lose the battle quickly."

"The Loon's men will join," Ed bellowed. "We're not ones

to pass up the opportunity to be in the van. Make Ultiir wish he was never a miracle child."

"What about the rivers?" Diero asked as he crossed his legs. "They could sneak Devro away on a boat, and we would never know since we'll be busy with the walls."

"Good point," Gordo said and wrote it done on a parchment that was full of ink.

"We also have to worry about reinforcements from the east," Cul said. "I hear his mother is still in Goldfield. If she sends an army to join the fray, we'll be trapped on both sides."

"Rila de'Tro and Ultiir have an … odd relationship." Urses played with his fingers. "It's possible she sends help, but I'm sure Ultiir isn't counting on it."

"Your Grace," Sir Rickart entered with a skinny man who was out of breath. "An urgent rider from the east. He has a letter"

"Hopefully no fight," Gordo said.

Yvanne walked over to the rider. "Why have you come? What's the letter say?"

The haggard man shook his head. "I can't read, milady, but I was told to give it to the red-haired one."

"Go find some food and water," she said before taking the letter. The seal was some strange symbol she had never seen, and she worried it was a marching lord coming to deal a blow to them in Whitefork, but when she opened it she saw Tundavik's signature at the bottom. "Tundavik and the lords of the Flewthlands are nearing the River Samosay. They're getting closer to Vigur."

Ed the Loon leaped from his chair, the others jumping from fright. "I must tell my men war is near! They will train extra hard!" he yelled as he ran from the tent.

"Shall we ready the troops?" Pollard asked.

Yvanne held up a hand. "We'll wait until tomorrow. The Samosay is still a hundred miles from Vigur. If we reach Vigur without Tundavik, then I'm not sure we win. Let's come up with our plan of attack tonight. Let's be ready." Yvanne went back to the table to plan a war with her family.

Ultiir

Fire crackled and smoke rose into the cloudy skies. Ultiir was lucky that the rain took a break so he could burn his enemies. "What a sight," he said to Edel de'Viere. The young lord was the chief informant of the city, but he was also in charge of commanding the city guard. Ever since Lord Geary's death, Ultiir hadn't trusted anyone else with the guard, but Edel was young and dumb. They hadn't been doing well of late. Angry peasants somehow overwhelmed them and took their weapons and rioted, destroying entire parts of the city. But when Ultiir told Edel his plan, the chief informant assured him the guards would be up for the task.

Ultiir held out his hands to warm himself. Not that he needed to. The flames were so bright and so hot that his face itched as the fire wisped toward him. The palace of Vigur rose high behind them, the smoke swirling round the towers as it vanished into the clouds. He had set the King's Brothel alight. The whores inside would never spy against him or anyone else again. Sophie would be without friends. "It's beautiful," he spoke again to the chief informant. Women and men inside the brothel were screaming. Some jumped from the windows dressed in nothing but burn marks and ashes. Others weren't so lucky. They raced down the street covered in flames. Dying somewhere among the marble homes of the wealthy nobles. In a gutter. *It's where they all belong,* he thought.

He had been stupid. His anger at Sophie for only doing her parents' bidding when marrying him caused him to fuck some whore. Atrice was her name. And she was Sophie's spy. Who knows what all she told the queen, but Ultiir wouldn't give in to temptation anymore. He wouldn't share secrets with just anyone. "Did you find a way to pay the guards?" He asked Edel. The city vaults had been emptied so much for the war that they sent word to lords for more coin.

"Some men were displeased," the young lord said, "but when they saw the girls and boys in the brothel, they decided that was payment enough. Not sure how many were bedded," he shrugged, "but my men seemed happy enough. Some even wanted to take the whores home, but I told them your command."

"After the war is over, there will be enough whores to go around," Ultiir said as the screams and the smoke twisted into the air. Water touched his brow. A light drizzle from the clouds above fell onto the city. "I guess the Four wish to see this fire go out. Let's go inside," Ultiir said. "We've much to discuss with the council."

Ultiir's new chief of his household guard, the old Sir Gid, led them over the paved roads as old puddles had new life breathed into them. The gate to the palace was closed. Dozens of men with shields and swords and bows stood on both sides of the portcullis. He didn't want any commoners breaking through. Though the rains of spring seemed to have deflated them. The worst of the rioting had happened in the winter, and Ultiir had burned the Rats Nest area of the city in retaliation. A huge chunk of land was gone. The houses and shops that teemed with vagrants and criminals and whores were in charred ruins.

As the portcullis lurched upward, he thought of how close the rioters had gotten. They had screamed and killed their way along the roads, and only the great wall of the palace stopped them. Some lords and ladies weren't lucky like he was. *If only Sophie had been one to die that day. I wouldn't be worrying about her and her spies and her plans.* He followed his knight through the gate and across the fields. Ultiir eyed everyone who passed. *Any of them could be the queen's spies.* But he only knew the whore, Atrice, was one for certain. And he had Sir Gid take care of that problem. He heard news that Sophie wretched and cried and screamed when she found the whore dead on her bed. The thought made Ultiir smile. *If only she loved me, then I wouldn't be so harsh.*

The tower atop the palace loomed over them. Ultiir couldn't see the top as it hid in the clouds and the rain hit his eyes. The spring rains always turned the marble of the palace dirty. Not pure white like summer. Usually the slaves would get to cleaning it, but they had all escaped. Broke free of their chains and raced across the rivers. "Any word on the slaves?" He asked Edel as they crossed the now empty fields of the palace lands.

The young boy scratched his head. "Perhaps Lord Hirons knows. Last I heard, they were amassing in the Eastlands. Maybe they want to sail east to Eotros. I don't think they're anything to worry about."

"And maybe they want to overthrow me," Ultiir clenched

his fist. "We can never be too careful. Enemies are everywhere, all wanting to harm me. Be sure your guards are on the lookout for any signs of a slave march toward the city."

"Of course, Your Grace," Edel bowed his head.

The rain beat them harder and faster before they entered the palace. When the wooden doors shut, it sounded like a thousand rocks were falling from the sky. His fire would certainly go out, but the whorehouse would never come back.

The palace was as barren as the empty fields. Rats tittered in the corners; spiders made homes in the rafters. The lords and ladies of the court hadn't been invited back in weeks, and he pushed them all out after they hid in the palace from the riots. It had been cramped and bursting at the seams. So he emptied it. Now, only guards remained. A few metal footsteps echoed in the halls; the queen's entourage were in her wing of the palace; and the lords of the king's council met every few days but otherwise they stayed in their chambers. *Probably plotting too.*

"Call for a council meeting," Ultiir told Edel as they neared the doors to the throne room. "I'll be waiting, and don't inform Lord Masson. That old shit can figure it out on his own." Lord Edel de'Viere bowed away and raced up the stairs. Sir Gid cracked his knuckles as he stayed with Ultiir. Ultiir motioned, and two guards with owl surcoats opened the door to the throne room.

The gray skies outside darkened the chamber, the stained glass windows not getting enough sunlight. No torches were lit either. The giant chandeliers that held candles hung still. It smelled of the earth. Mildew and moist. Ultiir hadn't sat on the throne much, and the court hadn't gathered in weeks. The marble throne rose out of the floor on the far side of the room, the cushion crooked. His and Gid's boots echoed like thunder as they made their way over the marble floor and between the spiraling columns that held the vaulted ceiling. A small mouse crept over Ultiir's shoe. He didn't kick it or track it. He was focused on the red cushion.

The cushion where his brother had once sat for two decades. Hurvir had been a warmonger. He had caused famine. Poverty. Illness. Ultiir was to fix all of it. *But the bastard followed in his father's footsteps. We'd be in an era of peace and prosperity if it weren't for him.* Beneath his feet, deep in the old mines, was the dungeon, and Devro was there. Rotting. Lord Drogue de'Vil had brought the bastard from Whitehall. *But the lord failed to take the town and end this war,* he thought with a clenched jaw.

"Remind me to speak to the bastard," Ultiir told Gid.

"Of course, Your Grace," the old knight said, his hand resting on his sword pommel. "My king, if I may, do you plan on holding court? The war is getting ever closer. I'm sure many lords and ladies are frightened."

"I know," Ultiir said. He reached his hand out and touched the cold marble of the throne. It felt like ice. It burned him. "If Hurvir were still around, we wouldn't even be in a war." Ultiir laughed, "Never thought I'd utter those words."

"You can't change the past, Your Grace, only the future. Now that the evil bastard is in your custody, you just need to take care of his followers and the realm will be at peace once more. I envision you as a masterful leader."

"If only others felt that way. If only mother did." Ultiir

didn't leave many knights and men in Goldfield to protect his mother, but she was a vile woman who didn't deserve their help, anyway.

Ultiir cleared his head. He didn't need to do much thinking at the moment. *Save that for the meeting.* He wandered to the wall behind the throne and pushed open a wooden door; it led to dozens of other doors and offices and chambers. His chamber wasn't too far, the place where he had Lord Gofrei Geary killed. The other offices were for his council. The doors were open, but no one was there. Empty. Like the rest of the palace.

"Stay here," he told Gid, and the knight stationed outside the door to the council chamber. Inside was the cracked wooden table that Hurvir had broken, chairs all pushed in nicely. Dust had settled on the cushions. The torches weren't lit, just like the rest of the corridors. Rain beat against the window. Ultiir traced a finger over the table and chairs until he reached the king's seat. It wasn't much more than the rest. A wooden chair with a leather cushion was the only difference. He sat in it, his body sinking, and tapped his foot while he waited in the dark.

Eventually the lords of his council appeared one by one. First came Lord de'Viere, he was always dutiful since Ultiir named him chief informant. Lord Dovi Lyons was next; the chief collector hadn't been doing a very good job at collecting taxes. Then came Lords Serle Verrier, the chief ambassador, and Alan Hirons. Lord Hirons' hair was graying. Last year it had been brown and lush. The stress of the war seemed to take more of a toll on the chief commander than even Ultiir himself.

"Welcome, my lords," Ultiir stretched his arms across the

table as they settled in. "I need to hear some good things about the war. Ever since Whitehall was lost, we haven't been doing too well, have we?"

Lord Verrier cleared his throat. "But, Your Grace, we captured the bastard. The war is nearly won if I say so myself." Ultiir just glared at him, willing him not to believe it. "Umm … we … King Anvrin hasn't written back in sometime. I worry he is forgetting who your queen is."

"Why wouldn't he help his daughter?" Edel asked. "Doesn't he want to see her succeed?"

Alan Hirons cleared his throat. "Maybe he is waiting for the rain to clear. I heard the Ters-Veck was surging. Not too safe to cross." Lord Hirons pulled out parchments from his sleeves and skimmed them over. "We received news from the Lands of Asara. Lord Edward Tall sent a message out saying the girl was ravaging the lowlands. It seems we've also lost control of the Brownfork and the Whitefork. Supposedly, her army is marching ever south."

Ultiir banged the table with his hand. It didn't crack like when his brother did it all those years ago, just rattled instead. His hand throbbed though. "And what is the chief commander doing about that?"

"There isn't much I can do," Alan said. "We're running out of coin. The planting season has started, and more and more of the men are wondering when they will return to their land and grow their crops. The war has been going on for too long. Winter certainly didn't—"

"Stop," Ultiir said as he rubbed his brow. "My lords, being on the king's council means you have immeasurable power. So I ask again, what are you going to do about it?"

Alan fingered his graying hair. "I say we move our

resources to defending the city. The wall only stops attacks from the east. If the girl's army can make boats, they can cross the Montla and be on our doorstep. But I'm not sure what to pay the men with. Whores don't always work," the lord said as his eyes settled on Edel de'Viere.

Edel looked around the room like Lord Hirons was talking to someone else. "My men do the job out of loyalty, not pay. Maybe the others should be reminded of that."

Lord Hirons snorted. "And I presume you're not making any coin?" Alan shook his head as he fingered the parchments. "We've also reports from the Flewthlands. Ever since the defeat in Storyah, our fleet has been sailing the Nokys searching for a place to rest and repair. My bet is they will go to Liari, but the captains have done crazier things before. The border with the Eastlands has seen heavy fighting. Good thing for us is that they're away from the Kinglands." Alan sighed as he continued looking through his papers. "The bad news is that the Flewthmen seem determined to win. Greencorse has been razed, along with other villages and hamlets. People are fleeing south, but flooding at the Three Rivers has stopped them. The flooding is also keeping the Flewthmen from marching south, so more good news."

"Lord Lyons," Ultiir looked to the chief collector. "Have you been able to find any coin? Surely we've some left in the city. I need enough to hire some mercenaries from Eotros. Those men are far more skilled and dangerous."

Lord Dovi Lyons licked his lips before biting them. "Well," the chief collected tapped his fingers, "with the slave revolts we've had to import more and more food; not to mention paying the city guards and our forces for their fighting;

taxes have also stalled due to the war; there's also the issue that two of our duchies are revolting, so even if we wanted to collect we'd be losing a lot of income. It's a dire situation, Your Grace."

Ultiir wanted to bang the table again, but his hand still ached. "How much is given to the dakenry in the city?"

"A few thousand a year, but—"

"Very well, take it from them and explain we'll give them more once the war is won. All the dakens should be in the field anyway."

"You would take money from the school that heals your people?" Lord Tedbalt Masson said in the doorway. "Why do I feel like that isn't a good idea, Your Grace?" Tedbalt said the last bit with annoyance.

"Welcome." Ultiir motioned to the empty seat. "We were wondering when you were going to join us?"

"I didn't receive word." The old lord said as he reached his seat and sat, fluffing out his gold cloak. "And since I was once chief daken, I feel it important to advocate for the dakenry."

"Good thing you are only chief consultant now," Ultiir rolled his eyes. Lord Masson had been integral in killing Hurvir, and in the plan to fight the bastard. But promoting him to chief consultant after Lord de'Marisco went to the Lands of Asara was a mistake that Ultiir would never forgive himself for.

"How much coin was given to Lord Henk Zazí and his failure to hold Redington?" Tedbalt asked. "How much spent searching for the slaves? The reason we are out of money is that, and forgive me, Your Grace, is that we keep wasting it on stupid endeavors."

"And what do you propose?"

"We need to offer independence to the Flewthlands. I know what you're all thinking, but the Flewthmen are strong. They've already revolted times before, one time coming so close that they got everything they wanted except freedom. Offer it to them, and watch as the lords question the fighting. They will go back to the Flewthlands and forget this. The bastard and his wife will have to rethink their strategy. Any coin and men sent to the north will instead flow back to the capital. We can bolster our defenses. Prepare for anything that may come. And forget the slaves. They won't last. You know how they are. They'll work together for a few months, then it will devolve into fighting. They're no better than dogs. Leave them to devour their pack."

Ultiir stretched his fingers. He hadn't realized he had been clenching his fists ever since Tedbalt walked in. "You would have me lose the Flewthlands? Lose the taxes? And let whole areas of my kingdom be turned over to slaves on the hopes they turn on one another?"

Lord Masson's eyes stared at him. The old man was holding in a smirk, Ultiir knew. *He wants me to destroy the kingdom. He wants me to grow unpopular and lose so he can marry Sophie and they can rule together. It won't happen.* "There's also the matter of succession," Tedbalt started, and Ultiir knew his thoughts were right. Tedbalt and Sophie were working together. Closely. Probably fucking too. The reason she had grown so distant from Ultiir was because of the old lord. "Some of the women feel like the bastard's side represents their interests more—"

"What women?" Ultiir snapped. "Name them." Lord

Masson cleared his throat and looked around the room. *No one will help you, you old bastard,* Ultiir thought.

"Well, there's the matter of Oceantree. We don't want to lose Lady Volles."

"Stand up, my lord," Ultiir said. Tedbalt did as he was told, his old knees wobbling and struggling to hold up his weight. "My lord, how long have you been working with the queen? Because this is the same nonsense she has spewed to me and the court. And you know what the court said, ladies included? That it was hogwash. No better than pig's shit. A stain on our legacy. An affront to our ancestors. If women were to be included in the succession, then it would've been written when the kingdom was founded. So I ask again, how long have you and the queen been fucking?"

Lord Masson's eyes grew wide, and his mouth dropped. "We never … we wouldn't … that would go against … against the Four …"

"Then why are you parroting her?"

The other councilors moved their heads, cleared their throats, let out an awkward cough while Tedbalt looked at each of them. "That is a vile accusation. The queen and I have always been close, but we do not talk politics or scheme or whatever it is you're trying to say."

"Madam Taire, before she burned, told me you and Sophie went to the King's Brothel together. Did you share a whore?" Ultiir stood as well. He towered over the old lord, who stood shaking and afraid. "Did Sophie like my present? Old Gid did good work, did he not?"

Lord Masson looked at the closed door. Sir Gid on the other side. "That knight … that monster …"

"My Lord Masson, I strip you of your rank as chief

consultant and banish you from this palace. Do not collect your things. They will find their way to you. I will have my guards escort you out."

"I've been in the palace for almost forty years. Longer than you. And you're going to banish me over unfounded accusations? Where will I go?"

"Well, the King's Brothel is burning as we speak, and the Noble Lands are full of lords and ladies who want nothing to do with you, so I guess the gutter. We'll clear your body."

"Outrageous," Tedbalt stomped for the door.

"My lord," Ultiir said, and Lord Masson stopped but never turned, "leave the cloak."

Lord Tedbalt Masson unfastened his golden cloak and threw it on the ground, stepping on it as he disappeared from the chamber.

Ultiir called out, "Sir Gid," and the knight bowed in the door. "How do you feel about being my new chief consultant?" The old man flushed red, but he picked up the golden cloak with footprints and bowed as he fastened it. "Now," Ultiir sat back down, "let's figure out this war on my terms, shall we?"

Bertin

He woke up screaming.

The death and destruction Bertin saw in Anha Jorbstah haunted him every day since his escape. Elves massacred by humans. A tale as old as time. A story told to him countless times since he was a boy, of humans saving the world from the treacherous monsters, humans making sure the elves were completely gone. That elves weren't to gain any of their land back. Humans were above all, especially elves. But what Bertin saw made him question who the monsters in the stories actually were.

"Need to keep moving," he told himself as the sun rose over the mountain peaks. He was somewhere in Rainvealand, far south of the Ters-Veck, and even farther from his home in Rowan. If he kept walking through the shrubs and hundreds of miles of grasslands that stretched to the west, then he didn't think about all the death. Of Thatar's broken skull, Ariad's sliced open flesh, the elvish children with severed heads, the burning and screaming that followed.

"No," he said. "Stop thinking about it. There's no reason to." He dragged his legs over the dusty grass. The grasslands were nothing like the ones to the north. It was dry, the grass barely taller than his ankles, with pockets of sand littered throughout. He was already sweating, snow only on the mountain peaks to his back. Spring brought warmer air in the lead up to summer. He didn't want to be in Rainvealand in the summer. *I'll die before summer. Die in the middle of nowhere in a foreign place while my family searches and never finds me. Die like Ioelena.*

Bertin gave an angry sigh to himself. Ioelena's death in the desert may have been months ago, but it was always on his mind, more than the deaths that were so recent. He had almost been free. Ioelena had saved him and was trying to get him to Salvalone for freedom. He'd already be in Rowan if that happened. But Kelltar killed Ioelena. Sliced her open and left her to bleed out in the sand. *Then I killed Kelltar.*

The screams of Kelltar as his flesh peeled off sent shivers down Bertin's spine. And he caused it. He pushed the elf into the dragon fire to watch him squirm and die. He did it for Ioelena. "Stop thinking about it, please," he pleaded with himself. "Focus on my goal. Survive. Get … somewhere." All he knew was to head west. Eventually he would hit the Bezir River. He hoped. He wasn't great at directions without a map, but he knew the river was too wide to miss. His first choice was to go back to Jorbstah. But after days of wandering around the fields, he realized he didn't know where it was, so he settled for west. *Back where I came from.*

"Once I reach the Bezir, I can take a boat north. Sail all the way to Rowan." But he didn't have any coin. "I can do work, catch some fish." But he wasn't a very good fisherman. Bertin rubbed his eyes and plopped onto a stump. A forest was once in the area. Wide stumps, all without the trunks.

The area was barren. The grass turned to sand and dirt. His eyelids slowly closed, but he wasn't ready for sleep, not while the southern sun was shining at noon. But he couldn't stop his body from sleeping.

Then he woke up screaming again.

He knew his eyes had dark circles; he could feel how heavy they were. His body ached. Not only from trying to sleep on the hard ground but also from his months of bruises. Bertin's cheek had been shattered, and there was no way it had healed properly. He could feel how rough the bones underneath were. One of his eyes still hurt when he opened it too wide from being punched. His legs were shaky, his knees buckled too many times to count, and his feet were covered in blisters from traveling hundreds of miles. Worst of all was his missing little finger. It was a symbol to the world that the prince of Rowan could be hurt. Hurt by elves of all things. *Then I watched little elf babies get their heads smashed,* he thought with a shudder before telling himself, "Stop thinking. Stop thinking. Stop thinking."

Bertin kicked the ground. A cloud of dust flew into the air, and he started coughing. He didn't think it could get any worse than facing Ih la Mat in the Delerous Desert, but he was very wrong. He let out a nervous chuckle. Wilclef, Robalt, Gordo. All of his guardsmen were dead. Their bodies somewhere in Lisan Biresdea. And who knew where Safír was? The desert guide probably made it to Salvalone, found somewhere to hide from the elvish attacks. Still alive. *At least I hope,* he thought as his cough went away.

Then his stomach rumbled, and he remembered how hungry he was. How dry his throat was. He didn't remember much about his teachings on Rainvealand except that it was drier than his home and that most of the rivers in Riorskè were south of the Kash Mountains. If Riorskè was still where he was. *But I haven't crossed the Bezir yet. I can't be in Attamek. Unless I missed the river in all my wanderings.* "No," he told himself, "I will not let my mind play tricks on me."

He tripped, and his face collected a pile of dirt. As he spat out the earth, he saw what he had tripped over. It was a deep rut. Then another a couple feet away. Wagons. He stood, figured out which way he needed to be heading, and followed the makeshift road until his body wanted to die on the spot from exhaustion.

Night couldn't have come fast enough. The lack of sun made him shiver, but it was better than the heat of the day. His tattered clothes had stuck to his skin from sweat. Now, he wished he would've found some elven clothes to change into. Clothes from Thatar. "Stop," he said before his mind even pictured the elf. But he couldn't stop it no matter how hard he tried. The arrow pierced through Thatar's skull the moment he saw Ariad be murdered. They died together. Bertin had vomited. Bertin had run. He couldn't save them. He fell to his knees and cried.

"The children weren't monsters," he wished he had said to the mites who cut them down, "they were laughing earlier. They were like human children. Having fun. Enjoying life," his tears turned to sobs as spit and snot ran down his face. "You killed them," he shouted into the black of night. "You monsters, you ..." *mites.*

But it wasn't just the mites who killed elves. His entire ancestry was full of elf killers. Elf murderers. He had lived in a palace constructed by elves, stone mined by elves. The humans took it. The humans murdered any elf in their way. "I'm a monster too. I laughed at the deeds of my ancestors. Basked in their glory. Live in the palace they stole." Bertin wiped his tears and tried to stand, but his knees wouldn't let him. His throat was hoarse. His stomach growled. "They just wanted to see their home again," Bertin sat and grabbed clumps of dirt and grass. "Just like me." He lay down and closed his eyes.

***

A soft touch on his cheek woke him this time. He had dreamt of fairies, not the ones being slaughtered in Anha Jorbstah, but ones flying and singing near the throne of Rowan. He touched his cheek, still ugly from being hit all those months ago. Whatever had touched him was gone. *Probably a rabbit.* The moon was in the sky now, but it was only a crescent, not much to light his way. He stood anyway. He had to keep moving. "I need to reach the river. I need … water."

Bertin felt with his feet for the ruts. When he found them, he kept his feet inside to keep from getting lost. The night dragged on as he walked for what felt like a hundred miles, but it surely wasn't. Bertin couldn't be sure of anything, though. His body ached. His head ached. There was nothing. No candlelight to signify a city or village or even a lone house. Rainvealand was supposed to be teeming with slaves, but there were no farms around him, no slaves. Nothing.

"I can't keep going," Bertin said as he collapsed to the ground. "Need … rest."

"You must continue," a familiar voice said to him. Bertin looked up and saw a glowing light; in front of it was his father. He wore a crown and was the brightest thing in the world. "Have you forgotten who you are?"

Bertin's breathing was quick. The voice, the sight, the smells. It was his father. But King Bartel was in Rowan. *No way he could find me here.*

"You're not real," he said as he opened and closed his eyes, but his father stayed in place. "You're in my head. The steppe has made me crazed."

"I'm right here, son," Bartel held out a hand, but Bertin wouldn't take it. He didn't want to touch whatever that was … or he didn't want to learn it was all a dream. Bertin hadn't noticed the tears that were falling down his face. He was seeing his father again after months away. After enduring so much pain and death and destruction, and having no one to turn to. No one to help him. Seeing his father's face felt like a hug. Like safety.

"Why are you here?" Bertin asked through his tears. "Have you come to help?"

"Only you can help yourself, my son. You are the king. You must be strong."

Bertin shook his head. "No. You're king; I'm just a prince who knows nothing. I didn't deserve to be born into this. I'm weak. Nothing."

"You are the king of Rowan. You knew the last time you saw me we would never see each other in this life again. Remember?"

"Not true … I—" but his father had looked sick. Sicker than before. The weight of the crown and kingdom and all his dead family burdened him. *Did I know? Is he really dead?*

"This isn't real. Ghosts aren't real."

"I'm no ghost," his father's voice soothed. "I'm here to make sure you find your river. Find the safety you so desire. Take my hand." Bertin blinked quickly. His father's hands seemed to turn from fingers to claws to fingers again. He shook his head. *My mind is playing tricks. My father is not here; he is safe in Rowan. Not dead.*

"If you aren't a ghost, then you will point me to the river. I just need to find the Bezir. I've been following these ruts for hours upon hours, and my legs are so tired. So tired," he repeated as he rubbed his calves.

"I will show you," his father's hand jerked out again. "Take it, and I will bring you to the river. I will save my son. Save you even when I couldn't save my mother, or your mother. I let her jump to those rocks. I should've been there." The apparition seemed to cry, and Bertin was even more confused. He cried as well.

"Why did you send me away?" Bertin choked. "Why didn't you trust me to run the kingdom? I would've done a fine job. I didn't need to see all this killing and maiming. Didn't need to be tortured. I needed my father to guide me. But you sent me away." He didn't care if the ghost was real or all in his head. His father entrusted Bertin's teachings to Blis and other tutors, to the councilors. He needed King Bartel to tell him how to rule. He didn't need a king in some desert to train him.

"All you learn will help you in life. Did you think I wanted to be sent to the North?" His father stepped closer, his legs shimmering. "To learn that my mother was killed and tossed in the river? To learn how my sister escaped prison just for me to never see her again? All the awful things made me a stronger king. A better man. It will do the same to you."

Bertin dug his hands into the ground beneath him. He had no more tears to cry, no water in his system. He had to find the river. Bertin stood without his father's hand, which shimmered to claws then back to fingers. "I will find the river," Bertin said. "I will." He walked past his father. King Bartel didn't have anyone to rely on when he was separated from his family, and Bertin didn't need anyone either. "I will become a better ruler by myself. I will get home by myself."

He didn't make it past the sunrise. Bertin fell into a heap on the dusty ground, his eyes blinking from seeing to darkness. He felt a burning sensation on his back but could do nothing. Could hardly feel. He blinked a few more times and heard shouts. A wheel. A horse. His father's voice. Ioelena's voice. That was the last thing he heard before everything went black.

Sophie

Her nightmares were full of blood and torture and of her own death. When Sophie woke, she would sweat or scream or cry. Her handmaids would comfort her, but she didn't want them to touch her.

"You're safe, Your Grace," Amalla said that morning when Sophie screamed herself awake. Her dream was about the dead woman. The dead whore. Atrice was mangled and bloody and left on the queen's bed for her to find.

"There's nothing to fear," Renna said in her Masani accent. "We have guards outside the door. You have us. You have weapons."

Sophie looked to the daggers and swords they had collected in the corner. "Yes," she said, hiding her hands under the wool blanket. Her fingers were shaking. It was as if the earth itself were moving, but it was just her. Always tense. Always afraid. "I worry too much," she said but couldn't stop a few tears from falling. Renna rubbed Sophie's back, but it didn't help. She stared at the fire in the hearth. *How warm it would be to jump in. I wouldn't have to worry about Ultiir or his sycophants anymore.*

"Sir Achen slipped this under the door earlier." Amalla handed her a letter. The seal a mountain. The king of

Terrop, Sophie's father, had written back.

"Thank you," Sophie said as she opened it and read. The letter ended with *I hope you know what you're doing.* She stood, wrapped herself in a silk robe, and threw the letter in the fire. The paper crumpled as it blackened and burned. She had written to her father after Atrice's death; after Sophie took the poison to be rid of the babe growing inside her. She didn't want her father to raise his troops and march to Viguran. Ultiir didn't deserve his help. Thousands of Terropian troops would instead stay in their kingdom, and Ultiir would have to muster new men to fight the bastard. "I need to stop being afraid," she told her handmaids. "My father listened to my advice, and I need the lords of the court to listen as well."

"Would you like to dress?" Renna asked, and Sophie nodded. They unlatched the door; a plethora of new locks had been added, so it took a few minutes. Sir Achen stood on the other side, in the corridor between the door that led to the palace and the queen's bedchamber. The knight bowed and watched them closely as they went over to the wardrobe and the handmaids started going through the clothes.

The mattress and frame were gone, leaving an empty hole in the room. Sophie had them removed due to the blood and guts that had soaked through. The smell. The memory. Atrice had been carved atop her bed and left to rot as a message. Sophie wiped a tear of remembrance. She hadn't been able to sleep anywhere other than with her handmaids. It was another layer of protection. She didn't think Ultiir would hurt her, but she didn't want to take the chance.

The handmaids dressed Sophie in a red gown with a hood

for the rain that never ended. It was spring after all. They added powder to her face to hide the tear stains, and she took Sir Achen's arm as they left the bedchamber. Her household guards all stood outside the door. Over two dozen. They had taken over the corridor outside her room. Cots and tables and sword racks and shields littered the hall. She was glad. Her own fort in the palace. Except her adversary wasn't in another town or kingdom. He was on another floor of the palace.

"Where are we off to today, Your Grace?" Achen asked.

"If Ultiir"—it hurt to say his name—"isn't calling court, then we will see the lords ourselves. To the Noble Lands." The knight nodded. She held his metal arm the entire way through the palace. A few guards trailed behind. If a battle was to be had, she would be ready.

They wandered through the walls and down the stairs. There were barely any guards left. Most fled with their lords when Ultiir closed the palace; and the slaves had left or been killed when they raced across the river. The ones who remained were outside in the barn. Getting beat or raped or killed. Sophie didn't like to think about it. She had Lord Masson take care of Sufar for spying on her, and Tedbalt killed the slave. At least, that's what she believed. He wouldn't tell her how the slave ended up dead outside. The slaves implicated were hanged, and a few weeks later the slaves revolted. She was in the palace as the fields caught fire. Luckily for her, a rainstorm gusted through. When the chaos was over, the slaves were gone. Running. To where? Sophie didn't know.

Ultiir had grown even more distant after that. He never wanted to talk to her. Even after the fight in Goldfield, they would exchange words. Now there was nothing. *How am I to win over lords loyal to him if he hates me? How am I supposed to interrupt court if he doesn't call it? I'll have to think of something before war descends on us.*

"Did you hear the news?" She asked her knight as the large palace doors were open and she finally took a breath of fresh air. It smelled of morning dew. Her hood kept the rain from hitting her hair, but it wasn't as hard as it used to be. Summer was getting closer. With it heat and bugs and fires and sweat. "The young duchess is marching south toward us."

"Some knights were telling me yestermorn," Achen said in a dry tone. "Are you worried? We will protect you. I *will* protect you."

"I know." She patted his arm. The guards and servants that were left would surely spread a rumor that Sophie and her chief guard were having an affair. It didn't matter to her as long as Ultiir didn't take any measures to rid her of Achen. She needed her knight. He was the only one she truly trusted. "Ultiir will have to defend the city and kingdom himself," she whispered. "My parents agreed with me. They actually listened. Terrop will stay out of the fight until I send word."

"Do you plan to send it?"

Sophie hadn't thought that far ahead. All she wanted was for Ultiir to lose in the little war brewing between them, but what if he were to lose the actual war? Devro would surely have her killed. "Let's see what happens when the duchess attacks."

"No one may leave without the king's consent," a guard with an owl surcoat said as they reached the gate to the palace walls. "Do you have a paper?"

"I am the queen. I come and go as I please."

The guard, a young, fat boy, shook his head, his jowls flinging about. "The king changed his mind. Go back and get the king, then we'll see."

Achen rested a hand on his sword. "Let us through, boy, or be sorry."

The boy laughed, and some of the other guards around the gate joined in. "Ya don't scare me. Why don't you and ta' queen go back to your rag of a kingdom?"

"Yeah," another yelled from inside the gatehouse, "go fuck some goats and be gone."

Achen sighed and drew his sword, and the boy's eyes grew for a split second. "How are we to go to our kingdom if we can't leave the palace grounds?"

"Well … I …" the boy shook his head and unsheathed a sword. "Ya don't scare me. You're nothing but a queen's man. You're not trained to deal with us."

"There's no reason for this to come to violence," Achen said as he shifted his stance. "You don't even have a helm on. It won't be pretty."

The boy looked around at the other guards, who either looked away or were watching with wide eyes and smiles. It didn't look like anyone was going to join the boy guard. "I'm not afraid of you. I'm gonna kill you than rape that cunt of yours," he looked to Sophie.

Achen ground his teeth. "Treason," was all he said before he stepped forward and in one stroke cut the boy's head clean off his body, his jowls flying into the air as blood spurted and caked the ground. Achen sheathed his sword and looked at the other guards, who watched in stunned silence. "Any other issues?" An older man shook his head and motioned for the portcullis to be raised. Achen bent and took the boy's fallen sword. "Be sure to let us back in when we come, or you all will be sorry." There were nods abound as Sophie stepped over the dead boy and his blood and left under the palace walls.

"Didn't have to be so violent," Sophie said as they entered the city streets. "You could've just nicked his cheek or something."

"I don't take kindly to threats of rape and insults. The boy got what he deserved." Achen said and puffed up his chest.

Sophie shook her head but smiled. *At least I have someone to protect me.* They made their way over the cobbled streets of the Noble Lands. The marble buildings built thousands of years ago by the elves usually reflected the sun, but now they looked gray from the clouds as rain echoed off the roofs. Then she saw the blackened husk of a building.

"That wasn't destroyed in the riots, was it?" She asked her knight.

Achen found a guard and got his attention. "What's this?"

"Whores," the guard spat, "raped and burned. Got off too easy if ya ask me." The guard said before going back to his patrol.

"The King's Brothel," Sophie said as her jaw dropped. "He's becoming more a monster," she whispered.

"Maybe it's time we went back to Udello," Achen said.

Sophie took a deep breath and let her chest and shoulders lift. "No. I've a plan, and I aim to see it through." She continued through the streets of marble homes.

Other city guards marched around, joked, spat, and

blocked roads. They had been given full rein of the area ever since the peasants rioted. There were still bloodstains. Luckily for her, she didn't see Lady Rila's death. But she cried with her other ladies-in-waiting that one of their close friends had been killed. *Because Ultiir had to get revenge,* she thought with a clenched jaw.

A large manor loomed in front of them as they turned down a small street. Two city guards were holding their helms and talking about their adventures the night before. Sophie tried to ignore them. Something about killing a lost soul and taking his girl to bed. The tone told her the girl had fought the entire time.

Sophie shook her head and knocked on the wooden door. A servant opened it and bowed his head. "Your Grace, the baroness will be down shortly. Come in, please." The young man ushered them in.

Baroness Mara's manor hadn't been looted, lucky for her. Colorful rugs made of wool and cotton and silk lined the white marble floors. Nude statues lined the halls. Mirrors hung from the ceiling. Paintings of gods and goddesses and ships and mountains followed a staircase up to the landing where Mara was fussing with her dress. "I'm coming," Mara called as she raced down the stairs.

Sophie took her boots off to keep the dirt from spoiling the floors, and Mara grabbed her hands and kissed her cheeks before bowing. "Welcome, Your Grace. I wasn't expecting you so soon. Lora was quick to put me in this dress." She fluffed a black velvet gown that matched her hair.

"We have much to discuss, do we not?" Sophie walked across the cold ground, her bare feet happy when they touched a carpet or rug. "Sir Achen, why don't you find some food?" The knight bowed, and the servant took him to the kitchens. "We had some trouble at the gate," Sophie told Mara. "His Grace doesn't want me leaving the palace."

"And he doesn't want us in," Mara shook her head. It would be treason for nobles to go against the king, but Sophie was asking her queen's council to commit treason on the daily. "Sounds like he doesn't wish for us to meet."

On the other side of an arch were fanciful couches. So thick with cushion that Sophie could get lost if she wanted. "Have you any news from Abre? I don't get many messages in the palace ever since ..." she didn't want to mention the death and mutilation of Atrice.

Mara gave a slow nod. "Our Abre Volles seems to be making a name for herself. Most of Oceantree has sided with her over the dispute. Probably the first time a woman has seen so much support since the days of Mertha Vandes. What was that?" Mara looked to the painted ceilings as she thought, "... some three hundred years ago?"

"Yes," Sophie said as she fell into a heap on a red couch, "but Mertha controlled much more than a small village."

"Then we can help her," Mara laughed. "Though I heard the Duke of the Woodlands hasn't been much help to either claimant. That nephew of Abre's hasn't even gotten support."

"And what is Lord Valles doing that he seems okay with a war in his duchy?"

Mara shrugged before slipping stockings onto her legs given to her by Lora. "No idea. I asked my husband, and he says that no lord from the Woodlands has heard from the duke in months. But he's supposedly still alive," she shrugged again. "Does it matter though?"

"And how comes the court?" Sophie asked. She had tasked her queen's council with figuring out which lord of the royal court would be the most sympathetic to her and her quest to add women to the laws of inheritance. So far the biggest supporter was a lord named Tylar, who had only a daughter to succeed him.

"I've been talking about a daughter with my husband," Mara said. "He swats away a baroness ruling over the lands around Sheplan, but I can see it on his face the more I bring it up. He would love to train his little daughter as his successor just as much as a boy." She touched her stomach. "Now I just need to give him a child. We've tried for many years, and I worry he will go to the High Doma for an … an …"

"He won't." Sophie said. But she thought of all the marriages Hurvir had annulled because of the lack of an heir. "Nothing to worry about right now anyhow."

Mara nodded and looked to the light drizzle outside. "I think Lord Mer Lasie would be a good one to talk with. He comes from Sayer's River and has much influence over lords from the Three Rivers, not as much as the lord of Raior but still. He also has four daughters. One of them nearing her majority and still not betrothed."

Sophie nodded and tried to remember anything about Lord Mer, but all she could picture was an older face. "Thank you, Mara." Sophie stood and took the baroness' hands this time. "I know I'm asking you to put yourself in danger, and Ultiir is only growing worse. The brothel," she stopped herself again. "I thank you."

"It's not a problem," Mara stood, and they embraced. "But

I wonder," she looked into the queen's eyes, "how do you plan on getting Ultiir to sign off on a law like this?"

"You'll just have to wait and see," Sophie smiled.

Tundavik

"I find this idea to be outrageous," Gordo told his son. "A squire? What do you think will happen out there on the battlefield? This isn't a story; this is real. You could die." Gordo was shouting now outside the small house. Glem's eyes were downcast, and his mother, Marya, was shaking her head at her son. "And you," Gordo turned to Tundavik, who leaned against the wooden house, "why would you agree to this?"

The sun felt warm on his face. The rain had stopped midmorning yesterday, now they were waiting for the river to stop rushing so they could ford it. Tundavik scratched his beard, which was growing longer and more tangled by the day. A bug had found its way in. "He wanted to go. We've younger boys than he already following us." He crushed the bug between his fingers. "It's his decision."

"It is not *his* decision," Gordo sneered. "Why should he go with you? You've given him nothing. We gave you a home so you could sleep, and your army ransacked what little we already had, and now you're taking my son. You're bringing him to war and death."

"Maybe we should go inside," Marya said to her husband. "People are staring."

Gordo said, "Let them stare." Whatever men weren't working on the fording were watching. They should've been training, but who doesn't love a show? Tundavik wanted to just roll his eyes and walk away, but that would do more harm than good, and he didn't want Glem to be beaten while he was away. "Glem sees how *noble* your cause is," sarcasm dripped like venom from Gordo's lips. "You fight for a bastard to be king. You come into the village and rape and loot anything you see. Whatever crop we had is now gone thanks to the flooding and your men. You've pillaged every village on the Nokys coast. Now I'm going to have to leave to find food, but I can't go to Redington because the war has reached there as well." Gordo spat at Tundavik's boot and headed inside after saying, "We'll all be dead come summer."

Marya and Glem just looked at one another. Tundavik could see the fury in her eyes as well, the way she glared, though there was a hint of tears in the corners. "I'm going to see to the crossing." Tundavik said quietly, then made his way down a shallow slope toward the river. Men were bringing buckets of dirt and any wooden planks they could find that weren't rotting. The River Samosay was getting closer to its former self every passing hour. Before long, they would head south to more war. *I wonder how Yvanne is doing. Are the men listening to her? Is she winning battles and skirmishes? Is she missing Devro? Guess I'll find out when we reach Vigur. Either I'll be alone, or she'll have an entire host behind her.*

"Well, everyone heard that," Sir Mar said from behind. "The yelling, I mean. Quite a spectacle for the army's commander to be admonished by some farmer."

Tundavik laughed and nodded. "I believe Gordo there is more of a fisherman."

The knight threw some loose pebbles into the water and watched them get taken downstream. Since Storyah, Mar had been getting along well enough with the other men. A few months ago he would've gotten drunk with them; Mar would've been one of the men sent naked into town from the whores. But he wanted to save Devro and find Raimund. And, like Tundavik told him, he couldn't do it with a bottle in hand. "Think we'll leave today?"

"Not sure," Tundavik said. The banks of the river had been eroded more than ever. Large clumps of earth and stone had fallen away. It had to have been a few feet wider than last year. "Where've you been? Feel like I haven't seen you since we reached the village."

"With some girls," Mar chuckled. Tundavik shook his head, and the knight held up his hands. "Relax. I can't pay women for their time? We're merely talking. Don't look at me like that, I swear it. I take care of my cock on my own." He said it as if it were some high honor. "They're good listeners."

"You pay them to talk to them? I'm sure you could've found someone for free."

"Yes, but would the free ones agree with everything I say? And sometimes they let me watch them play with each other." He laughed. "I heard Lord Toware is terrorizing the men. Think that could be a problem?"

"If that rumor spreads …" Tundavik didn't want Toware to be seen as a terror. He was merely keeping the men from finding girls. But he didn't need them fighting back. "Bad idea to keep the men and whores separate?" He asked as he watched some builders test the water. Creating mounds of dirt and seeing if they held. Some did, but others burst like a dam and flowed down the river.

Mar shrugged under his leather tunic. "Guess we'll find out." He reached into his pocket and pulled out some tack t chew. "You know, we should've waited a few months, then we could've taken the good fruit and stuff from these villages. I saw the bakers hand out old bread. It was covered in green mold with maggots; the men still ate it though, we've not much choice."

"Let me go back in time and tell Ultiir to kill Hurvir after winter." Tundavik sighed. To the south, they would see even more destruction. He didn't know how far the war had spread. He had heard rumors of slave revolts popping up all over the kingdom. And he knew Montlahead was now against Ultiir's forces, as well as Southcross and supposedly Redtop. The latter two were in the Kinglands, close to Ultiir. *Maybe we can win after all,* he thought as he looked at his men, who were either trying to build a crossing or playing like children. *First, we'll have to lose some first.* "How wrong is it to take the young ones?"

Mar's eyes trained on the men off to the side, some jumping in puddles, others throwing drying mud. "You mean like that boy whose father yelled at you?" he shrugged. "Could end badly. Could end well. We'll just have to find out."

"How did you react when you went to fight the mites?"

The knight picked at his nails; dirt had gotten underneath and didn't seem like it was any closer to coming out. "I was ecstatic, but what boy isn't? All we ever hear about growing up is the glory of war, the glory of men who vanquish their enemies. In times of peace, we yearn for the days of battle and death. Old men wonder why the young are weak, and the young men turn to robbing and raping to get the thrill." Mar cracked his neck. His growing hair swinging from side to side. "It's all a bunch of shit. Shit that old fucks like to tell people. War is awful, but we don't know until we fight. We forget. We forget what the smell of death is like — the rotting and blackened corpses. The ravens and crows pecking at eyes that will never blink again. Your friends dead. Your family dead. The trees dead. Then we begin another war to find glory, but all we end up finding is a pile of bodies shitting and pissing for the last time." Mar's eyes were lost to the south as well. Tundavik imagined him remembering all the horrors that came with the fight against the Rainvealandians. He never asked Mar about Vikry. How he became known as their savior. Mar cleared his throat. "So I was excited," he said as if he were actually happy, like his long speech never happened.

"Think we can get Devro?"

"I've seen Ultiir once or twice. That man doesn't know how to lead an army and couldn't hold a sword if his life depended on it. All we have to worry about is whether our numbers are greater than his."

"Let's hope Yvanne arrives when we do."

Over the next few days, the rainwater continued to dry and soak into the land. Small bursts of rain would happen, but none so bad that flooding took place. Tundavik stayed with Mar and his girls instead of Glem and his family. Mar had spoken true about only paying the girls to hear him talk. He told stories of Raimund and his travels in the North, sometimes stealing, and sometimes playing the hero to a helpless wench. Tundavik didn't know which was true. But the girls seemed to believe it, or pretended to so Mar would keep showering them in coin.

Tundavik even asked Mar why he didn't go back to drinking and fucking when the news of Devro's capture came. The knight said, "Trust me, I thought about it. When we got that letter, I thought, 'Then what the fuck are we fighting for?' But I decided to just find some beautiful women to talk with and decided I should fight to save him. More than I could do for Raimund." Mar shrugged with sad eyes that were usually reserved for Tundavik.

On the fourth day of waiting after the rain had cleared, the builders finally called out for Tundavik and other lords and showed off the ford. Dirt was piled to stop the water flow, and pieces of wood were atop it. Nothing special. But it would do. They tested it a few times with some oxen and horses pulling carts. It would take all day to get everyone over the river; the ford was only big enough for two oxen abreast at a time.

Glem had found Bera and Brun, and then washed and saddled them. He even found a mule for himself. "Where did you get that?" Tundavik had asked him.

"A gift from my father," Glem, garbed in a yellow gambeson, smiled. Somehow, Tundavik doubted that.

As Tundavik sat atop Bera, his cheeks burned from the sun, and he was happy for it. He was ready for the spring showers to be over and for the burning days of summer to arrive. *Hopefully, the war is over by then.*

Mar came trotting over on Brun, Raimund's horse that was entrusted with Mar's care. "The men found any sack they could and filled them with salt and fish and biscuits," the knight said. "They're excited to finally leave."

"The gods are looking down on us finally," Glem said to the knight before his mule headed for the river to drink much to the boy's objections.

"He may die before we reach the capital," Mar whispered.

Tundavik whipped his head around and almost gave himself whiplash. "Why would you say that? We haven't even left."

"He's young and naïve. I hope he doesn't die, but it wouldn't surprise me."

Tundavik shook his head. Gordo and Marya were in their home, watching out the door. It looked as if they had been crying. *Glad I never had to send my son to war,* was Tundavik's thought. *Too bad he had to die for that to happen.* "You can watch over him then," he told Mar, whose face dropped. "Make sure he reaches Vigur in one piece. You might want to start now," he pointed to Glem and the mule, who was trying to go into the water even with others coming to hold the stubborn beast back. Mar yanked on Brun's reins and muttered as he made his way to the boy. Tundavik only smiled.

Then he crossed the ford to the south. The army at his back. Who knew what lay before them? But Tundavik had a war to win.

Blis

Men untethered the boats, hoisted the anchors, and dropped the sails. The great masts of a rearing stallion would race through the ocean once more. Blis stood at the bow of the monarch's grand ship, the *Sea Glider*. It was a newer ship, built just after Queen Rouna's death. Her love of ships almost matched his. Blis loved the scent of the ocean, the salt and fish. The sound of gulls was music to him. "Ready to take to the seas once more?" A short worker said to him after unfurling a sail.

"Of course. I wasn't always this old or this fat. I captained the *Red Ember* during the war with the Rainvealandians and worked as crew for the *Sea Mare* much earlier when the Nowexerts were in Therirock. The salt of the sea is in my blood," Blis said.

"My father was on the *Red Ember*. He always said the captain was the best in Rowan. Knew everywhere to go and the best practices for blocking mite ships. He also told me the captain knew the best whorehouses when they took to land."

Blis laughed. "As I said, that was long ago. What was your father's name?"

"Raimund, a knight of Fairgrove. He fought to keep the mites from blockading the Ters-Veck. Unfortunately, he was killed some years later during a storm."

"A knight of Fairgrove does sound familiar." He lied. "What's your name, sailor?"

"Ormin, knight of nothing." Someone yelled Ormin's name and beckoned him over.

"That makes two of us," Blis said as the young sailor went back to work. He tried to think back to the *Red Ember* and all the crew aboard. The deaths of his friends and the bruises his ship took while fighting the mites. The great red sail with a yellow and orange flame plastered across. It was his favorite ship, given to him by royal decree, before the monarchy collapsed. But he couldn't remember any knight of Fairgrove. His old age had muddled his memory.

A commotion rang out on the gangplank. Blis turned and saw a young fellow with ragged clothes and the boy king being led by a royal guard. He sighed and sauntered over to the boys.

"Is there a problem with His Grace?" Blis asked the knight.

"These two were found in a brothel at the far end of Liari. Apparently, His Grace was escorted by this lowborn, Torbet. I was worried the king would miss our departure."

Blis shook his head. "I will deal with this nonsense." The knight bowed and worked his way to the stern. "You, Torbet, I will have you go to the *Fair Fellow*. Enjoy your work." The worst ship in the royal fleet. Blis was glad he never stepped foot on it. Torbet gave a slight bow and raced off the gangplank. Blis put his hand over Baldewin's shoulder and walked with him. "Should a king your age be found in a brothel?" The boy shook his head. "Then why were you there?"

The boy's eyes of honey grew wide. "Torbet told me a king needs a queen. We hoped to find one at the whorehouse. Torbet said to look for large breasts and wide hips."

"A child as young as you should worry about other things. And as king, you will have an arranged marriage. Your father, may the Four watch over him, was meant to choose, but the gods wanted to feast with him."

"Will this arranged wife have wide hips?"

Blis rolled his eyes. Baldewin never cared for girls or 'wide hips.' He knew that was Torbet talking. "I'm sure," he said anyway. "I'm also sure the people of Rowan would not like a Vigurite whore as their queen. Lords and ladies across the realm would question it, and men have gone to war for less."

"I don't want to start another war." Baldewin's voice was shaky.

"Good thing I'm here to stop you." Blis led Baldewin into his royal chambers with a laugh. Mari, Aveline's handmaid, pretended to clean. Baldewin and Blis were to keep her safe while the princess was away.

The room was fit only for a king. Purple drapes, gold etching, and a feather bed large enough for Blis himself. The king sat on a velvet chair, and Blis admired the wide window at the back. He could see the people of Liari. They differed from people on the continent. Fish and shipping dominated their lives. They wore hats to keep the sun and salt away. The roads were lined with open shops and tents selling goods from as far east as the maps went. They wore mostly light garments of silk or linen, different from the wool coats the Rowai had when they landed in Anhar. The people gave them strange looks, and they returned the favor.

"How are the councilors doing?" Baldewin asked as he plopped onto his bed. Mari went back to 'cleaning', but Blis knew she would listen to every word.

Why else would Aveline leave her here? She'll report every-thing she knows once the princess comes back. Blis stretched his arms and said, "They wish to leave sooner rather than later."

"And where did *they* decide to go?"

Blis sighed. "If you want to make decisions about our course of action, then I suggest you meet with the councilors instead of hiding in your cabin or whorehouses." Baldewin had done little since Aveline left, and after they won in Redington and Storyah, he was even less interested. The young king thought battles would bring him glory, but he never fought to gain any.

"You know they don't listen to me," the boy whined. "They didn't listen to Aveline either. They do whatever they wish, and I have to put up with it."

"Your Grace," Mari said with her head lowered; her words were soft. "If I may, why don't you show them some force? You are the king, after all. Aveline wouldn't want to see you isolating yourself."

Baldewin threw himself back on his bed. "Now even a handmaid is telling me what to do."

Blis nodded at Mari and cleared his throat. "Yes, but the handmaid is, of course, correct. You are king, and even though your regent is off somewhere else, you still have power, even if the councilors have a bit more now. Your father made sure of it when he healed the kingdom."

"And what do I tell them?" Baldewin traced the air. "'If you don't listen to me, I'll sic my hounds on you?' That will go over well." The young king sat up, his brown hair a mop on his head. "I don't even have hounds."

"You have knights," Mari said before bowing and wiping dust from her loose clothes.

"Shall we find Sir Delmar?" Blis asked. Baldewin, much to Blis' surprise, nodded.

As they left the king's quarters and made their way up one deck to the captain's quarters, shouts rang out from below and the ship lurched forward. Blis had to hold on to a railing to keep from falling into the sea below. Sails and oars worked together to pull the *Sea Glider* from port. He watched the window to see the other ships leave Liari. The *Queen's Tear* and the *Silent Kraken*, holding the lords of the east and west, followed closely behind as they moved farther from the island. He could see the painted masts of the forests of Lord Arin, the twin fish of Lord Monir, and the hills of Lord Ridas. Dozens of other sigils stared back at him, but his eyes were too old to see.

Delmar was wiping sweat from his brow when Blis found him. "Your Grace," he said to Baldewin, who was distracted by the ships cutting through the deep blue water. "What is it?"

Blis answered for the young king. "My good sir, we need you to come with us to the council meeting. Also, we must talk later about you forgetting your duties and letting the king here gallivant around Liari like a common lout."

The knight tensed, but bowed his head and followed them into the captain's room. Captain Pitor was busy at the helm, but the council was already discussing matters at a small table. As the door closed, the lords' voices dissipated.

"Your Grace," Wycleaf said in almost a whisper. "What brings you to a council meeting? You've missed quite a few in recent weeks."

"The king may go where he likes," Delmar said.

"Naturally," Jac chimed in, "we just weren't prepared for you, is all."

Baldewin's voice strained as he said, "I … I want to … join this one." Whatever force he was trying to convey certainly didn't come through. "I hope, my lords … that you don't mind."

"Never," Caxton said with a smile as his black hair fell to his face. "Stand by my side." He ushered for Baldewin, who took his place on the right of the councilor. Caxton worried Blis the most of all the royal councilors. He never knew what King Bartel saw in him, but Caxton had been a loyal servant to the crown for decades. He also wished for Blis to leave the *Sea Glider.* "I think you'll be better help to Lord Rean as he sails south. He'll need your knowledge of the seas. Plus, the North is far too cold for you," Caxton had told him as they docked in Anhar.

"I must stay near the king," Blis had said. "You already know I have advised his family for dozens of years. I cannot stop when I am needed most." And Blis never let Caxton bring it back up. *Why do you want the king alone?* was all he thought.

"So, what have you been discussing?" Baldewin asked as he looked over the maps. Blis could see the finger of the Flewth-Vet, where they would head; the city of Storyah, where they came from; and the many Glybelm Islands to the north.

Caxton pointed to the Nokys Ocean on the map. "We are discussing how the ships should be divided. We believe half of our fleet must search the southern waters, with a few ships following Lord Darry to the Island of Meret. The rest will follow us as we search the Glybelm."

"You think the fleet is there?" The young king asked. "Why would they go to frigid waters?"

"To hide and repair, of course," Wycleaf said as he slightly rolled his eyes, but Baldewin was looking at the map, not paying attention to the councilor's face. Blis crossed his arms, not able to say much.

"You don't think they went south?" Baldewin asked, tracing the coastline and up the Ters-Veck. "Perhaps back to Vigur? If my cousin's armies are heading to the capital, the usurper may want ships to defend it."

"Possibly." Caxton rubbed his chin. "Though north makes more sense to me. It's a perfect place to hide, and Viguran has controlled the Glybelm for centuries. So far, the islands have stayed out of the war."

"And we should bring them in?" Baldewin chewed on his lip. The ship moved with the waves of the open ocean as the wind carried it out. "Aveline would want that," he said as his eyes lit up. "She didn't want anymore of our people to be hurt in the war, but if the ships are in the Glybelm, maybe the raiders will take care of it. Isn't that right, Blis? The islanders hate the Vigurites. Maybe we can convince them to fight."

Blis didn't want to answer, but he gave a nod because His Grace was correct. But Aveline would surely want to return to Rowan.

"Perfect," Wycleaf said with a smile. "So, to Cahlun? That holds the islands' largest port. Might be the best place to start, Your Grace."

Baldewin nodded, and they discussed where the other ships were going, the plan once they reached Cahlun, and how Baldewin could help. The king was all smiles. Sir Delmar didn't need to use any force. Baldewin was happy to help. The councilors giddy for his involvement. But Blis couldn't shake a creeping feeling.

Flora

The letter had no crest in the wax seal, but it was sent for her husband, Barnet. It lay on Flora's trunk, stuffed with dresses. A candle melted next to the parchment, and she had to move the letter to keep more wax off it. Night and rain had fallen over Storyah, and Flora wrapped herself in a wool cloak as a fire blazed in her hearth.

"I rode for many miles, my lady." The rider said. "The rains and war have made it perilous, and I need to reach Ceal before the marsh becomes impassable." He handed her the letter. "This was delivered to me in the Catlands by a dark rider. I asked him nothing and let him be. He told me it was for your lord husband. I thought he was mistaken, but he told me he was never wrong."

"And where do you suppose it came from?"

"Perhaps your allies along the coast. I heard they were fording near the Three Rivers. Your lord husband may be of assistance."

Somehow she doubted that. Barnet was one of the few lords who kept their men in the Flewthlands to counter any attack from the Eastlands or the sea. Flora thanked the rider and sent him on his way with a gold piece.

She rubbed her eyes, and lightning lit the night sky. The rain knocked on the window so loudly she worried guards had come for her. No woman should have this much fear of her husband. But Flora did.

The letter called to her. It yelled out for her eyes to read the writing. Her father received letters every day when she was young; she was forbidden from reading them. The same happened when she went to Woodrun. But she wanted to break the rules, find out who was sending her husband a secret message. And it wasn't like she hadn't broken rules before. *I'm already an adulterer. What harm can come from reading a letter?*

But as she reached for the letter, there was a knock at her door. A guard opened it, and in came her father, the duke; and her daughter. Florance was asleep in his arms. Pyre gently woke her and let her down. "This little one fell asleep on my high chair … guess we can call it a throne now," he snickered. "She played with Lady Lueva's children all day. I'm sure she'll sleep well."

"I would hope," Flora smiled as Florance sat on her small bed. The hearth cast shadows over the room. "Have you any news from the south?"

Pyre clasped his hands and shook his head. "Not much, I'm afraid. Lord Vandes last wrote about the rains slowing them, and he could be in Vigur for all I know. Lord Rickart wrote he laid waste to Greencorse and Lord Hester's armies and is moving toward Ruwy. Other than that, I've not heard much. Swallow's rains have caused havoc, it seems."

Flora nodded as lightning lit up the rain outside. "Let us pray the Four stop these rains and Vigur falls with little bloodshed. It's time for this war to end."

"I'm not sure the Four care about bloodshed," Pyre scratched his chin. "Vigura led an army into deadly battle after all. Yes, it was to push back the forces of Veltoora, but nonetheless." Her father shrugged and gave Little Flora a kiss on the forehead. "Dream of the woods tonight, my little lady." He turned to Flora and said, "Have you seen your husband?"

"Not of late," she said as she glanced at the letter. "I know he spends hours walking the sands, but with the rain I'm not sure anymore."

"Well," Pyre said as he kissed her brow as well as if she were a child again, "if you see him, let him know both of you are welcome at court tomorrow. Lots happening." Her father disappeared out the door, but before the guard could go, Flora stood from her chair and grabbed the letter.

"My good sir, will you be so kind as to give this message to my lord husband?" She asked the guard, who nodded. "Also tell him I wish to see him at court tomorrow. It will be good for our family to stand together." He nodded once more and left down the corridor. Flora wished she had just a moment more to read the letter, but it wasn't hers. She didn't need to be treasonous to her husband once again. She turned to her yawning daughter and found a brush. Florance's hair was a tuft of blonde strands, all tangled from playing. "How is Lady Lueva?" Flora asked. Lueva had one of her legs cut off, and she hated being crippled. But Flora would tell her all the time how much her children needed her.

"The lady is good," Florance said as she kicked her legs. "Jac and I ran through the stables today. Usually there are giant horses, but they're all gone now."

"Off to war," Flora said as she finished brushing. "Who did we pray to yesternight?"

Little Flora tilted her head. "Umm, the south, to Mother Meret. Today we pray to the west, to Samosay."

Flora said, "Very good," as she brought Florance to the floor with her where they knelt to the west, placing four fingers on their hearts. "Who will lead the prayer?"

As they bowed, Florance yawned. "Too tired, and father isn't here, so you."

"I thought you'd want to do it," Flora giggled, "but okay." Flora and Florance both closed their eyes, the fire washing over them, the warmth filling them. "Dear Samosay, may the god of the west hear our prayers. We ask that you watch over us as we journey through our dreams, so that we find peace within. We ask that you protect those on foot who hope to serve the Four and the Many. We ask that you bless our words so they do no wrong, to bring no ill favor to the gods."

They both said, "We thank you, Samosay."

While Flora pulled the blankets over Florance, she prayed to herself. She wished for Samosay to protect those going to Vigur, and for the letter to be good words. Her dreams of fairies dancing over the whole of Viguran did not make her feel good about Sam the Sayer's intentions, though.

Court began as usual, though there were fewer ladies and lords than before. Most had either gone back home or to war. Wooden planks covered the holes left by the bolts from the attack on Storyah. Debris had been cleared away, though mud and dirt still tracked in. Lady Lueva sat in a chair with one leg on the ground and the other amputated and bandaged. Her eyes were soulless even as her children talked and joked with her.

Pyre Blume strolled over the black and white tiled floor to his throne. Knights and guards and messengers and peasants stepped up one by one for her father to hear. When Flora was young, court would be livelier, but people were starving now. Dying. Fighting. Instead of farming disputes and fishing rights, her father heard talk of war. Business as usual now.

Fighting near the Arner, skirmishes on the border. Raids into the Lands of Asara and the news from the duchess' army that marched south to Vigur. But the room grew quiet and cold when a knight with a bruised face bowed and said, "Lord Rickart is dead." Flora couldn't believe her ears. They had just received news that Rickart the Crazed had destroyed Greencorse. Now, he was gone. "He was slain just outside of Ruwy in his camp. His death caused a massive uproar. I was tasked with bringing the message to you, but as I was leaving, Ruwy was going up in smoke and flames. Lord Olette is now leading the armies. He has requested more men."

"More?" her father said as he tapped his leg. "Not sure if you've noticed, my good sir, but most of the troops left to fight. Any you need are either with Lord Vandes or along the border already. I fear you came this far for naught."

The knight nodded and kept his face tight. "Yes, my lord duke, but Lord Olette told me you had excellent guardsmen. He only asks because our need is too great."

Flora muttered under her breath, "Does Olette think the guardsmen can arrive in Ruwy in a couple hours?"

"What was that?" Her husband said. Lord Barnet Lovell wore an elegant black tunic with white embroidered trees.

"I can't hear you over this nonsense," he motioned to the duke and knight, who continued conversing.

"It will take over a week for the men to reach Ruwy. Lord Olette will either be dead or gone by then."

"Well, Olette was never the smart one," Barnet laughed. "There's a reason a man known as the Crazed was tasked with leading the fight and not him."

Flora couldn't help but smile along with him. "Florance was wondering where you were last night. She wished for you to pray with us."

"It's wartime. Leave the prayer to the doma."

"Your daughter missed you. We've not seen you much since coming here."

Sunlight shone through the arches, giving her husband a glow like the gods. Gray storm clouds gathered in the distance. "And whose fault is that? Tundavik is the reason we're here, the reason we're at war," he sneered. That was the husband she knew. "Did you tell Little Flora that I was busy with matters she nor you would understand? I see her around the castle. She is having fun with other children. What could she possibly want from her father? She would be bored as I pore over letters and scrolls she can't even read. Responding to messages and correspondence from all over the realm since your lover took us to war."

"You said aye." Flora reminded him. Somehow Tundavik convinced her husband to go along with the war, get almost all the lords on his side. Flora bit her lip. Part of her didn't want to know what the deal was.

Barnet's left eye twitched. "And you said aye when he wanted to be inside you and embarrass me."

Flora wished she could slap the twitch away, but it wasn't

a wife's place to hit their husbands. And she had already sinned so much. Instead she went quiet, not wanting to argue, not wanting gossip to spread. Lord Blume and the knight came to an agreement; half of his guard would travel south, leaving her father less protected. *Hopefully, the Rowai find the fleet and we don't have another battle here.*

Next, a peasant came before the throne. His clothes were gray and falling apart. Patches were sown into the fabric but didn't hide the many holes. His teeth, save a few, were missing, and the others yellow and black. He was skinny, and his stench filled the room. "Tell me your problems, my good sir." Her father said.

"I ain't be no sir." He knelt on a wobbly knee. "Mine own home and village were taken by a lord cursed by Veltoora. He raped and murdered o'er half the people."

"And which lord would this be?"

A guard, Sir Edmond Pomley, stepped forward. "We believe this man is speaking of the good Lord Poden Bruce." Flora remembered Lord Poden Bruce. He was always nice to her as a child, but sometimes she could hear the arguments he had with her father.

The peasant scratched his head. "Not a good lord anymore."

"Lord Poden lives in the Flit Levels, with his power around River Watch." Sir Edmond said. "This man accuses the forces of River Watch of claiming new lands outside the levels, including his home of Floodpan."

"I know of Lord Poden's holdings." Lord Blume sat up. "Tell me, my good man, why would Poden Bruce attack his neighbors?"

"I heard with mine ears knights talking. They said he

doesn't agree with the war, wants to take the Flewthlands for himself. He's takin' the power of villages before Storyah."

Her father looked at his guards. "And how are we to know this is true?"

"This man," Edmond said, "isn't the only one saying these things. Today a rider from the levels arrived and said the same. He was too tired to speak anymore."

Pyre Blume wore a look he hadn't in years. His eyes were downcast, his brow lowered, his forehead wrinkled. "Then we will march any knights and guards and send them to River Watch and show Lord Poden that I am still in charge!"

"My lord duke," Barnet said randomly. Flora wanted to stop him in case her father yelled, but Pyre's face relaxed. "Why send more to die? We're already losing hundreds if not thousands of men in the south. Why begin a civil war in the Flewthlands?"

"Poden would be the one starting it," Pyre said.

"Much the same, but either way we don't want another fight on our hands."

Flora's father straightened his back and sighed. "What do you propose? Go there yourself? Treat with Poden?"

"No," Barnet shook his head. "But Flora knew Poden Bruce as a child, did she not. Send her. Send her with armed guards and have her bring this foolish lord to heed with peace. No more blood."

Those in the court were watching her every move. Barnet was acting out, but no one else knew, for all they thought, Flora wanted to go. "I will not have my daughter near the fighting," Pyre said. "It's much too dange—"

"—I'll do it," Flora surprised herself by saying. "I know

Poden very well. He was always kind to me. Send me and I'll get this lord to lay his arms down, I promise."

"I could send Sir Edmond with you," Pyre said, his eyes lost in thought. "But any threat of violence and you flee, even if that means going to Plajul."

Barnet and Pyre continued discussing Flora's fate. She gulped and tried not to think of leaving her daughter behind. Trying to forget that there was a war. She prayed Lord Poden would look at her with kindness and end this folly.

As court ended and everyone went their ways, she and Barnet walked down the long tiled floor, a smile never leaving his face.

Yvanne

The sounds of swords and spears banging on shields reminded Yvanne of all the battles as they marched through the lowlands. She had rarely seen them. Either she was too sick or it was too dangerous. And just like those battles, she sat in a tent guarded by a dozen men with her handmaid and Tiro. This time though, at least Lady Lolly was there.

"It sounds horrible," her blonde-haired sister, Lolly, said as shouts filled the air. The tent flaps were closed, so they couldn't see if anything was going wrong. They just had to use their ears. "Never in my life did I think my husband and the men of River Tree would fight in this war."

Jacka was rubbing Yvanne's scalp and brushing her red hair. Never had Yvanne been so grateful for her handmaid. "I hope all is well. We had some difficulties in the lowlands," Yvanne said. "Don't tell the men that," she added. "I assume Goldfield will be even harder. Especially since they had already burned their fields awaiting our arrival." It took only a few days to march from the Whitefork to Goldfield. But it seemed like Rila de'Tro had been waiting. The fields gone, trees gone, barns destroyed, guards in the town. *How many people will I lose here when we're so close to Vigur?*

"Your Grace," the tent flap flew open, and she jumped as quickly as she could out of her chair, her belly slowing her down. Sir Loc stepped in.

Lady Lolly grabbed a knife and whipped around. "Is it my husband? Shall we go fight?"

"No, my lady," Loc said. "Your lord husband is quite alright. In fact, everyone is. The fighting is over. Lord de'Marisco sent me to fetch you."

"Over?" Tiro piped up.

When Yvanne exited the tent, she couldn't hear anymore fighting. No swords. No screams. Urses stood in his black traveling outfit and held the reins of Yvanne's mare, Snowfall. "Come," he called. "We've a town to explore."

The burned remains of wheat crunched under Snowfall's feet. Urses walked beside the mare, holding the reins and resting a hand on her neck. Sirs Loc, Tiro, and Rickart were near enough in case the battle wasn't actually over. Yvanne rested her hand on her stomach. She had taken to wearing loose-fitting clothes of black and blue. She had a half-cape on her back that flowed in the breeze of warm spring air as Snowfall glided.

"Excited for the babe?" Urses asked. "The daken in Vigur are the best. Giving birth there will mean a strong and healthy child."

"Do you think our plan will work? To take the city?"

Urses clicked his tongue. "If Goldfield is anything to go by, then yes. Though I'm not sure if Rila de'Tro is a good measure of how her son will do in a fight. He also has scores upon scores of more men and weapons. It seems Goldfield was left defenseless."

How odd, Yvanne thought. "Is it a ruse? Is Rila de'Tro

even here? What are we to do if we can't take her as hostage?" The plan was to capture Goldfield first, destroy one of Ultiir's strongholds before marching on Vigur, and to capture the almost dead Rila de'Tro. So far, the plan was going perfectly. Too perfect.

"If that's the case, then we attack Vigur just the same. Lord Cul's fighters are the strongest and are in the van. I don't see the wall lasting a day."

"You put a lot of faith in them. You've never even seen them fight, always off hiding somewhere." Yvanne giggled, but it was true. Urses had a knack for disappearing whenever a battle broke out, just to reappear afterward.

"Someone has to live," Urses smirked. "If everyone else dies in battle, who will be there to advise you on what to do next?"

"If everyone is dead, then there will be no next."

"I believe I can get you to safety if the need arises. I am lord of Keeland after all. The town of bandits. Men who have a knack for running away and hiding come through Keeland. I know many and more of their secrets." Urses paused as a dead body was being carried off. The knight was in gold plate. His helm had come off, and his neck was slit open, the blood oozing toward his chest. "Do you have any idea what you're going to do with your child?" Urses asked, and Yvanne puzzled at the lord. "If Vigur isn't taken? How do you plan to protect the babe and fight a war?"

Yvanne brushed her hair from her eyes. "I hadn't thought of that." She didn't like thinking of the giving birth part and what happened next. All her life she had heard the screams of birthing women in Whitehall; seen the lifeless eyes of those who didn't make it. As a child, it scared her. *Yet here*

I am, pregnant. Yvanne touched her belly again and felt a kick. "Luckily, I have an army at my back to protect us."

A horse trotted over the rolling hills toward Yvanne. She wasn't worried, though. She could see the red curls of her brother. "Too easy." Pollard said from his horse when he reached them. The dead crop had become dirt paths as they neared town. "It fell with almost no resistance."

"Maybe Rila de'Tro is afraid." Yvanne said back. "Maybe she knows her son is weak."

"They burned all the wheat fields that gave the town its name," Pollard said. "They must've been expecting us, but Gordo said only twenty men were slain on their side. All of ours still alive."

Urses stood back as Yvanne and Pollard and her knights went into town. Most of the men now made camp in the burnt fields near the Montla. A bridge was to be constructed to take them over the river and make it easier to reach Vigur. Ed the Loon would continue this side of the water. He would cut off Vigur from the north while Lord Cul led his fighters to the wall. Men who joined from the Crossing and other towns in the Duke's Pass would go south over the Ritae. With the capital surrounded, they hoped Devro wouldn't be snuck out. *I will get you back,* she told the imagined Devro in her head, *my child will not be without a father. This war will not end that way.*

The click-clack of the horses' shoes on the cobbled roads echoed in the silent town. Windows had been boarded. Shops closed. Homes cut off. Gordo and Diero were waiting on the streets with their hosts of men. Yvanne could hear a few whimpers escape from indoors from people hiding from the army. A few doors were bashed in. The homes stripped and rummaged through. Her men piled the twenty enemies who died into a burning mass just in front of the large manor that engulfed everything in shadow; the smell was horrendous. But Yvanne had gotten used to the smell of death since leaving Whitehall. It lingered. Everywhere she went, her nose was attacked by blood and piss and charred skin. At first, it made her sick. Now, she was just glad it wasn't her men she was smelling.

Gordo and Diero opened the large doors to the manor as Yvanne and Pollard dismounted their horses. "Is she still alive?" Yvanne asked.

"Alive and eager." Diero said, his lips tight.

"Well, let's see what she has to say," Yvanne said as the de'Tro manor swallowed her. It hadn't been looted yet. Jewels shone brightly as the sun bounced off them through the windows. Purple and green and red feathers lined the walls. And she thought she smelled cooked meat. *If the army smells that the manor will be overrun in seconds.* As she made her way between stone pillars that held up the high ceiling above her, she saw the oldest woman she had ever seen sitting on a chair of red velvet.

"Do you know how long I've been sitting here?" Rila de'Tro asked. Her skin was tight around her face, her skinniness bordering on sickly, and she looked like a wrong wind could break her. "Most times, whoever leads an army is in the lead, but I can tell by your *condition* you've never led an army a day in your life."

Yvanne glanced at Pollard next to her with a grin of disbelief. "I'm not sure you have the authority to speak to your queen like that," she said.

"My queen," Rila laughed and gasped for air. "As long as

my son is still alive and ruling from Vigur, you will never be my queen. I don't even see Sophie as my queen. In fact, I would say I was the last queen of Viguran. The kingdom has fallen apart since my rule ended."

"Hopefully you live to see the day I'm crowned in Vigur then."

"And what will you do after? Be a ruler? Command armies and navies? No," Rila de'Tro shook her head, her white wisps of hair flowing back and forth. "You will become the bastard's stress relief. Anytime someone upsets him, defeats him, mocks him, he will turn to you and beat you. Then he will fuck you. Ruin your body for a good twenty or thirty years, if you're anything like me, with babe after babe after babe. You'll wish you stayed in that shit-of-a-village Whitehall."

"Maybe that's what your time as queen was like, but Devro is not his grandfather or father. He will—"

"—don't associate the bastard with my husband and son," Rila interrupted. "He is nothing more than a cruel jape the evils of Veltoora played on my sweet Hurvir. Now, the entire kingdom is suffering because of it. War and disease. Slave revolt. Nothing is as it used to be. Peaceful? Good? Did you see my fields? All burnt. The slaves did that when they decided they were done having a good life. I gave them food and a place to sleep, and they were still ungrateful. Do you know how many beatings I told the masters were too much? Still, the slaves hated me." The old woman was shaking her head in disgust. She spat on the floor. "So now you've come to kill me? So be it. I'm old; I buried my parents and my husband and all of my children save for one, and the banished herself from my presence. I have nothing left. So end it."

Yvanne blinked. She didn't know how to respond. *This woman is insane, and I'm supposed to believe Ultiir will trade her for Devro? What have my brothers gotten me into?*

Luckily for her, Pollard was there. "We don't want to kill you, Your Grace," Pollard said. Yvanne liked the keeping of formalities. It showed the kooky old woman that she still had respect, even if it was fake. "We just wanted to talk."

"And why is a knight of some backwater addressing me?" Rila slowly crossed her legs like it was a struggle. "You still call me 'Your Grace,' and this girl-called-queen doesn't even have the dignity to speak to me. Pathetic. And the peasants are supposed to respect her?"

Yvanne again was at a loss for words. Never had she been spoken about in that way. Not even when she was marching against her enemies in the Lands did the lords resort to that. She was biting her tongue, watching a few servants far behind Rila, when Pollard whispered, "the old bitch."

Even though Rila de'Tro was ancient, her hearing apparently was still good. "What did you call me? How dare you say that about the queen mother! About the woman who ruled with her husband. Held back the mites. Held back the Nowexerts and their allies."

Yvanne motioned for Diero, and he escorted Pollard out as Rila raved and ranted. "Your Grace," Yvanne said, and the queen mother calmed herself, wiping tears. "That was uncalled for, don't you think?"

"Respect," the queen mother started, "my dear girl. It's the only thing that keeps us from being savages."

"Well, Your Grace," Yvanne let the words have a sting to

them. "The thing about respect is you must earn it, and, to be frank, my brother was right to call you what he did." Yvanne was trying very hard to keep her foot from tapping with nerves. Rila crossed her arms and leaned back in her chair, but her face was all fire. "This is what's going to happen. We have a wagon awaiting your arrival; it even has a pillow. You will be bound and taken there, and we will march to Vigur with you in tow. Then we'll see how much your son loves you."

Yvanne swirled around, letting her cape flow, and left the old queen mother to her bitter fate.

Tundavik

He was badly injured trying to protect the wagon," a lord named Tylo told Tundavik. "It's by the grace of the Four that he is still alive." The injured soldier withed in pain as the daken went to work bandaging his torso. It had been sliced open down the side, but not deep enough for death. The soldier had a black eye and a swollen cheek. Blood stained his gray trousers.

They were just a few miles outside of Forecreak if the maps were to be believed. The river to their north was thick with wood. That's where the bandits had attacked from. Three men were dead, the withering one the only to survive. The bandits had attacked near the rear of the baggage train, probably looking for food. *Can't find what we don't have,* Tundavik thought.

He had instructed the men to set up camp. Armed patrols would make their way through the tents and wagons throughout their stay. He didn't need anymore men dying before they crossed the River Fore. Then they would only be a two- or three-day journey to Vigur and hopefully Yvanne.

"So, what's the plan?" Lord Toware asked. "We can't just let these thugs come and steal what's ours and kill our men."

"They only took some helms and swords." Tundavik said, not wanting to go looking for a fight.

"Swords they can use to attack us again," Toware clenched his fist. "And who knows how many innocents they have terrorized on this road over the years. Dal knows Hurvir couldn't protect his people."

"I agree with Lord Toware," Lord Tylo said. Tylo was a manor lord of some land along the coast. He was once a knight. Hurvir had given him a lordship after the war with the Rainvealandians, and Tylo wished to repay the dead king by saving Devro. "Send us out and we will rout the bastards." Tylo's tight face reddened with anger.

Tundavik rubbed his eyes. *Just what I need. Vengeful lords.* "Fine," he conceded, "we'll go rout the *bastards*. My lords, bring your men. I'll lead the charge."

"Isn't that dangerous?" Glem had said from behind. He was standing with Lord Toware's blue-armored men. "M'lord, you're the commander of this army. You'll lead us to Vigur. If the bandits capture you … or worse …"

"Quiet," Tundavik snapped. The men would be expecting him to punish Glem, but Tundavik agreed with the boy. *I can't die here. I still have to reach Ritaeum and figure out this Nhamcaryn nonsense.* He shuddered at the ghosts that could be haunting his old home, and of the lady in his dreams awaiting him with more death and destruction than the war has already caused. "We'll follow this river — what's it called?"

"The River Clasp," Tylo said, "where Mother Meret clasped —"

"—very well," Tundavik interrupted. "We'll follow the Clasp to the east and see if we don't reach Forecreak. Bring some runners so we can deliver any news to the men."

"And who's in charge while you're away?"

"Probably Lord Furrow and Sir Mar," Tundavik said. He hoped Mar could handle a few rowdy men who were looking for trouble, and Furrow would give the command a more prestigious role. "Shall we go?"

***

Tundavik led a column of men through the thick wood. Sunlight struggled to cut through the canopy. Both thin and thick beech trees sprouted everywhere, making it difficult for Bera and the other horses to wander their way through. Tundavik had no idea where he was going. But the River Clasp was just to their north; eventually they would reach the confluence of the river with the Fore. By then they would be in Forecreak. Either met with arms or alms.

"I always loved King Hurvir," Tylo said to Toware atop their horses. "He was a kind man. A proper king. If not for him, the mites would've raided and raped the entire kingdom. When I heard the news of his passing — his murder — I cried and prayed for a week straight."

Tundavik rolled his eyes and imagined Toware was as well. Lord Toware was untangling a knot in his horse's mane. The horse armored in blue as well, looking like something out of a myth, like the horse was rising from the sea. "A week sounds rather long," he said to Tylo. "I didn't even mourn my father for that long."

"And how is it he met his end?"

Toware's horse rounded a rock, kicking dirt and flinging mud. The column of men behind were stepping carefully over a brook. The forest seemed to have flooded just like the River Samosay. Dried mud and pieces of debris that didn't belong littered the ground; rocks and trees had toppled over; birds' nests were strewn about. "He had raised Riverend in revolt against Hurvir," Toware said, and Tylo smacked his lips, "during Onto's Rebellion. Riverend was one of the first towns Hurvir encountered. I was lucky not to be there. I had gone on a fishing expedition in the Glybelm — gods, it was cold. No one in Riverend survived that day. Duke Blume told me that was one reason he sued for peace."

Tylo sat awkwardly atop his destrier, then scratched the small red beard on his chin. "I'm sorry to hear that, my good lord. My father was a drunk and a brute and would beat me and my siblings savagely. I'm sure the same excitement I felt at the news of his passing is what you felt when King Hurvir died."

"What of your father, Lord Vandes?" Toware asked. "Forgive me for not knowing my histories very well. We didn't learn much about the Woodlands in Riverend."

Tundavik rested one hand on his leg while the other held Bera's reins as they curved around tree trunk and rock aplenty. "My father was a fine man, much nicer than yours," he nodded at Tylo. "I'm sure he had a rough time raising all us children. He and my mother had ten in total. I the eldest. He fought toward the end of the Nowexerti Wars, helped free Ealna from the clasp," — he looked toward the river — "of the Hatets."

"Bloody traitors," Tylo spat.

"Then he died and I became lord." Tundavik remembered his father's death, though it was murky; all the death that followed clouded his memory. But his father, Elys, couldn't have been much older than Tundavik was at that moment. He had a graying beard and hair. The daken administered their ointments and poultices, and the doma prayed over him, but it was no use. Elys Vandes died just a day after he got sick. Rumors were that Elys was unfaithful while reinforcing Hurvir's massacre in Jorbstah, but Tundavik knew his father. He had too much love for his wife to do that. He was nothing like Hurvir.

"I'm sure you have many and more to tell," Toware said. "Good thing we still have a few days until Vigur."

They rode under the tall birch trees for what seemed like days, instead of only a few hours. The wood was too quiet. Even Toware and Tylo's men were silent save for a crunch of leaves or sticks and the occasional piercing sound of someone pissing. Bera was kicking underbrush. Squirrels and rodents scurried. Birds chirped. The River Clasp babbled. As they continued west, the river came closer to view. Tall grass and lilies littered the banks and shallow edge. Frogs croaked and occasionally splashed into the water. He didn't hear or see any ripples of fish.

Tundavik picked leaves and needles from his hair. The last time his hair had grown past his ears was during the war with the mites and the deaths of his family. *I need to shave it off as soon as Vigur is won. I don't need anymore bad omens with this lady already haunting me.* He scratched at his beard. He wondered how different he looked from last year when he was fishing in Attrima. Glodsteil the dwarf wouldn't recognize him.

Toware and Tylo were speaking of Vigur when Tundavik stopped taking in the sounds of nature. "When was the last time you saw the palace?" Lord Toware asked Tundavik. "Will it be a strange sight knowing your ancestors used to live there? That, if things went differently, you'd be king?"

"I don't think of it," Tundavik said, trying to even picture the palace in Vigur. He knew it was tall and had been built with marble by the elves all those centuries ago. *Maybe I saw it in a painting once.* "Never been. And being king doesn't seem the best job anyhow. Hurvir was killed. Ultiir and Devro are at war. I enjoyed living in Attrima, much more peaceful."

"But the wealth," Tylo drooled. "And what happened in Ritaeum to your family … well, it wouldn't've happened if you were king."

Tundavik didn't look at the lord. He didn't want Tylo to see the hurt and sadness and anger wash over his eyes. Much better to pretend like it didn't matter even if his heart ached.

"I found something!" a scout called as he ran toward the column from the west. "A village, my lords, some people. Could be bandits or not, hard to tell."

Toware unsheathed his sword and kicked his horse. "Then let's find out."

The lord of Riverend was quick, and his men followed in a flash while Tundavik and Tylo stayed still. The chorus of shouts and the shaking of the earth died as the army went west toward some village. Tundavik sighed. "That lord is going to get us in trouble someday. I'm not sure when."

Tylo nodded and said, "Perhaps he should bring up the rear when we reach Vigur. Keep them waiting."

"Maybe," Tundavik said as he kicked Bera forward and the rest of the army followed behind. "Though throwing the might of Riverend at Vigur's walls just might bring them crashing down."

"Then you've never seen the strength of my men," Tylo clenched his gloved fist.

Tundavik turned his head and saw the dozen men employed in Lord Tylo's service. None seemed eager. They were either very young or very old. "Where did you say your manor was?"

"Along the Nokys. Beautiful views of the islands, the birds are always a welcome sight. My manor didn't have a name nor a village near it, but I called it Heavensfield."

"I may have to see it sometime," Tundavik said as he wondered who would even return to Heavensfield.

The river grew louder as they neared it. Still no fish in sight, and the plants along the shore had been picked or torn up. As they continued along the south bank of the Clasp, the sounds of yelling echoed over the water. Tundavik rolled his eyes. "Let's see what Toware is doing?"

The village — more like a hamlet with a couple of houses made of dirt and grass — lay along the river. A small dock crumpled and rotted into the water; fishing lines were strewn about; nets tattered in the remaining weeds. Tundavik had been expecting to see cattails throughout the river, but they were gone, just like the fish. *Was everything eaten in the whole damned area?*

"Please," a shrill voice pierced the clear sky, "we've nothin'. Don't know nothin'. Just leave us be, please."

When Tundavik dropped from Bera, and Tylo followed, they found Lord Toware and his men looting whatever was left in the houses. Cabinets and dressers were thrown out, clothes ripped open, small rows of plowed earth were stomped and the roots pulled up. A blue-armored man held up a gloved fist to the woman screaming and crying. She had wrinkles on her face and liver-spotted hands covered her eyes. "Enough!" Tundavik shouted, and one of Tylo's men pulled the blue-armored man away. "Lord Toware?"

The lord of Riverend emerged from a house, pulling a young boy by the hair, his other hand holding a helm. "See!" He held up the helm. "Flewthmen metalwork. The bandits, the savages, live here."

"Drop the boy and control your men." Tundavik rested his hands on his hips. The lord's mouth was agape, but he dropped the boy in the freshly unearthed soil, and admonished the soldier for making the old woman cry. "I see you found what you were looking for," Tundavik said.

"Thieves, bandits," Toware spat on the boy. "What shall be down, commander? Lose a hand? Or a head for taking the helm?" The boy shuddered and cried and held his head like it was about to pop off.

"Tell your men to leave the village, then we'll talk." Tundavik said. Toware didn't hesitate. He did as he was told, which was good. Tundavik didn't have enough manpower to overcome Toware's forces if the lord decided he knew what was best. "Did you terrorize them enough?"

Toware chewed on his cheek like he didn't know what to say. "Not enough, I think. Three of our men are dead. Potentially a fourth when we return. So far we've killed no one in this village."

"Please, m'lord," an old man wobbled out from a house with a sunken roof, "we've just made home here. We've no issue with you and want no part in this war. Let us live, please."

"Did you catch all the fish and pick the wild fruit?" Tundavik asked the village, which had gotten larger now that people were emerging from their hidey-holes.

"No, m'lord," a girl maybe ten said. She had a broken and bleeding lip, and he wondered with fury which of the men had hit her, and what they would've done had he arrived any later. "The fish stopped a swimming this way. No creatures come this way now."

"The girl speaks true," the old man said. "Forecreak has been burnt to a crisp, and it threw the whole region into disarray. The town lay in smolders, the fields blackened, the Fore running red with blood. Now, beasts have come out of their dens, and bandits scour the land."

"Bandits?" Toware laughed. "You can't complain of highwaymen when you're doing the same. Stealing from our train? Killing our men?"

"We just wanted food," the boy in the soil said. "That's all we'se wanted."

"See?" Toware pointed. "He admits it. Tundavik, allow me to drag that boy back to camp and show him and everyone else what happens if you steal."

Tundavik rolled his eyes. The boy was just older than Glem, and he didn't see anyone else who looked dangerous or like a thief. "You wanted food, so you stole from an army on the march? That's how you end up killed."

"I'se searching for food is all," the boy said again. "I'se wasn't expecting no fight, m'lord; it just happened. We didn't mean for there to be any dead."

"Who is 'we'?"

"The boy must be talking about little Tito and Al," the old woman said as she brushed dirt from her face and clothes.

"Al was strong as a buck, but we buried him earlier." She pointed to a fresh mound of dirt. "Little Tito never made it back. We want to go searching for 'im and see if we can't find his body."

"He was bleeding real bad," the boy said.

Tundavik motioned for Toware. "Let's go. These people have suffered enough."

"But the men ..." Toware's face was covered in shock. "They died for nothing."

"We'll avenge them by taking Vigur and stopping the need for normal people to resort to banditry." Tundavik turned toward the small hamlet. "Next time, don't steal from an army. I can't promise you it will end well."

"You have our promises," the old man said, and the other villagers nodded. "New Vigur will be a place of peace, you will see."

"New Vigur? What's that?"

"It's where you're standing," the woman said. "The old capital is full of violence and fear. We want to begin anew. Make a capital and kingdom that brings peace to all. No more war."

Tundavik climbed atop Bera while the village emptied of soldiers. Toware stomped away with a pout. "It's a beautiful dream," Tundavik told the people as he departed.

Raimund

He dreamt he was flying through the clouds. Over oceans and islands. Mountains and rivers and steppes. The land came and went, as water swallowed it and cloud hid it. It was the best dream.

Except it had really happened.

Raimund awoke in a field of tall grass that tickled his ears. His face covered in flakes of pollen and flowers. Sneezing, he rose to get his bearings. *I am nowhere.* The field went on for miles in every direction. In the far distance, behind a haze of gray, he saw mountains. *The Noest.* Except those weren't snow-capped like the mountains he had climbed. Opposite the mountains, and just as far, he saw a forest. Dark sentinels rose, but looked smaller than any forest he had seen. *They will grow as I near,* he thought. *No way that forest is smaller than the ones in Viguran.* Nowhere in any haze, or far-off place, could he find the dragon. He had carried Raimund and left him for dead.

Raimund had no weapon to defend himself. No sword or dagger. He had only the small amount of fire his hands could make. If he had Valkyr, his sword, he would be ready for anything, but he was alone. His clothes were ripped and his hair disheveled. His stomach called for food and his throat for water. He slipped off his cloak and peeled away his gloves and the long stockings he wore under his boots. His ever-growing hair held the sweat from the heat, so he tore a piece from his cloak and tied it away from his face.

He could go either to the forest or to the mountains. Truth be told, he was tired of both. He wished for a city to appear, mainly Vigur. He would even take Redington. *I need to get back.* But in his heart, he knew that would never happen. He was so far away he would die before reaching Viguran. Never again see Mar or Devro, Yvanne or Tundavik. It was a mistake to listen to the voices in his head and climb atop the dragon's back. Now he would die for nothing.

The sun blistered the open grassland, and his winter clothing didn't help. Sweat drenched his body. He needed shade. The forest looked just a minuscule closer than the mountains. He kept his shirt on to act as armor in the event he was attacked, but he wished to take it off as his sweat clung to him. He reached the forest and was right about the trees growing. They reigned over him like a lord's tower. *If only a lord lived here.* He pushed through the thick brush and basked in the cool shade.

The trees went on in perfect rows and columns. Something he didn't expect. *A tree farm. Someone is here.* He went through the forest with his eyes ready to catch any movement. The only things he saw were insects and squirrels, a few all white like the snows of the Noest.

His throat was dry, and there was no water. *Maybe it will rain. Please rain.* He didn't know which god to pray to. He remembered some of the Many and a few of the Northern gods, but which was for rain? *Too many gods and no time.*

As he went deeper into the forest, some areas had a blue tint. He followed his eyes to see the cause. He stared into a pool of glowing liquid, not sure if he should drink it. *I am a knight. I will not die by a sickness,* but his body wanted to drink more than anything. He had to force his legs to move on. Other pools dotted the woods. He looked into the ones closest to him, hoping for water, but no luck.

Raimund leaned against the cool white stone that held the liquid. *Where is the fucking dragon? Why would he leave me after taking me on his back?* Raimund hardly remembered the flight. He wasn't sure if it took minutes or hours or weeks. But he was hungry and thirsty and tired all the same. *First, the beast kills my friends, then leaves me in a sea of grass.*

Raimund turned to the pool and stared inside. For a moment, he thought he saw his parents. The fire. Their charred skin. He cupped his hands and dipped them in the pool. As he was bringing the liquid to his dry mouth, a voice rang out. "Do not!" He dropped his hands and reached for his sword — he didn't have one. "The pools are not meant for drinking." The voice had a thick accent that Raimund had never heard before. Kruheshian? Or maybe he was in Eotros. Too far away from home was where he was. He looked for the source. "Here." The voice sang from the tree above him.

Raimund looked up and saw a creature with braided hair, skin slightly green, hair dark like the limbs of trees. He picked himself up and ran through the pools, hitting a few, trying not to fall in. His legs ached. He was so tired. His body was starved and dehydrated and falling apart. He fell to the grass between two pools, the blue hue lighting the trees above. As he panted, the creature came over to him.

"Stay back," he called out, but it didn't listen. He thought back to the mountain siren that almost killed him in the Noest. If not for Potter, he would be dead. This time he didn't have Potter to save him, nor a weapon. He felt his fingers grow hot, the fire wanting to fly out, but they stopped. His fingers cold. *The monster ...* he thought.

"I do not wish to harm you," the creature said in a high-pitched voice. As it got closer, the creature looked more and more like a woman, as if it was changing before his eyes. "I have come to help you."

"No, I don't want it," Raimund said through dry lips. Then he saw the creature's ears. They were pointed. "Are you an elf?"

"I am whatever humans wish to call me." The creature held out a hand; it had become completely a woman. Looking and sounding just like someone Raimund would've known back home.

"So if you're an elf, can you take me back home? Is Adedor east or west of here?"

She laughed. "North, south, east, west. Go any which way and you will find it."

Raimund gripped the soft grass beneath him. "I've no time for riddles." He let out a cough, his throat hoarse. "Just tell me, and I'll be on my way."

"It will take you far too long to reach your home. As of right now, you are near nothing and everything. But walk out and you will never return anywhere."

Raimund's head pounded. *This monster is crazed. She wishes to lure me closer. She wishes to —*

The creature said, "I wish nothing," and Raimund wanted

to vomit, but there was no food or water to come up. She had heard his thoughts. She was no ordinary elf; she was like some elf goddess. An elven witch. A demon. "Now," she looked forward toward an angelic light glowing through the trees. "I will see you to your home."

"Home?" Raimund backed up.

"You have much to learn while you are here. The others and I have set up a place for you to live for the time being. A place where we can teach you all you must know."

"And where is this place? Where are we?"

The demon smiled. "In time" was all she said as she carried her bare feet over the grass.

Raimund didn't walk with her, couldn't. The creature made her way through the trees while he stayed at the pools, clutching his stomach and tightening his jaw.

This is all a dream. I am asleep and will wake with the dragon near. Or it was a trap. Some deranged creatures wanted to feed him alive to lions or drown him in these pools. *She lies.* He had to repeat that in his head or he might have believed her. *She lies.* They are in Kruhesh. He would wait for night and the shining stars before following Dagmer's eye to the north. His throat burned and his lips chapped. *She lies.* But his thirst was overwhelming, and his hunger became unbearable.

She disappeared into the forest. Her green skin blended with the leaves and trees. *Last chance,* a voice told him, so he pushed himself up and followed the creature into the glowing light.

Aveline

Anha Jorbstah rose like a peak over the water and jagged mountains of the South. Stone reached for the sky, the sun shining bright over all. Spires and towers of stone created a great hulking presence of shadow over the valleys. But down below, thick, black tendrils had dried. Whatever streets under the layer of black were completely covered. It cracked and breathed and looked like waves.

"What do you think happened?" Aveline asked her guards. They all stood ready with weapons, looking to the mountains and into the large chasm of water below. There were no bridges to reach the city, so they could only look on from afar.

"Surely a dragon," Zoell said in her coral armor. "What else could do this?"

Dead trees had toppled over. Hands and arms and screaming faces had dried in the black rock, trying to break free. The largest stone tower looked like a candle dripping wax, dried black crust melted into the column.

"No time for jests," Bert said. He was her oldest guard, and he didn't believe in much.

Aveline also didn't believe in dragons, or at least that any were still alive, but she had no other way to explain the state of Anha Jorbstah. *If not a dragon, then something much worse. Something the elves have unleashed on the world,* she thought with a shudder.

"I have heard many stories of dragons returning to our world," Zoell said. "I do not say it as a jest."

"What do you think it could be?" Ivlin asked Bert.

Bert didn't answer. He merely shrugged. Tomas carefully stepped toward the chasm that led to water below. "I don't think we're making it across," he said.

"Do you think Bertin is there?" Aveline asked. She wasn't sad, even if he was her brother, just matter of fact. "Do you think he's dead?"

"We won't know," Dern the Third said. "This mission was always going to be a difficult one, and now that Anha Jorbstah is burnt to a crisp ..."

"It will be harder," Aveline said. "I know." Aveline wiped sweat from her brow. She had tied her hair to keep herself cool, but as summer grew near, the South baked under the sun. She sighed and sat on a rock. Tapped her foot. Looked to the clouds. It was like looking for an ant in a sea of grass. *Maybe I should've stayed with Mari. Protected Baldewin. Who knows what Caxton and the others are planning for him? How they mean to use him.*

Tomas whipped out his cock and pissed into the water far below in the ravine. The sound echoed throughout the mountains. Aveline shook her head at the knight, but was used to him by now. Even before the hard journey south from Ealna, Tomas was always crude. With the echo of piss came the ruffle of leaves in a densely wooded area a few hundred feet from them.

Bert stood with squinted eyes. Ivlin held up his hand to the old knight, telling him to stop. "Gonna wake a bear," Ivlin said. "Maybe we shouldn't investigate."

"I'll go," Dern said. "Maybe it's a tree nymph. Who knows what lives out here?" Dern grabbed his sword and traipsed over to the wood, disappearing into the trees.

"And if it is a girl, he'll blush and flirt and it still won't lead anywhere." Zoell asked as she rolled her eyes with a snicker.

"At least you've realized Dern is all talk," Tomas laughed.

"We've more important things to worry about anyway," Aveline said. She was used to her guards arguing and jesting and the like, but that was when she knew her family was safe. When her father still ruled in Rowan. When Bertin was off in Gereduss with Devro and Baldewin was playing games with some chancellor's children. Now they were all separated. Aveline and Baldewin might be the only two in their family still alive. She tried not to think about it, but Anha Jorbstah, being a mountain of dried magma, didn't help.

A scream pierced through the stillness. Her guards jumped up and faced the wood from which it came. "I guess Dern got his wish." Bert said, since the scream had sounded like a girl's.

"Look what I caught." Dern called out as he emerged from the dark pines. He was dragging a small elf girl by her arm. She kicked and punched at him while wearing an angry face, but she wasn't even half his size. "An elfling."

Aveline shook her head. "Let her go; you're scaring her."

Dern's face dropped, but he did as she said, and the little elf girl went running, but Dern caught her shoulder and dragged her back. "Oh, no you don't. Feisty."

Tomas shook his head. "You're a real hunter, Dern."

"What was she doing back there?" Zoell asked.

"Who knows?" Dern said with a shrug. He pushed the small elf forward. "Explain yourself. Are you a scout?"

"Siauf motai ad fotai fy," the little elf said as she stomped her foot.

"Anyone?" Dern asked, and everyone but Bert shook their head. The old guard tapped his lips as if he were deep in thought.

Aveline found a pack with some old bread they had bought from a merchant along the sea road. It looked clean enough. She stepped closer to the girl, who took a step back. Dern put his hand on the elf's back to keep her from running. "I don't want to hurt you," Aveline said. It was like talking to a startled horse. "Here," she threw the bread, and it landed at the girl's feet. Her ankles and legs were covered in dirt and burn marks. Like the fire had clawed at her. She had a bruise on her arm. Her hair caked in mud. Her eyes were a deep blue that looked even more like water with the tears that formed.

The elf plopped to the ground and stuffed her face with the bread as she crossed her legs. Aveline smiled at the sight. She looked a lot, almost identical, to the little girls back in Rowan. It was as if Aveline were seeing a reflection. Other than all the dirt and mud.

"She's been hurt," she told her guards as they too looked at the burn marks. "Maybe whatever happened over there." Aveline pointed to Anha Jorbstah. "If only we spoke elvish."

"Seàs," Bert said. Aveline eyed her guard while the others looked on in shock. "That's what she was speaking, Seàs.

I've no clue what she said in full, but it was something about her parents, I think. *Motai* means mother, I believe."

"And since when did you speak elvish?" Ivlin asked with a breathy laugh.

"I spent some time down south before I met any of you." Bert shrugged as if it were no big deal. "I had a life that was more than just guarding the princess."

"I'd never've guessed," Tomas said.

Aveline had forgotten some of her friends she had made while in the South as well, back in her rebellious day. The time she went against her father and learned the ancient tongue and went to temples to pray to Aldima Ahíd. *How could I forget?*

"I think I have an idea," she said. "We'll have to search for her too, but I know someone in Jorbstah. She can … see things. She might help us find Bertin. Tell us if he's dead or not."

"Mystics?" Bert laughed.

"I don't think you get to laugh this off," Ivlin said, "considering you can speak with elves or something."

"Yes, a mystic," said Aveline. "But first we should help this little girl find her parents."

"Elves," Dern said through a tight mouth. "Are you sure they'd be happy to see us? What if they think we've stolen her?"

"We'll just need to pray," Aveline shrugged.

The small elf, who stood and brushed her legs off as Aveline neared, barely came up to her knees. "Hello," Aveline said with a smile. She tried to appear as comforting as she could, but she hadn't been around children since Baldewin was little. The elf's lip was sweaty, as was her brow. Aveline pulled a handkerchief from her trousers and dabbed her head in mock demonstration.

When the elf didn't look scared, Aveline put the handkerchief on her small head and wiped. "It's alright, sweet thing." The cloth turned brown from dirt and a little red from a small, dried cut on the girl's head. "What happened to you?" Aveline bit her cheek as the elf's blue eyes stared into hers. Or looked to be staring into Aveline's eyes. Her eyelids fought to stay open. Her pupils were small. It was like the girl was looking at something beyond the guards, but there was nothing else.

Aveline pointed to Anha Jorbstah. What was left of it, anyway. "Are you from there?"

The girl followed her finger, and her eyes went wide at the sight of the ancient city. Tears fell down her cheeks even though she didn't make any noise. Aveline looked at her guards as she held back her own tears. Dern nodded, and Aveline knew he agreed to find the girl's family.

She held out her hand with a forced smile. The girl's brow was a little cleaner, but she really needed a bath fit for a princess. With soaps and scrubs of all kinds. "Come, let us find your parents. Your … *motai*." The little elf's eyes lit up for the first time at that word. She nodded and clasped Aveline's hand.

"Where should we go?" Bert asked.

"Maybe you can talk to her," Ivlin said as he pointed at the small elf. "Anything else you remember?"

Bert rubbed his chin again. Stubble had formed since they had left the ships back in Ealna. "Let me think," he said as everyone stared at him.

"We might as well go toward the pass." Aveline pointed to

a small opening between two peaks. It was a rugged place. As they had ventured south, she was worried about twisting her ankle on the dry dirt and falling rocks. "We have to go that way anyhow."

They hadn't made camp, so gathering their few belongings was easy. They all had a pack, and her guards had their weapons. Everything else was left with Baldewin and Mari.

"*Thecal?*" Bert said to the girl. The elf only shrugged. "Well, she's no help. I used the word for 'north' and nothing."

"Maybe the child will stay with us until we find the prince," Zoell said. "At least we could protect her."

Tomas shook his head and said, "That sounds like a great way for us to get killed. Carrying around a little elfling," he laughed. "The mites and elves themselves would hunt us down."

"Let's see what happens," Aveline said, "but stay close."

The group walked back the way they had come, leaving behind the ruined, blackened remains of Anha Jorbstah. It was supposed to be the largest and grandest elven city in centuries. All gone. Aveline had never been to Mi'rallen, the elven stronghold in the Saipta Isles, but she hadn't heard as many tales of it as she did of Anha Jorbstah. *Surely it's just as amazing,* she thought. *Surely the elves raced there whenever this destruction happened, and this little elf girl's parents are waiting her return.* But she gulped. In truth, she wasn't sure what she would do with the girl if they had to take her with them because Tomas was right. They would be killed.

It drizzled as they wound their way through the pass. North of the Kash Mountains was where the rain fell and flooded; south was much drier but where all the people lived. Aveline hadn't been to the Jorbstah Steppe much. A long time ago, she had gone with a few friends. The dialect was harsh, a mix of Rainvealandian and dwarvish words. She'd never heard anything like it. But in Jorbstah, she had a few more friends. Hopefully, they would help her find her brother.

"Here you are." Ivlin handed the girl an apple. The elf looked at it for a moment before biting into the skin. It looked dry, but they had little on this journey.

"*Locti,*" the girl nodded as she wiped her mouth.

Everyone turned to Bert, who shrugged. "She either said *thanks* or she wants to kill you. I'm not sure."

"Name?" Aveline looked into the girl's bright blue eyes. "My name is Aveline," she pointed to herself. "Aveline." She pointed to the girl and shrugged.

"Badyn." The girl said.

"We'll say that's her name," Dern said.

Aveline nodded. "Badyn?" The girl smiled. "Pretty name," she said and held out her hand, which the elf took again. There wasn't much else she could ask. The little elf didn't know where to go, or couldn't tell them, at least.

They passed rodents scurrying, mountain goats jumping, and snakes slithering. There was nothing in the pass besides them and pests. Small rocks would fall as their footsteps echoed. It wasn't the safest path, but it was the only one she knew. Whatever had happened to Anha Jorbstah could happen to them. If it was a dragon or not. Aveline didn't want to face it.

"Shall I pray for elves to show up?" Tomas laughed. "It might make this quicker."

Zoell tugged on her pack. "Only if they plan on helping us. Who has the map?"

Ivlin looked around the valley. Red rocks grew all around them, small brooks cut through the dry land, shrubs lined the floor. "We're not lost. We've been this way before." He dug into his pack and brought out the map. Aveline gathered water from a brook into her skin and gave some to Badyn. "See," Ivlin said. "Once we get out of this pass, we just turn west for a while. We'll have to find a hood for her," he pointed to Badyn's ears, "before we see any people, though. Just to be safe."

"And how long will this take?" Bert asked.

"A few weeks," Ivlin said with a sigh.

"As long as Bertin isn't dead, we should be fine," said Aveline. "If he is dead though …" she didn't want to think about it though. The thought was enough to make her cry, but Badyn was only smiling, which made Aveline smile too. "… we'll find him."

"You should hand the daughter of the trees over," a thunderous voice called out. It echoed in the valley, and Aveline saw half a dozen elves pop out of shrubs with bows in hand. They were all in greens and browns and blended with the land. Their white eyes were blinding, but every time they blinked, they disappeared again.

Aveline had to put her hands up and clear her throat for her guards before they found weapons. "You speak our tongue?"

"Do I have a choice?" The same voice said.

"We didn't steal her," Dern said.

"Defensive," another voice said. It was soft, like someone singing.

The one with the loud voice looked at Aveline, then at Badyn. Out of the corner of Aveline's eye, she could see the little elf eyeing her. Her eyes danced across the elves, and Aveline knew she was searching for her parents.

"It's alright, Maddel." The elf stepped forward and lowered his bow. "My name is Chel." He wiped sweat from his face. "What are you doing here?"

"Just traveling through," Bert said.

"No," Aveline stepped forward, still holding Badyn's hand. "We were looking for another human in Anha Jorbstah, but it was … destroyed. We found Badyn here in some trees. Now, we wish to find her parents."

"Parents?" another said. Now, all the elves had shown themselves. If worse came to worst, Aveline's guard could probably fight them off. Probably.

"Badyn, you said?" Chel asked. He waved a hand, and the other elves all lowered their bows. His eyes darkened. "We're lucky she can't understand your language," he said with a deep breath. "Her parents are dead. Killed by the attackers. I saw it myself."

Aveline bit her lip and nodded as she squeezed the little elf girl's hand. "I understand. My parents are dead too, though not killed by attackers. What happened? Why did Anha Jorbstah look the way it did?"

Maddel sighed and looked at the sky. "We usually have plenty of notice when humans are coming. This pass is the only way to the city, but they came through one of the dwarves' tunnels. You need a word to get through, but they burst in somehow. It was a travesty. The things we saw."

"When the dragon fire flowed," Chel said, "the doors were closed." Aveline's eyes widened at the thought of a dragon flying over these mountains. For just a moment she looked to the sky to make sure it wasn't here again. "All inside would survive, but we had to run. It was either cross the bridge or fall to our deaths in the water. I saw Badyn's parents …" he swallowed hard. "I saw them catch fire, or rather, their bodies catch fire. We were lucky. Badyn was lucky. Many of the children are dead now."

"A terrible thing," Maddel added.

Aveline smiled at Badyn, whose face had shrunk. "We came to give her back. We just wanted to find her parents, but I guess we won't be able to do that."

"We'll gladly take her." Chel said. "We need to get through this pass so we can sail back to Mi'rallen and away from this mess."

Maddel spoke to the other elves in their language. They all nodded in agreement. "You wish to go to the human city of Jorbstah?" She asked, and Aveline nodded. "We will gladly cut a week off your time if you wish. As a thank you for helping Badyn here."

"That would be great." Aveline said. Badyn still looked lost, like she was expecting to see her parents already. Aveline squeezed her hand just a little more before letting go. The little elf's eyes found Aveline. Still deep blue with tears. Still the long stare. Aveline kept her tears in too as the girl ran over to the elves.

They all started talking in their language, the girl giggling as Chel laughed with her. Aveline dabbed the corner of her eyes at the thought of little Badyn finding out about her parents. She thought of her own. Dead. But at least she was older when her father died. Badyn would have to grow up an orphan. Aveline took a large breath. "When are we leaving?" She asked the elves. She had to find Bertin.

Bertin

A bump woke him. His eyes burned as the sun beat down on his face. He could hardly move, his body rigid. He thought he was dead, but then he heard the sounds of men. His neck and back ached as he lifted his head to see two Rainvealandians conversing and laughing. They were driving a wagon pulled by two mules. The winds of the steppe left them covered in dust, but they didn't seem to mind, didn't seem to notice Bertin either.

Mites, he thought, *couldn't get me in Anha Jorbstah, so they had to find me later. Fucking animals.* He went to jump out of the wagon, but he fell back in pain, not caring if the men saw him now. He grunted and clenched his jaw as his hands found his back. It was as if a lion had scratched him. He felt ridges of torn skin and dried blood. His shirt was off. Torn next to him. He had never known mites to have talons, and the image of his father played in his head. The ghost he saw ... maybe it had talons. Maybe it was a monster, and all Bertin saw was fake.

He had been dreaming, and it was hard to tell reality from his nightmares. Ioelena had come to him in his dreams. "You're in danger." She repeated as she bled to death under the scorching desert sun. Thatar said the same as he held

Ariad's lifeless body. Kelltar echoed them as he was set aflame.

Then he saw one last image. His own death. His heart stabbed by a wicked, elvish blade.

Now, the sun baked the wagon. Bertin didn't know where he was. He couldn't see forests or mountains, nor any cities. The large steppe stretched to the horizon; not even farms dotted the dry land.

One mite must've heard him groaning. He said, *"gul olkoi,"* and Bertin had never wished so much for Aveline to be with him to translate in his life. He didn't know if that meant they were going to kill him or just beat him. They looked like murderers the way they tore at the meat. Their creeping smirks and hard faces. Bertin would rather travel with the elves at the moment. He saw what the mites did in Anha Jorbstah. He didn't want the same to happen to him. To be pierced by a bolt that exploded from a crossbow, ripped apart like the meat at their fingers.

It took Bertin a few minutes of deep breaths before he was ready. The men laughed and sang as they continued on their path. The smell of spices permeated his nose. He wanted to be back in his castle having lunch with his siblings — there was no time for that. He had to escape or risk his death.

His hand raised, then his other until he lifted his head as quiet as a mouse. He turned ever so slightly to see the men who drove the wagon. The two of them sat together on the bench, ripping at cooked game.

Bertin thought of his dead mother and his ... dead father. He couldn't leave Rowan without a king, not after having that vision with his father, or that talk with his ghost, or the monster, or whatever it was. He found his courage deep in the depths of his gut and flung himself over the side of the wooden cart.

He hit the ground hard, his chest sore, any breath gone from his lungs. His body ached and screamed as he stood. The wagon stopped, the mites looking around and dropping from their bench. That's when Bertin saw the blood in the back of the wagon, a deer carcass rotting in the sun. He wanted to vomit at the thought of sleeping next to death, but instead he ran, not wanting to end up like that poor deer. He ran just as fast as when he had escaped the fire in the ancient city. The steppe was vast. Endless. But he wouldn't stop, not while he could still see the wagon behind him.

Finally, after minutes, hours, days — he didn't know — he collapsed. His ripped clothes were sticky with sweat, lips tasting like salt. His heart beat faster than a drum. If he looked hard enough, he could see it trying to rip out of his chest. The wagon was gone, as were the mites. He couldn't see them or anything else. Bertin was alone again in the grasslands of the South, hoping another ghost wouldn't find him. He crawled forward a bit. The sun was past noon, so at least he knew where west was. He would have to follow the sun until he hit a river or town or more people. Hopefully, they wouldn't want to kill him.

The ground gave way as he tried to stand, and he tumbled with rocks and pebbles and dry grass into a small ravine. He cried out as he hit the bottom. "Now I'm stuck," he panted. Bertin went to the edge to climb out, but then he realized where he was. The slope of the banks, the grass and bushes that congregated in the center of the ravine. He was in a riverbed, just without the river. It was too dry, he guessed, the water all gone.

He laughed at his luck. Eventually, it had to reach the Bezir. "It has to," he said.

So he was off again, his feet aching worst of all. With the elves they had turned bloody, but this time he had boots. He touched his back again. Luckily he didn't open any old wounds, but the scars felt like the ridge of the river, and they still burned. "If only I had been a herbalist's son," he said as he bent down to examine the brush. "I'd know what to eat and what heals." He sighed instead of picking a plant. None of it had fruit anyhow, and he didn't want to get this far to die by self-inflicted poisoning.

There was a squish beneath his boot. Water. A small stream had formed. The water came from somewhere west. He had never been so happy. He dropped to the bottom of the riverbed and didn't even use his hands, instead putting his face in the small stream, collecting a pile of dirt and water. But it didn't matter. He was happy. His throat and lips weren't as dry. His body sighed in relief as the water made its way throughout.

As if by some miracle, more water kept trickling down the riverbed. It couldn't have been more than an inch deep, but it was never-ending. He had an endless supply. His prayers answered. Either the Four or the Dragon or the Ancient One was looking out for him.

The gray overcast turned black. The sun hid as day seemingly turned to night, but it wasn't evening yet. A roar. He didn't know what kind of animal could make such a loud noise, and hoped it wasn't a lion stalking him. Then he realized it wasn't an animal roaring. It was water.

He looked forward and saw it. The riverbed wasn't dry. A giant wave of water crashed toward him. Huge soaking rain beyond that. It was a flood. And he had been stupid to think the gods answered his prayers.

Instead of screaming and freezing and letting the water take him to his grave. He raced to the bank of the riverbed. His boots slipped in the small stream of water that was growing larger. He grabbed an exposed root, dug the toe of his shoe into the dry dirt, and pulled with all the strength of his ancestors and the elves and his friends who died.

He had to survive for them. The whole time wandering the expanse of steppeland, his mind was on his own death. Of joining his mother and grandparents and Thatar and Ariad and Ioelena. But when his death was imminent, his mind changed.

The rushing water sounded like claps of thunder as it ate at the banks of the bed, as it destroyed all the plants and killed all the animals, as it set its sights on Bertin. He let out a raspy scream and pulled himself up. A cloud of dust formed where he threw his body. Then the rain hit.

Huge, cold raindrops pelted him and the ground. It reminded him of the exploding crossbows the mites used in Anha Jorbstah. The sound was deafening compared to the quiet of the grass. The riverbed came to life with the water. It grew and grew until it eroded the shore. Clumps of rock and dirt and grass falling into the water. Bertin thought he saw pieces of a house in the river, but he didn't have time to find out. The water was overflowing the banks. The rain dumped millions of gallons onto the dry land. He had to get away before the river took him.

He clambered away from the bank, but the water was

too quick. His foot caught on the ground, and he fell in a heap. It wasn't too high to rip him away from the land, but a white tree limb crashed into him, then a wooden plank, some stone. Bertin tried to move away, but the water held him in its grip, not wanting to let go. His side bruised, the cuts on his back burning and bleeding once again.

Bertin knew he wouldn't be able to escape this time. He was caught. He was going to die in a barren wasteland, his body mangled by a river. "What are you doing?" A voice said. He wiped his eyes and saw a boot in front of him. As he followed the leg up, he saw his sister. Aveline stood over him, her heels dug into the ground, not swaying with the water, not getting wet from the rain. "Grab my hand and let's go."

Bertin reached his fingers out and grasped her arm. She yanked with all her might as he fought off the water's grasp. He stood, the icy rain beating him on the head, blood trickling down his back, bruises lining his torso, but he could still stand. Aveline took off running, a tree in the distance making itself known. Bertin followed. He could barely hear his boots splashing through the water as the river roared and the rain drummed.

He grabbed the tree, a tall birch. His arms wrapped around it as the river surged behind him. The tree lurched with the wind, leaves and branches falling all around. He didn't want to turn back; he didn't want to know if the water was coming for him or not, so he just held on to keep himself from dying. Aveline stood next to him. "Where did you come from?" He asked his sister. Her hair caught in her face. "I can't believe you're here," he said as he reached out to feel her again.

But she was gone.

I'm not crazy, I'm not crazy. She was here, helped me flee the river. She helped me. She helped ... There was no sign of her. The water surged over the riverbed, but it wasn't close to him anymore. He was safe. His sister had saved him ... something had saved him. He knew he couldn't have saved himself. *I couldn't.* He was weak. *I'm weak.* But he was alone. *All alone.*

Ultiir

Olier unlocked the metal door and handed Ultiir a torch to light his way. "Stay here," Ultiir told the fat jailer. He wandered into the dungeon that was once elven mines. Rocks protruding between the dark cells, pieces of rubble on the dirty floor, rats scurrying to their nests. At the far end was where the bastard would be. Ultiir hadn't spoken to him since he arrived weeks ago. *I don't need to see him. I owe him nothing. He started a war against me, and letting him live is a mercy.* But as he turned to the cell and saw the blond-haired young boy, he knew the real reason he hadn't yet seen him.

The bastard looked like Hurvir.

The blond hair that grew past his ears. The blue eyes of a Bruthaki. A weak chin and small nose. All his nephew needed was a few years of training, and he would look like Hurvir did when he was first crowned. If Devro weren't a bastard, he would've made for a fine heir.

Ultiir was transported back to his days as a child. Hurvir was learning how to be king from their father, who was old and gray and full of wrinkles. Hurvir walked with his hands behind his back, listening intently, while Ultiir played with the palace dogs. His brother was nice to Ultiir. They only saw each other a few times a year, and every time he would sneak sweets to him. Hurvir would listen to Ultiir cry about Goldfield and mother and father. He was a good brother. Back then, Hurvir seemed like he would make a great king. But he dragged the kingdom into war upon war and famine and death.

Ultiir took a deep breath to keep tears from forming. Devro was whispering to himself, but Ultiir couldn't make out what he was saying. "You've only been here a few weeks. Not the time to go insane." His nephew glanced and squinted at the light before turning around to face the jagged wall of rocks. Ultiir fixed the torch to a sconce and bent down. His red cloak dragging the dirt. He made sure to wear his small golden crown today to show Devro who was the king and who was the subject. "This is the first time you've been in the palace for, what, seven, eight years? How are you liking it?" Still, the bastard didn't speak. "Have time to talk to yourself but not to me?" Ultiir wiped dirt from his boot. "Truth be told, I didn't think it would be this easy to capture you. If I'd've known I would've had Urses snatch you in the night months ago when I sent him to Whitehall with Gofrei's head." Devro turned ever so slightly at that. "What did Lord de'Marisco tell you? He ran away? After I killed Gofrei ..." Ultiir remembered the dead Sir Lird killed by Lord Geary and how Sir Lovis killed the mage. The same Lovis killed by the mob. "After I killed Gofrei, I sent Urses to deliver the head as a show of force. Never did I think that lord would still be in Whitehall after all this time. Did you take him captive? Or is he biding his time before jumping back to me? Guess we'll find out soon enough.

"Your bitch wife and her host are paving a way through

the Lands of Asara. Getting ever closer. Some of my advisors think she's coming this way, that we need to defend the city more. But I know she'll lose if she steps foot outside the walls. I have the best archers, the best cavalry, the best swordsmen, and thousands of peasants to throw at her." Ultiir grabbed the bars, a chill running through him, to get as close as he could to the bastard. "You will stay in here forever."

Devro's hair fell to his face as he looked to the ground. *Sniffling?* Ultiir thought. *Of course not. Just another trick by a bastard from Veltoora.* Then he saw a tear hit the ground, staining the stone. Ultiir almost fell back, but caught himself with his hand before standing. The bastard was still a child, still his nephew. Ultiir was there when Hurvir brought the babe home. Devro had smiled when Ultiir had held him and bounced him on his knee. He had been tasked with finding the best milkmaids for the newborn. Ultiir had scoured the city until he found a woman named Jama. The babe was healthy. Strong. Adorable. His nephew. His family's legacy. A bastard.

Ultiir rubbed his head as he felt tears from the memories well up in his eyes, but he willed them to stay in place; he wouldn't show weakness … couldn't show his weakness.

"Why don't you just … kill me …" Devro said as he wiped his nose, but still had his back turned. He sounded like Hurvir when he spoke, and Ultiir couldn't keep the tears in anymore. His nails dug into his palms as he clenched fists. His head ached. His eyes burned. His gray tunic became stained with tears.

Hurvir was a few years older than Devro when he told Ultiir not to worry about Goldfield. "Don't let the monsters make you sad," he had said as he wiped Ultiir's tears and held a cold cloth to his bruised cheek. "One day we'll be the ones in charge. There won't be anyone stopping us from taking revenge. Killing them all." Ultiir had been too young to fathom what his brother was saying, but Hurvir's eyes were steel. He was a protector. The only one who cared for Ultiir. "Just remember every servant and guard and anyone else who lays a hand on you or our sisters," Hurvir had said, "I'll take care of them in a few years." And he did. Once Hurvir was crowned, Goldfield was purged, much to their mother's objections. Seeing the abusers and rapists put to the sword was one of the first times Ultiir had been happy.

Ultiir wiped his eyes and masked his sniffles in fits of coughing. "I …" he started but his voice croaked. "I remember when your father brought you home. I …" he cleared his throat. "We were all confused. Hurvir was said not to be able to father a child, and everyone thought if he did it would be a girl who couldn't succeed him. But when we found out who your mother was, it made sense to those who believed in curses." Devro's head slightly turned again, his ears perked. "Hurvir had stayed in Maertan for far too long. No one knew why. Eventually he told me he had meant a whore and stayed with her when she told him she was pregnant. At first he didn't believe her, but then her stomach started growing. He would write every now and again, but didn't mention you at all. A year after he had left for Maertan, he came back with you. He told me your mother had died of some sickness carried by horses." Ultiir shrugged even though Devro wasn't looking. "Who knows if that was true."

He sighed as he bent over again, wishing Devro would

look him in the eyes, so he could see if they were like Hurvir's, so he could remember his brother more. "Never in my life did I think we'd be warring against each other," Ultiir said. "You the little babe that I would hold sometimes when Hurvir got bored. I was the one who put you on your first horse. I doubt you remember. Truth be told, you were much too young, but you kept grabbing her mane." Ultiir giggled through a dry mouth. He looked at nothing but Devro's back. The jagged walls and the iron bars and the torch weren't there. Only Devro. Only his one nephew. "I've done terrible things to get to where I'm at. The war only made me do more.

"It doesn't have to be this way. You can surrender, and I can let you live out the rest of your life in Goldfield or anywhere else you wish. I'll even let your wife go with you. No one else has to die." Devro didn't answer. Instead, he turned his head away more. Anger took hold of Ultiir now. "Fine. I tried for peace, but you didn't accept. Let the histories show it. And if your bitch wife comes here, I'll bring her head to you." Ultiir flew to his feet and stomped away, tears still in his eyes, his heart beating through his chest, still wishing that Devro had looked at him.

He made his way past Olier and kept Old Gid a few steps from him. He wanted to talk to no one. See no one. His head screamed in pain. He wanted sleep; his eyes were puffy, and holding them open was a chore.

"Your Grace," Dele squeaked as they topped the stairs from the dungeon. He was the only page not frightened by Ultiir.

"What is it?" Ultiir asked as he rubbed his temples.

"I just heard from Lord Hirons that he saw your sister in

the city."

Analere actually listened to me. She came. "Is she in the palace already? Have you found a room to her liking?"

Dele shook his head. "No, Your Grace, Lord Hirons saw her in the dakenry."

***

Ultiir rolled his eyes as he entered the white building in the center of town. He hadn't come this far since the rioting was at its worst, but this time he came with only a few guards so not to make a scene. Sir Gid was always at his side. He didn't wear the new gold cloak much, especially out in the city. Ultiir had grown fond of the old man since his mother sent him away. *And he listens to everything I say. At least I know why Mother hung onto him for so many years.*

Aches and groans escaped from the door as it opened, and the smell of blood and vinegar and herbs filled his nose. Inside were dozens of people — men, women, and children atop cots or even on the hard, wooden floor. Some bandaged. Some bleeding. Others coughed or sneezed or wiped their watery eyes. There were about a dozen daken all fluttering around the room. There were no windows so everything was lit by torches, but even with the lack of light, Ultiir could still make out his sister.

Analere was kneeling near a young man and conversing with another daken. Ultiir motioned for his guards to stay behind as he walked over agonized men and pregnant women and sickly children. "I assumed you would come to the palace." He told his sister, who didn't turn around and didn't stop her conversation.

"I agree," she told the other daken, who was an old, graying man who reminded Ultiir of Tedbalt. "Fetch the saw." Another daken raced to a supply room and came back with a jagged saw. The torchlight reflected off the sharp teeth. "When I read your letter," Analere said to Ultiir as she wrapped a tourniquet around the boy's thigh, "I was confused. *Commanded.* I've never been commanded to do anything in years. But I listened. Then I heard how awful everything has been in Viguran—" she tightened the cloth and the boy screamed in pain. "That's not even the worst part." She patted the young man's leg.

"—so I decided to help with the dakenry for a couple days." Analere grabbed the saw. "Bite this," she said and handed a cloth to the boy, who bit so hard veins bulged from his head. Then she got to sawing while the other daken held the writhing boy down. But he screamed all the same. Ultiir wanted to wretch, but not in front of a room full of people. Sick people. He held his hand to his nose to escape the smell.

Once the sound of bones crunching and tissue tearing stopped, and the boy fainted from the pain, the daken burned the gaping wound to stop the bleeding and kill the dead skin. The leg was carted off. Ultiir was sure his face was green.

Analere finally stood and let the others work on the fainted boy. She wiped the blood on her white robes and put her hands on her hips. "How is everything with you? Because what I saw was a burnt city and men marching to battle."

Ultiir let out a long breath he hadn't known he was holding in. Seeing his sister calmed him. Reminded him of a simple life. "I've been better. Hurvir dies, I become king, and it seems like nothing changed."

"I was sorry I missed his burial." She blew blonde hair from her eyes. "And your coronation." She walked over the sick people, some holding out their hands for help. "What luck that Hurvir choked on a chicken bone and you became king. Never did I think you would have the crown and the throne and the queen." She wiped her hands with a towel, the red smearing.

"What I would give to have Hurvir and relinquish it all back to him." Ultiir said. He wasn't sure he was telling the truth or not. "We should really leave this place. It makes me miss Goldfield …. almost."

Analere rolled her eyes. "How is mother? The messenger said your letter came from that wretched place. Is she as awful as ever?"

"Yes," Ultiir didn't hesitate. "I was trying to bring her back to the safety of our walls, don't worry she isn't here, she said no. Instead, she's out in her town with almost no defense since the Flewthlands have now joined the war and the Asaramen are pushing south."

"You think she'll be killed?" Analere didn't sound sad when she said that, just matter of fact. Like it meant nothing to her. Ultiir didn't know if Rila de'Tro's death would mean anything to him or not.

"So far, nothing has killed her. Not the Nowexerts, not the mites," Ultiir was telling himself just as much as Analere. "She'll be fine. You can see her again if you desire."

Analere dumped some herbs into a mortar and ground them. "Your city is falling apart," she said, ignoring anymore talk of their mother. "The sick and starving here remind me of Pleat Isle, and they had the pox there. I guess this war hasn't been easy."

"We're close to winning," he lied. "Devro is in the dungeons as we speak."

She almost dropped the mortar and pestle. "Our nephew is here? Have you spoken with him? Figured out his plans? Why he started the war?"

Ultiir rolled his eyes. "He's a bastard. They are evil spawn."

Analere shook her head and gave a pinch of her herbal concoction to a child with a coughing fit. "You haven't asked those questions, have you?"

"He won't …" Ultiir chewed his lip and sighed. "He won't talk to me, just sits in silence all day and night. The happy child that ran around the palace a decade ago isn't there anymore." He felt tears form in the corners of his eyes. *I will not cry over a bastard,* he told himself. "He started a war and is now my prisoner. There's nothing to discuss."

Analere nodded slowly, and her lips pursed. "Why did you call me back? I was doing fine on the isle, traveling and helping." Her hands found her hips again. "Why the letter?"

Ultiir scratched his chin. *To tell you I killed Hurvir. Murdered our brother. Destroyed our family and plunged the realm into war. To beg for forgiveness.* He shook the thoughts away and said, "I need a new chief daken on my council. You're the only person I trust in the whole world."

His sister laughed, but Ultiir didn't. She stopped and stared into his eyes. It was like he was looking at a younger version of his mother. "A woman on the King's Council? I don't know."

"You don't have a choice." Ultiir smiled.

Yvanne

She vomited as they hit a bump in the road. Lady Lolly rubbed a hand on Yvanne's back and took the bucket from her. "Thank you," Yvanne said as she wiped her mouth. The wagon was stuffy. Sweat clung to her like a babe to a mother. *I want the pregnancy to be over and for the war to be over and to be back in the cold embrace of Whitehall and ... and ...*

Yvanne quieted her mind. There was no reason to go on and on. "How close do you think we are?" She asked her sister, who went to rubbing Yvanne's leg. Jacka sat across from them, mending a hole in some lord's trousers. The column had left Goldfield days ago. Vigur didn't look too far on the map, but hills and streams and the thousands of people in her army slowed them.

Lolly looked out the window, her hair getting caught in the breeze, shimmering in the light. "I don't see the walls yet, but I'm sure within the next few hours." She turned her head and scanned the army behind them. "Lots of people."

"We need anyone we can get," Yvanne hiccuped and rubbed her eyes as a headache set in. "Lord de'Marisco says the fighting might be over quickly."

"Let's hope." Lolly brought her head back into the covered

wagon. "I see too many whores following us. Lord Aimora just rode past and screamed at a Lodean for fucking instead of marching."

Yvanne waved her hand. "I've more important things to worry about. As long as the men are satisfied, then so be it. We might have more bastards running around is all."

Lolly smiled, but it didn't reach her doe eyes. "How do you feel about Devro? I mean, we haven't had a bastard king since the Bastard Wars. That was centuries ago. Do you think he'll be able to handle it?"

"Worried we're straying away from the Four?" Yvanne giggled, but Lady Lolly didn't move, which meant she was serious. "Devro has some of the best lords and ladies in Viguran helping him. His ancestors had been kings of Viguran and Rowan. What's to worry about? It's in his blood."

"Whore's blood as well," Lolly muttered.

"For all we know, the whore was of noble birth," Yvanne shrugged. "What does it matter? Those who follow me don't seem to care. Why should you? Why me?"

Lolly played with her hair. "You're right, of course. It's just the teachings of the Four forbid laying with a whore, and bastards are evil spawns. What if Devro plunges us into more war? Into famine? Or poverty? I don't want to lose River Tree."

"His uncle caused this war. The last wars by his father. They aren't bastards, unless Rila de'Tro is a liar, but something tells me she didn't have many suitors. Hurvir also caused famines and plagues to run rampant. Whole towns destroyed. I don't think Devro is capable of that."

The wagon jerked to a halt when Lolly said, "True," but

her voice cracked.

"Why are we stopping?" Yvanne shouted out the window to a passing knight. He was from the Brownfork with the brown river running down his surcoat.

"The lord's said a break, Your Grace. There's some streams up ahead to drink before we cross them."

"Very well," Yvanne said and didn't wait for anyone to open the door. She flung it open and hopped out of the wagon.

Tiro jumped from beside the driver and ran to her. "My queen, are you alright? Should I get your horse?" Snowfall was being tended to by some grooms in the back of the column. Yvanne wanted to ride her, but she didn't want anyone to see her get sick either.

"No, Tiro," she held up a hand. The headache pounded. "I just want water. Don't run. I'll get it myself." The ground was uneven as she made her way, along with too many armed men, to the streams. Rocky hills rose to their south. The Montla just to the north. Men had drank out of it, but some had gotten sick or even died. Gordo forbade anyone else from drinking the dirty water. The stream, on the other hand, was as clear as a blue sky. Small pebbles tumbled over one another as the water raced downhill to the river of life.

Lord Aimora, holding his helm that had a blue ribbon flowing from the top, was talking with his Lodean. Yvanne only knew Besta and Orra by name. The others she had forgotten. *Bad leader,* she thought of herself. "My sister," Yvanne said to Aimora, "told me one of your men was whoring around? How did the punishment go?"

The Lodean bowed before collecting water in their skins. Besta gave his to Yvanne, and she took a drink. It was the best water she had ever had. Her headache vanished, and her insides felt full, and her child kicked. Lord Aimora chuckled. "Not much punishment to be had. I told him to wait until the next time we stop. If I were to guess, he's probably with the same woman right now."

"But he doesn't have much coin," Besta said. "He'll have to find other ways to pay."

"Don't some women complain of Girgo's cock? Too big?" Orra laughed, then his face stilled when Yvanne turned to him. "Sorry, Your Grace."

Yvanne swatted that away and smiled. "Tell me later if the whore finds Girgo's cock to her liking." Then she turned to Aimora. "So, your Lodean are ready for the fight? I hope it's a smashing success."

"We all do, my queen," the lord said. "I do worry about Lord Cul. He hasn't been happy since finding out he's leading the vanguard. I don't want him to make a mistake that could cost us the battle."

Cul was upstream a way, where the stream made a tiny waterfall. He scowled as he talked with Lord de'Marisco. "Well, Urses thinks it's a great idea."

Aimora smirked and sighed. "People like him come up with grand plans and think everything will go as smooth as butter. But has he ever fought? I never see him in the battles. He doesn't lead any men. And I believe his only contribution to the war with the Rainvealandians was blocking the Iron Gate."

"He's been good to us so far," Yvanne said as she took the waterskin again. "His information about Ultiir's tactics and plans has been correct. I think trusting his judgment will be for the better. We'd never've known that the lord of

Blackrock was named duke if not for him."

"I just think you should be careful with whom you trust."

Yvanne nodded. "My father said the same of you. He told me to 'never trust a Lodean'. Where would I be if I listened to him?"

"Probably for the better," Orra joked.

Lord Aimora smiled and thought for a moment, his eyes following the stream. "Your father didn't trust us because of who we are. I distrust the Lord de'Marisco because of *how* he is. None of us chooses our parents. I didn't choose to be born a Lodean, just like you didn't choose to be born a Veck'kop or the daughter of a duke. I do not distrust Urses because he was born along the river. Lords who have known him for years have told me stories."

"And what do they say?" Yvanne didn't like the thought that Aimora or other lords believed she was putting too much trust in Urses de'Marisco. She wasn't a child. She knew that the lord of Keeland held secrets and revealed only what he needed to.

"He enjoys climbing the ladder," Aimora said, "and pushing it down after he's reached the top."

"Let him scale the walls of Vigur," Besta said after he took a swig, "let him see how much he likes ladders then."

Yvanne rolled her eyes; she didn't need to be told any of that. She was smart enough to know. She was a duchess. A queen. "Let me go see for myself," she said to get away from the conversation. So she marched up the hill to where Urses and Cul were chatting. "My lords," Yvanne said as she wiped sweat from her brow, "how goes it? Lord Cul, I hear you aren't fond of the van? I thought your warriors would excel."

Lord Cul didn't bow his head or straighten his back. He drank water and let it drip from the corners of his mouth. "Would you be happy? It will bring me even closer to death than I already am."

Urses smirked. "Cul and I were discussing our grievances," the lord's voice was soft. "He was wondering why the Loon wasn't taken up on his offer of leading the van."

"The plan is simple," Yvanne said. "My brothers think it will work best. Cul and his fighters attack first; try to pry open the gates while we lob rocks and whatever else we can find. Ed awaits our signal and attacks from the north across the river. Then it's a full charge into the walls, hopefully Tundavik will be there as well to add to our numbers. What's not to like?"

"My fighters were told we would stay in Whitehall," Cul itched an eye. "But you decided to leave the protection of the duchy to your sister. We didn't complain when we marched. In fact, we found glory in the battles. My warriors are strong, ferocious, but toppling a wall a hundred feet high is nigh impossible. I still think going straight into a siege is a better idea. And we'll lose less of our army that way."

"And I told Lord Cul here," Urses said, "that Ultiir has enough food stored to last until winter. I'm sure the Terropians have sent shiploads of goods. We also risk the threat that King Anvrin will join Ultiir. They've been in contact since Hurvir's death through Sophie. I don't want to take that risk. More of our men will die that way."

Yvanne looked at the lords. *When was the last time either of them actually fought? If Urses has never then does he actually know? And Cul is so old he probably hasn't yielded a sword since the Nowexerts.* She scratched her hair; the coming heat of summer made it sticky. *But Diero and Gordo and Ed agreed on the plan. They've fought recently, and I must trust in family.*

"We will fight. Lord Cul, your people will lead the van. I'm sorry, but it must be this way. Their strength is unmatched." Cul didn't nod. Instead, he just yawned. A horn blew in the distance, signaling the break to be over. Yvanne waddled back to her wagon and pulled at her nails as it started bumping over the hills and streams again.

Sophie

Lord Mer Lasie wasn't too old, but his face was hard, his brow wrinkled, his gait slow. Sophie had pictured him as old as Lord Masson, but Lord Mer had been wounded in the war with the Rainvealandians and never recovered. He was actually only a decade or so older than she. "That's very kind," Sophie said as they walked the palace halls. No one stopped Sophie and her guards from coming and going through the gates. Sophie brought whomever she wished with her now, Sir Achen always a few steps away. Lord Mer had complimented Sophie's handling of Lady Rila's tragic death. Sophie had been buttering Mer up as they wandered the halls together. Passing the throne room and entering the back halls where the councilor's offices were located.

"But I must say I'm surprised your mind is on this," Mer said after Sophie brought up succession. "I would think that the war would be worrying you too much. I've heard that the traitors are closing in on the Montla. Any more, and we'll have to escape the city. I think we've more to worry about."

"Yes," Sophie said as she took a sip of wine. She had a page dig through the cellars to find the very last cask of wine. No more until the war was won. Lord Mer sipped his goblet as well. "My lord, wasn't your grandfather the lord of Raior?" He nodded. "But he died with no male heirs, only your mother, and you weren't born yet. So, some greedy lord swooped in and snatched your lands. Our laws do not allow you to press a claim through your mother. But if we changed that, then you could expand your holdings from the measly Sayer's River all the way to the coast. Take our second-greatest port city. I see immeasurable wealth in your future if that were the case."

Mer nodded again, his head slow, his eyes blinking. "I fear you are too smart, my queen." He gave a smile. "You know much and more about my family. It's true, Raior should be mine, but what can you do when laws are in place?"

"You change the laws. You are a lord of the royal court, are you not? Right now the only power I have is my words, but you have the authority to change whatever you see fit." As she said that, they passed Lord Masson's old chamber, the door covered in dust, with spiders making their homes in the corners. He had been stripped of his role and sent away by Ultiir.

"And if the other lords do not agree? I would be upending hundreds of years of tradition. They would never look at me the same. His Grace would cast me out," Lord Mer shook his head. "It would be the end of my family legacy."

"But you should try." Sophie shrugged as they stopped in front of the king's council chamber. The door was slightly ajar, but she heard no one inside. Dirt had settled near the base of the door; a rat scurried inside. "Valor the Iron wasn't afraid when he ended the wars between the various peoples of Viguran. He took the crown and united the realm. He didn't worry about some king."

Lord Mer cleared his throat. "This wine isn't very good," he laughed as he drank. "Perhaps if someone brought your motion to a vote …" he let that hang in the air. Sophie needed a lord to champion her idea. Lord Tylar was her best bet at the moment. "But you know how our kingdom works? The king must approve any new laws even if passed unanimously by the court. I've a feeling he won't like his one."

"Of course," Sophie blushed. *I just need to get Ultiir out of the city for a bit.* "That's actually why I've come here," she motioned to the council chamber. "I'm to meet with His Grace, my husband, and discuss matters of state. He likes to hear my advice."

Lord Mer said nothing, only smirked. "Then I will talk with you later." He bowed, trying not to spill his wine, and kissed her hand before finding his way out.

"You'll be right outside?" Sophie asked Sir Achen, whose hand never left his sword.

"I'll be sure nothing happens," her knight said.

Sophie pushed the door open, dust from the ground littering her view. The chairs weren't even pushed in. Watermarks stained the windows from the spring rains; a wasp was building its nest in the corner. The council still held sessions, though fewer times than before, but the state of the room looked like a crypt. *Guess the slaves really did clean everything,* she thought as she sat in the chair at the head of the table. She stretched her palms over the wooden table, cracked from where Hurvir had hit it. A red stain where Lord Gofrei Geary's headless corpse had lain. Tedbalt had told her so much of the happenings in this room, but she had never sat in the chairs. Old Rila de'Tro could sit at her husband's right side, but Sophie was relegated to the gossip outside. To talk of dresses and marriages like she was taught.

"No more," she told herself.

In the frame of the door was Ultiir cast in shadow, the torches behind him silhouetting his body. His hair was longer, unkempt, growing a million different ways. He slouched just slightly. His back bent. He looked frail, as if a wind could shatter him. *Just like his mother.* The old knight who followed behind him even looked younger.

"Not even going to stand?" Ultiir said with a dry voice. The door was closed behind him. The two knights would stare each other down, Sophie knew. Ready to fight if the queen or king called for help. "Nor bow? Usually my subjects bow."

"I am the queen," she said, cracking her knuckles.

"Am I supposed to take this as an insult?" He motioned to her sitting in the head chair. "And sending some page to collect me. You're lucky I even came."

"Why did you?"

Ultiir pulled out the seat across from her and sat. They were only a few feet away from one another, but Sophie could feel the gulf. "I wanted to hear what you'd say."

Sophie moved her brown hair behind her shoulder. "Do you think I'll tell you this was all a misunderstanding? That I love you? That I want us to come back together and be seen as king and queen?" Ultiir said nothing. Sunlight peaked through the gray clouds, barely enough to light the room, but she could see his eyes were low. Sad. "I regret nothing, but we're still married, so we have things to discuss.

First, I would like to know why you stripped Lord Masson of his rank."

He laughed, but his eyes didn't change from their sadness. "We can call him Tedbalt. We both know that's what you call him in bed." Ultiir gave a smug smile. "He committed treason. Luckily for him, I didn't carry out the full sentence. There's a lot going on. I don't want to waste my time killing an old man."

"Replaced one old man with another," she said as she pointed to the door. Old Gid on the other side. "Could drop dead at any moment."

"We are at war," Ultiir snickered. "But I trust Gid far more than Tedbalt. My mother trusted the knight for decades; I think that speaks for something. He also doesn't ask questions, does what he's told, and never complains. My sister, Analere, is also joining the council as chief daken. It will be nice to have people I can count on."

"Replacing the whole council? What of Lord Hirons? Lord Masson told me he is still in the dark about Hurvir's murder. Shame if I told him and turned him against you." Sophie picked at her nails. She didn't want Ultiir too angry, but it was so easy, and she needed him alone. "Who's to say I haven't already?"

Ultiir stood as fast as he could, his chair falling back. Sophie tensed as she imagined him crossing the room and beating her like Hurvir would do at dinner. Slap her like he did after the riots. But the king just stood and smiled. It was wicked. "Did you enjoy Sir Gid's present? There can be plenty more where that came from. You don't want your bed sullied further, do you?"

Sophie couldn't say anything. Her body froze. Her

thoughts stopped racing. All she could picture was Atrice's naked body, bloodied and tortured and on her bed. Red stains. The smell. Vomit. She clasped her hands together to stop them from shaking.

The door opened, and the monster walked in with Lord Hirons. The old knight looked like a grandfather, but his armor was steel, his heart was bitter. "Your Grace," the lord said. "I'm sorry to interrupt, but it's gravely important. A secret letter from Lord de'Marisco."

"What is it?" Ultiir didn't look to Alan Hirons but instead to Sir Gid, his new chief consultant.

"Lord Hirons here says that the bastard's wife has an army marching this way. The Asaramen took Goldfield, captured your mother," he paused. If Gid was waiting for Ultiir to be upset, it never came. "Goldfield allegedly fell rather quickly. Your mother didn't put up much of a defense," the old knight looked far sadder than Ultiir. "He wishes to slow her march."

Ultiir nodded and waved his hands in annoyance. "Fine. We'll burn the fields. Burn everything beyond the gates."

"Also, Your Grace," Lord Hirons interrupted. "Lord de'Marisco claims the plan is to offer a trade between your mother for the bastard."

Ultiir just continued as if he never heard the lord. "Have any men who wish for safety to get to building weapons. We have a battle to win."

The king, his knight, and the chief commander all left the room. Sophie was alone in the dark chamber. Sir Achen peeked inside. "Your Grace?" He asked, but she said nothing. Her thoughts were stuck on Atrice. She had handpicked the woman. Made her fuck Ultiir. Made her spy. Old Gid murdered her, but Sophie helped. The blood. The cuts. The mutilation. The horror. *It was my fault.*

She cried.

Achen looked confused, but his hand dropped his sword, and he slowly put an arm around her shoulder. The queen sobbed into her knight's chest.

Tundavik

W ell, I would say we're stuck," Mar whispered from the bushes as the moonlight cascaded over them.

Tundavik only sighed to signal agreement. They had crossed the River Fore only few days ago. Another bout of terrible rain slowed their progress so much snails would be faster. The Fore was filled with blood, like the people of New Vigur said. Broken bodies and limbs floated atop, and the grass had been soaked so red you couldn't see any green. Once they were able to go around the flooding river of death, they marched on west.

Now, they were at the Fall. And the village was completely cut off from the road. Giant wooden spikes and trenches had been set up and dug outside the low stone walls of town. Archers and crossbowmen stood atop the walls at all hours. He had sent scouts with Lord Tylo to find a way around. So far, all the reports were that the land was so muddy from the rain that a few scouts had to be rescued before being sucked down to an agonizing death. That didn't include the armies and bandits that prowled the region. As well as more and more defenses to slow an approaching army as they descended on Vigur. It was working. Tundavik's army slowed once more.

"I say we attack and test how good their defenses are," Mar said.

"And if we lose?" Tundavik asked, pushing leaves and branches from his view. "We don't need any men to die when we're so close to the capital." Tundavik left their vantage point atop a small, wooded hill. Glem was tending the horses when they arrived, brushing their hair and checking for ticks.

"Will we fight?" The boy asked with glee, and Tundavik rolled his eyes.

"Not yet, at least." He climbed atop his mare and trotted toward camp. *No way the people in the Fall haven't seen our fires. Heard our men. They're just waiting for us to strike first.* "Glem, do you know who the lord of the Fall is?"

"No, my lord, in fact I've never heard of the Fall before."

"Great help you are," Mar chuckled atop Brun. "Don't ask me either. I was in Gereduss for half a decade, remember?"

Tundavik didn't even know the past lords of the Fall. He had only seen the town once, not as grand as Goldfield, but in a few decades he could imagine the roads would be paved for miles as more and more settled the area, at least if the war didn't destroy it first. Its name came from the small waterfall on the River Montla. It was the last river port. No one could sail any further upstream with the rocks and rapids and shallow waters that appeared.

Lord Furrow and the men of Nye were standing watch. The camp looked like a mirror image of the night sky. Like a thousand stars had fallen in the dark, destroyed fields along the river. Men were collecting water. Others pissing in the Montla. The bakers were going around and passing out whatever crumbs they had left. Mostly hardtack and the occasional fish to a highborn lord.

"What news?" Furrow asked as Tundavik handed the reins of Bera to Glem. "Will we pass through on the morrow?"

Tundavik scratched his head. "Who's the lord of the Fall? You must know."

Furrow nodded and said, "Yes," like it was the stupidest question he had ever heard. "It's Lady Ceala. She's ruled over these lands for a couple decades at least. Even took command of a regiment during the war with the mites. It was a sight to behold. A woman leading a column of battle-hardened men," he laughed.

And how will you react when you see Yvanne? is what Tundavik wanted to say. Instead he said, "And do you think this Lady Ceala will treat with me?"

"Well," Furrow tapped his chin, "the lady is an odd woman. I think if we send you in alone, you might be able to seduce her. She's never married, the whore. Want's to spread her legs for any man she can find and not be faithful."

Tundavik looked to the river; the dark water churning, it was too wide to ford. He would have to talk to Ceala if no other way was found. "And you know this how?" he asked the lord.

"Why," Furrow said, "I asked for her hand in marriage a decade or more ago. Her reasons for the rejection were that she didn't see any strategic need in marrying someone in the Eastlands. When I tell you I cursed that woman ..." he seemed to lose his train of thought. Tundavik just wanted the lord to get on with it. "Anyhow, the real reason is all the men she wished to bed. Apparently, she was fucking the commander of her guard while entertaining my proposal." The lord shook his head and was quiet after that.

"So what will you do?" Mar asked later as they took the aforementioned hardtack from the bakers.

"I'll have to see if she'll let us through." Tundavik said as he bit the tack and was surprised at how soft it had gotten. *We've been traveling for so long,* he thought. "Guess we'll see what this Lady Ceala is really like."

"And the seduction part?" Mar asked with a raised eye. "I know you had your ways with Flora in Storyah, so how hard can this be?"

Tundavik shook his head with a smirk as he wondered how Flora was doing. The smirk turned to a frown as he thought of Barnet and if he had carried through with his plans. "I just want to speak with her. Besides," he chewed on the flavorless cracker, "maybe she has some salt pork."

***

"I request an audience with the lady of the Fall," Tundavik shouted to the town the next morning. "I'm the commander of an army the other side of the hill and wish to pass through." Lords Furrow, Toware, and a few others from the Eastlands stood beside him. Maybe a dozen guards were with them. Mar, in full metal, beside Tundavik.

"And if they don't listen?" Mar whispered. Tundavik didn't want to think of that. Audiences were common in war, and he didn't think Lady Ceala without decency. But he looked at Lord Toware. *That would be the perfect man to lead the assault. Brash. And without remorse.*

There was a rattle and few minutes later, a bald man

151

dressed in chainmail appeared alone. "Put down your arms." The bald man called. Tundavik nodded, and the few guards who held a sword sheathed or dropped it. "Who comes to the Fall?"

"My name is Tundavik. I fight on behalf of King Hurvir the Third. My army wishes to pass, but you've made the land an obstacle and are slowing my progress. We wish you no harm."

The bald man stepped forward and held out a hand for Tundavik to take, which he did. "My lady was wondering when you would come visit her. You shall come alone, and I promise you safe return as the commander of the city guard."

"Very well," Tundavik said, drowning out any protests from the lords.

"You weren't very quiet," the commander of the guard said as they dodged spikes and stakes toward the gate. "We knew youse was coming the moment you crossed the Fore." The commander, Wright, said.

"We had to go around the Fore. Flooded." Tundavik said. They stood outside the town walls, the line of archers watching his every move. "Did it flood here?"

"Flood here?" The commander laughed. "Of course it did, but that happens every year, and we thank Swallow for sending the rains to replenish our crop." Commander Wright motioned for the portcullis to be opened.

"What crop?" Tundavik said. The burned fields outside the town had turned to dried mud and decaying bodies. Ravens and crows and buzzards pecked out the innards. The wooded hill was the last remnant of whatever was left.

"That was Lord Leur." He said it with venom and spat

as he walked under the rising portcullis with Tundavik following. "The whoreson has always hated Lady Ceala and wants nothing more than to take the Fall and all the lands and wealth that comes with it. Saltcreek isn't as great as he had hoped when his father died. The war hasn't helped."

Tundavik was being gawked at by the people of the Fall. Men walked around in mail and leather and some in plate armor. Smiths were hammering away in their forges. Women and children were sewing garments. The bakery was empty. Looted, it seemed. Everyone was wiping their brows of sweat, Tundavik doing the same. He wasn't prepared for the worst of summer. The whole town dripped with rain and was full of mud. Footprints and puddles littered the ground. The occasional chicken would run by, pecking at the ground, just as hungry as the people. "So he attacks Lady Ceala for her land?"

"Well, Ultiir has also put him up to it, we believe. Lord Leur was happy to go along with the king killer, but Lady Ceala sees neutrality as the best course of action." Soldiers nodded and bowed as Wright walked. They all looked tired. Like they had been fighting for decades instead of a few months. Some men watched Tundavik with glares or sad eyes. *Because they hate Devro? Or because I'm bringing the war ever closer?*

Tundavik followed Wright to a stone square of a building in the center of town. "So the odds she joins Devro's side ..."

"Is very small," the commander put his index and thumb close together as he walked up the steps, "but not impossible."

As they entered the stone castle, Tundavik was glad to feel

cooler air. The stones seemed to protect the inside from the humidity that would eventually choke them during summer. It was nothing grand. The castle was purely for defense. Torches lit their way as there were no windows. They twisted and turned between walls, and Tundavik was sure he'd be lost if not for the commander. Murder-holes occasionally surprised him. The ceiling with a hole for the defenders to dump whatever they could on the attackers.

Then they turned a final corner and a small room in the center emerged. Sat in a high chair, up a few steps, was the lady. Lady Ceala was older than he imagined. Wrinkles formed, and the skin was loose on her arms. She was dressed in gray. The entire room reminded him of the overcast of clouds he had seen the past weeks.

"My lady," Wright bowed, "this is Lord Tundavik. He wishes to speak with you."

"Leave us," the lady said in a stern voice. Wright didn't need to be asked twice. There were no guards in the room, no arrowslits, no murder-holes. *Good thing I didn't come to murder you,* Tundavik thought. "I would ask you to state your business," she said, "but I heard of the hundreds of men you have at your back, the wagon train of weaponry and armor. Do you wish to intimidate me? Because you're out of luck if that is the goal."

Tundavik shook his head. "You've got it wrong, my lady. I merely wish to pass through. Your lands, unfortunately," he added to not slight her, "are barren and dead and not fit for my army. I need to get to Vigur quickly. Through town is the fastest way."

"And I'm supposed to believe you won't ransack my city? Rape my people? I do not trust armies, my Lord Tundavik.

I want them nowhere near the Fall." Lady Ceala tapped her fingers on the stone chair, which echoed throughout the stone room, while wearing a face of stone. "I fear Lord Leur has done much damage to my trust."

"I don't know this Lord Leur and certainly do not work for him, couldn't even point out Saltcreek on a map, your commander told me about him," Tundavik added when Ceala's face puzzled. "I serve Dev—King Hurvir de'Tro the Third. It's imperative I get through this blockade and march on Vigur."

"I've heard of your so-called king. Captured is he not?"

Tundavik shuffled his boots. The gray stone floors hid the dirt. "That's why it's imperative. Believe me, I would gladly go around the Fall, but the lands outside are dangerous. The Montla cannot be forded. We risk another flood of rain if we sit here."

"And how is that my problem?" The lady asked. "I sit in this castle, waiting to open the doors to my people if Lord Leur is to attack. My crops are burned. My livestock taken. My river polluted. And I'm supposed to let you through? Perhaps we could come to an arrangement." The lady's eyes sparkled, and Tundavik was afraid to find out why.

"Lord Furrow warned me," he muttered, but the echo of the stone carried the sound.

"Furrow?" Ceala's ears perked. Her face flushed with youthfulness for a moment, her eyes widened and a grin appeared. "Of Nye? What's that coot doing here?"

Tundavik scratched his beard, dead skin falling away. "He's with the army, leading his men."

"And what is Lord Furrow saying about this old woman?" She said through giggles.

He cleared his throat. *Either she'll take my head or go find Furrow's, or maybe she'll just laugh. I hope she laughs.* "He said you were … promiscuous. That you …"

"Out with it."

"… that you fuck a lot of men." He chewed his lip waiting for a reaction. But it was as he had hoped. The lady just laughed and laughed, the room shaking with the echo. "He told me I should try to seduce you, but I would never. I told him that."

"Unfortunately, just like I told Furrow all those years ago. I've no want or need to marry nor to fuck. I enjoy my life just fine without it, thank you. My parents never agreed. They wanted to make sure their descendants inherited this town, but what kind of law is that? If the kings of Viguran have shown us anything, it's that sometimes our descendants are no better than pigshit." Ceala wiped her eyes, which had teared up during her laughing fit. "No, the arrangement I was thinking involved you and your men and the lord of Saltcreek, who wants nothing more than to see me and my town under his rule."

As if on cue, a horn blared from outside, and the shouts, which were no more than whispers in the stone castle, called the men to their defenses. "Not now," Tundavik said and cursed under his breath.

"I guess that makes your decision all the more imperative." Lady Ceala of the Fall smiled.

Flora

Rain fell from the gods and turned the road to mush and mud. Flora didn't care. She was used to the rain by now, but her feet sank with every step. Strong destriers pulled the carriage near her, but still the wheels dredged the flooded road.

"Perhaps you should come under the cover, my lady," Sir Edmond said from within the carriage, the wooden roof protecting him from the worst of the rain. "Your lord father wouldn't want the cold to bite you."

Flora wiped water from her face and glimpsed her blonde hair turning dark. Still, the rain wasn't the worst it's been. "I heard that the rain washes any sickness away. Besides, the carriage is cramped, and the rain makes it reek of mildew."

"But it is safer, my lady," Edmond said with his sword at his side. "Rains and wars bring out the worst in people. Thieves and bandits and rapers. They all emerge from their holes to take whatever they can find. Not to mention we're getting closer to Lord Poden and his men. Wouldn't want to be hit by a stray arrow."

They had been traveling for a few days now, the rain and mud slowing them. Her company spent two days in River's Edge weathering a downpour that flooded and destroyed almost everything it touched. They had left Storyah with only a few wagons and men. Nothing to arouse Poden Bruce into believing they were coming to fight. Some wagons were hauling whatever food they could find. Mostly for her and her guards, but some as a peace offering to Poden. *Hopefully, he takes it, and we get this over with quickly.* Hard rain near the Flit, along with flooding fields, turned them inland on a winding road. It wasn't as direct, and the roads smaller, but they took the flooded path to Grass Ridge, where the road forked. Now they were heading north toward the River Flit. Toward Floodpan.

Flora relented and stepped into the carriage with Sir Edmond's help. It was damp and the cushions wet from the rain that came sideways, but her feet were aching, so she was glad to sit. As they passed a flooded grove of trees, she thought of Woodrun and how the floods would submerge the trees. The people would scurry to Mya's Hill, the wife of a lord of Woodrun who ruled for one hundred years. The people would have to follow young Sir Ollyver Ponce, left in charge by her husband. Hopefully, the war hadn't touched them yet.

"Sir Edmond, you come from Uphain, correct? How does it fare with the Flit's wrath?"

The knight looked at the rain and shivered. "They will fare well in Uphain. The town was built to survive the floods by the elves of old. But I'm sure Nopra and Rin will dance together and push on the great grass walls."

"I hope the Many look down on those in danger," Flora said. "Especially us."

Floodpan was empty when they arrived. The land was a shell of the former town. The shops were looted and the houses empty. Thatched and wooden roofs were burned, but the rain must have stopped the spreading flames. The swollen fields were also empty save water. The few men in her train searched for wheat or barley but found nothing. Floodpan had everything taken, and now the rain washed away the horror. Flora wondered where Lord Poden's force had moved. What did they leave in Floodpan? Were the villagers all killed or some taken? *Why would Poden decide now to attack this place? There's nothing here to gain.*

Edmond didn't like it, but Flora stepped out of the carriage. She lifted a headscarf and wandered the town. The river surged while rain beat down. Debris was pulled into the Flit, a mess of wood and stone and weaponry. She even saw an arm floating in the river. The train came to a halt near a burnt shed. Runes and other symbols from elves and dryads decorated the wood boards. She rubbed her hand over them, feeling the indents and following the curves.

"To the mountains." A voice came from behind. At first it sounded like her husband, but it turned almost angelic. "The ancient creatures must've posted this warning a thousand years ago." The man wore a green cloak and hood over his brown tunic. His blue eyes hidden in the shadows.

"Forgive me, but I do not know you."

"Sir Marbert of the Seeded Field. I joined your train at Grass Ridge." He lowered his hood and let the rain wash over his golden hair.

"May I ask what enticed you to join us? We aren't on some mythical adventure."

"You're going to Lord Poden. I had an uncle who lived

in Floodpan, and seeing what has become of it sickens me. He's most likely dead unless Poden Bruce needed a one-legged sickly man as a soldier."

"And how do you know the ancient runes? I have never met anyone who could read them, not even in Storyah." She stepped closer to the man. The rain made his face shine in the broken sunlight.

"I studied in Edincassone." He rubbed his fingers over the wooden boards. "Did I mention my uncle was also the lord of admissions before an accident that involved a captured lion for study?"

"From a scholar to a knight in my company. How did you ever have time for it all?"

"I was a very busy child. Now, I work the fields of my home, but the rain has put a stop to that." Sir Marbert gazed over the ruined Floodpan. "Do you think Lord Poden will return?"

"I do not know." She looked over the ruins as well. The rain and clouds only made the village more desolate. "I hope he is done with his raping and pillaging. Why a lord would do this to his lands, I cannot say."

"Just like those that attack their own kingdoms?" He rustled through a batch of dead petunias before finding the only live one. "For my lady."

Flora was going to thank him, but Sir Edmond's voice cut through the air. "We best leave soon. We don't want Lord Poden to come back with his men. Instead, we need to surprise them in River Watch."

"There will be no surprises here," a voice shouted as the ground shook. Lord Poden Bruce led a dozen or so men on horseback, all carrying spears or clubs. Both Sir

Edmond and Marbert unsheathed their swords. Edmond was blocked by Lord Poden's midnight-colored mare, so Marbert clung to Flora.

Lord Poden Bruce was older than she remembered. His face had new wrinkles and seemed to be stuck in a scowl. His and the horse's armor were bluer than Marbert's eyes with black streaks.

"Lady Flora," his voice was scratchy, "I do not mean to intrude on whatever it is you are doing, but you have set foot on my newly acquired lands. I have to ask you to leave and take your men with you unless you seek a fight."

Flora took a deep breath. "If you expect much fighting from my small company than your men are not very well trained. My lord father, your old friend, sent me here to broker peace."

Poden Bruce scoffed, and his horse shook her head. "Lord Pyre Blume has never been a friend, no matter what he tells you. We fought and fought over small and large items alike. Pyre wanted to go to war. I did not. He wished to fight for independence. I kept him from suicide. One of the few times he heeded my council. So why should I treat with his daughter of all people?"

"You know me as well. I remember seeing your face as a young girl in the maze of the castle." She looked at Floodpan once more. "You also destroyed a village which was causing you no harm."

"This land was in favor of your father. I came to make sure they didn't rise against me." He shrugged. "They resisted my calls for peace, and the same will happen to your father if he does not bow to me. And to you."

Marbert scowled and said, "A threat to a defenseless

woman?"

Flora put a hand in front of Marbert, who gripped his sword. "No bloodshed, remember? We only wish to talk peace terms with you. That is why my father sent me with only a few men. I even have food for you and yours. I'm sure they're hungry." The few riders not wearing helms, licked their lips. "We should get out of this rain."

Lord Poden glanced at his cavalry. "I will hear what you want to say, but only in River Watch. Your men will give up their swords, and you will be held as a captive until we are done."

"Captives?" Marbert laughed. "You mean to hold us as ransom to force Lord Blume into submission."

"I only need her, so watch your tongue before I rip it out." Poden growled. "What do you say, my lady?"

Flora licked the rain from her lips. Her throat was dry even with the water. *It's idiotic of me to follow this man. He destroyed an entire village and killed who knows how many.* But she wanted her father to take back control. And she needed to prove to Barnet that she could bring peace. "Take me to River Watch," she said.

Bertin

Strange plants surrounded him. They grew and climbed all around his legs. *Is this what it's like to be buried? A feeling of closeness with the earth?*

"Na mayku?" A voice said to his right, but Bertin knew the voices were never real. It was only his mind playing tricks on him. Everything that had happened since leaving Anha Jorbstah hadn't been real. He had just been walking. It wasn't possible for him to have fought a river and won, or to have his back ripped to shreds and still walk fine. To be captured by mites and escape. No, it hadn't happened. His mind was playing tricks.

"Hama?" the voice said again.

"Leave me alone," Bertin answered. "I've no reason to speak with you. All you'll do is trick me again. Make me think you're here and real but disappear when I need you. I will not fall for it again."

A butterfly landed on his boot. It had torn so badly he could see his feet underneath. His trousers shredded at the hem. He laughed as the butterfly took off and brushed against his nose. *What I would give to fly. I'd be home in no time at all.*

"What are you doing?" An unfamiliar voice said. This

ghost was a large man, sun-soaked and bulging with muscles. "My slave says you wandered into our fields and won't move? Says you speak," he spat at Bertin's boots, "the Veck'kop language. Why are you here?"

"Just let me pass through," Bertin said. "I'm tired of dealing with ghosts and visions."

"Ghosts?" the man said. *"Insaki içkoll,"* he belted out a laugh with his apparent slaves who surrounded Bertin. "Come with us and we'll get you talking straight once more."

"I will go nowhere with you," Bertin said. "I'm fine right here."

The large man snapped, and the ghosts grabbed Bertin by the arms and started dragging him across the field. Bertin flailed, but he was stuck. *Spirits are always strong,* he thought as they drug him over the fields of brown and white plants toward a barn and a home. Beyond that, a large river reflected the light of the sun into his eyes. His mind was playing tricks again. Bertin could make out red towers rising from the other bank of the river, smoke rising to the sky, scents of bread and fish and piss filling his nose. But that would mean a city, and Bertin was still too far away. *I'm too far away.*

He tried to kick away as they sat him on a chair in the barn. Inside, animals filled the stalls. On one side, horses whinnied for food; the other had large heifers lying down with pregnant bellies. The large man stayed over him, keeping him down, as he called out in his venom tongue. A woman came over, dwarfed by the big man, but that made her look kinder. Bertin shook his head at yet another ghost. He wanted to wake up and be back with the plants tickling his legs. The butterflies. The birds.

Bertin hardly noticed as the large man pried his mouth open and the woman made him drink some dark liquid. Bertin coughed, but whatever it was had already made its way down. His vision grew blurry. He tried to speak but couldn't. The ghosts were finally killing him.

***

He dreamt that his brother was king. Never in his life did he imagine little Baldewin sitting on the throne, waging war. His crown slipped from his small head and shattered into a million pieces. Aveline stood at his side. Her eyes were empty sockets. Her body pale as if she were lifeless. Below them were skulls as far as the eye could see. Bertin walked over them. Crushing the bones and hearing screams as he did it. Aveline and Baldewin only watched from afar. As Bertin neared the throne, a boney hand reached up and wrapped around his leg. He couldn't scream as the bones of the dead pulled him down. Forever gone.

When Bertin woke, he was covered in hay and dripping sweat. The woman stood over him with a small smile. *"Al ahí da,"* she said, *"teku geldi."* Bertin had no idea what she was saying other than the usual prayer of "al ahí da." Aveline had explained it once before, but he didn't bother to listen. Something to do with their god.

That's when he realized where he was. A barn. Rainvealand. The river and the ghosts. *I was going insane. What happened out there?* He reached for the scars on his back but only felt cotton wrappings. He plucked hay from his hair and sat up, but the rush to his head caused him to fall back dizzy. The woman shook her head and spoke softly before handing him an herb.

She mimicked chewing and said, *"nemeku."* So Bertin took the green herb and put it in his mouth. It crunched between his teeth and tasted like a river polluted with shit. But the dizziness went away, and this time he carefully sat up, putting a pile of hay behind his back.

"Thank you," Bertin said as a cow mooed. That's when the smell hit his nose. The burning scent of fresh horse and cow shit. How that didn't wake him earlier he didn't know.

"Sin tesukku," the woman motioned for Bertin to say it.

"Sin tesukku," Bertin said, and the lady nodded with a sweet smile. Never did he think he'd speak the Ancient Tongue of Rainvealand, but he also didn't think he'd ever speak any elvish words. *Far from home,* he thought.

"Finally awake," the big man said as he barreled over the woman. "I see my sweet Faci did a wonderful job with you," he kissed the woman's hand. "We've been married for merely two months, but already I can feel she will have strong children who will take over the farm for me when I am long gone with *Aldima Ahid.*"

Bertin wanted to stand to face the man, to not look so weak, but his legs were shaking. He wore nothing but pants and the bandage on his back. His tattered clothes in a pile near him, a chicken pecking at them. "I believe I thanked her already. I'm not sure what she did, but I feel much better."

"Thanked her?" The man laughed. "You should be thanking me. If not for me, the slaves would've had you killed, probably devoured you as well with how hungry they are," he laughed and clutched his wife's shoulder for support. "You were raving like a madman. We thought you were some lost *veckart* come to murder us. Of course you wouldn't be able to, but nonetheless. So, how did you come to find my farm?"

Bertin took a deep breath. He remembered the river, and something that looked like Aveline had helped him. Then he had walked once the land was dry once more. Walked and walked. *That's why my legs are so sore,* he thought as he touched his calf gingerly; bruises made their way up his leg. "It was a long journey," he said. "But it's not important. I need to get to Suktir or Panscar or whatever the closest city is. I shouldn't be here."

Big man shook his head, and the wife mashed some herbs with a pestle. "Suktir is right over the river. We on this side supply them with all they need to eat and drink and feel better."

Bertin pushed himself up, wishing he could jump with excitement. *So, it was a city I saw. I've never been closer to going home.* "Then you must have a boat to get across the Bezir? Do you mind if I use it?"

"You wander into my fields, stomp my crop, scare my slaves, cause me to bring you to my wife to heal, and you want to take a boat? And I get nothing in return?"

"I don't have any coin," Bertin said as he felt his pockets.

"I know," Big Man laughed, "we searched your clothes while you slept. Toss and turn a lot, you do," he added. "Why don't you do some work for me for a few days?"

"A few days?" Bertin shook his head. "I've places to be, I nee—"

"—You slept in my barn for three days. Faci here was always watching over you. I didn't get to bed her. Those days could've been the perfect time to make children. Some work would surely put things right."

The lady spoke, and the language actually sounded sweet, but then Big Man spoke, and it was venom and hate. "What's she saying?" Bertin asked.

"She thinks you need food." He looked Bertin up and down. "Which I would say you don't deserve, but you look like you haven't eaten anything in years. Almost like a walking skeleton, I say." Big Man said some more words to his wife and left them alone. Faci smiled and left as well.

Now is my time to leave, Bertin thought as he took a couple steps, but his stomach roared and the lack of energy caused him to plop on the hay again. The big man was right. Bertin held up his arms and could see the veins and bones. His legs were like a chicken's. His stomach gone. He counted every one of his ribs and felt a scar where he had been punched. His fingers found his cheek and felt all the imperfections from when it was broken. Nothing on his body had healed any proper way. Bertin shuddered at the thought of seeing his reflection.

Faci brought in a circular bread covered in poppy seeds. Bertin drooled as he took it before devouring it. He relished the crunch. The softness. Faci looked almost surprised he ate it so fast. "Sin te… tesukku," he said, and Faci nodded a smile.

Faci laid a bowl of stew that burned his nose with spice. *"Valti,"* she said. He didn't care what it was; he spooned handfuls at a time. Spicy eggs and vegetables made his eyes water, but the sweat cooled him from the heat outside.

Once he was finished, his stomach still hungry, and he wondered how long it would take to fill the vast chasm, Faci helped him stand. She slipped him into some Rainvealandian clothing. Loose white pants that had turned brown at the hem, dark pointed shoes, and a long red robe of cashmere. He hadn't looked this put together since his father held an audience with him in Rowan. *Months ago, and he might be dead ... No, just nightmares telling me that.*

"Nie bepiku," Faci motioned for him to follow. She held his arm as they left the barn, his legs still wobbly. Once outside, when his lungs filled with fresh air that didn't smell of animal waste, he felt strong again. For the first time since he ate with Ariad and Thatar, he felt like he could take on the world. Now he just waited for it to come crashing down again. Faci took him to the shore of Bezir. On the other side, a giant wall rose from the bank. A small port just to the north. The mutterings of townsfolk filled the air and carried over the water.

"Suktir," he said, and Faci nodded. "I must work," he said as if she could understand. "I don't want to make your husband mad, and I don't want to run anymore."

Faci went to the cattails growing along the river and found a flat stone. She came back and gave him the rock, then motioned for him to throw it into the river. Bertin scoffed, but Faci's eyes were sweet. So he skipped the rock across the water until it sank away. She clapped and turned her head to a small dock with a tied boat. *"Mekoi,"* she said and gave him a small push.

Bertin looked to the fields and saw only slaves working. Big Man was nowhere to be seen. He knew he had to do it. It was the only way to get home, the only way to keep from getting get trapped working a field until the large man decided it was enough. No one was looking, and Faci walked away. *"Sin tesukku,"* he said just loud enough for her to hear. She clasped her hands and gave a quick bow before returning to the barn. *If only I knew how to say goodbye.*

He quickly untied the boat, grabbed an oar, and jumped in. He hadn't rowed a boat in all his life; every vessel he had traveled on had sails. Bertin used whatever was left of his muscles and pushed off the dock. He rowed as fast as he could, switching the side he paddled on to not turn. There were other riverboats in the water; he made sure not to hit them, though came close and heard some Rainvealandian curses.

Bertin heard shouting and turned to see Big Man yelling at his wife and motioning to Bertin, but he was too far gone for anyone to catch him. The river docks for Suktir were already within his reach, and there didn't seem to be another boat that side of the river. He climbed out and looked back at Faci. Big Man had clambered away. Bertin gave a smile and wave, Faci returning the favor, and turned to enter the city.

Yvanne

Vigur rose high above blackened ground. The fields had turned to charred remains miles outside the walls. Any shack or home or barn burned. Ruined goods floated in the Montla. No doubt Ultiir ordered everything and more destroyed. *Give us no advantages, but we've the numbers and strength,* Yvanne thought. As they neared the city, she had taken leave of the wagon and sat atop Snowfall. Her mare's elegant white coat blinding as the sun hit it. She wanted Ultiir to know an army was coming, and that she was the leader.

"I've no sign of Tundavik," Pollard scowled. "The scouts found nothing either. He must've got lost."

Snowfall crested a small hill, and the black fields extended all the way to the walls of the city. "He'll be here, I'm sure." But she was getting nervous, especially as the roofs of homes and shops and towers emerged from beyond the wall. Hundreds of thousands of people were there. Yvanne didn't know how many would fight.

Diero, clad in brown leather that hid his mail and stark white helm, said, "Even without Lord Tundavik we'll still be able to win before the day is done."

"I wish I shared your optimism," Yvanne said. "You really

believe that?"

"Our army is powerful. You told me about their fighting in the passes of the Asara and the lowlands. We've been marching through enemy lands for weeks now, not a problem we couldn't solve. Goldfield fell in minutes. We'll easily beat the men who hide behind stone all day."

"These will help," Gordo said at her side while pointing behind. Wagons were coupled together, and teams of horses were pulling siege engines: ballistae, catapults, ladders, rams, the beginnings of trebuchets and towers. Loads of lumber from any forest they could find followed them. "Hopefully, this makes our victory easier."

Pollard pulled ahead on his horse and motioned for Yvanne to follow, which she did. The city wall got larger and larger the closer they got; it was suffocating. The wall was sheer gray stone, rising over the land like a cliffside out of a black ocean. Torched homes and a small village a mile from the city were empty. Atop the walls were soldiers with bows and crossbows and shields. Who knew how many with sword and spear were on the other side of the gates. "You're sure about this?" Pollard asked. "You don't think Lord Cul's plan would work at all?"

"I worry about Terrop, don't you?" Yvanne said as a warm breeze caught her off guard. In the far distance, over the Asara Mountains, storm clouds brewed. "We will try for peace, but when that doesn't work, our plan will begin. We just need Tundavik to arrive in the coming days. If not …" she didn't want to think about Tundavik not coming with his host of Flewthmen and stragglers. The difficulty will increase tenfold. *I want Devro back, though. I can't wait around forever.* "If not, then we might have to attack."

Pollard shook his head. "I think you are being misled."

Yvanne bit her cheeks. *Not him too.* "I am tired of being treated like a child," she snapped, hoping only Pollard could hear. "Everyone looks at me and sees weakness, but I am not weak. I am not a stupid girl. Why does everyone think Urses has some huge sway over me? Would you say the same if I were father? Or would you trust I knew what I was doing?"

Pollard's eyes were big and his brow raised, but he said nothing, instead keeping his head down as they rode toward the city. Wooden spikes rose from the ground, making fences. Holes and trenches were dug, some filled with rainwater. Yvanne and Pollard had to be careful where they rode. Snowfall trotted cautiously. Once the Gate of Vigura was within sight, and the army behind them was patiently waiting, Pollard said, "Ready to make peace?"

"Let's just hope Ultiir is," she said.

"Stop there," a man shouted from atop the wall in gold plate, probably the commander. "The gates are closed. No one else may enter." He pointed to the army. "And turn them around? We want no trouble here."

Yvanne closed her eyes and cleared her throat. Her baby kicked. "Release the rightful king and we will leave. No one will be harmed."

"The rightful king is Ultiir de'Tro," the commander said, "now turn around."

"You say that as Hurvir de'Tro's own son rots in your dungeons? We want no trouble. We want peace the same as you." Yvanne's throat hurt from yelling at the top of the wall. "If it would please the false king, I think we can negotiate. A prisoner trade."

The commander laughed, his gold plate shaking. "And who do you have that's as important as the king's nephew and enemy?"

"Tell Ultiir I have his mother, Rila de'Tro," Yvanne said with a smile.

***

"How is she?" Yvanne asked Sir Robern as she and Tiro neared the wagon that housed Rila de'Tro.

"Your Grace," he stood and bowed, his long, black beard shaking. He usually shaved it off, but weeks on the road stopped that practice. "Forgive me, but she is an old, bitter woman. How do you think she's doing?" Yvanne chuckled and had Robern open the wagon door.

"We've made it to Vigur," Yvanne said as she peered inside. Tiro stood behind her, his hand on a new dagger found in the rubble. The old woman looked dead; her eyes sunken, skin white, body shaking. "Don't you want to see your son?"

Rila leaned her head forward. "I'd much rather see the sun. Help me," she snapped at Robern,had made who begrudgingly grabbed her hand and helped her out of the wagon. Rila held onto the large wheel. "That's better. I feel almost whole again." She looked around at the buildings, all of them burned, just husks of their former selves. They had made camp in the burnt village just outside Vigur. Urses said it was called Fielding. Well, Fielding was no more. "This doesn't look like Vigur," Rila said. "Unless my son and that bastard have reduced it to rubble."

"Not yet," Yvanne said. "We're waiting to see if Ultiir will agree to our terms."

"Shit terms, aren't they?" Rila mused with a thin smile. "Find me a chair," she told Robern. Yvanne nodded at him when he refused, so he left and returned with a chest full of clothes. Rila sat with her hard shoulders slumped. "Better. If I were Ultiir, I would never trade a bastard who styles himself king for an old queen mother. Who would?"

"I'm sure your son loves you, so he would."

"Then you know nothing of my son. He is of my blood, remember? We've tougher hearts than others. Carrying over a hundred years of ancestral pressure will do that."

"If my mother were behind those walls, I would trade anything to see her again." Yvanne thought of her mother's red hair and how it smelled of strawberries in the autumn months. She rubbed the stone on her necklace. With all the traveling and fighting and sick morns, she almost forgot her power. *I wonder if the baby can feel it? Can he sense the power I wield? Will he wield it? Maybe the kingdom will have an éithrio ruler and be the better for it.* "But I loved my mother. Are you saying Ultiir doesn't love you?"

Rila coughed as she laughed, reminding Yvanne of her father and the last few months of his life. "Ultiir and I have had our share of troubles. The last time he saw me, he told me how much he didn't care for me." Yvanne's face must've shown disappointment because Rila said, "Surprised? Is your plan going awry already? He had some choice words about how I raised him and his siblings, but, as you will soon learn, being a mother is hard. They had all the coin and power in the world, and still they complained. Never happy, those ones." Rila's eyes got lost as she watched the floor, ashes blowing in the breeze. "How did you find Goldfield? Was it to your liking?"

Yvanne shook her head at the odd question. "It was fine."

"My children hated it. Do hate it. It baffles me how they could hate their ancestral home. The de'Tros have lived there for centuries and they turned their backs on it. Why? Because they say I was a harsh mother. Me," her voice cracked with shock. "I never beat them. Never laid a hand on them. Neither did their father. That's what the servants were for. We had the servants beat them so our children would hate them and not us. Didn't work, I guess."

Yvanne held her stomach. She couldn't imagine tasking servants with beating her child. Jacka or Helge. They would never lay a hand on her babe, and if they did, it would be the last thing they touched, no matter how much Yvanne cared for them. "I can see why Ultiir might not be too fond of you. Still, I'm sure this plan will work. Just a few more hours."

Rila seemed lost in her mind, or her hearing was gone since she didn't acknowledge Yvanne at all. "My daughters even cried rape sometimes." She shook her head, and Yvanne thought she could see tears forming. "Of course they lied. Why? I do not know. Analla and Philla pretended as if they didn't like the attention," she laughed and looked at Yvanne. Any tears gone. "And Analere was always a whore, even as a young child. I'm sure she lured the servants into her bed."

Yvanne didn't let go of her belly. As she felt a kick, she wanted to vomit. From the thought of poor Rila's daughters or from the pregnancy she could not say. "Sir Robern," it was her turn to hold back tears, "put this monster back in her cage and don't let her out until Ultiir comes with his terms."

Robern didn't hesitate as he grabbed the old, frail woman and put her in the wagon. Yvanne walked away from the burned buildings so as not to hear the bickering and whining that Rila de'Tro would let loose.

Fielding looked like a small hamlet. As she walked over the ruined remains, Tiro always behind her, she imagined how it looked before Ultiir had it burned, the people and the children and the carts and the horses all crisscrossing and shouting and playing. "Do you know anything about this place?" She asked Tiro.

"My father would sometimes bring bread to the capital if he had an overabundance and wanted to sell for a higher price," the boy knight said, his voice squeaking, reminding Yvanne how young he was, even compared to her. "He said Fielding was full of markets. Something about less tax than behind the city walls."

"Shame what's happened." She said as the debris broke and crunched beneath her boots. "I'm sure it was a beautiful little town. Have you been to Vigur?"

"Never, my qu—," he cleared his throat, probably remembering what Yvanne had said about formalities. "Never."

"Do you miss Whitehall?" She asked as a warm breeze came over her, which made her miss the cold airs of the mountains. The goats that climbed mountainsides. Eagles that circled. Wolves that howled. "Wish you never came?"

"I would never," Tiro said like a child. "Serving you has been one of the greatest things in my life. What would I be doing? Watching as my father can't get enough wheat to bake bread. I'd rather be here."

Yvanne turned to face her guard. *What was I thinking knighting him? He saved me, but can I save him?* "I want you to stay by my side during the battle. Don't go chasing glory. I wish to see you and Tito reunited in Whitehall when this is all done."

"Whatever you say," he said as he gave a salute of his hand.

That night, Yvanne made her home in a pile of rubble. There was one stone wall standing, so fabric was draped over to make her a room. She didn't know how much protection a leaning wall would give, but she felt a little safer. Strong men had carried buckets of water from the Montla to be heated for her bath. Lady Lolly didn't want Yvanne to bathe in the waters of the Ritae, the river of death, even though it was closer. Jacka got her bath all ready, found a smooth rock, and got to scrubbing.

Yvanne leaned back in the warm water, her hair dangling outside the wooden tub. "I feel like I haven't bathed in ages."

"You smelled like it too," Lolly giggled from the other side of the room. She was readying their beds. "We'll need washerwomen to clean these hides once the war is won." She said as she brushed dirt and bugs from the wool and cowhides.

There was a knock on the stone wall, and Jacka stood to cover Yvanne while Lolly went to see who it was. "It's too late for visitors," her handmaid said.

"Perhaps it's Ultiir," Yvanne said as she placed her hands on her belly shiny with water. "I'll make time for him."

Lolly came back in with a letter. It had already been opened as the seal of an owl was broken. Yvanne didn't want to take it. She motioned for Lolly to tell her the news. "Ultiir doesn't want to meet. He doesn't want to make the trade." Lolly sounded sad, afraid.

"Very well then, I guess it's war." Yvanne didn't want to

say those words, but she had no choice; she had to show Ultiir she meant what was said. "We just need Tundavik to show up as quickly as he can," she said as she sank lower into the water, some of it splashing onto the ruined floor. "Who gave you the news?"

"Pollard."

"Good," said Yvanne, "means the council knows. The meeting tomorrow will be lively as they all try to get me to act or freeze or run."

Lolly put the letter on a side table and leaned over the tub where she grabbed Yvanne's hand. "The good thing about you being queen is that it's your decision. It doesn't matter what Lord Cul says, or Diero or Gordo or Pollard, a Lodean, or even me. The Four will guide you to the correct decision. We will all be better for it."

Yvanne smiled and kissed her sister's hand. "Thank you."

Eventually, Yvanne felt clean enough to dry off and crawl into bed. The bugs that swarmed and bit made her feel dirty again. Lolly and Jacka slept beside her. Some guards outside were talking. She had sent Tiro to get some food and talk to others. *Wonder how he's getting along,* was her final thought before her eyes closed.

"Your Grace," Robern yelled her awake. "Your Grace, there's been an attack. Come quickly."

Yvanne groaned as she stood. Jacka slipped a coat over her nightgown and boots on Yvanne's feet. Not very modest for a queen, but she was confused, stumbling around, not caring who was around as she made her way through Fielding. She realized as they neared the grass where they were going. *Rila de'Tro. Ultiir tried to free his mother.*

Soon enough she found out she was right. Hundreds of

men and lords and even some camp followers gathered round the wagon, torches in hand, lighting the field like stars. Three men clad in black were on the ground dead. Blood oozing from their torsos, one with his throat sliced open still spraying bits of red phlegm. There was a saw beneath the wagon, but Rila de'Tro was still inside. Her face was whiter than snow. Her eyes wide as she took deep breaths.

"What happened here?" Yvanne said slowly. Her mind was still playing catch-up.

Aimora stepped forward. "The wagon guards were killed; it wasn't until Rila screamed that we knew what was happening. Ultiir must've sent them. That's the only explanation."

Diero was looking at the dead. One of them with the banner of Weathers Edge on his surcoat. "They killed five of our men. Seems Ultiir lied about not wanting his mother."

"We'll bury the dead soon," Gordo came from the shadows. "Terrible affair."

"Who were the dead?" Yvanne asked. The bodies were covered in shadows and blankets, but she could see the red stains beneath them.

"I think it's best we wait until the morn to identify them." Gordo kicked his feet, dirt floating into the air. "We don't want to be wrong."

Yvanne motioned to all the torches. "The sun seems to have come up already. Surely we can find someone to identify them." Gordo gulped so loudly she was sure they could hear it in Vigur. "What?" Yvanne asked. "Afraid I won't like what I see?"

Gordo waved a finger to Diero, who shook his head as he

pulled the blankets from the faces of the dead men. Orra was one of them, and Yvanne could feel Aimora's sadness. The Lodean had an open wound across his chest; blood had dried. She had traveled with Orra for months, never expecting him to die, especially in the night at the hands of a group of assassins. *I need to be prepared for even more death. For faces I'll never see again.*

But nothing prepared her for who came after. As Diero pulled the blanket down, Yvanne's stomach turned to knots. Her head screamed with pain. And she felt faint. Her legs ready to buckle at any moment. Sir Tiro — Little Tiro — was dead. His eyes closed forever. His throat slit open. The white bear on his surcoat red.

No one said anything. The crackle of fire was the only thing she heard before she said, "Whether or not Tundavik arrives tomorrow," she took in a deep breath of air that smelled of smoke and dried blood, "we attack Vigur at daybreak."

Blis

Northern winds hit the *Sea Glider* with great strength. It didn't feel close to summer or even spring on the water; it was as if winter never left. The boat lurched as the waves crashed against the bow. Men vomited over the sides of the rails, others laughing at their misfortune. Captain Pitor was directing his sailors on where to go to stay out of the storm that looked to be moving toward them. The northern winds offered a challenge, but nothing an experienced commander couldn't deal with.

Blis had been one of those commanders many decades ago, before even Queen Amalia was named regent and the flames broke out. Catching pirates in the northern waters off the coast of Gerot-Staller. A dozen ships had left with him, only four made it home. One of those was his. The king at the time, Anton, gave him a medal. *I wonder where that medal is now?* he thought as a wave hit and sprayed water over the deck.

Blis stood with Delmar near Baldewin as he watched the icy waves and the ship turn to stay in its good graces. "Do you remember your studies of the North?" Blis asked the young king.

Baldewin straightened his crown; his hair blew across his face, a halfcloak behind him fluttering. His clothes had a smattering of ocean on them. "Somewhat, though Aveline and Bertin know more than me." His eyes dropped after mentioning his sister and brother.

"They've had longer to learn," Blis said. He put a large hand on Baldewin's shoulder. "They'll be fine. We'll see both of your siblings again, I can feel it. When we get back to Rowan, they'll be waiting for us."

Baldewin sniffled, then sighed. "What do you want to know about the North?"

"Just tell me about the Glybelm." Blis rested his hands on his belt.

"What's there to say? They were raiders. Raided the coast from Viguran to Semadia. Eventually, the Vigurites took control."

"While true," Blis said, "you may want to know more about the people. You do want them as allies, do you not? You may need to spend our time sailing with a book in hand."

Baldewin brushed that off. As a child, the boy loved learning history and of the many people of Adedor, but he was getting older, focusing more on wars and fame. Blis missed the small boy who would run around the palace. Play with his brother and bastard cousin. Afraid to go near the palace gates. Always smiling. That boy had been full of nerves as of late. Biting his lip and nails. Legs shaking. "This isn't fair to you," Blis said, "becoming king at such a young age. You're only a boy, but we expect you to behave like a man grown."

"Do I act like a man?" Baldewin asked. "I try to be brave

and to listen, but sometimes I wonder if that's all it is. At least now the councilors seem to respect me. Maybe it was just Aveline they disliked."

Blis wanted to shake his head at the young boy playing dress-up as a monarch. Instead, he only smiled, keeping a deep sigh inside. "Perhaps," he said to placate Baldewin, "but you must remember that the councilors are not your family. Aveline should be trusted more than they."

"If she were here with Bertin, I would gladly give them the power. Have you seen some of the fish that fly along the water?" Baldewin gave a little dance as a wave smacked the ship. "I could catch the world's largest fish out here."

"I've heard the fish in the Drewogh are even larger."

Baldewin leaned on the railing, his hair screeching with the wind. "How do you think the Glybelm will feel about us? Will they think we're there to free them?"

"Or take them over," Blis said. "How would you feel if a fleet of warships descended on your home?"

"They wouldn't make it to Rowan," Baldewin clenched his fist. "The moment they crossed the waters near Edincassone, I would have them destroyed. They don't like the Vigurites, so maybe they'll see us as saviors. Hopefully, convincing them to help won't be a problem." Baldewin pushed off the rail and started for his cabin. Sailors were shouting, and masts were fluttering, and the captain was laughing. "I might let Caxton speak, though. I know I'm king, but it's much easier if he does it, and he was able to get the House of Awaran on our side more than Aveline," he said with a shrug.

"Let us wait to see what happens. Maybe you'll be more confident by then."

Baldewin yawned with a nod. "I'm going to sleep. Wake me for supper."

Blis nodded and let the young king go into his cabin alone. Delmar stood outside the door. The knight wasn't leaving Baldewin alone anymore, not since Blis told him he'd feed the knight to the sharks for letting the king out of his sight.

Blis took in the salt air as he made his way to the stern.

The captain was speaking with the helmsman when Blis found him. Pitor wore a vermilion coat with golden buttons and a hat decorated with rubies and two white feathers. His brown beard was shaved in the traditional sailor's way; past his chin and to a point. The captain looked as Blis did in his youth, other than the goose crest on his underclothes. "My lord of ..." Captain Pitor said as Blis approached, "what are you lord of again?"

"Not a lord of anything. Though I was once a captain like you."

Pitor's eyes beamed. "A fellow knight of the seas. I am surprised at how little we've spoken. Although you are with the king most days."

"It has been a busy few months. And I'm not sure I would be considered a knight. The kings of Rowan never bestowed that honor upon me."

"A knight of the seas needs no king's sword. We fight the gods, the beasts of Veltoora; krakens and great whales. That is more than any land-bearing knight could ever say. Usually I laugh in their faces. They think it is hard fighting a few men in mail, come to the ocean and best a storm." The captain bellowed out laughter.

"I suppose you're right." Blis said. "My best day was maneuvering a bursting ship through clouds and winds only Vigura would allow."

Pitor hit Blis' back. "See! We fight more danger than even a king. And what do we get? Not even proper gold, and most don't become advisers to great kings of Adedor like yourself."

"Just one advisor of many." Blis chuckled. "Actually, I came to ask when you think we'll reach the islands. To be honest, I've no idea where we are. I would hug the coast on my voyages. You're much braver than I am to face the open ocean."

Pitor let the wind rush over his face. "It depends on our speed. Nopro doesn't seem to enjoy working with Balanir to give us favorable conditions. But I would say less than five days. Perhaps closer to three. If I fail at that, you may throw me in the frigid northern waters."

Blis rolled his eyes with amusement before turning to the railing. Captain Pitor descended the stairs, leaving the steering to the many helmsmen about. He watched over the water and the many ships behind it. Fish jumped to the surface; even a dolphin swam past. He loved to jump into the water during times of peace. To swim with the salt creatures and his crew. Fun days under the scorching sun in the cool waters of the Western Ocean.

A clap of thunder moved over the water. Blis turned to the sky and saw ominous clouds in the north. The ships wouldn't be able to stay away from the storm forever without going days out of the way. Blis entered the king's cabin, Baldewin already asleep under his wool blanket. Mari slept on a cot in the corner. She didn't want to be alone with the sailors, and Blis didn't blame her.

No one got much sleep. The ship eventually hit the

northern storm and crashed through rough waves. Blis stood away from the window as wind battered the glass and wood. The storms in the west were what Blis knew, not these eastern gales. The boat needed to reach Cahlun, not get lost at sea, so they could find themselves on Eotrosi shores.

Blis wrapped his large hand around a tree-shaped candlestick, its limbs holding the light. He made his way out the door, blocking the strong winds from the flames. The deck was empty save for a few unlucky souls who needed to watch for rocks. He wasn't sure how they would see anything as the rain came down sideways. The mixture of wind and rain made the sky impossible to see. *Was it day or night? Could a clearing be near?*

He went back to the chamber and shook off his coat of rain, happy to be back in the room's warmth. "It's much too dangerous out there," he said as he saw Baldewin sitting on his bed awake. "I don't want to fall overboard."

Baldewin seemed to shake. "Is this the Mist of Men from the stories? Has it come to pull us to Veltoora?"

Blis made his way to the boy king, almost falling as a wave slammed the ship. He rested his hand on the king. "Those are only stories told to scare children. My ships never encountered such a mist. The worst thing I saw was mites salivating at the thought of my death."

"Mites do not scare me as much as the mist. Old Bria would tell stories of men going mad when the fog appeared. Ships would overrun with fools; even the captains would turn crazed. Ships would sink and crash, and no one would know." Baldewin held his breath as lightning turned the room blue and white. "I even heard Captain Pitor speaking of the mist."

"I heard the mist only comes in the West," Mari said from her cot, jolting as thunder clapped. "So we should be fine here."

Blis scoffed. "It isn't true." He felt sorry for Baldewin. A king should be old enough not to believe such stories. He wished he could say that, but knew it was the furthest thing Baldewin needed to hear. "The storm will end shortly. And you will see the mist for what it is. A falsehood."

And the storm did end ... eventually. The ship had one more violent rock from a wave, then the skies were painted blue by the hands of gods. The deck was full of life when Blis and Baldewin emerged. Water and salt made the wood glisten as midday occurred. The crew went to work, fixing any damaged boards and checking the sails for tears. Others leaned over the railings to vomit or check for men overboard.

That's when the screams reached them. Blis was blinded by the sun for a moment as he looked over the ocean. Through the waves and foam, he found the source. Men cried for help as their ship slowly sank, the hull breaking and water filling the interior, the wood peeling away, men jumping to the water or climbing as high as they could on the masts. Blis saw the pale sword painted on the sails. The *Fair Fellow*. The ship he had sent Torbet. It was crying out for nearby vessels to save the crew.

The *Boar's Head* was first to the destruction. Blis watched as a ladder was thrown to the fallen sailors and worked their way to safety.

"Where are the others?" Baldewin was gazing over the water as well. Blis followed his eyes and saw nothing. There were no other ships.

"I'm sure they're close. The storm couldn't have blown them too far off course." He knew how discouraged he sounded. They wouldn't stand a chance against the Vigurites in the Glybelm if they only had a few ships.

There was a commotion behind Blis. The sailors were yelling and pointing to the wreckage where half-a-dozen black ships descended. He gritted his teeth. "Pirates."

Blis had heard stories of eastern marauders. The way they put their victims' heads on the bows, or the way they drank from skulls and used the bones of the dead as sword handles. Blis had dealt with western pirates, but they were mostly smugglers selling slaves from Kruhesh. They were easy to take care of, but these black ships looked as though they came straight from Veltoora.

Captain Pitor shouted from the stern, "My king, what shall we do?"

Baldewin's face went flush. He turned to his adviser, then to the pirates. He was mumbling, and Blis could not hear. So another stepped forward.

"Get us over there as fast as you can, Captain," Caxton yelled, "and men, find any bow and quiver you can below deck." The men and the other councilors didn't even hesitate when it wasn't their king speaking. They now looked to Caxton for command. He turned to two others named Edin and Wis and said, "Man the ballista and aim for those ships."

The deck erupted in chaos. Men went to find arrows and bows. Edin and Wis loaded the ballista as they did in Storyah. Baldewin shook as Blis took hold of him and made their way to Pitor to get out of everyone's way. "Have you fended off pirates, Captain?" Blis asked.

"Only once near Decaro. A kraken pulled their ship down the moment I set eyes on it. A beautiful sight it was." The captain reeled the ship around and caught the wind. *Sea Glider* leapt into action. The ocean parted as the ship aimed for the pirates.

Edin carried a large bolt to Wis as he cocked the ballista with a winch. They loaded the iron-tipped weapon and had it ready to fire. The *Boar's Head* had the same idea. Small rocks and boulders flung from its bow to the pirates. Blis couldn't see any damage, but hoped the stone would scare the sea raiders away. Instead of leaving, the pirates pressed on. Captain Pitor shouted commands as they drew near. Caxton readied the archers to loose on the crew of the pirate ships.

"Perhaps we should wait out this battle in your cabin?" Blis said, remembering the times he held the infant Baldewin. So small in his hands. Now almost too big for comfort. The king said nothing; he just nodded a jittery head.

They made their way down the steps, Blis keeping his eyes on the soon to be battle. A crackle ripped through the air, and the ballista was being reloaded. There was a blunt noise off the hull of the black ship, but no damage. Single bolts would take time to destroy another ship, Blis knew.

Caxton shouted, and Pitor spun the wheel and the ship along with it. Blis felt like he could hurl, but it was worse the second time. Blis fell into the rails with a thud. It was as if a wave broke the hull. His leg had slammed into the wood, and he held a sore knee as he stood looking at the battle and then for the king. Baldewin was gone.

That's when the screams registered in Blis' ears.

He saw over the railing a crying Baldewin as he held onto the ship with all his young might. Blis tried to move, but his knee was so bruised it hurt to walk. *I need to! I cannot let this boy die. I cannot fail his father and his sister.*

But Blis didn't need to move anymore. Mari had emerged from nowhere, and she gripped her arms around the young king as his crown went falling into the kraken's domain. She grunted and yelled as she used all her might to lift him back on deck. Baldewin dug his nails in as he clung to her.

Delmar found them as well. "We must get to safety," he shouted over the fighting and the jolts of the ballista. The knight helped Blis, as Mari helped Baldewin. When they were in the king's cabin and the fighting grew quieter, the crownless king sobbed.

Bertin

Suktir was bustling under the hot noon sun. People were fanning themselves with large fronds, bathing in the public waters, drinking from the wells. Bertin was happy to drink with them. Cold. It almost hurt how good it made him feel. He wondered if the mites could tell he wasn't one of them. His skin was paler, but some mites had pale skin too, and his hair was brown along with most of theirs. He was also wearing what Faci had given him. The long robe with tight sleeves matched many of the townsfolk. Some men wore enormous hats that doubled their size. Red and yellow and orange were the dominant colors people wore, and it looked as if the city was on fire. His red robe blended him in as well. But he still didn't speak the language. He spoke the language of their longtime enemies. Luckily for him, his father had sacked Bardekan and not Suktir. *Maybe they won't hate me as much as they hate the Vigurites.*

Bertin had never seen so much brick. The shops and homes and storehouses were all red. Spires that lined the top of the city were spiraling columns of red brick. The city walls, wells, bathhouses, towers, and armories were all brick too. It made him miss the elven marble of the palace in Rowan. Rainvealandian cities were mostly human-built.

The clean cuts and perfect edges of the elf's craftsmanship were too perfect for the mites' city. Some bricks were falling apart, others not perfectly aligned, mortar spilling out and not being cleaned. The roads, a mix of brick and cobble, had unpaved sections of dirt, grass growing in the cracks, and roots of trees breaking through. It caused an uneven mess for Bertin's tired feet to walk over. He almost tripped a few times. The gutters along the side of the roads were full of piss and shit and animal bones, scavengers picking at them. Pigs walked through the streets, devouring as much trash as they could. Merchants shouted and sold; donkeys dragged carts full of goods. Some people were sweeping the mess. A woman waved from atop her balcony at Bertin. A man came from behind and romantically gripped her hips and pulled her inside.

He was glad when he had marched up from the Bezir that the city gate was open. Guards and knights stood to protect the city. Their surcoats were plastered with snakes, eagles, and lions. They watched him through their helms made of twisted faces. But merchants traveling with their goods kept Bertin hidden among the crowd. He listened carefully to hear any of the common language, but all he heard was the grunts and growls of the mites' tongue. Once he was on the safe side of the walls, he was lost. He had no idea what he was doing. His entire plan for weeks or months or however long he was in the barren waste was to get to a city and charter a way home. But the docks didn't have large ships. Merchants didn't look to be traveling north; in fact, he heard a few say something about Kahdar and figured they would continue south after finishing in Suktir.

Open-air altars blazed with fire as he crossed through.

Guards stood near the flames with stoic masks that made the twisted faces that Bertin believed were based on their god's many forms. He finally found a tavern with people sitting and drinking in the cool shade outside, but he wanted to be indoors, just in case anyone or anything came after him. It was small compared to the villas near it, and the red bricks made it conspicuous, but he knew a tavern by the smell. The fruity smell of brewed ale reminded him of apples. He followed his nose to the barkeep.

Once there, he saw barrels of ale stacked behind the counter. The barkeep stared as he waited. Bertin said, "A drink?" before realizing the man wouldn't be able to understand him. He pointed to an empty mug and then to the barrels. The man nodded and poured the drink.

The barkeep held up one finger and then placed out his palm. He wanted money. Bertin searched his new clothes, praying Faci dropped a few coins into the pockets. Nothing. He shrugged. "Sorry. No coin."

The man kept his palm flat out but pulled the mug back. Bertin knew he wouldn't find what he needed. He was about to leave when five coins with the Ancient One's twisted face filled the barkeep's hand. "*Siné cu orunu kin.*" The man set down another coin. "*Ria suvéc.*" The barkeep turned and filled a clay bowl with stew. He handed it to Bertin along with his ale.

Bertin wanted to cheer, but he could feel the stranger's eyes on him. He curled his fingers to keep his missing little finger from being a source of conversation. The man leaned against the wooden counter as he sipped his ale. "A traveler?"

Someone accidentally bumped into Bertin, and the man

motioned for him to follow. "You could say that," Bertin said as he followed the stranger.

They found a table, and the man set down his two drinks and two bowls of stew, before rubbing his square jaw. "And why would a Seler come all the way to Suktir?" he asked in his heavy mite accent, the words almost sticking to his tongue.

"Adventure," Bertin lied as he drank his ale and then shoveled stew into his mouth. It was spiced with peppers and full of beef; he couldn't help but drool. "Do you not travel much? Just to see the world?"

The man looked Bertin up and down. They almost matched in what they were wearing. Both in long robes, but the man's had fancy embroidery that looked silver, his boots freshly shined. No bruises. "I travel but mostly to hunt," he said, then drank. "So you won't tell me how you found your way south of the Ters-Veck with little coin and a damaged face?"

Bertin touched his cheek lightly. "I ran into some trouble, but that happens sometimes." The man's eyes bore into Bertin, and he knew the man would not relent unless Bertin told him something. "Elves," he told the truth. "I ran into some elves, and they weren't very kind."

"That's to be expected," another voice said. The man's friend sat at the table and got to eating.

"This is Barhi, I am Torlem," the man from the counter said. "Please excuse my friend; they are not very polite sometimes, forgetting to introduce themselves."

"He doesn't need my introduction," Barhi said between bites. "Besides, who is he?"

They both looked to Bertin for an answer. *I can either be*

completely honest and hope they see some value in me, or lie and run away. He chewed his cheek before he said, "My name is Bertin. I'm from Rowan."

"Well, Bertin," Barhi said, "welcome to Suktir. Do you not speak our language?" Bertin shook his head. "I guess it's a good thing we've been north of the *Tuyuk Ehir.* You'd've been alone here."

"Bertin was just telling me of his travels," Torlem said. "Something of elves, yes?"

Bertin nodded. "I found myself in …" he thought for a moment. *They're just strangers. I can tell them it won't matter. Maybe they can help me find a way home.* "I was in Anha Jorbstah. My adventure found me there. The elves …"

"No need to say what they did to you," Torlem said. "We can see with our own eyes."

"May Aldima Ahíd strike them down." Barhi added.

"Al ahí da," Torlem prayed. "We've run into elves before. The *adér* are a frightful lot. Using their witchery to destroy and take from us. They are nothing but wretched heathens. If only our kings felt the same. They allow the elves to take land from them, revolt against them," Torlem's face twisted, his brows low and eyes scrunched. "They all deserve death."

There's the mites I know, Bertin thought as he imagined Ariad and Thatar lying dead together. "When you say you travel to hunt, do you mean?" He didn't want to say it, but the flashes of Anha Jorbstah were too much for him. He had to clench his jaw to keep his eyes from filling with tears. All the dead elves at the hands of the hunters.

"We hunt the elves," Torlem nodded.

Bertin stared into his stew. He didn't need to react to anything Torlem or Barhi said. He needed to look composed, like the murder of innocent elven babies didn't bother him. "Have you ever gone to Rowan?" he asked in a monotone voice.

"Never," Barhi said. "We've no reason to go to *Açlar.* Unless you think there are elves that the king can't be rid of. Though we haven't heard of many elves above the Tuyuk of late. Your people know how to push them out."

We do, Bertin thought as his mind clouded. "I should be going." He stood. *"Sin tesukku."*

Torlem chuckled. "Before you go, we always need a third to carry our things. Why not come with us? Get some revenge."

"Sorry to tell you, but I don't think you'll find many elves left in Anha Jorbstah, and I don't wish to go back."

"Of course not," Torlem said over some drunken shouting in the tavern's corner. "But that's not where we're going. We're headed west to *Sritik,* I believe your people call in Sruhq? Elves galore are there. Maybe some who hurt you have traveled there, or have demon families there. What do you say?"

"I'm sorry," Bertin said, "but I need to get to Rowan."

"Well," Barhi said, "if you change your mind, we'll be here until the morn. Then we set off."

Bertin looked around the tavern. Drunkards fell off seats, men fought over drinks while women sat on their laps, and others played cards. None looked like travelers like Torlem and Barhi did. Bertin took one last sip of ale and set off with a sigh.

"I'm never making it home," Bertin told himself when he was outside the tavern. There was a fistfight happening in the street between two drunk men as the sun started setting behind them. The sky made every punch pink and purple. *Maybe I can do it myself. I traveled all the way from Anha Jorbstah to here, and now I know I'm in Suktir. If I walk north, I'll be in Panscar by next week ... hopefully.* "Surely there are ships in Panscar."

An old man beside Bertin must have heard him speak, because hatred grew in his eyes and he said, *"Siniuz meku git!"* and spat. He pushed Bertin, who went stumbling out of the crowd and into the fighters.

He was pushed again. Then again. He lost sight of what was happening, but heard the crack of fists meeting skin and bone. The bated breaths. Yells and curses. Bertin didn't know how to get away from the fighters. Luckily for him, they were focused on the other, but he was caught in the midst of it. Thrown around like a toy doll. Finally, he tripped and hit the hard brick of the street. Welts started forming on his face and chest. He prayed to the Four and the Dragon and even the Ancient One for protection.

His prayers seemed answered. Torlem and Barhi stumbled from the tavern with swords on their hips. They both shouted in their language, threatened with their swords, and pulled Bertin up to his feet, wiping blood from his cheeks and arms. "Caught in the wrong place," Barhi said as they drug him toward the tavern.

Bertin could feel tears in the corners of his eyes, but he was tired of crying and feeling hopeless. "I will go with you," he told the hunters. "I will travel to Sruhq."

Raimund

I am glad you followed." The creature-turned-woman said. "This is very important. As you are."

Raimund grabbed his stomach. He could feel the bones beneath his skin. He hadn't been this starved since he had entered the fighting pits almost two decades ago. "Important how?" he asked. "I'm no king or lord. Just a knight."

"Knights protect the innocent, do they not?"

Raimund gave a hesitant nod, though he wanted to say no. All he wanted was food and water and shelter. He didn't want to tell his whole life story to this … thing. An insect landed on the creature's hand before she sent it away.

"Now you will protect even more than before."

Raimund shook his head at all the riddles. He stopped talking to keep from getting confused. The forest seemed to go on forever. Never ending. Rows of great, bright green trees, all the same size, surrounded them. He grew tired of the pattern, and of the blue pools that dotted the ground.

As they walked, Raimund felt his feet were going to fall off. Sweat covered his brow. Any relief the shade from the trees brought was gone as he followed the creature deeper into the woods. The glow in the distance was too soft to be sunlight. It reminded him of the stained windows of the palace in Vigur. *Perhaps that's where all this leads. Back to Vigur. Maybe I'm dead and the gods wish for me to see it one last time, and this creature is leading me to the feast.*

"You are not dead," she said, Raimund forgetting his thoughts could be heard. "I am leading you nowhere you do not wish to go."

"I wish to go home, so this isn't exactly somewhere I want to be."

The creature giggled like a young girl. "You may not know it, but your fate is tied to this place. It was not an accident that you were found and compelled to mount your beast. It was not an accident that you wound up here. That your legs decided to come with me."

Raimund stopped walking, but the creature — demon — didn't. "So I've no say in the matter? No say in my life?"

She shrugged, but kept moving. Raimund watched his legs. They weren't following. He was the one in control, not some fate nor the gods nor this demon. If he stopped, then he could make his way home. Or die trying. Succumb to his hunger, or get lost in the trees, or get killed by a monster he had never heard of before. He sighed as he moved his legs one by one behind the monster, giving in. "I'd like to know when we're going to reach it," Raimund said. "I'm not sure I can keep going much longer."

"We've barely moved an inch," she laughed and pushed through the trees, the glow taking her over as she disappeared. Raimund let out a laugh and a cough at the same time. He turned and found out she was right. He could still see the imprint his body made while lying near the pool. It was maybe ten feet away. Even if he ran, who knew how far he'd get? How long would it take? So he plunged into the light as well.

On the other side was a large clearing. Small wooden buildings built in the center, but on the outer parts, the trees had been turned into homes and shops. Creatures that looked like men and women and even children ran out of their houses and onto the road. They all had greenish skin like the she-creature, all brown cloths, their hair braided and some adorned with leaves and flowers. "What..."

"You will see," she said before letting Raimund finish his thought. "They are excited to see you; never have I seen them so joyous."

"Surely elves have seen humans before."

"We are not elves," she laughed.

"Then what are you?" Raimund asked as small monsters stared at him with sparkling eyes, like he was a thing of beauty, and not a smelly, disheveled man who hadn't had a proper grooming in months.

"You may call us *arym* if you wish, though that is not what we call ourselves. Humans wouldn't be able to say our name. You may call me Nostara if you wish, though demon seems to be preferred."

This dem—Raimund caught his thought. "And why do you look like a human woman with elf ears? I find this all confusing."

"Humans are easily confused," the creature, Nostara, laughed. She always laughed. "We make ourselves look ... familiar to those around us. Our true forms are too much for your eyes."

"Would I go blind?" Raimund scoffed. The green woman shrugged. As Raimund was pulled along, green beasts threw flowers at his feet. He scrunched his face as they clapped and shouted in words he did not understand. "And what are they saying?"

They stopped near a towering tree. Its leaves were full of green and life, and the trunk was a dark, rich brown. There were small cutouts to make windows and doors. "They cheer is all." She moved right and said, "The Elders wish for you to make this your home."

"Living in a tree? Who are these Elders?"

The door swung open, and Nostara beckoned him inside. Luckily, the people didn't follow. The home had nothing but a bed of leaves in one corner and a chamber pot in the other. "The Elders are our leaders. What more is there to know?"

Raimund took a deep breath. If he had his sword, he could burn the entire forest, the Elders and everyone with it, but he would be stuck in the middle of nowhere, stuck in this hell. "You've been very cryptic, and I don't enjoy that. I've been away from my family for months and just want to go back there," he wanted to cry, but his body was failing him. He could feel it. Any longer, and this monster would have to bury him. "I've seen death, and that damned dragon killed a friend. I want some answers. Need answers."

"All will be revealed in time," Nostara said.

As she made her way to the door, Raimund shouted, "No! Do not leave me here with nothing. I want food and water and to be told what is going on. Do not leave me."

"I was going to take you to an old friend," she said, and Raimund's chest hurt as she left.

"Do you mean Mar?" Raimund chased after her. "Or Devro? Are we closer than you're letting on?"

"Just see," she said. The crowd had departed, and Raimund was thankful. They went past a tree ten times larger than his. "The Elders live there." The green woman said. That tree was the tallest he had ever seen, taller than the mountains in the North, the palace in Vigur, and the cliffs in Gereduss.

They continued to the other side of the forest, where there were fewer buildings and hollow trees. Raimund sighed. *Maybe she'll show me the way out of this hell.*

"I will not," Nostara replied to his thoughts. She pushed through a thicket and waved him on. "Through here."

He was excited to see a friend, even if it was just the young Potter who had helped him track down the dragon. He wanted to hug and reminiscence and feel safe again, wanted to let his shoulders drop instead of always being on guard. But it wasn't a friend he saw.

The dragon lay coiled in the grass, basking in the hot sun. The black scales seemed to have turned red with the daylight. Raimund felt like crying again. "This beast killed a friend. I never wanted to see it again unless I was driving a sword through its snout."

"Yet you climbed atop his back, did you not?"

The dragon woke and uncoiled his tail and neck. He moaned and stretched as small puffs of smoke escaped his sharp teeth. Yellow eyes found Raimund again. The last time that happened, he thought he was going to die, that the beast was going to be the last thing he ever saw, but now he didn't know what the future held.

"My dear Raimund," Nostara said, and he realized he had never told her his name. "How can you not understand? You climb atop the dragon and ride his back a million and more miles. He saved you from certain death in the frozen mountains. He led you here. Led you to me."

Raimund held his head. "No, I don't understand. I was perfectly fine in the mountains. I had a plan to escape and get back to Viguran to help my friends."

"You are far more important than some crown."

"You have the wrong man," he said, shaking his aching head. "I'm just a knight."

The dragon roared as he devoured a four-legged creature that looked to be full of meat. Nostara stared back at the towering home of the Elders, the canopy swaying like a giant in the wind. "They have seen it. Darkness shall fall over this land once more. Your world is at risk. You will lead the *Vareel* and *Marvaerth*. With evil reborn, so shall a savior walk amongst us. He will ride on the back of Nardal," she pointed to the dragon, "as he did in the tales of yore."

Raimund scratched his head. *This forest has* driven *her mad.*

"I am not mad," she said. "We arym see the world differently than humans. We know what is coming, and what will be lost if you do not lead your armies. Raimund, you are not just some knight who needs to fight for a king. You are Ryobas reborn."

Aveline

Her speckled eyes watched the brothel. The whores found men and women and anyone else and all the coin along with them. Wine and ale were poured and drunk and dumped on tables. It was as hot as ever in the cramped space along the Street of Dragons. Smoke from candles and pipes wafted about. She drank wine from a glass in the shape of a dragon taking flight. The most beautiful cup Aveline had ever seen. "Enjoying the drink?" Dern the Third returned from a back room, more sweat than usual.

Aveline took a sip of the spiced wine, cumin leaving traces on her tongue. "Just as good as I remember. I haven't been to Jorbstah in years. That time, it was still rebuilding from the war. Nice to see it's gotten better."

"If you say so," Dern said as he ordered a drink the best he could.

Her guards had stayed close to her earlier in the day as they had entered through the Headwater Gate, the *Kollapi*. A long line of wagons, carts, and peddlers with grapes, big and small; wheat and dough; beets; and cherries that matched the red bricks of Rainvealand, waited to be let in. Mountains rose on either side of the city wall. Specks of snow at the top. The elves had led them through an old dwarven tunnel, not wanting to appear with them. Once Aveline went to leave, she gave little Badyn a hug and the tunnel door closed. She could only hope that the little elf would have a good life from now on. Though she wasn't sure.

The city guards in their red steel had looked at them with disgust as they entered the city. Luckily for Aveline, swords surrounded her. As they had made their way down the *Sovas,* Aveline was struck with how different it all had seemed. When she was young, it was difficult to find a home by the gate, but people continued to be born and move in. The streets had gotten filthy, and the gate more guarded, the fields made smaller.

"You seem to enjoy the whores well enough," Aveline said to Dern. "Maybe you've a soft spot for *mites* after all."

"Fucking is different," Dern crossed his arms.

Tomas took a break from flirting to say, "He just doesn't want to admit it," and slammed his chalice before drinking and laughing.

Zoell pushed her way through the crowd, hands trying to grab her, as she brought a plate of food. "We couldn't've found a quieter place?" She asked as she took a bite of goat cheese. "Do you know how many people have tried to pay me if I do unspeakable things to them?"

"We might need the coin," Ivlin said, "and aren't you a maid? You can charge triple." Zoell averted her eyes as Ivlin laughed while he went for some mutton. "Maybe I should find some rich fuck to shower me with silver and gold."

"I think we'll be alright, and Zoell would never sell her body." Aveline said. "She isn't like you, Ivlin."

"I only sell my sword and talent. Women don't need to be paid to bed me," Ivlin boasted as he puffed his chest. "Haven't you heard of men praying to the Four for my cock? I've heard Dern and Bert at night asking our sweet Mother Meret to be as gifted as me."

"I only pray for your foul mouth to be ripped off by wolves." Bert took a piece of mutton. He wasn't angry, but his voice was monotonous. "And a princess doesn't need to hear your filth."

"Have we been traveling with a different princess all this time? She's the one who finds the brothels," Ivlin said while gesturing to the smoky, sweaty room.

Aveline hiccuped as she giggled. "It wasn't my first choice. We're only here because of an old friend. She calls this place home."

"And where is this old friend?" Bert asked with his sour face. "Have you asked about?"

"The brothel owner told me she should be back in the morn to sell some goods, so enjoy your night."

Tomas stood with two men. "I will." He disappeared up the stairs of the hot brothel.

"It's a good thing you know your way around these mess of streets," Bert said. He was the only one not drinking. Aveline knew the sword at his hip would be burning. "How a princess can love a southern place I will never understand. It reminds me of the rat-infested, shit-stained warehouses of the docks."

Aveline sighed as she drank. "Tomorrow I will drag you to the Square of Empires to change your mind. The pillars were sacked during an old war with the Deleri, the stone cut away from the mountains of Saipta. Jewels decorating the buildings taken from the Reds of old."

"I doubt that will do much, princess." Bert said.

"Stop." Zoell stood and gripped her sword pommel. Aveline didn't know who she was talking to until she turned and saw a man with a curved back standing over her.

"It's fine, I know him," Aveline said as she stood. Zoell didn't take her eyes off him, but Aveline laid a hand on her shoulder while she spoke. "So, Filik, how have you been?"

Filik snorted and kissed her hand, leaving spit running down her fingers. "After all this time, you are still as ever beautiful." He said in the Rainvealandian tongue. "What are you doing in Jorbstah?"

Aveline let the hunched man sit next to her on the red velvet couch. "I'm looking for my brother and was hoping your sister would know where to find him. I came here since she knows the owner."

"Sayla lives here now," Filik said, wiping drool from his lips. He was a bald, skinny man. Older, but still with too many wrinkles and sagging skin for his age. "She's no whore, though, but people from all over still pay for her visions." His slender fingers reached out to the food, and he bit off some pomegranate, the juices exploding and running down his chin. "She told me a few weeks ago you would be here. I almost didn't believe her."

"You always believe her." Aveline rolled her eyes with a laugh.

Filik laughed too. "Well, Sayla's been right more than she's been wrong," he said and shrugged. "You said you were looking for your brother? Which one is that? And why would either of them come here, of all places? You always spoke about their hatred for us."

"My baby brother doesn't hate anyone yet. And I'm looking for Bertin, but he didn't come here willingly. Elves took him across the steppe to Anha Jorbstah, but it was ... gone." Aveline blew her hair off her face. "I've no idea where to go next."

"Why don't I bring you to Sayla's room to wait?" Filik wisped his fingers through the smoky air. "Unless you want to find a companion?"

"I already have one," Aveline said as she thought of Mari. *Hopefully, she's safe and watching Baldewin close.*

"Well, in that case," Filik stood, his knees never stretching entirely, and he waddled over to the staircase, a half naked woman pushed past him. "Coming?"

Aveline nodded to her guards and stood to follow. Zoell and Bert stood as well. "The rest of you can stay," she told Ivlin and Dern, who were looking sad, "and keep an eye on one another, and any dangers that might come our way."

She followed Filik as he slowly made his way up the wooden stairs. They creaked and drooped under all the weight. Upstairs the air was fresher; the smoke hadn't yet made its way up, but the sounds of fucking were like drums in Aveline's ears. Filik stammered along the hall. Some doors were open, and Aveline didn't want to see what was going on inside. The moans and screams were enough to fill her imagination. There was another staircase and a door at the top. Filik played with a set of keys.

Inside the room, it was quiet. The window opened to let in the moonlit sky. There was no moaning or smoke or drunkards. Aveline let out a large breath she didn't know she was holding in. "Sayla will not care if you sleep in here." Filik motioned to the bed and spoke in the common language. "Unfortunately, there is only one bed, which I feel the princess deserves."

Bert said, "That makes two of us," and looked around the small bedchamber. There was a vanity, a small balcony, slatted ceilings, and red curtains. It was nothing fancy. But Aveline was glad to at least have a bed.

Filik smoothed the sheets and closed the window. Outside, midnight had washed over the city; hearths blazed with fire on the Street of Dragons. It was still busy out. The street was always busy with taverns and brothels and fighting rings and gambling. Men and women wore either loose clothes with hoods, or almost nothing at all. Beads of sweat ran down their heads and over their coarse black hair, even with the sun below the horizon. They drank from wells that dotted the city squares. Guards were under the shadows of the red towers to protect against the dragon's breath. The same breath that consumed Anha Jorbstah, according to the elves, at least.

Aveline and her guards told Filik all they remembered. First, what Bertin looked like. His brown hair that never went past his ears, and his milky skin that matched Aveline's. Their journey from Ealna down the marsh coast and over the Pywaln Mountains to Anha Jorbstah. The way the ancient city was a mess of melted bodies. The little elf girl.

"And now we await Sayla," Aveline finished.

Filik rubbed his chin as he sat in a cushioned chair. "There are always a plethora of men who have those features. Some of us Rainvealandians even look that way. I'm afraid that won't narrow down your search."

"And you've seen no elves?" Bert asked.

"Elves don't enjoy the company of Rainvealandians. They'd rather risk the coast of cliffs than the townsfolk. No pointed ears in this brothel."

"*Sin tesukku,*" Aveline said. "It all comes down to Sayla, then." She wanted to be out of Jorbstah quickly. Bertin could be another hundred miles away by now. "One more night and we'll be on our way."

Aveline lay in the large feather bed with a white headboard and a ring of blue flowers. Her fingers played with the wispy curtains as she made her way to the shutters. The streets had emptied as it grew later and later. Only to be filled again with whores and thieves. She could barely sleep, Bertin and Baldewin and Mari on her mind. She didn't know where any of them were now. *Hopefully, Redington is free and they are sailing back to Rowan. And maybe Bertin could find a way to the Ters-Veck. Maybe I'm all this way south for no reason.* That was a happy thought, and it put her to sleep.

A butterfly woke her that morning. It landed on her nose and sent shivers down her back. She was alone in the room. Filik and her guards gone. She found her clothes, brown and gray, to hide the dirt and filth that covered them, and bumped into Zoell's back outside the door. "They're outside enjoying the sun," Zoell said before she even asked.

Just outside the brothel, Bert picked his teeth; Ivlin sat near a brick well; Dern the Third handed Aveline a stick with meat.

"The bakers won't sell us any bread." Her guard ended his fast with the same meat. "Some festival is beginning this week and the roads are clogging."

"Like the sewers of Rowan." Ivlin carried a flagon of

water.

"It's almost a moonless night," Aveline said. *"Uzu tir Sekin.* We'll want to leave before the bonfires and parties begin. Where is Filik?"

Tomas, still swaying from his drink, pointed to the hunched man near the wall. "He went to pray and now he's getting you something to drink."

"Let's hope he doesn't poison it." Ivlin added.

Aveline shook her head, and sweat dripped onto her nose. Even with the morning sun, it was still too hot for her. *My guards will mutiny if we're here until the worst of summer,* she thought with a chuckle.

Filik brought a cup of water over and handed to Aveline, but first he blessed it by saying, *"Uran tir nuç artír, deçaran tir vída, Uyuk Dism tomir."*

"Al ahí da," Aveline took the cup and drank.

"Beautiful that you still know our customs," a woman's voice said. Sayla was wrapped in a shawl, her hair hidden, and she hugged Aveline. "I've been waiting for you. My visions didn't tell me exactly when, but I knew you'd be here."

"You're never wrong," Aveline hugged her back. "How has life been treating you?"

"Well enough," Sayla said. "Shall we go to my room?" Sayla led the way, and Aveline followed with her guards and Filik behind her. "I sense a great loss in you," Sayla said as they stomped up the stairs.

Yes, but which one, Aveline thought to herself as images of her mother and father's dead bodies flashed in her mind, then Bertin and Baldewin and Mari and everything else she's lost so far. "That's why I'm here. I need your help to find my brother."

Sayla pushed open the door to her bedchamber and said, "Then let us find him."

Filik and Dern helped Sayla push a small table to the center of the room. Aveline sat in a velvet chair, Sayla opposite her. Aveline's guards crowded around the room while Filik opened the window to let in some morning air.

"Hold out your palms," Sayla said, and Aveline did as instructed. Sayla ran her fingers over the lines, and Aveline had to keep from pulling her hands back as they tickled. "Yes, a great loss." Sayla closed her eyes and gripped Aveline's hands. The red curtains blew in the mountain breeze. "You are looking for Bertin. You are tracking him. Oh my, you saw terrible things in the elven city." Sayla's face twisted. "Yes, yes. She is safe, too." Aveline blinked away tears at the thought of Mari, but she was glad she was safe. "I see him, your brother Bertin, not the little one. Bertin was here; he was. He made it through the gate with elves. Oh, he lost a dear friend. Then another. And another." Aveline didn't know who could be Bertin's dear friends, but she would not interrupt Sayla while she worked. "He is lost. His mind wanders from him. His mind tricks him. He is going … going … I see something else. I see—" suddenly Sayla's eyes opened with pure white. She shook and convulsed, and it felt like she might rip Aveline's hands off.

"What's happening?" Bert asked from behind. The table rattled, and candles and books fell from shelves. It was like an earthquake, but only in this one room. Aveline couldn't free herself, and her guards stumbled behind her.

"Sister," Filik said, and he stammered over to her.

When Filik shook Sayla's arm, her mouth dropped, and she said, *"abhai senn ... abhai senn .... abhai senn ...."* Then she fell out of her chair.

"Princess," Dern came over and pulled her away. "Are you alright?"

"Fine," she said, with bruised wrists.

Sayla sat up with Filik and Zoell's help. Tears streamed down her face. "It was awful ... it was ... I saw the ... The world was gone. Destroyed. Bertin was there. He helped .... He caused it."

"Nonsense," Bert growled.

"He was there," Sayla held her head. "I know where he's going. You will find him where all the elves and dwarves and nymphs and fairies live. He is going to the Sruhq Forest. To a dark place."

Sophie

Sophie didn't expect the war to reach them so soon, but the young duchess was quick. The night before she went to sleep, hoping Ultiir would make peace. *I should've known he would trade no one for his mother, that rotten old bitch.* She peered out the window with her handmaids, Sir Achen, and Lady Ficca. "Oh, this is terrible," Ficca said with a tear in her eye.

Stones flew over the wall and crashed into homes and shops. Screams from peasants carried over the city. Small black arrows were exchanged between the wall and the ground. Sophie could barely see the thousands of men that filled the battlements. They formed a mob of steel that reflected the sun. They would have to hold the capital for who knew how long. The young men of this city, and those yanked from the fields. Those who hated Ultiir would have to protect him. Though they would be killed either way.

"What do you think Mara is doing?" Ficca asked as she started pacing around the room, biting her nails. "Oh, we should've called all of your ladies-in-waiting. I don't want more to die."

"The bastard's army won't reach us," Achen said. He had become the voice of assurance as of late. Sophie had to put her foot down to keep her personal guards from going to the vanguard, even though Ultiir insisted. She wouldn't let him strip her of her protection. Instead, they kept her safe. Hopefully, just from Ultiir and not from the attacking army.

"We'll be okay, Ficca," Sophie said and gave the woman a hug. She had gotten larger since Lady Rila's death. *Always eating.* Sophie was the opposite. She felt like eating nothing. "As much as I hate to say it, Ultiir is strong, his army stronger. The lords want to live to see their family just as much as you." Sophie looked to the edge of the city once more. The burned fields and destroyed villages did little to slow the advancing army. She wondered how long it would take for Ultiir's reinforcements to arrive. So many of them were off fighting the Flewthmen or in the mountains. *I wonder where Yvanne is out there?* She tried her hardest, but it would take a miracle to see the girl so far away. "I would admire her for leading her husband's army if she didn't want my head on a pike as well."

"That would be awful," Ficca said, and Sophie's handmaids agreed.

"Has a war ever come to Vigur?" Renna asked.

"The mites laid siege," Sophie said. "I wasn't here yet, but I've heard stories. It was a tough time. I don't think the young duchess can hold out for as long, though. If the battle turns to a siege, hopefully it's short."

Sir Velle came to the room and bowed. Beside him was Lord Masson. "He insisted," Velle said, "Your Grace, I assumed you wouldn't mind."

Sophie nodded and allowed Tedbalt to join them in the handmaids' room. "Forgive me for saying," the old lord said, "but Ultiir did an awful job at stopping this." He shook his jowls with anger. Ever since the gold cloak came off that man's shoulders, he seemed to have aged twenty years. Now, Sophie could see how old he really was. He was fatter from years of gluttony, shorter than some boys, moved with a limp, and his skin was as white as a ghost. "He was to negotiate. Instead, that imbecile tried to free his mother with some peasants-for-hire, and they ended up dead. The bastard's army sent the commander on the wall a letter calling for Ultiir's head. I just hope it won't be a bloodbath."

Everyone was quiet. It was treason to speak about the king in that way, but Sophie had done worse. "I was just telling them we've nothing to fear," she said.

"Of course not," Tedbalt shook his head, wisps of white hair shaking. "May I speak to you in private, Your Grace?"

Sophie followed Lord Masson to the hall and into her old bedchamber, the place where her spy was gutted like a fish and left to bleed. She took a deep breath to rid herself of the thoughts. "What is it? Here to tell me we're all going to die?"

"Maybe," Tedbalt said. At first she thought it was a joke, but the old lord wasn't laughing. "If you wish, I can get you out of this city. There are secret passages all over the palace, some that even go under the rivers. Barnet the Wise of old used them to sneak off to his Rainvealandian lover. We can change clothes and set off south. Find refuge in Hazari."

Sophie rolled her eyes. "You wouldn't make it past Vigura's Wrath. No. We stay here and see what happens. If Yvanne wins, then I will beg for mercy. Maybe she'll grant it or maybe she won't." She chewed her cheek. *Perhaps she'll treat me like I did Atrice.*

"I'm not sure that is wise. The palace walls haven't been well maintained in two decades, the city walls not much better. Sophie," his cloudy eyes looked deep into her soul, "if you stay here, you will die."

She grabbed Tedbalt's liver-spotted hand and held it close. "What kind of queen would I be if I ran away scared? It shows everyone that Yvanne is braver than I. Powerful. Fearless. Why would the peasants follow a weak queen?"

"What kind of queen?" Tedbalt stepped back; his mouth couldn't close. "You'd be alive! Forget about the people and the armies and Ultiir and your pride. You will be hanged in Meret's Square like a common criminal. You will be talked about in the histories as being hanged next to your husband. We can change that. Live a life away from all this. You go back to Terrop, and I spend my last few years on some island somewhere. Alive." Sophie pulled on her hair. She couldn't leave the city. These people — her people. She shook her head. "At least let me show you one tunnel. Just in case."

She nodded to entertain the old lord. Achen quickly followed. They wandered the barren corridors and staircases of the palace, walking down flight after flight until they reached the office of the old chief watcher. "No one's been in here for a while," Tedbalt said as he pushed the squeaky door open. "Ultiir didn't want things touched."

Webs and dust and nests covered the desks and shelves. Tedbalt lit a candle, and the light illuminated the old tunics and trousers and papers and ink spills. A mighty river emerging from rocks was the sigil above the chair. Swords and precious stones collected dust as they hung on the wall. "He thought we'd forget," Tedbalt said as he went toward a bookshelf and felt the wall.

"Why would he keep all this the same?" Sophie asked after a cough. "He cut the man's head off but didn't want his things moved?"

"Perhaps he's sentimental." Tedbalt shrugged. He pushed in a stone, and the wall slid open like a door. "Gofrei's favorite way to hide his whores when his wife would visit from Montlahead. Come," he ushered her and Achen through the darkness, using only the small candle to light their way.

"How long have you known about this?" She asked as they turned a tight corner.

"For years," he shrugged once more. "This tunnel only reaches the gardens though; others stretch for what seems like miles. Haven't needed to use those much." They stopped at a wall, and Tedbalt pushed another stone. Light cascaded over them as the wall opened. They emerged through a marble arch into the gardens. Everything was dead, even though it was spring.

In the distance, the Asara Mountains loomed over the Montla-Ritae. A ship just on the horizon. "The Awarites," Tedbalt said. "Somehow the regent of Rowan was able to convince them to block the river. Guess they heard the fighting too."

"So if all goes bad, this is where I escape? This is where I leave my friends and allies to die."

"I know you wish to help them all, to change their minds, to change this kingdom," Tedbalt's eyes were wide, tears formed, "but you must live. If that means running away, then so be it."

"You've been a very kind ally of mine, Lord Masson."

She kissed his hand as a rock smashed into the city and the capital shook. "I should've trusted you sooner. You could've helped with Hurvir."

"I'm sorry I didn't," he blushed. "Shall we go see what your husband is up to? If he knows what he's doing?"

"I think we should," she said. But before they could even get inside, an iron bolt ripped across the sky and blasted the palace walls. They were using ballistae. And it was up to Ultiir to save them.

Ultiir

The streets of Vigur were quiet. Guards around him shooed away the occasional beggar, threw vagrants out of the way, but no one else was out. Bakeries and taverns were closed. Warehouses not already looted were boarded up. Guild halls abandoned. The city was shrouded in a fog of silence. That is until a rock or bolt flew into the city walls.

As they neared the great gray stone wall, the noise grew louder. Shouts from the other side of the wall filled the air. Commanders this side were quieting their battalions. Hundreds of men, some just ripped from their homes, were clad in whatever armor they could find. Some plate or leather or just a regular wool tunic. There weren't nearly enough supplies to go around. Swords and spears and clubs and butter knives were among the weaponry. The wall protected them for now. But at any moment, a flood of the bastard's soldiers could break through the gates.

Ultiir and his guards, Sir Gid always next to him with sword in hand, reached the Gate of Vigura and pushed through the crowd of troops. Vigura's gate was the main entrance to the city. The River Gate to the north and the Shadow Gate to the south. Vigura's held a large gatehouse over the portcullis. It was adorned with four-pointed stars. A bolt struck the wall, and the world shook as a door opened. A guard bowed at the sight of Ultiir's small crown. There were a few shouts of terror from the men, but a commander said, "Show the king you are no coward!"

Ultiir followed Gid up a tight staircase in the wall. Hopefully, *I see some dead men the other side of the wall. I don't need this city falling.* He would be an even bigger embarrassment to history than his brother or father if he let Vigur fall. Vigur had stood for hundreds of years. The last time it was sacked was when Valor the Betrayer turned his back on his allies. Ultiir would not be remembered in the same breath as the Betrayer.

The staircase was dark, but Ultiir liked it more than the outside right now. It was too hectic below the wall. Too much for him to think about. At least using the stairs he could count. He reached sixty-five before the hatch on the top opened and blinded him. "What are you expecting us to see?" Ultiir asked Gid.

Sir Gid gripped the hilt of sword and said, "Hopefully the bitch is losing and arrows fill her men. I wish to see my lady, Rila de'Tro, once more."

"Of course," Ultiir nodded. He cared for his mother, wanted her to be okay, but if he never saw her again, that would be alright. He didn't need to hear how much he was failing. How he was letting his ancestors down. "If Yvanne dies, at least the war ends."

"Then you can have revenge on all those who turned against you," Gid said.

They exited the gatehouse and were on the stone wall. It was damp from the spring rains. Outside, the burned fields had turned to mud. A good sign. A few wagons had gotten stuck. Tents were constructed just near Fielding, a mile or so away, the village destroyed so the enemy couldn't use it for defense. The villagers taken in to Vigur and ordered to fight. Below horses and knights stood ready for any opponents. A knight in all white steel plate checked the formation. A few dead bodies littered the field. Catapults and one trebuchet were throwing rocks big and small. The wall shook as another projectile hit. A ballista was further back, firing bolts every few minutes. Arrows rained down; those without helms were surely dead.

"I'm surprised you came," Lord Alan Hirons said beneath a helm of steel. "I didn't take you for a fighter." Alan was standing with other commanders near the archers. The bowmen were in leather while the commanders wore steel, some shinier and more taken care of than the others. "The queen told me you were going to stay in the palace."

So, *Sophie is talking to Alan,* he thought, but couldn't let his wife play tricks on his mind. "I think the king of Viguran should make sure his capital is protected." He turned briefly to see the palace rising and piercing through the clouds. *So far away.*

"The girl's army," a commander with a blue stripe running the length of his armor started, "is trying to climb the wall with ladders. Brave ones they are. So far, we're holding them off."

"Should we not talk in the gatehouse?" Gid asked. The gatehouse was at least covered with wood and stone reinforcements. Out on the wall was nothing. Some men were holding shields over themselves, but arrows from the ground still came arcing over, and a few archers let out screams as they were pierced. "No deaths up here yet," the blue-striped commander said as an archer was taken away with an arrow in his arm. "We're putting up a good fight."

"This is Commander Fince de'Gul." Lord Hirons said of the blue-striped man. "He oversees the gatehouse here."

"Loose!" another man shouted, and arrows flew down in the hundreds. Once one set of archers was finished, they left the arrowslits to nock an arrow, and another battalion pushed forward to loose their strings. It was well coordinated. Ultiir just hoped they had enough arrows.

He jumped a foot as a grapple came over a crenellation. Commander de'Gul raced over to it and ripped it free with metal gauntlets. There was a scream and a crash after the commander threw it over the wall. "It's busy work, but they seem to be focusing on the Gate of Vigura more than the others," Fince said. "As long as they don't come over the wall, then we should be fine."

Ultiir placed his hand on a wooden beam of the gatehouse. "And the gates are all secure?"

The commander nodded. "There are men at the ready, the iron bars are down, and archers line the walls. Do not doubt your men, Your Grace, we are strong."

"I don't doubt them," he said. *And I don't doubt the ones on the ground either.* He took a deep breath and put just a bit more weight on the beam to see if it was sturdy.

That's when the entire gatehouse came crashing down.

As he blinked and saw debris and men running and screaming and bleeding, he saw his father. The old man he barely knew. His once-blond hair was white, his skin was pale; he hovered over all at the head of a table with a brilliant crown. His oldest brothers were mumbling beside him; their faces were nothing. Philla and Analla looked at Ultiir with said eyes. Both were playing with dolls. Then there was Hurvir. He looked the same as he did at the feast, blue liquid oozing from his mouth. He had just been seated at the long table, and worst of all, Hurvir never looked at Ultiir.

He blinked and saw his mother. She held out a hand and said, "Follow me," but he couldn't, wouldn't. He didn't want to follow his mother. He didn't want to face Hurvir and his sisters and brothers and father and tell them what he had done. Ultiir shook his head and cried out, "No," as his mother's hand touched his shoulder, "do not take me!" He screamed.

"Your Grace," Old Gid lifted Ultiir as best he could to his feet. "Are you alright?" Ultiir nodded, but in truth he had no idea where he was. He could be dead or alive. The knight brushed dust and dirt from Ultiir's clothes. Once he saw the knight's old eyes, he remembered where he was. The Gate of Vigura. A boulder the size of a shack had destroyed it. Nothing but splinters remained, and there was a great hole in the upper half of the wall.

Commander de'Gul's face was gone from a plank that pierced through his skull. Lord Hirons was crawling in agony with a fragment of wood in his leg, blood trailing behind him. "Help me," he said.

"We need to get you out of here," Gid told Ultiir. "They are bombarding us." Rocks, big and small, flew to what was left of the gatehouse. Luckily, the wall hadn't collapsed. The portcullis below would still be standing. "Quickly," Gid threw Ultiir behind him and found his sword. Men had climbed up with ladders and grapples. Old Gid went to work, cutting down one man, then another, then another. Blood spewed all around.

"Get me out of here!" Alan called from the ground as he tried to stand. The bastard's men were racing toward him, fighting off the archers who grabbed for their swords. "Ultiir, please," he pleaded. But Ultiir did not save him. Lord Alan Hirons was stabbed three times in the chest. Blood soaked the walkway. The chief commander's eyes stared at Ultiir.

But he had no time to think about the dead commander. Men from the mountains, in poor armor with poor blades, stood poised to attack. Ultiir knew he couldn't fight off all of them. He couldn't call his men either. They were fighting their own battles. He looked at those he might be able to fend off. There was an old man without a helm, and a boy no more than ten cowering in fear.

Ultiir would go after the old man first. He wrapped his fingers tightly around the hilt and blew out a strong breath.

The old man's head came clean off. It flew over the battlements and out of the city. Old Gid stood behind where the other man once was. The body dropped with a clang of armor. Ultiir wasn't the focus anymore. It was Sir Gid, the oldest knight Ultiir had ever seen.

Gid picked up the headless man's sword, while still holding his own. Yvanne's men attacked at once. The old knight spun with both swords, swinging them around his head, deflecting every deadly blow. More came from behind, but he was able to extend his sword like an arm and push them back.

He was flanked on both sides. The blades spun in the air and clashed with steel. Gid's feet moved with every strike, never standing still. A helmless man was sliced across the face, the skin peeling away. Another behind lost his sword after Gid twirled them round. He stood no chance as the old man swung at his feet and made him lose his balance. He fell screaming.

Gid continued on his rampage. He cut another down who was wielding a small axe. Another's helm was knocked off, giving the Gid the perfect opportunity. He dropped one of his swords, grabbed and threw the axe, and picked up the sword again in one fatal move. The axe buried itself inside the man's skull.

As the old knight moved past the young kid, he picked the boy up and threw him over the wall. At first Ultiir imagined Devro being the young boy, but quickly he remembered where he was. *No time for remorse or anything else. I must survive.* Gid then went to another knight. This one in steel plate.

Gid used both of his swords to confuse the knight. His opponent flipped his sword in the air, trying his best to deflect the blows, but it was no use. Gid beat down on the man's plate. The knight buckled under the attacks and fell to his knees. Gid kicked with all his might at the man's head, and he fell into a heap.

He threw down a sword and unsheathed his dagger. The last man also threw down his weapon. "No!" the man screamed. "I surrender." Gid didn't listen. He jabbed the dagger through the slit of the helm, and the men whimpered away.

Ultiir looked at his shoes, now covered in red. The stairs were dripping as if a wave of blood had just washed over them. He picked up a dead man's sword; he hadn't picked up a weapon in ages. It was heavier than he remembered; his arm could barely hold it straight. The men of the wall surrounded the ladder and the Asaramen who poured over. Clashes of steel rang from swords. Axes and spears were used to push the attackers back. Men were thrown from both sides of the wall. Wood planks from the destroyed gatehouse were used as weapons.

Ultiir stayed by Old Gid, both clutching their swords. A man came at the king, but Gid pulled out a dagger, spun it round, and jabbed it into his neck. The blood spurted, and Gid wiped the blade with his surcoat. Ultiir swung his sword at another. The weapon bounced off the man's own blade. Ultiir didn't know what he was doing. He swung the steel as best he could, making sure not to cut himself or his men. Luckily, his opponent wasn't very skilled either.

The man sliced and cut like he was a child. Missing every blow, Ultiir was able to slap the blade on the boy's hands. He dropped his sword, and Ultiir hit him with the pommel, knocking the enemy to the stone. Ultiir cheered as his men pushed the ladder from the wall. He watched as it stood straight up. The men at the bottom jumped, the ones on top screamed and prayed as the ladder continued back crashing into the siege engine below. The men atop the wall cried in victory while cutting down their enemy.

More ladders reached the top of the wall. Men wearing leather and mail and plate climbed over the battlements. Ultiir turned and saw the same happening on the far side. He heard the slap of ladders and looked over to see more and more contact the wall. He grabbed the top rung of the one nearest him and pushed with all his might. All of those men fell thirty feet and crashed onto fallen rocks and bodies.

His men shouted a battle cry and went to war. Those from below kept piling onto the narrow wall. It was easy to be thrown off, both into and out of the city.

Ultiir looked where the Gate of the Four once stood. A man in a steel cap was attempting to descend the stairs. Ultiir clenched his fist and kicked the man back. He was young, looked as though he had never seen battle, he seemed useless for battle, but it showed how desperate Yvanne was to get the bastard back.

The boy kept his hands up to block the final blow. "Please, no," he pleaded and morphed into Devro. Running around the palace. Chasing cats. Tripping over servants. Ultiir was shaking as he turned away. He couldn't do it, but he heard Gid come from behind with his sword. The boy choked on his own blood.

Yvanne

Ed the Loon was supposed to have crossed the Montla and attacked the River Gate when Yvanne gave the signal. Now a bonfire burned outside Fielding, and his army still hadn't arrived. Her other brothers were all fighting. Yvanne was safe at the camp around the destroyed village. She watched from her tent as the fighting raged. Her army was trying to break through the walls of Vigur. And they were one step closer.

Rocks destroyed the main gate of the city. It crumpled and fell. Her men were using ladders and siege engines to vault into Vigur. Ultiir's guards were putting up a fight, but she saw more and more of her people on the walls. Ed would distract them if he ever showed. "Maybe this fight will be over quickly," she said aloud.

"I hope so," Lady Lolly said as she blew her nose into a handkerchief from her chair. Tears had stained her face.

Jacka put a hand on Lolly's shoulder and said, "Your husband looked very strong. I'm sure he'll be just fine. Fighting off dozens of men. He'll come back to you." Lady Lolly nodded with a tearful smile at the handmaid.

Gordo, the only brother to stay behind to protect Yvanne with a few of his guards, nodded his head. "If there's one thing I know about River Tree, it's that the men are strong. The water gives them strength." He bit at his nails. "Where is the Loon?"

"Relax," Urses' soft voice said as he entered the tent. "So far, all is going well. The Shadow Gate is under attack as we speak." He pointed to the Ritae River. The gate was being hit with rocks and arrows. The men atop the wall were in a frenzy. No reinforcements looked to be coming. "Once Ed attacks, it will be the final blow."

Yvanne wanted to believe, but her men were still being pushed from the wall. Even with the Gate of Vigura in shambles, the portcullis remained, and her men couldn't get through. Ladders fell from the wall. Men fell to their deaths. Someone threw a torch into a siege tower, and now a fire was breaking out. And she couldn't find Pollard. In all that mess, her brother was gone. Off fighting. Or dying.

Chilling screams rang out, and Yvanne wandered outside for a better look. Boiling liquid was pouring onto her men from what was left of the Gate of Vigura. Yvanne wanted to look away but couldn't. She could barely see it, but it was prominent. The skin seemed to peel away like butter. The helms melted and meshed with the skin beneath. White bones emerged where skin once covered. More liquid dumped, this time followed by rocks and arrows. The gate was looking like a pyramid of chaos, men climbing over one another and the dead to break through.

"We should get back inside," Sir Robern said. Gordo agreed, and Urses stood watching.

Yvanne was going to turn back to her tent, but the sight of the barred wagon stopped her. A few guards, including Sir Loc, stood at the ready. "One moment," she told Robern before setting off to Rila de'Tro.

Inside the wagon, Rila was nodding off. *Not even the sounds of dying can move this woman,* Yvanne thought.

"See what chaos your son has caused?" Yvanne said, and the ancient woman shook awake. "All this fighting and death because he didn't want to trade for you."

"Smart," Rila rolled her wrists and they popped. "You will not win today. Vigur has stood the test of time; it will not fall to a bunch of traitors from the mountains."

"Then we will besiege the city," Yvanne said. "Ultiir will beg as the city starves and the people turn against him. I'll be sure you two see each other again."

"What is this cockiness? You sound so sure," Rila laughed. "Just come to goad me? Get under my skin? I lived in Vigur when the mites laid siege to the city. Do you know how awful it was? All the wheatstores empty, warehouses looted, every cat and dog and rat found and eaten. Even some resorted to cannibalism. Despite that, no one rose against the crown. It only brought the city together."

"We'll see," Yvanne said. She wished she could laugh in the old hag's face, but Rila de'Tro was probably correct. Yvanne didn't know how long a siege could actually last. "I came here to see how you were handling the fighting. I wanted to see how it felt to see your beloved city being tarnished."

Rila yawned. "You think if you can get me out and in front of my son that he'll stop this? That I wish for this to stop? You should've left me in Goldfield. How many times must I tell you Ultiir doesn't care one lick for me? Hopefully, your bastard child doesn't follow in his footsteps."

Yvanne held her ever-growing stomach and turned as

there was a commotion on the river, but not the Montla, not Ed. The Ritae stirred with small boats rowing up the river from the city. Arrows from the men from the Duke's Pass flew toward the boats from the southern bank of the river, but it didn't matter, the boats lurched on the northern bank and all those trying to break through the Shadow Gate now had a fight on their hands. Men in mail and leather shouted as they ran toward her people with swords and axes, shields and spears.

Pollard, in his gleaming white armor, was above all with his horse. He commanded the men at the Shadow Gate. He whipped them into a frenzy and started fighting off the attackers. The Lodean were with Pollard as well; Sir Aimora Dore's blue-ribboned helm leading his mountain men.

Her brother charged at the soldiers who had made landfall. He didn't give them a chance to gain their footing. He rode his horse into the water, swinging his sword as he went. Spears met armor, swords clanged against swords, and axes crushed helms. The river splashed all around as they fought off the invaders. The Lodean were proving how strong they were. Each one could take at least two, possibly three. There were still more boats coming, but Yvanne had hope. Then there was movement on the other river. The river she needed.

Ed the Loon crossed with his men. Blood stained their armor and surcoats, but they were coming. They made their way to the River Gate. The Loon disembarked first, then his men followed. They had their weapons clutched and climbed the side of the long wooden gatehouse. Helping each other, they eventually reached the top.

Yvanne watched as Ed quietly moved with his men along the wall. No one saw them. They were busy fighting near the Gate of Vigura. They entered the gatehouse and she lost them.

There was no movement. Her eyes darted around the northern portion of the wall. Gordo tapped his sword. "What is it?"

"The Loon," she smiled. "He's entered the gatehouse. The portcullis should raise any moment." They needed only one gate open to bring Ultiir to his knees. Her army would rush the River Gate and sweep through the city, opening the other gates as well. It would be over quickly. The wall would fall, and the city next. All Ed had to do was open the gate.

So he did.

The portcullis lurched open. Shouts rang out from the wall in warning, but her people also shouted and cheered and took aim at the River Gate. They raced to the opening portcullis. Fought off the guards defending the tunnel through the wall. Dashed under the iron teeth. Pollard had finished with the men at the Shadow Gate and kicked his horse towards the Montla. Lord Cul's fighters noticed the opening of the gate and left the Gate of Vigura.

Her men clashed with the guards of the city. They funneled through the gate in a dangerous move. She knew hundreds, possibly thousands, would die for their victory.

But the portcullis screamed and fell. Yvanne's jaw dropped as it smashed through her men, the spikes impaling their armor. Those on the other side banged on the iron bars to get out, but it was no use. The city guards began their slaughter. There was nothing she could do from the tent.

"What happened to the Loon?" Lady Lolly asked. "Do you think he's alright?"

"I'm sure all is well." Urses whispered. "He is strong."

As if Urses had predicted it, the portcullis rose again, impaled bodies being brought up with it. This time the gate was open all the way, and her men didn't hesitate to go to battle. Then she saw Ed and his men emerge from the gatehouse atop the wall.

Some loosed arrows; others fended off an attack. They were protecting the gatehouse and the raised portcullis. Men chopped and sliced at them, but the Loon's men ducked and dodged. Ed picked up his battleaxe and swung hard at the attackers. He didn't miss. Blood spewed; those without good armor regretted it as pieces of their bodies severed. The fight was bloody, but not as bloody as the one happening at the portcullis.

Pollard barked orders at the men in front of him. The army was once again funneling through the River Gate. Lord Cul and his fighters pushed with all their strength at the men protecting the city.

Blood and innards spilled over the grass and sprayed up the walls. Swords, axes, spears, daggers, even rocks, anything that could be a weapon was in hand. She saw one man beating the bloody face of another with a metal boot.

Yvanne turned her attention back to Ed the Loon, who was still fighting to protect the gatehouse. He used his battleaxe as a warhammer and struck one man so hard his armor shattered and he flew into a thatched roof. His men were fighting just as well as he. Their swords kept men at bay with their slices and swings. Sliced skin fell in heaps, and blood stained the stone wall.

While Ed was finishing a man by bashing his head in, another approached from behind ... then another. Before long, Ed the Loon was surrounded, and Yvanne could do nothing but watch.

The Loon spun his axe and contacted steel plate. He ripped it out and swung again, this time striking a head off. He was too slow to dodge the next attack. A spear tore at his flesh behind the knee. Ed spun in anger, knocked the man down with the face of his axe, and continued to beat until his helm was covered in blood.

A man jumped on Ed from behind and wrapped his hands around the Loon's face. He struggled, but the only way free was to unlatch his helm. A helmless Ed got away and clenched his battleaxe tighter. He screamed as he swung the blade at the man.

Ed the Loon could do nothing to stop it. Before he reached the man, a sword cut a tendon near his foot. He fell to his knees and dropped his axe. The man in front and the man behind approached the Loon. They used daggers to stab ... and stab ... and stab.

Ed the Loon's face turned to mush. Blood and entrails spilled from the dozens of holes in his face. The men picked up the lifeless Loon and threw his body off the wall. Ed crashed into the horde below, never to be seen again.

Lolly screamed, and tears filled her eyes; Urses shook his head; Gordo cursed. Yvanne did nothing. There wasn't anything she could do. Not even with her powers could she bring Ed back from the dead, nor would she be able to burn the stone wall. If she did, then her men would turn on her, call her a monster, a traitor.

Lady Lolly was about to speak when a long bellow rushed over the land.

Yvanne was too preoccupied in her mind to notice the rumble of the ground. Cups rattled and fell from tables. She trembled. The noise didn't come from the city, but from behind. She turned to see the most amazing thing.

Tundavik Vandes leading an army.

Tundavik

The stone wall was overbearing as they rode across the blackened grass. His allies had taken over a small village.

He couldn't focus on that. He needed to keep his attention on the battle. Tundavik's army drowned out all noise. The battle was nothing compared to the horde at his back. Men in all kinds of armor, cheap and expensive, ran on their boots, or rode on their horses. More horses and oxen pulled catapults. They lined them with the ones already hurling rocks at the city.

To his right was Mar. His helm already down, spear extended from his arm, ready to fight. Glem was on the left. He was small, but he wanted to fight, and he rode a horse into battle. His armor was only boiled leather. The Flewthmen followed behind. Their many sigils and insignias flowing on flags and surcoats. Lord Toware broke away with his men to lead the van. The lord of Riverend promised he would be the first to reach the palace, and Tundavik took him up on that offer. Lord Furrow and his men from Nye also broke away. They took aim at the Gate of Vigura, which, surprisingly, was falling apart.

As Tundavik dropped his visor, he saw men he didn't

know. Some with blue ribbons, some with banners of leaves or fields or fish or peaks. He knew they were friendly only by the smiles that formed as he passed them. Through the slits in his helm, he saw Commander Wright follow Lord Toware with the men of the Fall behind him. Lady Ceala agreed to let them follow Tundavik after they defeated Lord Leur of Saltcreek. He was forever grateful to the lady.

He took a deep breath and looked at Glem one last time. The boy still did not have a helm. Tundavik motioned, and Glem found a steel cap. He worried the squire would not make it out alive, but the boy begged to fight, and Tundavik had told him it was his choice.

Another deep breath. It felt good to feel his lungs move under his heavy plate. He wished for the breathing to never stop. He did not want to die in Vigur without taking the city, and he wouldn't leave this city like he did Suktir.

The white towers of the palace turned to red spires. Panscar entered his mind, then the assault on Suktir. The journey down the Bezir and all the cities and villages sacked. In his mind, Mar and Glem turned to his comrades from Ritaeum. His subjects fought a war they deemed just. They wanted to win; they didn't want to die either. The spires and red bricks grew larger as he came to them. Blood ran under his horse's legs. The screams echoed through his helm.

The stone wall reemerged as he descended upon his enemy.

Yvanne's men parted as they came through. The gate was open for them to take, so they did just that. Tundavik lowered his spear, and others on horseback followed. The men on the other side of the wall dropped their jaws when they saw what was coming. Their death.

He trampled through the gate, crushing as many men as he could, his spear piercing and bludgeoning anyone in his way. The light of the city grew closer and brighter. Lord Toware was thrown from his horse, and the last whinny escaped with screams. Tundavik realized Bera would trample his men and get stuck in the tunnel. He didn't want her to die in agony, so he did something stupid and dropped from her. As he ran under the portcullis, a bombardment of hits and kicks and swords banged at him. Someone kicked the back of his knee, and he lurched to the ground.

The sound of fighting grew unbearable. Ringing, pounding, screaming, and chanting. The boulders that smashed into the wall and city echoed like thunder in the tunnel. Tundavik wanted to cover his ears, but the steel helm was in the way. It amplified the noise, the chokes of blood, the coughs of last breath.

He steadied his breathing while he lay on his stomach. His breath became the only thing he could hear. He stretched his arm to his side and unsheathed his sword.

A foot stepped on his back, and Tundavik whirled up and jabbed the steel below the hauberk into his spine. The man fell to his knees, and Tundavik kicked him over.

He saw the mess in front of the gate. The horses could only make it so far. The city defenders pushed as hard as they could to stop the advancing army. Behind him came more soldiers. They locked eyes with him, and he knew he was in danger.

His sword flew on its own at the attackers. Dodge, strike, deflect, strike. Tundavik couldn't hold all of them off. They advanced more quickly with every step. Their swords cascaded onto him like bolts of lightning.

Tundavik found himself back on the ground after a boot met his breastplate. His helm had come halfway off his face, the cold tunnel air piercing his skin. The helm was stuck where it was, no coming off his face. He clawed at the metal but stopped when a warm wave washed over his hands and lips.

The helm came off with all his strength. He looked up and saw a hand wrapping around his arm. Mar had taken out the man. He was using one hand to defend them by fighting off those who wanted them dead. The knight kicked open a wooden door and slipped inside. He barred the door and threw Tundavik onto a set of wooden steps.

Mar dropped his sword and shield and leaned on the door that was being bashed on by fists. "We only have a few moments." He lifted his helm and spat blood. "This tunnel will kill us all."

"We're almost through. The men are doing a fine job." Tundavik matched the hard breathing of Sir Mar. "It will all be over soon."

"It was almost over for you already. We haven't been here five minutes and you're already trying to die." Mar pushed back on the door that was being hit. They both looked up the stairs to where sunlight came through. Screams traveled down the steps. "We have to get out of here; it isn't safe."

Mar lowered his helm, held up his shield, and clenched his pommel. Tundavik wiped away the blood that stained his cheeks before putting his helm back on. "You think we can make it past this door?"

"No," Mar didn't mince his words. "But we can try. Are you ready?"

Tundavik wanted to say no. He wanted to stay hidden until the battle was over. But a commander would never leave his men. He would stay until the battle was won or lost, life or death. He took a deep breath and held it before nodding.

The door burst open with hammers and pommels. Mar wasted no time. He attacked the door in a frenzy, pushing those on the other side back. Tundavik watched in awe before heading to the door himself. Mar threw it open and began his attack. Tundavik pushed a man in mail against the stone wall before turning.

His men were stuck at the gate. Above them hung the iron bars. He looked to the other side. Empty. The city was open for them to take. Mar finished the last soldier and followed Tundavik's gaze. The knight shook his head. And he was right.

Tundavik went to the wall of men and started pulling the attackers from his host. Mar followed his lead, leaping to sword fights, pulling attackers from defenders. They took out as many as they could before the tunnel was a mess again. Behind them, from the burned fields, came a dozen men with lions on their surcoats.

A hand squeezed Tundavik's shoulder and pulled him away from the fighting for a moment while the tunnel bloodied. Lord Tylo smacked him on his back. "Told you you've never seen our strength."

Lord Tylo gripped his sword and moved to the front with a war cry. His men followed his every move and they got lost in the mess of fighting.

Tundavik made his way to the light. He fell to the ground once outside, twisting the broken blades of grass in his hand. He didn't need to turn to know what was happening. The chokes and screams matched the fury of steel. The sound of boots squishing on blood and flesh echoed in his helm. Shouts for help escaped the tunnel. He couldn't stay down.

He grabbed a fallen man's shield and turned to face the tunnel. His men fought with all their strength, but they could not take the gate. He didn't want to admit any failure. He had to take the city as he had taken Panscar. But he couldn't.

"Fall back!" he cried out, hoping for others to hear. Eventually, the lords and knights echoed Tundavik. The tunnel emptied as the fighting erupted outside the wall.

Pollard rode in with his followers behind. Their spears skewered the enemy's armor. They stayed atop their horses as they trampled the guards of Vigur. Pollard's wooden spear snapped in half. He dodged all the attacks as he reached for his sword. Once he had it, he cut down as many as he could.

The red-haired knight found his way to Tundavik. "You looked like you could use some help."

Tundavik slipped off his helm with a nervous laugh. "Is it that bad?" He didn't need Pollard to answer. "We'll have to find another way in. We need another gate to open, preferably both."

Pollard shook his head. "I don't think that's going to happen. The fighting atop the wall has stopped. No one wants to climb a ladder to their death."

Tundavik looked for another way. He saw the water

glisten. "It won't be too deep near the bank. If we cross the river, we can pour in from the sides."

Sir Pollard patted his bloodstained horse. "We can't make it past the defenses on the river. A spiked wall keeps us from doing that."

"So we're supposed to funnel in like cows and watch as our men get slaughtered?"

"I think you can come up with another idea." Pollard looked to the fighting. "But you'll need to think while you fight."

Tundavik followed his gaze. More men spilled from the open gate. Instead of dozens, there were hundreds. They seemed never to stop.

He put his helm back on once again, raised his shield and sword, and braced for battle.

The hundreds swept over them like a waterfall. Chants and cries drowned out the noise of the world. He used every technique he had learned all those years ago as a boy. He spun his sword and hit with the pommel, beat one with his shield until he didn't move, and attacked the least equipped men.

Those without helms or gauntlets, gambesons or mail, met their death. Tundavik cut off any piece of body he saw. He stabbed through the openings with a dagger he found and watched the blood empty.

He saw Mar employ some of the same tricks. He stayed near the tunnel, fending off any man who came through. Lord Toware and Commander Wright were with him. Their men falling all around. Pollard was also a force on the field. He rode his horse through the madness, using his sword like a clipper; pieces of flesh were like unknowing plants.

Arrows from above hit Pollard's stallion. They crashed and shot up blood. He worried for a moment, but Pollard stood, dragging his sword across the grass. He went back to work, hacking at anything that moved. Others weren't so lucky. They fell and never recovered. He had to stop this carnage.

Tundavik looked around with every free moment he had. Glem was nowhere to be seen. He just wanted to know if the boy was still alive. He wanted to prove Mar wrong; the boy could be useful; he didn't want Gordo and Marya to mourn their son either.

Then he breathed a sigh of relief.

Glem was still riding his horse along the wall. He tried his best to spear those in different surcoats. Men in their own army jumped so as not to be trampled. Tundavik threw down his helm and waved at Glem. The boy's horse whinnied and bucked him off. Tundavik fetched the reins before helping him up. "I'm glad you're okay." He put a hand on Glem's shoulder.

"How's it going? I feel I'm doing well out here." Glem said as he gasped for air.

Tundavik looked at their only opening. "There's no time." He jumped on the horse and calmed it before he was thrown too. "Stay safe. I'll come back for you."

Tundavik raced across the bloodied grass and onto the ashy dirt. It felt good to be out of the tunnel, away from the fighting. The sound of death and metal grew quieter as he made his way farther from battle. He headed to the village where his allies' tents were plastered over the burned remains.

As he got closer, guards whipped out their swords, and a man in full plate armor jumped in front of the horse. Glem's horse frightened and nearly threw Tundavik off. "Stop!" The man shouted.

At least they're giving me time to explain myself, Tundavik thought. He climbed down off the horse with his hands up and said, "I need to see Yvanne."

"Not one more step," the man said as he clutched his sword.

"It's alright," Yvanne said as she emerged from her tent with ladies and guards and Lord de'Marisco. "Gordo," she said to the man, "it's Lord Tundavik Vandes."

Gordo let out a breath that he had been holding and said, "Thank the gods. But you scared me coming so fast like that."

"What is it you need?" Urses said. How the lord who brought Gofrei's head to Whitehall was allowed so near Yvanne he would never understand.

Tundavik coughed through his aching body, sore and bruised from the fight. "I wouldn't be here if it weren't important." He looked to the wall, all three of the gates still being protected. Mud and dirt soaked with blood, the blood of their army. "The men are struggling to push through. They don't have enough momentum to take the gate. We may outnumber them, but it isn't enough."

Yvanne sighed. "I worried this would happen. My fears subsided when I saw your horde."

"We've tried. Even with thousands of men, catapults, and a boat on the river, we cannot win." Tundavik saw the masses of wood piled high, enough to build any weapons they needed. "At least not today."

Her handmaid helped Yvanne stay upright as she looked dizzy. She rubbed her brow. "What do you suppose we do?"

"We'll have to begin a siege." He saw her brother nod in agreement. "If we can stop shipments into the city, we can starve them out. Wait a few weeks and then agree to Ultiir's surrender, or we attack once more."

"Weeks?" Yvanne chuckled. She rubbed her ever-growing stomach. "I don't have weeks. This needs to end today, and if not today, then tomorrow. We will keep hitting the wall until it crumbles."

"Lord Vandes is right." Gordo added. "A siege would be for the best. We have enough wood for siege towers and other engines. The men will be well rested and ready for battle in a few weeks if Ultiir wishes for another fight."

"You think Ultiir will surrender?" Yvanne said while chewing a fingernail. She looked over at a wagon lined with iron bars. "We could be here for months if we underestimate the number of stores they have in the city."

"We just have to outlast Ultiir," Tundavik said. "Daily rock throws. Raids and attacks on any riverboats or wagons we see. Trust me."

Yvanne blinked and looked around the burned area and then took a deep breath. "Fine," she said. "Call the men. We will begin a siege."

Flora

The road to River Watch was short but full of rain and mud. There was no escaping the water and ever-flooding river. Her carriage had to be abandoned when the mud swallowed a wooden wheel. She rode on the back of Sir Marbert's mare, Spider. "Why choose that name?" She had asked when comfortable on the mare's back.

Marbert giggled and said, "Black and red and brown spiders infest the Seeded Field. Great spiders traverse the fields on their way to the sea. The name reminds me of home." She shivered at the thought of spiders in the ocean. As they continued on the road, Sir Marbert would loudly sigh and roll his eyes. A long hempen rope tied Spider to Lord Poden's horse so they couldn't race off. "Shall I spur Spider and pull the old prick across the mud?"

Flora gave a quiet laugh. "I want to go to River Watch. No one is forcing me."

"Except the man we're being led by. Remember, my lady, you're a captive." Marbert sighed. "Will your father come riding across the flooded fields to your rescue if you do not return?"

"I would hope." Though she wasn't sure. Would Lord

Blume even be able to lead a host through the mud-caked lands? Maybe her husband would come. The thought only made her sad. Barnet would rather she stayed far away from him and the court than risk his life to save hers. Hopefully, Florance was happy. She wiped away bubbling tears. "Go closer to the lord." She told Marbert. Once Spider was in line with Poden's horse, she said, "How have the floods treated your home?"

"The Flit Levels flood like this after Samosay's feast every year, and it's only getting worse," the lord said. "River Watch was constructed to keep the waters out, but even our levy's break. If only your father had sent men in the autumn, like I inquired. Perhaps my home wouldn't have a foot of river in it."

"You are the lord. It is your responsibility to gather and train men to fight the Flit. You cannot blame my father for your every woe."

"Lord Blume promised aid should I need it when he sent me to River Watch all those years ago." Lord Poden snapped. "I should have known his promise was as good as horse shite."

"If you had left Storyah on better terms—"

"Better terms?" Poden spat. "Your father was weak. I tried to strengthen him, and I see he has not changed. Bowing to the whims of a bastard who calls himself king. Sending our men to fight in another war because of Hurvir de'Tro. First for the dead king's hatred of mites, now for the young boy he sired. Pyre could never light the way out of his father's shadow. The Flewthlands was independent for weeks as the Vigurites pushed the Nowexerts north through the swamps. The gods gave us those days. So full of hope and happiness only for it to be taken away, just as the gods do. Then Sir Garth and Lord Onto Blume tried to bring us back to those beautiful weeks, only for your father to sue for peace. Make terms with that *Veck'kop* king," he said it like a curse.

"Have you received word of the war of late? How are our people doing fighting with the Veck'kops?"

Poden smirked and shook his head like she had told a joke. "I have seen neither riders nor letters from the capital. Though I know the armies are slow on the border with the Eastlands. No one can make ground while the whole duchy floods. The Asaramen have used that to their advantage. They descend from the mountain and wrap around their enemy. Last I heard, they were marching toward Riverton once more. Duke Gallient has been fighting traitors in Montlahead. Who knows what's happened since, but the young king and his queen seem to be making strides."

"So shouldn't you be helping instead of taking these lands? If the bastard wins, you don't think my father will turn him and his armies loose on you?"

"I did not ask for this war. If I had known why Lord Blume called the lords to vote, I'd've never sent my envoy. Good thing I didn't send a few hundred men like the other lords. They would be going to war instead of helping me. And now my envoy, Fenton, rides to Vigur with none of my support."

"You don't care if he dies?"

"He was a ward sent to me by some large family in Plajul hoping it would better align us across the Flit. I never wanted their son and am glad he's gone."

"And of what your family?" Flora tried to remember Poden's family when he would visit Storyah. "You had a wife and some kids, no? Is River Watch treating them well?"

Poden Bruce took a deep breath. "Poden the Younger is training as a knight. I think he is in Caiag Rock at the moment. Luk is awaiting my return. He is my eldest and heir. Ceres was sent to Gamm Lars to meet her betrothed. His grandsire still holds the city until his old neck finally breaks. Then some loon gets the city before my sweet daughter becomes lady. I'll be lucky to be alive."

"And your wife?"

"Enough about that." He motioned in front of them, beyond his cavalry and the mud-soaked road. "River Watch."

The town was small, a few homes or shops. *Or has the river washed them away?* The horses stepped into the foot of water, and she saw the broken levees and the men trying to fight the river. She had a feeling they would lose. River Watch was mostly built out of wood taken from the foothills of the Asara, but some flooded dirt huts dotted the outskirts. The people were watching them from the small four-pointed domaton that rose off the ground on stilts. Flora could hear preaching and recognized the Book of Mother Meret. The doma wished for safety from the river, but Nopra, the goddess of freshwater, wasn't beholden to Meret.

They rode into a raised barn and tied many horses to loose wooden poles. The others would have to deal with the river licking at their shoes. Poden took the supplies from Storyah and gave them to bakeries, butcheries, and the doma before going to a black stone castle on the edge of the Flit, small walls surrounding it. A watermill spun as fast as it could with the rushing water.

Poden stopped at the top of the steps. The sun was setting behind gray clouds, and a slight drizzle fell. "Your people will find accommodations around town. The doma is full and not fit to handle you, so you might be sleeping on a flooded bed."

"I won't be in the castle?" Flora asked.

"That is my home." The lord laughed and brought forward a young man in mail. "Sir Len will watch over you and bring you to me when I call. Do treat this place well, and it will be good to you."

Flora doubted that as she looked around at hidden faces that glared at the newcomers.

She found herself in the only whorehouse in town. It smelled of mildew and rotting wood as water leaked through the ceiling. The inn and tavern were bursting at the seams, so Sir Len decided the brothel would be the best place for her to rest. The naked women surely helped his thought process. Sirs Edmond and Marbert kicked some girls out of the room next door to see to Flora's protection. "You shouldn't bunk with a whore," Edmond told her, but she didn't mind. In her room was a woman named Vanette. She was a young girl, maybe twenty, with blackish-blue eyes.

"My ma told me to sell myself so we could afford chickens," Vanette had told her. "Not sure where Ma is now."

Flora was lucky; only Vanette was in the room. Moans of pleasure from other rooms made her feel sick, reminded her of Tundavik. "An adulterer."

"What was that?" Vanette said as she slipped under a blanket of horsehair.

"Nothing," Flora said as she followed suit. *No reason to be thinking of Tundavik at all. He did awful things in Panscar,* she thought, *but I wonder how he's doing on the march to Vigur?* "He never cared for you," she muttered to herself, "merely used me to get Barnet's vote."

"You talk a lot," Vanette said. She blew out a candle, and darkness overwhelmed them. Clouds of rain and thunder hid the moon. "Who never cared for you? Your husband? Your father? My pa never cared for me neither. Went off to fight a war, but I guess that war was only a couple villages over because he was found dead in an inn," she shrugged. "You've a husband, right?"

Flora said, "yes. He is the lord of Woodrun. He's in Storyah right now with my … our daughter."

"I almost had a husband. But his lord doesn't wish to have anymore wives."

Flora sat up on the hard bed. It was too dark to see anything, which made her glad. Vanette didn't need to see her wide eyes. "Do you mean Lord Poden?"

"Who else?" Vanette giggled. "He said I looked like his wife when she was younger. I would be in his bed every night; he'd play with my hair. He loved my hair. I even let him spill inside me," she laughed some more, but her voice was lower. "Who wouldn't want a child to grow old in a fancy keep around fancy people? I never had a child, though. Then his heir yelled at Lord Poden for disgracing the family name. I was sent back here and haven't been with him since."

"And where is his wife?" Flora asked.

"Veltoora, for all I know. She died some time ago. Lord Poden never told no one what happened. One day his lady wife walked the town, and the next she was being buried outside. Hopefully, the water hasn't brought her back. Sometimes that happens, ya know? The dead walk. Scary thing with all the rains."

That morning she was out of bed before anyone else. As she wandered the halls of the brothel, she heard some beds shaking. Even though she lived in Storyah for so long, she had never been in a brothel, even with all the whorehouses around the main square. She found it disturbing. Not peaceful. There was always noise. A moan, the sound of a whip, cries. She hated it. Even more so when she saw the young girls and boys sleeping half naked in the main room, waiting for patrons to come buy them.

"Looking for someone?" Marbert said from behind. "You shouldn't wander off without your guard. Remember, we're not welcome here."

"I just want to find Sir Len. I would like to speak to Poden first thing. Before his men get to his ear and turn him against my father even more."

"The first door on the left," Marbert pointed down a short hall.

Flora didn't like the noises she heard from the room, but she needed to speak to the lord sooner rather than later. When she opened the door, she found Sir Len pounding into a black-haired woman. It took a moment for them to realize she was there.

"Come to join?" Len laughed through bated breath. "I've never had two before."

"I need to see Lord Poden. You're the only one who can get me into the keep."

He sighed and pulled his hard self out of the girl. She played with herself as he dressed. "Do you usually spoil a man's good time?"

She thought of her husband and the nights they never shared. *There was nothing for me to spoil.* She put her hands on her hips while she waited. Sir Len lifted his hood and walked Flora to the small castle. A guard let them into the bailey, and Flora had to lift her knees high to keep her shoes from getting stuck in the mud. Luckily, it wasn't raining as much as yesterday.

"I can still see the moon and most of the village sleeps," Sir Len said as they walked up a few wooden steps that creaked and almost buckled. "What makes you think Lord Poden will want to see you?"

"I'm here to make peace," Flora said. "Why wouldn't he?"

Sir Len spoke with the guard at the door to the castle, so Flora was allowed to stand in the great room to dry off. A serving lady helped pat her dry. The room was dark, with shadows from candles dancing over the wood planks. The lord's chair was raised off the ground, and behind was a tapestry of a trout swimming through the reeds. A small map of the Flewthlands strewn across a table, the Flit Levels clearly marked, with hamlets and towns being colored blue or red. She could see Storyah on the coast, Grass Ridge in the center, River Watch on the Flit, and Woodrun in the west. She tried to bury the thought of her husband, but she still said to herself, *so eager to send me away.*

The knight came down the stairs and motioned up. "He is ready for you. Also, he just woke, so do not get upset if he growls." The serving lady helped Flora up the steep wooden stairs until they came to a door with a trout plastered in the middle. It swung open, and Lord Poden waved Flora in and the serving lady away.

"Would you like broth?" He grabbed two bowls while she sat at a small table in the center of the room. "It shouldn't be too cool. I just took it off the fire." She didn't get to answer. The lord ladled cloudy broth into the bowls and gave one to Flora with a spoon. Without his armor and helm, she could see where his hair parted, leaving a large bald spot; his clothes were baggy like he had lost weight, and his skin sagged. "Sir Len said you wished to talk peace. I'm sorry, but I've nothing to say."

Flora spooned some broth. It was made from vegetables and tasted like nothing. "Well, what kind of envoy would I be if I didn't at least try?"

"One who knew her place," Poden smiled as he ate.

"You sound like my husband," she said before realizing it.

Poden Bruce laughed. "The lords of Woodrun have always been crotchety bastards, good to know Barnet is following in tradition." The lord took Flora's empty bowl and set it near the hearth. "How is Lord Barnet? Enjoying Storyah? How does he like your father?"

"Looking to recruit?" She asked as she clasped her hands together in her lap. "I'm sorry to say, but my lord husband would never turn on his father-by-law, no matter what you said or did. Doesn't that worry you? The combined strength of Storyah and Woodrun raining down on River Watch? It needn't come to that."

The lord cocked his head as he scratched his chin. "I have dreamt of my winning. I have heard the words of the gods. No threats you make will change destiny."

"And what have the gods said?" Flora asked. Usually, the Four and the Many would only speak to her in a domaton, never in her dreams. "Why would they want you to go against my father? He's been a good follower of the faith."

"They tell me of the end of the world." His face darkened as clouds covered the morning sun. "The only way to stop it is to unseat the duke and take control. I am the savior. The world will be fine if I rule."

Flora scrunched up her nose as if his words stank. It was blasphemous. It was treason. "I do not think the gods would say that to you. They don't wish for war to wash over our lands again. Enough destruction was had when they beat back the forces of Veltoora."

There was a thumping sound above them, like a knock on the ceiling. She looked outside and saw the beginnings of a rainstorm. Poden gulped. "Time for you to go. We will discuss this some other time." He grabbed Flora's wrist and hauled her up and out the door. "I do not take this burden lightly," he said as they made their way down the stairs. "The gods have chosen me and me alone. Now," he let go of her as they reached the door. The pitter-patter of rain hitting the steps outside. "I must pray."

As Flora was ushered outside, the door slamming behind her, she thought, *This lord is going to get us all killed, and there doesn't seem to be anything I can do about it.*

Bertin

Throwing their things to the ground, Bertin settled in for a long night of sleeplessness. Torlem and Barhi constructed both their tents and fire, leaving only a cowhide for Bertin. He used the skin as a blanket and lay near the flames. His eyes closed, but no sleep came. Throughout the night he opened them, only to close them again.

Paranoia was growing in his heart. With every sound, his ears perked. Will the big man find him and take him as a slave? Will ghosts and demons find him again? Or would Torlem and Barhi decide he needs to be hunted instead of the elves?

Owls hooted, and memories of Devro came to him. *I hope he's drinking with Mar in Gereduss and having a good time. Hell, anything would be better than where I'm at.* The hooting continued, and he tossed and turned. He didn't know where they were—somewhere to the west of Suktir. It wasn't as dry as it was east of the Bezir; he had seen more farms popping up along creeks and brooks and small rivers. The landscape had turned more green than barren the farther they went. Bertin held his eyes closed until he drifted to sleep, though he thought he could hear the birds wake as he dreamt.

When Bertin woke, Torlem was skinning a boar, and Barhi disassembled the tents. He didn't want to, but Bertin packed the bags. He needed the hunters to stay happy with him if he was ever going to have the chance of reaching Rowan.

After a long morning of clearing the land, the boar was ready. The scent of smoke filled his nose like the butcher's in Rowan. His mouth was awash with juice as he bit into the slab. Bertin reached for a knife to cut a chunk of meat, but it was pulled away. Torlem shook his head and sliced the boar.

The boar was salted, wrapped, and packed away with care. Bertin carried that too. Their journey to Sruhq began as the sun broke away from the horizon. The elves and dwarves and whatever else who lived in the Sruhq Forest were seeing the same sunrise; their happiness would turn to horror once the hunters reached the forest. Maybe Torlem and Barhi weren't like that; perhaps they wanted to go to the kingdom to meet the nonhumans. He sighed helplessly.

"What is Sruhq like?" Bertin caught up to Torlem. "Does it look like other forests?"

"Sure," Torlem said in his thick accent, "but all trees look the same to me. The difference is this wood is overrun with wickedness, and wickedness has no place in this world, not with us humans."

Bertin gulped, remembering the ancient streets of Anha Jorbstah flooding with elven blood. "And how does one rid the world of wickedness?"

Torlem smiled and swirled a long knife with a hooked edge. "You exterminate all who bring the evil and impurity.

Elves have long brought darkness to this world, and our kings have allowed them to take the forest for themselves, so it is up to us to take on the job. This would not be happening had they stayed hidden. Had they kept their sorcery to themselves."

"They're not the only evil in this world," Bertin said, watching Torlem's face to see if he got angry. His face never moved. "The Rainvealandians have done countless deeds that have killed thousands."

Torlem chuckled. "While true, we fight for our land. Those north of the Ters-Veck wish to push us out again."

"The only good thing about those northern kings is that they kill elves just as we do," Barhi said. "I'm sure they would love to send people along with us on this hunt."

Bertin went silent as he thought of his father and all those who came before him. All the death his ancestors caused. *I wonder how many they killed were little elven babies ...* "How long have you been traveling to Sruhq?" he asked to break the silence.

"About once a year," Torlem answered. "The last elf I killed has his head mounted on my wall," he laughed, and Bertin shivered. "Barhi, *lettakus siné giné?*"

Barhi's eyes lit up as they remembered. "*Nim giné nir adé olkat lettak.*" Barhi looked to Bertin and changed their tongue. "It was one of our first hunts. I got lucky; the elf was half dead. Another elf had shot an arrow at his back. Infighting, I guess," Barhi shrugged. "Ever killed anything on your travels?"

"I killed an elf once." Bertin said as his memories filled with muffled screaming.

"Truly?" Barhi clapped. "You are full of surprises."

"It was in Anha Jorbstah. I burned the ancient city and everyone who lived in it," Bertin said with a dry mouth. Kelltar's terrified look burned into Bertin's mind like the dragon fire. Hopefully, *they can't see my sadness,* he thought, but Torlem and Barhi both hollered and laughed.

Torlem smelled the air as if he could smell the charred elf. "I hope you get another kill in Sruhq. It's teeming with prey."

"Not without a weapon." Bertin needed a sword, but Torlem would not answer.

The days grew longer as they crossed the hills of Attamek. Small streams kept their thirst quenched; leftover boar helped their stomachs from aching. Flowers bloomed all around. Barhi picked some red and yellow petals and stuffed them in a tunic pocket. Every so often they would smell the sweet scent.

The rows of flowers brought his mother back. He rarely thought of her, but the time of Swallow always reminded him of her soft touch and voice. He thought she would live forever. Her body was covered with roses as they laid her to rest below the domaton. Maybe his father was buried the same.

The night came in time for him to forget again. He helped make camp while fighting the thoughts of his dead parents. The mites could not see him cry. He needed them to think he was strong, and not to find out who his parents were. They shared what was left of the dark meat before enjoying the fire.

Bertin watched Torlem and Barhi bicker and joke in their ancient tongue. Sometimes he wished he could join in but knew it would be better to stay silent. Vigura's star shone bright in the northern sky. "Always find Vigura and he will lead you home," Blis had told him during one of his studies. Bertin thought little of it at the time. Why would he be gone? He would be prince then king, no reason to go south except war. Now, he sat in a field surrounded by wilderness.

"What's the closest town to here?" Bertin asked.

Torlem glanced at the wildflowers. "Ansehar is on the western border, Panscar is to the north, and Suktir is back east. I would say a few days' journey to either. Why? Miss the whores already?"

"Suktir was the first city built by men I had stepped foot in for a long while. It was nice."

Barhi laughed. "That's because Suktir is nice. Ansehar is shit, but we'll pay for food and some supplies to last us the hunt. After Sruhq, we'll go to Bardekan. You can find a ship to take you north."

Bertin was almost at a loss for words. "You're going to take me to Rowan?"

"Not a chance." Torlem scoffed. "Barhi and I will stay in Bardekan for a few weeks; you'll go to Rowan. If that's really where you want to be."

"I have business there."

Torlem stretched and entered his tent. "I'm sure." He said as he lay down to sleep.

The night was full of sounds which kept Bertin awake. To pass the time, he watched the stars, counting as many as he could. Finding any constellations he remembered. There were brighter objects he had never noticed. Whether they were stars or not, he did not know. Five bright orbs almost aligned. He didn't have time to care; he would leave that to the stargazers.

He twisted and turned until on his side. The cowhide did not make the ground any more comfortable. He watched with envy as the mites stuffed their tents with wool. In the palace, his bed was made of the finest cotton, covered with the best silks of faraway lands; now he lay on dirt.

Bertin's ears perked at the rustling of flowers. *Maybe someone is taking a shit.* Then, the steps grew closer. He turned onto his back and saw looming shadows descend on the camp. With skill and caution, they went through any pack they could find, taking all the food and supplies. Bertin acted asleep, but the shadows drew near. His eyes darted for weapons but found only roses. The flowers let out a cry of death to warn Bertin what was coming.

Fingers tightened around his collar, and up he went. The man laughed and licked his lips. Bertin could smell the ale coming out of his pores. *"Sazim imliko iré amak emtekun raya."* Bertin squirmed, but the clasp was too strong. He lifted a small dagger and brushed the cool blade along Bertin's neck.

Blood poured, and Bertin fell to the ground. His hands searched for his throat only to find no wound. The blood came from the bandit. His head concaving as he slumped down.

Barhi whipped a bloodied sword around like a crazed fool. Torlem followed with a hooked sword to match his dagger. He parried and dodged and sliced the muscles of a bandit's shoulder. Bertin crawled away from the fighting. He grabbed a stick, but it would be no match for steel blades; besides, he was bruised and broken and would be of no help.

Torlem and Barhi didn't seem to care. They both used

their swords and daggers to slice everyone who surrounded the camp. No one was safe; they would've cut down women and children alike if it meant they'd reach the men. Strike after strike, step after step, sparks flew to light the night as steel rang. Bertin couldn't see who fell or how they died, but he could hear. The gushing of blood echoed that of a waterfall. The dark brimmed with moans and grunts.

The scratch of wood lit a torch. The mites stood over the dead, everything bloodied by battle. Torlem lifted Bertin to his feet. "You nearly died." Torlem seemed to laugh. "You're not much of a fighter."

Bertin wiped dust and blood from his ragged tunic. "I've seen my fair share, but no, I'm not a fighter like you two." He scanned the flowers. "You must've taken out ten men together."

"We've a lot of practice."

Bertin clutched a dagger from the ground. "I could practice too."

Torlem shook his head. "We still do not fully trust you." He swiped the knife away. "You can't blame us. We found you lost in Suktir, with nowhere to go. Then you join us after first saying no and have yet to tell us why you want to go to Rowan."

"I just want to get home. I've been traveling for far too long and miss my family."

"You've a family?" Barhi asked as they looked through the pockets of the dead. "And you left them?"

Bertin shook his head but said, "Yes. It wasn't much of a choice at the time, but now I fear my sister and brother are all alone and I need to be there for them."

Torlem sat on a log, playing with the embers of the

campfire. "Barhi and I are lucky; both of our families are gone. My parents died when I was young. My sister decided she wanted to travel to the North, *Ahtalez,* I believe it's called in our tongue. You see, my sister was born to a different body, and in the image of Aldima Ahíd she was able to change her ways. They didn't appreciate it in the North, luckily someone sent her body back South." Torlem scratched his neck. "It was an awful image."

"And mine died in a flood," Barhi said. "I was in Sruhq. The entire village I was born in was gone from the map in an instant." Barhi stood and wiped their hands. "All this fighting is making me hungry. I'll return in a moment."

Bertin sat by a now-roaring fire. His fists and jaw clenched. His eyes trained on the bodies and the weapons the mites left behind. He itched his little finger … there was nothing. "A great king must be a great warrior." His father's words rang hollow. He would never fight as well as the late king, evidenced by the many welts and fractures he had all over his body since stepping foot in Vaandet. He would always be at a disadvantage.

Barhi returned from their night hunt with a small dog-like beast, its snout long and colored brown. They cut the skin and peeled whatever they could. Bertin stared at the ground. His eyes hazed with the sorrow that wouldn't escape him.

"You know," Torlem started as he stared at Bertin, "I also once had a woman. She was kind and soft. Treated me any way I wanted, and I did the same to her. I was working in Cluo, on the docks, the day she died. The elves had broken through the gate and raided the inland. I could do nothing to stop them. I fought with a carving knife, smaller than this one." He lifted his shirt to unveil the long scar that stretched from his sternum to pelvis. "They said Aldima Ahíd smiled favorably upon me that day. It was a miracle I lived." Torlem looked at Bertin's missing finger. "How did it happen? A whore bite it off?"

The fires and sacrifices came back to him. The desert seemed so long ago. "An elf chopped it off and threw it in the fire. Some strange tradition or the like. I wish it were a whore." He managed a chuckle.

"An elf mangled you, and you killed an elf with flames. The same one?"

"No, they were very different."

"You've had a lot of run-ins with elves, it seems," Barhi said as they readied a spit. "How did they find you? How was one able to steal a finger from you?"

Bertin's eyes closed as Telemaw came back. "I was captured during an expedition. They left me to rot while they sacrificed the other humans. I was just able to escape, but only with help. I ran as far as I could until they found me." Ioelena's corpse seemed to form in the fire. "They killed the woman with me ..."

Torlem cleaned his hunting knife with a cloth. His eyes were cold as the night. "A woman you loved?"

"I ..." He didn't love Ioelena in the way Torlem was talking about, but she helped him escape, let him see Wilclef one last time. If not for her than he never would have killed Kelltar. He would be weaker than he was now. "In a way," he finally said.

"Do you think about her every time you close your eyes? Then again, when you open them? Do you dream of her night and day? That's how I am with my lovely Asin." The name rolled off his tongue as if he were reciting poetry.

"I think of her mangled body and see how lucky I am. They took one finger; they took her life. I see the way they left her in the bloodied sand. I dream of it every night."

Torlem shuffled his feet. "What was her name? As beautiful as Asin?"

Bertin had to think quickly; he didn't want to say an elven name. "Rouna." His mother's name. "After that, they drug me wherever they went, but I killed the elf who killed Rouna. I pushed him into a fire. I was able to get free and lost my way. Now, I sit by the fire with you and Barhi, hoping to find my way back to where I come from."

The Rainvealandian looked at the last of the stars before the sun rose. He reached for a small knife and outstretched it to Bertin. He wrapped his good hand around the leather handle. "You're going to need this for when we find them."

Sophie

I didn't think this would happen again in my lifetime," Lord Masson said. "I definitely didn't think it would be by the hands of our own people." Sophie stood with him atop the wall of the palace grounds. In the far distance, they watched as boulders occasionally flew over the city and crashed into the houses below. Asaramen were on the north and south banks of the rivers as well, keeping small boats from crossing. A ship from Awaran blockaded the city from the trade along the Montla-Ritae. They were under siege.

Fires raged in the distant. Everything near the city wall — the houses and shops and the like — all destroyed from the fighting. The only good in the city was that the palace wouldn't catch fire. The elves built it to withstand an attack by dragons. She prayed it wasn't just a myth.

"Ultiir wanted to fix this kingdom, but all he did was bring more war and anguish." Sophie said as she wiped sweat from her brow. Her hair was pulled back, but even that couldn't keep the heat of summer away. Vigura was bringing his season even as she prayed for him not to.

Tedbalt nodded. "Hurvir would be proud."

Sophie sucked her teeth. Her guards stood around her,

afraid any stray arrow could find her. Sir Achen hadn't let go of his sword hilt in weeks. But she was glad to have protection. The people below had nothing, and the city would starve eventually, and the people would react. She shuddered at the thought of cannibalism. *I'd rather they break down the palace walls than turn on each other.*

"This will be the end of us, won't it?" Sophie said as she outstretched her gloved hands and rested them on the gray stone.

Lord Masson scrunched up his face. He had gone back to wearing white robes after Ultiir stripped him of his title. Sophie was just glad he hadn't been named a mage and hanged … yet. "I hope not," he said. "Losing to an army led by a young girl, pregnant at that, would be the most embarrassing moment of our lives."

Sophie laughed. "Perhaps if I led instead of Ultiir, she would go easy on me."

"Have you spoken with the bastard?"

"I've no desire to," she answered.

"Ultiir told us that the bastard despises you. That you turned your back on him and his father. Who knows what the Lady of Whitehall has heard about you."

"I'll never understand why Devro holds any love for his father," Sophie said with a sigh. "The man who beat him when he was just a toddler."

"Bastards are odd creatures. That's all you need to know."

Sophie rubbed her fingers through her hair. All she felt was sweat. "Do you think a duke will come to us? Lord Gallient or even Lord Valles? I'd like this siege to be over so we can move on to more important things."

"Securing the throne?" Tedbalt smirked. "That girl has

cut us off. The North could explode in war again, and we would never know. They shoot down our birds, capture our riders. No one is coming, and we certainly aren't leaving."

"Then we must sue for peace. Force Ultiir to make the deal. Stop anymore killing. Surely the lords of the court want that."

"I'm not sure if you've noticed, Your Grace," Tedbalt chuckled, "but Ultiir hasn't called the court into session in months."

"Then the lords will have to demand it."

"And how do you propose they do that? Ultiir has closed the palace, and all the lords are lying in fear in the Noble Lands. The only way would be to open the gates and do so without Ultiir knowing."

The white houses of the Noble Lands reflected the sun. Pristine and clean and guarded, unlike the rest of the city. "We'll convince them," she said with a smile.

***

Sophie made her way through the halls. Paintings of her predecessors followed down the corridor. Their stares did not make her feel confident. The queens of old never had a say in kingly matters; she had to change that.

The throne room was empty. Only the spiders and mice had taken over. *If the siege holds too* long, *then those mice will have another problem.* She turned away from the throne, not wanting to look at it, not wanting to remind herself of Hurvir and Ultiir and all the horror they caused. Instead, she walked along the corridor behind the throne room with Sir Achen, chambers lining the walls. When she opened the door to her new office, where the chief watcher used to sit, Ultiir was on the chair waiting.

He looked smaller, skinnier, his hair getting lighter with every stressful minute. He had looked so young the year prior, but now his wrinkles and drooping eyes reminded her of Rila de'Tro. "Nervous?" Sophie asked as she slipped off her heels after walking all day. "Do you need my advice? This that why you're in my office?"

"Yours?" He scoffed and twiddled with a quill. "No one has used this room since that traitor from Montlahead occupied it. When did it become yours?"

Achen seemed glued to Sophie as she pulled a dusty chair from the corner and sat on it. Her guard never took his eyes off Ultiir. *I will not let him make me cry today. He will not get to me. Never again.*

Sophie cleared her throat. "When I decided it would be better to conduct my affairs somewhere other than my room. The room you bloodied."

"You don't want anyone else to realize you've been fucking Tedbalt and his old, shriveled cock?" Ultiir smirked as he stood. He leaned on the desk in front of Sophie, crossing his arms, trying to look mighty. But Sophie knew he was terrified. His brow was sweaty. He licked his lips. His legs shook. "I thought you wanted to be away from me?"

"The closer to you, the more I can watch you."

"No more defenseless whores sent my way? Too bad," he clicked his tongue. "I liked that one. Sir Gid liked her more, though."

Images of blood and rape and entrails and beatings and screaming and crying flashed in her mind. *I will not ... he will not get to me.* Sophie only smirked. "Well, that was the point, wasn't it? For you to like her and tell her all of your secrets. Luckily, I didn't need her anymore."

"Of course," Ultiir said as he pushed himself off the table and looked at the dusty and web-covered trinkets hanging on the walls. Decorative swords and shields and tapestries from far away. "I heard rumblings from some of my people that you, the old fuck Tedbalt, and the bitches of your council are trying to get the lords to convene court. Is that true?"

There was a knock on the door, and Mara walked in, freezing when her eyes found Ultiir. She bowed with a, "Your Grace," then turned to Sophie. "They're waiting."

Sophie stood, brushed her dress, and slipped into her shoes. "Why don't you find out?" She said to Ultiir. As she left the room, a smile cascaded over her lips. She never turned to see if Ultiir was following; she didn't have to. He was too proud, too paranoid. He needed everything to go his way.

The throne room wasn't empty any longer. The lords of the royal court and their ladies and guards filled the room. They squeezed tight between the arched walls; a million colors rained on them from the stained windows. It was a beautiful sight. Somehow, Sophie and Mara and Tedbalt and anyone else on her side were able to convince them to come together. To defy the king. They were laughing and cursing and bickering as they filled the room. Lord Tylar bowed his head to Sophie as they made eye contact. The ladies of her queen's council also peppered about the room. Mara stood with Filra as they whispered. Alba was with her husband. Lady Ficca stood with some other ladies. The room echoed for the first time in months, like thunder over the palace. She couldn't even hear Ultiir walk up next to her.

"Defying their king," Ultiir rubbed his chin. "How did they make it past the gate? I've had it closed and guarded since I sent them all away."

Sophie motioned to her guard. "Sir Achen can be very persuasive."

"Your Grace," the old monster, Sir Gid, said as he raced in with the other councilors. Ultiir's sister among them in a white robe. "We couldn't stop their entering. It seems the guards let them in."

"Then I guess we'll have to find new guards," Ultiir bit. "My lords," he turned to the crowd of people who didn't silence. His face grew red until he stomped his foot and yelled, "My lords!" like a child throwing a tantrum. The throne room quieted, echoes stopped. "My lords, welcome back, but I must ask what is this for? As you know, only the king can call the court into session, and I don't remember doing that."

The room was even quieter now, Sophie thought she heard gulps in the crowd. *Be strong,* she thought.

Lord Tylar craned his neck and said, "It's doing with the siege, Your Grace, we feel you're not handling it well."

Ultiir's jaw strained. "Would you like to take over for me? I would happily name you the chief commander; let us pray you do not die like the last one, or like your father."

It was like a wave crashed over the room. There were wide eyes, gasps and murmurs, gulps and shifts. They were uncomfortable, and that was exactly what Sophie needed. Lord Tylar's face reddened as much as his red clothes. "How

…" he said the rest so soft that she couldn't hear.

"How dare you!" cried Count Ompter, an old rival of Tylar and his dead father. But it wasn't directed at the lord; it was directed at the king. "Never in my life have I seen a lord of the court disrespected in such a manner."

Now, there were nods in the room. Ultiir shifted back. "It was merely a jest."

"Jesting about a dead father?" Called out a lord named Ripple.

A lady said, "What a heinous joke." Another said, "Such cruelty." Then more chimed in with their disappointment. "You should've called the court back into session months ago," a lord said. "What gives you the right?" "We are noble!" "We have armies!"

The room was erupting in a frenzy of shouts and raised fists. The entire palace was shaking, dust fluttering from the ceiling and chandeliers. "Stop this siege! Stop the madness!" yelled Lord Wilt.

Old Gid, the beast, strutted over to Ultiir and whispered to him. The councilors were all stepping back. The king's sister came over to Sophie, her white cloak floating over the insults. "Quite a scene," Analere said. "Who knew the lords felt this way?"

"Anyone with eyes and hears would've known," Sophie said with a bow of her head. "Your brother kept himself shut in instead of conversing with them. And it caused this." She motioned to the yells and argues. Some tried their best to get Ultiir's attention, but the king looked like a boy, like the bastard he fought against. Completely out of his element. "But I am glad he has someone like you to trust fully now," Sophie said to Analere. "Let's hope he isn't able to break that."

"I'm not sure anything could come between a brother and sister."

"Your mother probably said the same thing about you and her." Sophie smirked as she walked to the edge of the lords. "My lords!" She strained her voice. "My lords!" She tried again. Sir Achen was at her back, and he pounded his metal boot on the floor. The room quieted once again. "My lords, it is imperative that we hear you, but we cannot while you all shout. What is it you want?" She heard cries for safety and food and for the war to end and their coin to grow again. "Would you like the siege to end?" The room mostly nodded. "Then let us focus on that."

She turned and walked up the steps to the throne. It took all of her power not to sit on the red velvet. Instead, she did as was tradition and went over to the smaller chair for the queen. "Your Grace," she waved a hand at the throne. Ultiir crinkled his nose but followed her lead. He looked so small under the stained glass and beams. How something that conveyed so much power could make a man look so weak she didn't understand.

"First," Ultiir started, "I must say my apologies to the Lord Tylar. It was not an offense I wished to make. Now, about the siege. There is very little I can do. If it were up to me, I would make the bitch from Whitehall and her armies leave the city and return our kingdom back to peace, but she will not leave."

"Have you made any negotiations?" Asked Lord Clye. "Does she want the bastard? How much use is he to us here if it brings a siege?"

Ultiir took a large breath. "There is nothing I can do; the

girl will not meet with me."

"Your Grace," Sophie leaned forward, "are you going to tell the court that the Asaramen have your mother?"

Again gasps. *Just what I want,* Sophie thought as she tried to hide a smirk.

"They captured the Queen Mother?" asked a lord old enough to remember when Rila de'Tro stalked the palace halls. "Then you must save her."

"You must release your prisoner for her!" Another shouted. This time even the monster Sir Gid nodded. There was more yelling, more pleading. Ultiir's eyes glazed over, but Sophie's were burning bright. She needed the lords to turn on Ultiir, to be angry, to hate him. As she took a breath, she set her sights on the throne. There, Ultiir's red eyes glared at the world.

Yvanne

Her screams drowned out the war beyond. Her belly heaved as her servants and guards and siblings gathered round. Yvanne gripped the edges of the bed, spit flying from her mouth. It wouldn't come out. It was stuck. She screamed some more. The world was dark around her. Flames licked at the foot of her bed. She would be dead soon. Her baby dead too. But she kept screaming and pushing and screaming and pushing until she heard the gasps from her entourage.

Ladies screamed and men cried, children ran and the elderly fainted. The dark world burned as the flames surrounded her. Lady Marla Mae held up Yvanne's child. Neither boy nor girl. Not a human nor a demon. Her child was plopped onto her belly, the sack breaking and dousing the flames. Yvanne's child, the heir to Viguran, was nothing she had ever seen. It curled and twisted, its fingers like claws, its skin like scales. She was looking at a monster. She gave birth to a beast. And as blood spilled from the womb, Yvanne's eyes closed. Sir Tiro reached out a childish hand and took her toward a blinding light—

Yvanne woke herself with a scream. She felt her body and cried as she felt her bulging, soft belly. The baby kicked.

More tears escaped.

"What is it?" The tent flap flew open, and in came Sir Mar, his gray eyes scanning the room.

"Nothing," Yvanne sighed and wiped her eyes. "Just nightmares." Jacka followed Mar inside, the sun peering through the holes in the tent and the charred wall Yvanne's tent had been set against.

Mar averted his eyes, and Jacka helped Yvanne out of bed and into loose-fitting clothes. "You gave the entire camp a fright," Mar said. "Your handmaid had just gone out to get water when you started screaming."

"Was it the baby?" Jacka's soft voice asked. Yvanne nodded. "Do not listen to bad omens. I have delivered countless babes whose mothers were afflicted with nightmares. They didn't think their children would survive, but most of them have grown up to be big and strong."

"Most," Yvanne whispered as a blue shawl draped over her shoulders.

Jacka found a brush and untangled Yvanne's red hair. "If the Four will it, then there is nothing we can do."

Yvanne bit her lip. Through a small gap in the tent flap, she could see her armies getting ready for another day of siege. She stopped counting the days and hours a while ago. *I was foolish to think Ultiir would surrender so quickly, especially for his mother of all people.*

She said, "Sir Mar?" The knight stood at attention, not needing to hide his eyes any longer. "Did you ever think of having children? That is before you became a knight?"

"Your Grace," Mar began, "you should know there are certain parts of my knightly vows I don't take as seriously as others."

Yvanne nodded and slipped into her shoes, much too small for her swollen ankles, but she hadn't a choice. "I've heard you and Jacka flirting late at night." Her handmaid's eyes dropped, and she became pale. "It's alright," Yvanne smiled. "We've more important things to worry about. So?" She looked to Mar.

"No," he shook his head and pursed his lips. "The world is much too cruel to bring a child into it. Besides, what kind of father would I be? I enjoy the comforts of men and women too much."

Jacka giggled. Yvanne did too before saying to her handmaid, "Water would be nice." Jacka bowed and scurried out of the tent.

Mar took a step forward, his boots leaving mud stains on her carpet. "I haven't … bedded your handmaid if you're worried about that." He said when they were alone. "Tundavik told me to stay close to you and keep you safe, not fuck some girl."

"And I thank you for that," she said as she sat on her bed. "So is it a mistake?" Mar cocked his head. "To bring a child into this world? Am I dooming it to a life of pain? And what if I don't win … if Devro doesn't win the war? We'll be butchered. The babe will be an orphan; and that's only if I give birth before being killed."

"Don't think like that," Mar said, and stood over her. "Ultiir hasn't killed Devro yet, has he? Then you shouldn't think of your death just yet. Wait until he lops the bastard's head over the wall," Mar chuckled, but Yvanne wasn't laughing. "Sorry, humor allows me to be ready for anything." His voice cracked.

"I'm sure it's better to laugh than to always stress." Yvanne held her head. Everything about her was sore at the moment, and she didn't know how much longer she could handle the pregnancy. Her breasts were sore and oh so heavy, her belly was being kicked, her insides cramped, her legs and feet always tired. "I just want this babe to be out of me already. For Devro to have his son and heir so we can plan for the future. I want to know my child is healthy."

"Everything will be fine," Mar said. "And I remember when Devro was young. Actually, I was in the palace the first day Hurvir arrived with his bastard from Maertan," Mar chortled. "The whole place was abuzz with gossip and rumors. It was too scandalous, even for Hurvir, who had already defied the Four and annulled multiple marriages. I found it idiotic — the gossip. Hurvir was stupid too, but I had already grown to hate that wretched king.

"I saw Devro on the last day I was in Vigur, when I left the guard to travel anywhere else. He was a chubby, purply baby. Giggling and grabbing and crying. Hurvir had left him with some maids for the night, so they let me see the bastard. He was a healthy boy. His hair was almost full already, and I could see the very beginnings of a tooth. If I had known then what I know now about Hurvir, I would've stolen him. Taken Devro north and raised him properly. Instead of the beating and yelling. But you can't change the past. And I got the boy when he was seven anyway. But Devro is a strong kid; he's becoming a strong man, I guess. You and he will raise a fine heir, I know it."

Yvanne smiled as Mar licked his teeth and cleared his throat. His eyes shiny. "Hopefully, you'll be around to help. You and Raimund and everyone else. In the palace or in Eotros if we have to run away. Will you come with us? No matter what?"

Mar scratched his chin. It was newly shaven and stubbly. "I'm not sure."

Jacka came in with a bucket of water and filled Yvanne's skin with it. Her handmaid made sure to fetch from a small brook in the hills. The men were pissing and shitting in the Montla and Ritae, and they had dumped dead bodies in the rivers as well. Which reminded her of poor Tiro. The young knight who had followed Yvanne was dead. Ed the Loon was dead too. She was lucky more of her brothers didn't die in the fighting.

There was a crash outside, and she knew her men were reloading the trebuchets. They were trying to beat Vigur into submission. She didn't know if it would work, but she prayed it would. "Shall we go outside?" Yvanne asked as her handmaid helped her up. "See if we've made any progress?"

Mar bowed, his mail rattling. "I do enjoy the smell of death in the morning."

Once the sun hid behind soft clouds, Yvanne could see the camp that sat atop the charred remains of Fielding. The Asaramen were to the west. They loaded catapults and trebuchets and gathered boulders. The large siege towers sat empty, collecting dust. Men pulled wood from the bottom to make fires; almost nothing could be used in Fielding. Knights and men-at-arms sat and chatted, their armor lying by the wayside, their weapons littered about. There wasn't much to do during a siege as they waited. Sooner or later, the city would run out of food. Hopefully, *the people revolt and open the gates for us.*

Her people bowed as she walked through the town. Diero and Gordo were off in a flat meadow training the young fighters with swords and shields. Lady Lolly said, "Hello," in her sweet voice as she helped the few daken they had with the wounded. The scent of dried blood turned to cooking fish as she passed by the cooks. Mar grimaced at the smell. "I would've thought you'd be used to fish since you lived in Gereduss."

"Not two-headed ones," Mar pointed, and sure enough, a dead fish was staring at her with four eyes. She rubbed her belly as she kept her vomit down. "How do you think Tundavik and Pollard are doing?"

Yvanne strained her neck to see through the burned fields and homes and shops, but only multi-color tents stretched to the horizon. The Flewthmen had taken up the eastern parts of town, and Tundavik and Pollard were reinforcing the edges of the camp for fear that the Eastlanders would launch a surprise attack. She just shrugged.

To the south was the Ritae, the river of death. Gravediggers were busy filling their giant holes. Yvanne said, "Jacka, will you find us some food? Preferably not tack." Her handmaid bowed away, and Yvanne continued to the river.

"Your brothers would hate your being out here," Mar said as he followed, "especially Pollard. He would have my head. One brave archer from Vigur and you're dead."

The wall of Vigur had woodwork to repair the damage, though more boulders broke through, some of the builders' bodies were rotting under the sun. City guards lined the top. But they were too far away to hit her with an arrow, she hoped. "Good thing Pollard isn't around." They sloped down with the bank, smiling at the workers, and came upon rocks that formed a four-pointed star. "This is my brother, Ed the Loon. He would laugh at me for taking a risk. Pollard buried him here, away from the mass graves. The Four don't let those buried en masse feast with them." She looked to the large holes still being filled. "Stupid rule." She muttered.

"I'm sure the gods don't care about that." Mar leaned over the water. "There are far more important things to worry about."

"I hope they find Tiro's soul," Yvanne said softly.

"Another brother?"

She shook her head. "A new friend. If the Four are as great as my doma taught me, they would find that poor boy and lift him to a high seat." Whatever lurked below the river disturbed her reflection. "Tundavik hasn't told me what happened in Storyah. All I know is you two got the Flewthlands to join us."

"That's the most important." Mar smiled. "The rest was bloody awful. Too many lords bickering for me to enjoy it, and I stopped visiting the brothels as much," Mar motioned to the graves, "probably a mistake on my part."

"Did you enjoy being tucked away in Gereduss? Away from the lords and ladies?"

Mar's smile faded. His eyes turned sad. "It was fine. Though sometimes I wonder what my life would be like if Hurvir had chosen me to be his commander. Would I be dead with him? Would I have ever met Raimund?"

Yvanne rubbed her belly before gripping the locket around her neck. The energy of the stone pulsed under her hand like a heartbeat. "Do you think Raimund is still alive?"

The knight didn't answer. Instead, he skipped a rock over the river; it bounced a few times before sinking, never to be seen again. The south bank was vast emptiness. *If only I could swim over there. Give birth in peace and come back. Maybe Vigur will've fallen by then.*

"Maybe that's what I'll do after the war is won," Mar said, "go to Redington and track down Raimund. Surely Devro and Tundavik would help as well."

"I'm sure," Yvanne said as she peered east again. This time she saw Tundavik and her brother atop their horses, inspecting the battlements. "What do you think of Lord Vandes? You've spent so much time with him. Devro trusts him, as do I, but just wondering."

Mar seemed to smile at the thoughts that filled his head. "He can sometimes be cranky like the old man he is; he doesn't enjoy a lot of things, and he likes to disrupt others' joy as well." The knight looked to the capital as a boulder flew over the wall and crashed into some building below. "He's smart, was born to lead." Mar then looked at the grave of Ed. His gray eyes turned to rain clouds. "He's also experienced terrible loss, and that drives him to do things he might not always be proud of."

"I expect Devro to give him control of the Woodlands once again when the war is over. If not, I'll have a talk with him."

Mar laughed. "I'm not sure Tundavik would want that. I don't think he ever wants to step foot in Ritaeum again. He might've been born there, but there are too many terrible memories. I guess I understand that, though my past isn't nearly as bad as his, I just complain a lot," he laughed again.

"How did Hurvir find you?" Yvanne asked. When Jacka was struggling to juggle three bowls in her hands, they went to help. Small patches of green came through the charred ground as they walked back toward camp. "You saved Vikry, didn't you?"

"There isn't much more to the story," Mar said. "It wasn't as glorious as everyone made it out to be. Vikry had been saved once before, by men much older and better than me. Hurvir had held a tourney the year before to get away from war; he was impressed with me. I guess he liked winners, so he gave me a battalion. At the time, I was as excited as ever. I was the youngest knight to win a tourney, then the youngest to be named commander." Mar took a deep breath. She could tell the memories were flooding like a river. "Vikry fell again once the Rainvealandians thought they would lose. No one was expecting it. Hurvir was more pissed than I'd ever seen. He sent every man with a ship down the Montla.

"The mites had blockaded the city. They used their new ballistae mounted on their ships to keep all at bay. Somehow, I got a ship," Mar chuckled, "I don't actually remember how. But I commanded that ship as best I could. We neared the city at night and, with swords drawn, pounced, ramming our ship into the grandest one, which had a twisted face for a sail. We jumped aboard and took it with ease. One by one, the ships fell to us. Our allies were able to get through the blockade. I led the charge to the Houses of Awaran and liberated the lords and ladies." Mar proudly smiled. "Vikry never fell again."

"If I go by that, then we need ships." Yvanne said as they reached Jacka, and she took her bowl of stew. "I need ideas. I need this siege to end quickly. We don't need hungry soldiers."

A bugle played from the destroyed Gate of Vigur. The

men stood and looked over the destroyed town. Yvanne could barely make anything out, but she could hear the portcullis raising over the quiet of the camp. "Maybe you got your wish," Mar said.

Tundavik

The morning air was crisp as it hit his skin. Tundavik was thankful for a breeze as summer was coming. He had to carry a cloth with him to wipe his sweat as the days got longer and warmer. It didn't help that he was doing so much work, but he didn't want the soldiers to feel like the commanders were looking down on them. Yvanne would deal with the sick and dying. Tundavik would help reinforce the eastern part of camp.

Tundavik held the large spike with a few other men while some dug. They straightened it as best they could. The large piece of wood was taken from the burnt remains of the village. *Hopefully it holds,* Tundavik thought as wiped his brow. Hundreds of men were busy ramming spikes into the ground, digging dry moats and trenches, building small platforms for archers. He was terrified that Ultiir would be able to get a message to Lord Gallient and have the forces of the Eastlands descend on them. *I won't let that happen.*

"Already tired?" Sir Pollard said as he handed Tundavik some tack. It was hard and stale, and he missed real food. "We've still a long day ahead of us. Your Lord Toware wants a trench dug around Fielding, and since you've lowered yourself to manual labor, I'm sure you're going to join."

Tundavik's back ached. He wasn't young anymore. Between the fighting under the gate and building defenses, Tundavik felt his age. His bones were slow, his joints popped, his muscles always sore. If he looked in a mirror, he wouldn't be surprised to see a fully white beard. He scratched at the hair on his chin. He was tiring of it, and now with the heat it made his face too warm. "I'll talk Toware out of that. We won't be here long enough, and our men can protect Fielding just fine."

Pollard crunched on his hard biscuit. "Yes, but that man is stubborn. I should know," he smirked. "Sometimes I think he's going to work the men to death."

Tundavik thought back to New Vigur, that small hamlet where Toware would've been happy to kill every single villager. Young and old. "That wouldn't surprise me either." Tundavik wiped dirt from his hands and then massaged his eyelids. His headaches had gotten worse; his dreams more intense. He hated that woman for telling him he needed to go to Ritaeum. He'd rather go to Attrima, where his head wasn't always throbbing. "Heard any news from your sister?"

"Well," Pollard said as he pursed his lips, "how would I hear anything when you forced me to be with you? I'm not Sir Mar remember?"

Tundavik crossed his arms. "I know you didn't like that I split you up, but you're a much better commander than Mar, and I trust him to protect your sister until his dying breath."

"Hopefully, that last breath comes quickly," Pollard giggled. "Sorry. I'm not too upset; it's just that I've been protecting my sister since before you even came through the Swallow Pass. Then we had the march here, and I had to be close to her. If anything happened to her, I'd … I'd …"

"I understand," Tundavik said. *The poor boy has already lost his mother and father. To lose his sister …* he cleared his throat to stop his mind from wandering. If he wasn't careful, he would think of his own children. Brother and sister. Dead. "Later today we can go see them. I want to hear of the happenings around camp."

"Well, I heard, just from soldiers so probably gossip, that Lord Cul has been crying ever since the battle. He lost dozens of his warriors." Pollard shook his head. "Of course the Peakmen were supposed to be the best in the realm," he shrugged.

"I don't care for a crying old man. I want to make sure everything is running smoothly. The Asaramen are growing tired with every passing day; the Flewthmen won't be far behind, but they haven't been warring as long. I want to make sure the men are ready for anything. We don't know what Ultiir is planning."

"You don't think he's planning to trade Devro for his mother? I know she's a bitch, but she is still his mother."

Tundavik rubbed the bridge of his nose as Glem brought over Bera and Sir Pollard's horse. "That whole family is a disaster," Tundavik said as he threw his leg over Bera. "I'm probably the only person in the world who thinks Devro is lucky to be born a bastard. At least he has someone else's blood as well."

"Whore's blood." Pollard said, climbing his horse. He squinted his eyes in the bright sun.

"Let's hope Devro takes after his mother more than his father," Tundavik said before looking down at Glem. "How is everything?"

"Fine," Glem said with a straight back. "Though we are running out of horse feed. I've looked through town and the barns to see if any escaped the fires, but so far, nothing."

"We'll figure it out. Why don't you stay here? We're just going to check the progress along this line and be right back," Tundavik said, and the boy nodded. He clicked his mouth, and Bera trotted, Pollard bringing up the rear.

Defensive walls of wood and broken brick formed rows along the battle line. Spikes, all pointed at the tip, emerged from the ground. The Flewthmen were dressed in their armor, shields on their backs, swords at their hips. It was like a sea of metal and leather as the men went about their day, building, laughing, foraging. Lord Furrow was calling out to his men as they hammered away at wooden pegs.

Lord Tylo was swinging his sword with his men. "My lord," he called out as Tundavik went by. "My lord, have you given anymore thought to my men becoming guards for you? It would keep them out of the battle, and the Four know I can't lose more of them." Most of Tylo's men had died in the assault. The lord of Heavensfield didn't emerge from his tent for days.

"Once the east is secure, then we'll talk," Tundavik said as he rode on.

Pollard snorted with laughter. "Some men you found on your march don't seem like they enjoy war that much. Just shows that the Asaramen are even stronger."

"Lord Tylo is young," Tundavik said as he watched a man skin a rabbit. "He was hoping for glory and a peaceful end, much like Devro."

"Of course, Tylo is over half the bastard's age." Pollard

rolled his eyes. "You'd think he was smarter."

Tundavik couldn't argue with that. As he stretched his neck, he saw a woman and a man in the distance near the Ritae. If it weren't for the red hair of the woman, he would never have guessed it was Yvanne and Mar. Tundavik was going to call attention to it, but he cleared his throat. He didn't need an upset Pollard. "So how do you think the defenses are coming?"

Pollard laughed. "You're the seasoned commander, not me. But they seem fine, and I highly doubt Lord Gallient or any other lord is going to be coming to Ultiir's help. That man will turn on anyone, haven't you heard? Accusing someone of witchcraft and having them executed. Surely he's made no friends." Tundavik nodded in agreement. The day was just beginning, and he was excited for night to fall, even though he got little sleep with the flying rocks barraging the city and his dreams. "Is that Yvanne?" Pollard said, his eyes scanning the river. "Makes me wonder why you would trust that man to keep her safe. Doesn't Mar know she isn't to leave the town? I'll go over there—"

"No," Tundavik interrupted. "We can watch from a distance, but Yvanne seems perfectly safe to me." Then a bugle played from the walls of Vigur.

"Surrender?" Pollard's jaw dropped. "Do you think Ultiir has had enough?"

"Let's find out," Tundavik said, and he spurred Bera into a run, Pollard following suit.

They raced over the burned fields, fighting hard to grow back greener and fuller. Soldiers were slipping into their armor, readying their weapons; other lords were also heading toward the gate. Yvanne and Mar were trying their best to hurry from the river.

Under the woodwork of the Gate of Four, there weren't as many people as Tundavik expected to see. The lack of guards made him doubt it was Ultiir. *But who else would come speak with us? Surely not the queen.* It wasn't the queen he saw. Instead, it was an old man, graying hair and sagging skin, dragging a white cloak over the debris and bloodstains.

Tundavik was dripping sweat by the time he reached the old man. Pollard wiped his face and said, "Who are you? Where's the usurper?"

"His Grace," the old man said it like a curse, "couldn't be bothered to end this siege." He projected his voice, the archers along the wall watching.

He's saying this more for them than *for us,* Tundavik thought. "Then why are you here?"

"To make peace," the old man bowed. "I am Lord Tedbalt Masson. I was once the chief consultant, though Ultiir decided he didn't need me anymore, so now I am but a humble daken."

Pollard scoffed and threw his red curls out of his eyes. "We don't make peace with disgraced lords, and certainly not a daken. How are you going to convince Ultiir if he won't listen to you?"

Lord Masson swayed on his feet. "Well, the queen herself asked me to speak with you. She wishes for this to end, and she claims she can get Ultiir to free Devro if that's what it takes."

"We already know how to free Devro," Pollard grimaced. "Tell the queen and king that Rila de'Tro isn't getting any special treatment from us. That she starves just as much as the city, and that she cries out for her son to save her."

"I hardly doubt that," the lord laughed. "Even so, the queen and I," he said in a softer tone, "have devised somewhat of a plan, but again, we will need your help to put it into motion."

"And that would be?" Yvanne said as she walked up beside Tundavik. Mar held her as she gasped for breath. Lord Cul from the Peaks, Lords Furrow and Toware, Diero and Gordo all appeared at the wall. They watched the old lord with hands on their weapons.

Tedbalt Masson gulped. "If you start the attack again, then Sophie and I will smuggle the bastard out of the city. This seems the easiest way. Ultiir is stubborn; he takes after his mother. He doesn't care if the whole peasantry starves to death. He will not give in."

"So you want more of our soldiers to die?" Yvanne asked.

"This sounds like a trap," Pollard said.

"Why?" Tundavik said louder than the rest. "Why do you want to help rescue Devro? Why now? You had our first attack to smuggle him out. He's been in the dungeon for months. Are you afraid that we will win? That the people of Vigur will storm the palace and depose Ultiir and you?"

"I'm just trying to end this before hundreds if not thousands die," Lord Masson said with a blank face. "I've been to the dakenry. You don't see it all because you're out here, but there are children looking for anything to eat. Dogs and cats have been butchered. Looting. Rioting. The rivers have no fish. Birds don't come into the city anymore. We've no bread—"

"Sounds like us," Pollard said.

Tundavik pulled his tunic tighter; he could feel the sweat pooling in the cloth. "I understand where you're coming from, but the only way is if Ultiir agrees to the trade. Rila de'Tro is waiting. And we're ready for Devro. So convince your king. Then we'll talk." Tundavik didn't wait for anymore words; he kicked Bera and rode back to Fielding, trying not to think about the starving children.

Blis

The moonlight shone through the windows, illuminating the king's chamber. Baldewin slept in his goose feather stuffed bed while Blis sat on his smaller bed of wool, and Mari hummed to herself. Caxton and the councilors were first off the ship as it arrived in Cahlun. "To make sure it was safe," they had said. Stadvik, the small capital of the Glybelm, welcomed them. But the actual king was still inside. Sleeping. *Caxton is probably undermining Baldewin as we sit here,* Blis thought with crossed arms.

When the pirates were taken care of, everyone had shouted, "Caxton!" The other Rowai ships that arrived in Stadvik didn't seem to question Caxton as the leader they should follow.

"What did Aveline think?" Blis asked the handmaid.

Mari rubbed sleepy eyes and said, "About what? She holds a lot of opinions."

"I know," Blis giggled, "about Caxton. How did she feel about the council?"

"That they were buttering Baldewin up before sticking him in the hearth."

"And you feel the same way?"

Mari flipped her dark hair from her face. "What does it matter? I'm just a handmaid." But Blis kept his eyes on her until she nodded. "I see it the same. The councilors were drooling when the old king died. Those months you were gone and Aveline was up North, I heard many rumblings around the palace. King Bartel would be late to meetings, or the councilors and the Royal Chancellery would meet and decide on things without him. I'm sure they were thrilled when a boy of twelve became king."

"I'm sure they were." Blis shook his head. A cool breeze from the northern waters washed over his balding head. "Aveline and Bertin are gone. Their father and mother are gone. Caxton tried to get rid of me. What are we going to do?" They both watched as Baldewin slept. His stomach rising and falling, and a small snore escaping from his mouth. His crown was gone, at the bottom of the ocean, the kraken feasting on it. Blis didn't want the kraken to feast on the kingdom of Rowan as well. "You were quick to save His Grace when the pirates attacked," Blis said to Mari. "You do much more than I do." He rubbed his knee. It was still sore, but he could walk; a small limp never stopped him.

"I had ran out when I heard shouting. I'd never seen pirates before, especially from Eotros. Then Baldewin went overboard, and I was imagining myself telling Aveline that I failed her. That her brother slipped out of my grasp and into the waters. She would be alone in this world. She'd never forgive me."

"What do you think she's up to?"

"Hopefully, she's found Bertin and we can put all of this behind us." Mari's eyes fluttered. "She said she would leave with me. We'd still visit, of course, but she said she would travel the world and be with me."

"That's a nice thought," Blis said. *If we make it out of this alive. If Aveline comes back in one piece.* "Her brother … brothers would miss her, though. You'd need to bring back exotic goods to make them happy."

"We will," Mari said.

Baldewin stirred awake. "Aveline?" He said as he stretched, and his shadow from the candlelight grew like a giant. "I thought I heard her."

"No, my king," Blis said. "Mari and I were talking. Sorry for waking you."

"Is it night already?" Baldewin looked out the window. "Guess I slept all day. Did the councilors come back with news?"

"No," Blis said curtly. He was tired of Baldewin trusting those men. They allowed him to sit in on one meeting, and now he believed they would never betray him. "We should go into town," he said.

"Town?" Baldewin yawned. "Caxton said it would be safer if we stayed here."

"But it was your idea to get help from the Glybelm people. Who knows what Caxton is telling them? He could be turning them against you."

Baldewin climbed out of bed and found his clothes. "I doubt it. I know you don't, but I trust him and the other councilors. They've never done anything to go against me. They've only done what is best for Rowan, even if I don't know the correct direction to go."

"I'm sure your grandmother thought the same thing when Talland took over the military and laid siege to the city."

Blis could feel his face getting red. He didn't want to get angry at the child, but he needed the young king to realize the danger. "We cannot let Caxton and the other councilors bring about their own Brutahki Flames. We cannot let them dispose of you. Kill you."

"That won't happen." Baldewin rubbed his eyes while Mari fixed his bedhead. "Father held this council close for a reason. Isn't that enough for you to trust them?"

Blis went over to the window. The dark Drewogh Sea stared back. The mouth of the kraken. "No," he stood there silently until he said, "but I will listen to my king."

"Then we can go into town," Baldewin said with a smile. "I'm starved, and I'm sure you are too. Mari, will you come?"

"I … umm …" Mari stammered. "If you want me to."

Baldewin nodded, and they were off to find food. Blis off to find the councilors.

They wore black cloaks with hoods over their heads. Sir Delmar wore a large cloak to hide his mail and stabbing sword underneath. Behind them were the many Rowai ships that took over the harbor, gangplanks and anchors down with sails hoisted.

The town of Stadvik was small and rocky.

Off in the distance stood the mountains that made up the island chain. The salt breeze turned to a breeze of mead and meat. Blis couldn't complain. He wanted that food. The ship was only home to old bread and tack. He wanted to be home eating in the castle with Baldewin. Peacock or venison with Western wine or Northern ale always made Blis forget his responsibilities.

The four made their way through the town. Tents with exotic wares lined the main street, all the color of storm clouds. Men spoke to them in their foreign language. Behind them there were one or two blacksmiths, a masonry with a bakery attached, and a few brothels. Most made of stone, with a few wooden buildings mixed in. Blis figured the masons had a fine business in Stadvik.

Baldewin kept getting distracted by the merchants, playing with their trinkets and pretending to understand them. He felt rugs from Eotros and dolls from Okros. Mari almost dropped a Kruheshian vase.

The people seemed odd as well. Gray and black seemed to be all they owned, to match the stone and stormy sky. Some wore leather vests, and others had wool cloaks with trousers of cotton. Even if it wasn't as hot as the South, wool seemed too much. Blis would faint from the heat in that getup. He was surprised to see a man wearing blue velvet, then deduced the man hailed from Eotros. His face and body smaller.

"There." Delmar pointed to a tavern with Rowai men vomiting outside.

Their steps made a sort of song as they walked on the cobblestones. Blis didn't want to see the town; he wanted Caxton. Nothing would stop him.

"You!" a shaky voice rang out in the common language. Blis searched but saw no one. "You four from Rowan." Blis looked again and saw a little lady, barely large enough to see over her counter, and old enough to remember the days of the Glybelm raids.

"How do you know we're from Rowan?" Baldewin asked.

"I know a lot of things." She jumped onto a chair and matched the king's height. "And the island is teeming with Southerners today." She spat at the word.

"We don't wish to bother you," Blis pulled Baldewin. "We're going to the tavern and will leave you alone."

She spat again. "If I wanted to be left alone, would I have called you?" She turned to Delmar. "No need to touch your sword. An old woman like me won't do no harm." Delmar seemed to release his hand beneath his cloak. "Come closer." She said to Baldewin.

"Just give her a coin and we'll be on our way," Blis said.

"Your Southern coin don't matter here." She spat and held out her hand to Baldewin. "I was talking to the boy anyhow. First of all, I want to tell you that your friends have been making a mess of this place since they've arrived. Looting and drinking and whoring. I've had my wares stolen more times than I can count. There's a reason we hate you Southerners," she spat.

Baldewin tried to say, "we're not from the South—"

"—south of here, though?" The old crone went on. "Second, I see grave things in your future, young man." Baldewin stepped back when she said that.

Blis rolled his eyes. "Don't listen to her."

"A great fire," the old lady said as the glow of fire seemed to fill her eyes. "Your mark claims you will lose everything."

"My mark?" Baldewin's voice was high as he gulped.

"Oh yes, one by one they will fall."

Blis pushed forward and separated the young king from the old witch. "Enough of this rubbish. I've been around long enough to know when to spot a charlatan. Keep your Northern mystique away from us."

The crone held out a hand. "Shall I see your mark? Or your knight's? To tell you what's to come. Perhaps death will come from a sword fight or tumbling down the stairs like a sow." She glared at Blis. "Those who learn of the mark will believe. The gods made it so."

"I'll believe when I see this great fire that engulfs the world," Blis rolled his eyes. "Now, we should be on our way. Delmar, give the woman a stallion."

The knight reached for copper, but the lady shooed it away. "I told you I've no need for Southern coin. Go find your people and be out of my sight."

Blis wanted nothing more than to do as she said. "Witch." He said as they continued on the dirt road. "Do not believe a word said to you, my king."

"But I don't even know what she meant," he whined. "Should we see her again?" Baldewin turned before Blis could say anything, but the gods had already removed the crone from the island.

"Shall we find those who don't speak in riddles, Your Grace?" Sir Delmar said, and Blis chuckled to himself that the knight thought the councilors didn't spew riddles.

As they made their way across the hilly town, Mari stepped closer to the king. "There are some who see things normal humans cannot," she said, and Blis rolled his eyes. "But just because the woman saw a fire doesn't mean it will happen. Your sister told me about those who saw Rowan wash away in fire before your grandmother was forced out of the palace. But Rowan did not truly burn." Baldewin nodded as he listened to her, looking over his shoulder every so often to where the crone had been. He seemed to shake with fright. "Perhaps she means a fire will grow within your heart and you'll become the brave and noble king we all believe you can be. Or that your enemies will burn. Or maybe it means you will meet a red-haired maiden.

Who can tell?"

Baldewin nodded, and his shaking stopped. Blis quietly snorted. *A handmaid becoming an adviser to the king. What's next?*

The tavern was made of wood and surrounded by stumps of trees. It towered higher than any other building on the island, ending at a point. A statue stood at the top. Not one of the Four that the Veck'kop kept, but a false Northern god. Behind the statue was black smoke from a chimney.

As they made their way inside, a Northman spat at Baldewin's feet. *"Zeika Krovski."* Delmar pushed the man outside and flashed his sword. The Northerner kept walking after that, cursing under his breath.

"Do you know what he said?" Baldewin asked the knight in his innocent voice.

Sir Delmar shook his head. "I speak no Heller, not high nor low. It's of no value to me." Blis had to agree. He just assumed the Northman meant disrespect.

"Do we get to drink while we eat?" Mari whispered as drunk men stammered about, some flirting with her, but she ignored them.

Blis did feel like a flagon of the island mead. "Care for a drink, sir?" Delmar said no, and Blis was off to the bar with Mari. "Give me your best and biggest; the Four know I need it. We also need some of your stew. I can smell it cooking in the back." The server stared at him and the handmaid with wide gray eyes. *He cannot understand the common language.* Blis turned to another Northerner. "Do you know what I'm saying?" The man gave a nod. "Can you tell the server I want a drink?"

The Northerner laughed and finished his ale. "He

understands you fine enough," he said in a harsh accent. "He doesn't serve Southern mice, especially after the others stole a barrel."

"A barrel?" Blis asked.

"There." Mari pointed to the other side of the room. Wycleaf and Jac were drinking with wenches on their laps, laughing and cursing. Caxton was with them, but he was merely sipping at his mead as he spoke with a Northerner dressed in white furs. "Did you want to say hi?" Mari asked him.

The councilors' shoulders dropped as Blis and Mari approached. Baldewin and Delmar came over as well. Caxton put on a smile and said, "Didn't I leave you on the ship?"

Blis said, "The king wanted to explore the island and see the Northerners. There was no reason for us to stay on the *Sea Glider.*"

"It was for your own safety." Caxton poured mead and passed the cups around to them. "To the king and our friend here, Leader Ohtala." Ohtala nodded as they all drank. "He was installed some years ago by the king of Viguran to oversee this island. Ohtala tells me he has seen no ships that aren't his."

"I … know …" the Northern leader said in his broken tongue. "I … see ship … know all ships. None from *Kürinstya.*"

"So we came all this way for nothing?" Baldewin dropped his eyes. "Waste of our time."

"Nonsense, Your Grace," Jac laughed. "We fought pirates!" He stood atop his chair, and the women and men cheered for him. The barkeep glared.

Caxton cleared his throat. "What Jac means, Your Grace, is that the Glybelm is more than just one island. Cahlun made the most sense logistically speaking, but there is another port further to the east. We may need to sail to Khana, find out if the ships are there or not."

"And if they're not?" Blis asked, letting the words bite. "Then we're in the middle of the ocean, running out of food and water, while the Vigurite fleet could set sail to take back Redington or attack Storyah again."

"I understand your worries," Caxton said, "but what else are we to do?"

"We've done all we can," Blis said. "Perhaps it's time to sail back south, maybe even home."

"William is doing a fine job as king, I bet," Jac hiccuped and laughed.

"Of course," Wycleaf hesitated with a smile, "he is not king. Jac is being funny."

Is he? Blis thought. *Or is this all a ruse to keep us from Rowan so William can consolidate power?*

"Well, if we're having a discussion about it," Blis said, "then I vote going back home."

"There is no discussion," Caxton whispered, "unless His Grace wishes there to be one."

Baldewin's eyes darted over the room. "No ... I mean ... I trust you, Caxton. If you and this Ohtala believe the ships could be on Khana, then so be it. What's a few more days at sea?"

Blis shuffled his feet. "I need fresh air." He left the group behind and went outside alone. Drunken men spilled from the tavern. He heard women cry in their homes as the sailors had their way. If they didn't leave Cahlun quickly, then the islanders would surely fight back. That was the last thing they needed.

The door of the tavern swung open, and Blis thought Baldewin was coming to see him. Instead, it was Jac and Wycleaf cursing and kissing the women they were with, laughing and stumbling. They went opposite Blis, but he could still hear them. "Shh," Jac laughed, "don't be so loud, Wycleaf."

"So sorry," Wycleaf fondled the girl. "I just wanted the girls to know the future. They could be queens!" He shouted as they disappeared into the night with giggles.

Blis didn't like that. His chest burned. *Just drunken fools,* he told himself, *but powerful drunken fools.* Who knew what they were planning? They looked to Caxton for advice, much like the rest of the crew.

"On dry land?" Captain Pitor said as he carried a torch to light his way. "I hate dry land," he laughed.

"I've grown accustomed," Blis said. "Why aren't you on the *Sea Glider?*"

"Needed a drink, and most of my men are here. Not much to do in this town." Pitor wiped sweat from his brow as the torch fire whipped toward his face. "Guessing we aren't finding the fleet here?"

Blis shook his head. "We're going to Khana next. *Caxton,*" he said it like a curse, "thinks the fleet could be there."

The captain nodded. "I've only been to that island once or twice. Nothing fancy. Even smaller villages than Stadvik here. How these people raided the coast for a hundred years, I'll never understand."

"You, of all people, should know how powerful ships make you."

"Aye," Pitor laughed. "You got me—" the captain turned his nose to the sky. "Smell that?"

Blis did. It was the smell of burning wood. He whipped around, but the tavern was still intact. Then Pitor took off down the hilly paths of Stadvik, and Blis followed as best he could.

Before they could even get to the docks, a black funnel covered the moon. Blis still couldn't tell where, but then the *Sea Glider's* wood blackened in the dim light of orange. A fire on the royal ship.

Men raced from the town and tavern. The Rowai were too drunk to do anything, and the Northerners didn't care. Delmar, Baldewin, and Mari came running. "What happened?" The young king asked.

Sailors had to keep Pitor from climbing his ship as the fire spread. He yelled out, "My beautiful girl," as flames took it. Blis' eyes watered, but from sadness or the smoke he did not know. The great masts, taller than gods themselves, snapped and crashed into the harbor. The stallion sails couldn't stop the yellow licks from engulfing them. Then the cabin's windows burst and the goose beds charred.

As other ships kept the fire from taking their hulls, Blis turned. He didn't want to watch even if the entire fleet burned. He didn't want to know if he'd be stuck in the Glybelm any longer. At the top of the hill stood Caxton, a smirk sneaking across his face.

Raimund

ou are Ryobas reborn. He kept repeating that to himself. He had no idea what the demon-creature was talking about.

But the people ... monsters ... creatures seemed to believe it. Every morning, outside Raimund's door, would be baskets of fruits and berries and nuts. He ate better here than he had in a very long time. He would take a leathery leaf and find a small stream that ran through the clearing. Insects that sparkled in the sun would fly near his head, and he would drink the best water he had ever tasted. *It is strengthening me,* he would think, and he was happy for it.

When he slept, he dreamt of Sile's burned corpse speaking with Yvanne. He hoped that didn't mean the young girl had died. Yvanne and Devro and everyone else had to be safe. *They have to be.* He even dreamt of Potter a few times. Slaying the dragon and parading the head to thunderous applause, but when he woke, he could still see the dragon in the distance, curled and smoking.

Now, it was night; the moon gone from the sky, and Raimund had to escape.

He prayed Nostara or any other monster hadn't heard his thoughts as he tied a large leaf full of fruits to his back.

He had no weapon, so he quietly carved a point at the end of a stick. It would have to do if they hunted him. He had to get back home, and this was his only way.

Raimund tiptoed outside his home in the trees and carefully took a peek. There was no one around. The wooden huts were dark. The trees were quiet. They shook only every once in a while with the wind. He left his boots behind, walking barefoot across the grass. It was soft, but more importantly, it was quiet. He didn't need a monster child to come running over and praise him or give him gifts. But he couldn't see anything, and hoped they couldn't either.

He had planned his escape over the last few days. Nostara had been meeting with the Elders, leaving Raimund to wander the clearing alone. He would walk toward the dragon and look into the trees. He would see the blue hue of the pools, and even farther were the mountains he turned away from. *What would've happened if I'd gone there instead?* He would wonder. *Maybe those mountains were actually the Asara, and I turned my back on my friends.*

But he couldn't think like that now. He had a job to do, and he had to do it quickly. The moon might not stay away forever, and he wanted to be far in the trees if that happened. He counted two hundred paces and turned slightly left. He needed to be as accurate as he could in the dark. Any other time he would light a fire in his hand, but he didn't need anyone to catch him, nor burn the forest down much as he wanted to.

Raimund pushed through familiar leaves, blowing bugs from his lips, and saw a red glow escaping the sleeping dragon's nostrils. With every exhale, a mix of smoke and fire would puff into the night sky. *Must stay quiet, but if I had a sword it would be over. I'd never see you again.* He half wanted to climb atop the dragon and fly away, back to the Noest and Sile's burnt cabin. The other half wanted to kill the monster. Even if this thing was Nardal and Nostara thought he was part of some prophecy. *Let me ride a horse instead. At least Brun back home has never killed anyone I care about.* He cleared his throat to stop thinking of Viguran. Mar was to keep Brun safe. Raimund wished he knew whether they were all still alive or if Ultiir had won. Killed them all.

The throat clearing must've been too loud, because the dragon's eyes opened and he groaned, his throat shuddering as his teeth smacked together. The beast looked around. Raimund stood as still as a statue, praying not to be seen. As he held his breath, the dragon went back to sleep on the moonless night.

Raimund let out a shaky breath, his jaw sore from clenching. He took quiet steps and moved on from the beast. After another hundred paces and he would be in the trees; then he had to follow the light.

As the glowing blue aura of the pools came into view, Raimund smiled, his eyes tearing up. He wanted to run as fast as his legs could carry him, but didn't need to tire himself so early in his escape. It was a small step, but a giant one to take him back home. The trees were planted linearly; the pools dotted the horizon. He wiped his eyes as his feet took him over the soft grass. Closer and closer. The mountains across the large flat expanse came into view, a blue light cascading over them. Beyond was the palace of Vigur, where Devro sat on the throne. Yvanne at his side.

Mar and Tundavik, his commanders. Brun whinnied.

And Raimund saw the dragon again.

"No," he let the word escape his mouth. All of his walking since seeing the beast hadn't been real. It was as if he were dreaming.

The dragon's yellow eyes burned Raimund as the giant beast stood, his four legs shaking the world and causing Raimund to fall, his makeshift leaf basket breaking on his back. Fruit staining his loose shirt, his makeshift weapon rolling away.

"No," Raimund cried out again. "Why? Why? Let me leave!"

The dragon's steps shook every tree, every rock, every insect. Raimund could see it all. Flames escaped his mouth as his snout came down to Raimund's face. *Now he's finally going to kill me. Char me like Sile.* But the beast was supposed to be Nardal, and Raimund supposedly some savior of the world. He stood and brushed his pants off. "Stop," he said to the dragon, but the beast didn't listen. "I said enough! Leave me alone. Let me be!"

The black dragon let out a low hum as his warm breath blew over Raimund. But he stopped moving. *He's listening.*

"Go back and let me leave this place." The dragon didn't move. Now it was his turn to act like a statue. Raimund looked at his squashed fruits, his dirty ankles, his tangled hair. "Why did you bring me here? This is no place for me. I was a fool to listen to ghosts and voices. A fool. I've damned myself to the deepest depths of some hell that plays with my mind. Listen to witches talk all day. Find myself speaking to a dragon." He kicked the grass. "You're not even supposed to be real. Only a myth. What happened to myths?"

The dragon sighed as he dropped to the ground, his eyes level with Raimund's. "And you can't answer my questions either. Dragons are supposed to be intelligent, but I've found that to be a pile of shit. So intelligent that when I wanted to go south to Viguran, you took me here." Raimund threw his hands up. "I don't even know where here is."

There was a ruffle through the trees, and the dragon hurled himself around, a deep growl echoing from his throat, flames licking his teeth. His tail almost whacked Raimund in the face, but he bent down in time. "It's alright." The glowing lady said. It was Nostara, but she looked to be in daylight while everything else was at night. The dragon slunk off to his usual spot, but he didn't lie down this time. He watched them with his eyes. "Whatever you're doing, it seems to have worked."

"What are you talking about?" Raimund asked. Not even mentioning he was trying to run away.

"The dragon," she looked to the colossal beast, "he was protecting you."

Raimund rolled his eyes. "I'm sure he was."

"Believe what you will." Nostara's green skin shone as bright as a distant star as she frowned. "Why are you out here?"

Raimund smacked his lips. The demon surely knew why; she probably heard all his thoughts long before he left. "I was going back home."

"I am sorry," she said with no hint of emotion, "but this is your home for the time being. You must learn how to repel the darkness. The *Ravadak* are coming, and you are Ryobas. You must stop them."

"None of what you're saying means anything to me, can't you see that?" Raimund said as he threw his arms in the air. "I don't care to beat back some darkness when I can't even see my friends."

Nostara's eyes were lost looking past him. She waved a hand and started toward the blue pools. "If I must convince you, then I will. This is more important than any family or friends or kings." Raimund followed, though he wasn't sure if it would be like last time and it would all be an illusion.

Nostara went between the dark sentinels and looked into a pool, waving her hand and causing an image to emerge. It was Devro, weeping in the dark. Then Mar, drenched in blood. Tundavik, weeping at a headstone. Raimund's parents, burning to death. He kept his eyes on the pool. If he blinked, tears would fall, and he didn't want to cry over witchcraft.

"Humans believe they posses all the knowledge of the world. But they are wrong. This world has entire continents yet to be explored by your people." She waved her hand again, and the image changed from his friends … his family.

Four rings came to life, all with different images. The top left was a human, the one next to it an elf, below was some beast, and the last a lone dwarf. The rings slowly morphed into one. "This is the world we stand on today. The binding brought us all together, though some stayed on their world."

Nothing makes sense, he thought.

"That is why I must teach you," she said to his thoughts. "Long ago, when four became one for a short time, the different creatures walked across the realms, through magical portals, bringing us all in contact with one another. Eventually though, the world started to break. It was too much. So Ryobas and his children led armies to close the link to the other worlds. It could only be done by destroying the different portals." Nostara moved her hand once more, and a bright, glowing orb blinded him. It was deep in a swamp. The trees were twisting and dying all around it. "It is your fate to close the link once again, or else you doom everyone on this world to certain and horrible deaths."

His head was spinning as he watched the ring break into four. "And you think Ryobas has come back. Me? Why if he has already stopped it?"

"The binding will continue until complete. The elves call it the Coming of the Dragon. It happens every five thousand elvish years, though it seems to be quickening." She leaned Raimund's head over the pool. "Look closer." He did, and he saw a desolate place. The countryside burned, and cities turned to ash. "The Coming of the Dragon. Nhamcaryn. Whatever you wish to call it. The only ones who can stop it are Ryobas and his beast Nardal."

"The dragon," Raimund nodded, that was the easy part to understand. "And I'm supposed to believe that this prophecy is true?"

"It is no prophecy," Nostara said. "It is true. Would you like to see what happens when a world is unable to stop the binding?"

"Do I have a choice?"

Nostara cleared her throat and looked to the forest. "First, you must join with Nardal. Become one. Then I will show you what will happen."

"With the dragon?"

Nostara said nothing, only nodded. Raimund followed her gaze to the trees. The dragon watched them. Yellow eyes burning bright.

Aveline

Ivlin found a basket of figs unattended and threw the fruit in his pack. "I'll leave a copper." He told the group, but Aveline had her doubts, though she was happy to have more food. They had been traveling for far too long, on foot nonetheless. She and her guards took a break near a pond. The water was fresh from a small creek and soothed her sore ankles.

Bert, grunting as he sat his aching body on the ground, said, "Feels we've been traveling half a year. I guess I'm only getting older."

"Right you are," Dern the Third laughed as he stretched and jumped. "I still feel as strong as a bull. Your bones are just getting more brittle as you gray."

Zoell splashed water on him. "Bert will be just fine."

Tomas was naked, bathing in the pond and floating around. "They always talk about the healing properties of mite water. The stories better be true, because I'm just as sore as Bert."

"I believe those stories are of the hot springs," Ivlin said as he bit into a fig. He handed one to Aveline, who shook her head. "They're good. I can't believe someone would leave them behind."

"Did you ever think they're coming back?" Zoell asked. "Or maybe they were in a hurry. Running away."

"From what?" Ivlin gestured to the barren landscape. Not even the Kash Mountains were close. They could still be seen, but nothing like before. The mountains were probably a day's journey from where Aveline was. But other than the Kash to the south, they could see for miles in any direction. There were only shrubs and dirt.

"Zoell believes in ghosts," Tomas laughed. "At least half of her stories of Moon Bay involve one of some sort."

"If you're going to make fun of me," Zoell said, "at least hide your cock while doing so."

The men laughed, even Tomas himself, and continued their bickering and joking and cursing. Aveline rubbed her shins and splashed water on her face. She wanted Bertin to emerge from the water so she could finally go home. She wanted everything to be back to the way it was before the winter. Her father alive. Her brothers safe. Mari in her arms again.

"Have you listened to Sayla's visions before?" Zoell asked while the men tended to themselves. "Can we trust her?"

Aveline shrugged. "She's never steered me wrong before." Zoell's eyes squinted with a question. "Back when I first came to Rainvealand," Aveline said, "I met some … troublemakers, we'll call them. Sayla was one of those. She would use her visions to help us find a rich fuck to rob, or food for the night, or anything, really."

"I've heard stories of your time here, but never about that."

"It was a long time ago," Aveline said. But it had been just barely five years since she was running with her gang of misfits, trying to fit in with them, and forget about her palace and riches. "I never should've done it, but it's all in the past now."

Far off in the distance, wains hobbled from the mountains carrying goods to far-off places. Aveline found Ivlin's bag and took a fig. The juice was sweet as it filled her mouth. As much as she missed the banquets in the palace, she enjoyed eating on the road. Food was more of a luxury now and not a given. "Let's just sleep here for the night," Aveline said. "The forest is still days away, and here we have water. Sound good?" Her guards all nodded.

After the tents were set up and a small fire lit, they gathered in for the night. Tomas would take first watch, but they were so far off the road, it didn't even matter.

Dern the Third was practicing his swordplay with a dead tree while the sun lowered in the west. Chips broke as he slashed. "Expect the forest to be full of master swordsmen?" Aveline asked.

"I can never stop practicing," Dern laughed through his sweat. "If I did, then I could end up like the Knight of the Yellow Coast when I beat him in the tourney." He sheathed his blade. "You remember that?"

"How could I forget? It was the last tourney my mother attended."

Dern's face grew in shadow. "I'm sorry, I shouldn't've brought it up."

"It's alright," Aveline said with a wave of her hand. "Right now, my brothers are all that matter."

Ivlin picked at his teeth. "How do you think the little one is getting on with the council?"

"He could be all the way in Eotros by now," she shrugged.

"Caxton probably sent him there to be rid of him."

"Baldewin is young," Bert said. "Boy kings are always subjected to the whims of others."

"Let us hope your brother is more like King Rickart the Tame and not the young Artur of Millstone." Tomas added as he cleaned his blade.

Zoell fed the fire and cooked a small rodent she had caught. Bert and Ivlin conversed and argued over maps and roads while Dern continued his training. Aveline stretched her legs and wiped her brow. She prayed Bertin would just pop out of the mountains and save them the trouble of looking, but her prayers weren't answered.

The night didn't want to come. The sun breathed its flames until the last minute. Finally, as Lendia blanketed them in darkness, the South cooled. Aveline imagined the chorus of cheers that would fill Jorbstah as the night was dark with no moon. The feast would happen with hundreds of thousands in attendance. The changing of their ancient one's face.

She didn't want to sleep, or couldn't. Baldewin and Bertin and Mari were always on her mind. She told Mari that she would leave Rowan and the palace behind. *But what about my brothers? Just leave them to fend off the vultures themselves.*

"Did I do wrong?" She asked Zoell near the fire. "Looking for Bertin instead of helping Baldewin? One's older than the other."

Zoell sighed as she looked to the stars. The great stallion looked down on them with twinkling blue eyes. "What more could you have done with King Baldewin? Time and time again, he sided with the councilors over you. What would've changed that?"

"Well, abandoning him certainly didn't help."

"If you wish to go back, then so be it. We all follow wherever you go," Zoell said as Bert's snores filled the air. "My blade is yours."

"Do you miss your family?"

"Of course, Princess. I pray to my Lady to keep them safe. Once we return to Rowan, I will ride to Moon Bay and embrace them."

Aveline was going to speak, but wheels hobbled on dirt and rocks. Her guards woke and grabbed their blades. Tomas slipped on a gray helm and went into the darkness. His back glowed as fire danced on his armor.

The wagon stopped after making its way through the brush. Aveline stood near Dern and Bert. She could see no mouth, but only red eyes staring back at her like a demon.

Zoell took a few steps forward to be with Tomas. "State your business." Snickers escaped the wagons and whoever was aboard spoke to each other. Aveline couldn't make out the whispers. Zoell tightened the grip on her sword. "I will ask you again."

One demon cleared his throat. "Fuck off." His accent was thick.

Tomas cleared his throat as he unsheathed his weapon. "The road is farther north. Head that way," he pointed, "and we won't have to fight."

"But," another demon said as blackness rose from the wagon, "we saw a fire and wanted to trade."

Bert grabbed Aveline's arm and pulled her back a step. "Bandits," he whispered.

The demons dropped from their wagon, and the horses whinnied. "You don't have to make this difficult," the first one with red eyes said. His voice was dripping with accent. He turned to his friend and said, *"Ilmeks nim olka oke sor le?"* They both laughed. But it *was* only two of them. Aveline's guards would surely be enough.

"Ayrlmakan." Aveline said trying to get them to leave.

Red eyes grew in shock, and as the fire lit the two bandits, she saw lips curl into a smile. "You understand us?" he asked in the ancient tongue. Aveline nodded but said nothing. As they got closer, her guards were digging their feet into the harsh ground.

The other demon said, "We just want some supplies. Saw your fire and thought you'd be alone. Didn't expect a fight."

"And you should know," Red Eyes said, "that we're some of the best fighters this side of the Bezir."

"What are they saying?" Bert growled.

"Nothing important," Aveline said. "They want to rob us."

"Well," Dern said as whipped his sword around, "that's enough for me."

The bandits weren't even prepared; in fact, they looked shocked as their eyes grew in fear. The red-eyed one was the first to die, his head chopped clean off his body. Zoell had moved to the other one, but he was running, and Zoell stopped the chase. Unfortunately for that man, Ivlin wasn't as honorable. Ivlin found him and sliced open his guts. The sound gushed through the night air. The horses were whinnying and crying, but they couldn't move from the wagon they were attached to, and as they ran in different directions, they couldn't pull it either.

"Calm," Aveline said as she started toward them. There were three horses. The bandits probably stole an extra one. *"Sakinmaku."* She said. One horse settled as Aveline brought a fig to her. *"Sakinmaku."* she said again, and she brushed the horse's muzzle. *"Sakinmaku nim kiz."* The horse stopped trying to get away and happily ate the fig. The other horses weren't nearly as crazy either.

"I think we've found a quicker way to the forest," Aveline told her guards.

Ultiir

They want me to fail," Ultiir said as darkness swallowed him. The torch was slowing dying, and he told his men not to disturb him. "They want me to release you," he told his bastard nephew. Ultiir was sitting on the cold stone of the dungeons. The bars of Devro's cell across from him. Even if the light went out, Ultiir would know the way. He was used to the tight corridor. Where to turn, to duck, to walk. Sir Gid would wait on the other side with Olier. *Probably talking about me.*

Devro didn't speak. He sat with dried tears on his cheeks, away from the bars. It was good that he was at the back of the cell. Ultiir didn't want to see his face anyway. He didn't need to be reminded of Hurvir and the poison and of a little Devro and the war.

"You'll probably say something after this," Ultiir said as he swatted a bug from his hair. "All that ruckus you hear above us, that's your wife. She and her armies have come to the city to rescue you, and now my lords want me to release you to her." His neph—the bastard's—eyes widened in the dark, damp dungeon. "They descended upon me with thousands of men and horses and weapons. They destroyed a tower and almost breached the wall." Ultiir thought he saw a grin. "Don't be too happy. I knew they were coming. I have correspondence with someone in your camp. My knight, Old Gid, killed dozens of your followers. Now they hold a ruined Fielding and live off burned lands." Ultiir smiled as he thought of them starving as well. How could the lords of the court get upset with him when they are in the middle of a war? "This is a nice place, though. Quiet. Much better than the palace and all the gossip and my bitch wife. You get your own quarters with no one to bother you in the night." Ultiir took a whiff. He let out a long breath. "It reeks in here, though. I should probably have you cleaned."

He thought of all the blood that he had to wash off himself after the fighting at the gate. Lord Hirons dead. The Gate of Vigura forever changed. "I told myself I would never be like your father. I would never wage an endless and costly war. Now, I'm fighting your wife," he chuckled and waited, but the boy didn't reply. "Hurvir would be proud of me, wouldn't he? I'm just following in his footsteps. In our father's footsteps as well. A de'Tro can hardly be king for one day before a war breaks out." He let out a sigh, and the small flame whipped. Shadows danced all around him. "Maybe that's the curse. Forget Hurvir's poisoned seed, in the end he could still have a child. But some curse was put on us hundreds of years ago; that our family would cause nothing but hurt and chaos.

"Your grandmother caused the same hurt, just to her children. You know that's who they want me to trade you with?" Ultiir laughed as tears welled in his eyes, his throat scratched, his jaw ached. "Why would I trade you for my mother? She is an awful woman who deserves everything she gets. If she didn't want to be captured, then she should have retired to a small cabin on the ocean somewhere, instead of trying to do my job and control Goldfield. Why would I send my little baby nephew out—" he stopped himself as he felt tears hit his arms. He blinked and wiped and never wanted to cry over his bastard nephew. No, not his nephew. Merely a bastard. A demon. Hurvir's son … "I killed him, a warmonger, a mass murderer. The man who thought war was more important than feeding his own people," he sniffled and couldn't stop the tears from falling. His brother's dead face plastered in his mind. "I killed him." The once great Hurvir the Warrior, brought down by a bit of poison.

"Now I too have people starving in the streets, dying for a war they don't want. I have more rebellion than any other king of Viguran in history. Now I'm seen as the warmonger, even though it was you who declared war. You marched first, and now I deal with the aftermath. I killed your father just to become him."

Ultiir pushed himself up, grabbing the jagged wall to help, but a rock broke. And Ultiir crashed to the ground in a puddle of his tears. "Don't laugh," he said. But not even the bastard was laughing. When Ultiir used the light to look closer, he saw fresh tear stains on his nephew's face. "I must go."

As Ultiir pushed through the small corridor of rocks, he heard Devro say, "Yes, I agree," to no one.

The metal door opened, and Sir Gid led him away from the dungeons. The coolness of the dark vanished as the coming summer heat washed over him. Ultiir touched his face over and over to make sure his tears were gone.

Old Gid cleared his throat. "You aren't like your brother, Your Grace. He went to war because of old hatreds. You're only fighting to keep your kingdom secure."

Ultiir didn't respond. He kept pretending Gid had heard nothing. He wanted sunlight, and luckily for him, Vigura was bringing summer early. They journeyed through the long corridors and flights of stairs until he was outside. The sun burned. The palace gate was open as lords were going in and out.

"They've trapped me," Ultiir told his guard and chief consultant. "They've won."

Sir Gid shook his head, and his jowls flew. "No, Your Grace. Remember, they are beneath you. You are king. If you want, you can have me and your guards clear them out."

"No," Ultiir chewed his lip. "That will make them angrier. They've already promised not to leave the palace until the siege is lifted. We don't want them to grab anymore power." As he said that, one of Sophie's guards entered through the gate. "We need to stop them as well."

"Your wife has done heinous things to you," Gid agreed. "Shall I treat her like the whore? I'll have my men fuck her to death as well."

Ultiir shook his head. "No. We can do worse to her."

"Your Grace," Lord Edel de'Viere said as some city guards followed with a small boy in hand. "We've just arrested this child for trying to open the gate."

The young boy cried as his head was pushed down. "Please! Please! I didn't mean anything by it. I would never—" A guard punched the boy's mouth before he could finish.

Ultiir pushed the guard back. "I want to hear." He bent down to be at eye level with the child who had tears streaming down his face. "What is it? What did you do?"

The boy spat blood. "They're accusing me of treachery. They say I planned to open the gates, but that is not true."

"It is true." Edel interjected. "We found him and others trying to open the portcullis of the Shadow Gate."

"Liar." The boy spat again. "You are lying to your king." He sobbed uncontrollably.

"We haven't found the others, and he won't tell us where they are." The chief informant explained. "But this presents a bigger problem. Those sympathetic to the bastard's cause may try to help his wife. We'll have to put trusted guards at the remaining gates."

Ultiir nodded. He waited for the boy to stop crying. He looked into the watery eyes of fear. "Where are you from?"

"The Whitefork, Your Grace."

"From the Lands," Gid said from behind. "Now we know why he wants to betray us all."

"Just tell His Grace who helped you," one guard shouted with a metal gauntlet at the boy's head. "We know you had help. You're just some stupid peasant vagrant."

"No help, no help," the boy cried, and his voice cracked. Ultiir cleared his throat, but he needed to know how many of his people, his soldiers, were traitors. "The gate was opened the day before … I wanted to leave then but couldn't … so I tried … tried again," he fell into a heap of tears and snot and blood.

"Leave him," Ultiir told the men. "What is he talking about? Why was the gate opened?"

"Lord Mass—" Edel started then said, "Tedbalt, Your

Grace, he went out of the city. I was told you knew."

"Of course," Ultiir lied. "It's been a long few days with the court and the siege and everything." He turned to Gid and said, "Come," and they headed toward the gate. Behind them, the boy sobbed as his head was placed on a block and a sword swung down.

"We need to feed their hatred," Sir Gid said as they exited the safety of the palace. "Tell the soldiers that the Asaramen rape their wives and daughters. Castrate their men. Murder animals. Anything."

"We'll worry about that later," Ultiir said. "Right now I want to talk to that traitor Tedbalt and feed him to the dogs if I have to."

The Noble Lands were empty, the lords and ladies protesting by sleeping and eating and shitting in the palace. City guards still made their rounds, shoving out the occasional vagrant or starving child. Ultiir had to remember which manse was Tedbalt's. All the houses were white, but there was one where the door was slightly ajar. Gid went first and poked his head in before waving Ultiir through.

Tedbalt was coming down the stairs with a potted plant. "Your Grace," he said as if nothing was wrong. "Just redecorating since I seem to be the only one banished from the palace at the moment. He left a trail of dirt on his marble floor as he set the pink, flowing plant outside."

"Why did you go outside the city?"

Tedbalt clicked his tongue and nodded in understanding. "As you can see from my neighbors, I thought it was time to rethink this siege."

"You've embarrassed me." Ultiir closed the door so the streets wouldn't hear. "You went behind my back. This is treason." He felt his face bulge. "Give me a reason I shouldn't have Sir Gid cut you down."

"I did what was best for the city," Tedbalt said with a puffed chest.

"You want me to surrender?" Ultiir raged. "Surrender to a girl who leads my nephew's army? Peasants would remember me with jokes, when I should be revered like Valor the Iron."

"You would rather care about your reputation than the thousands who starve? Why do you think there won't be another riot? Imagine all the death the peasants could cause if they found out you have more food than them." Tedbalt held his head high, as if he were winning. "It is time to be a good and noble king. Tell the girl you will talk with her. Make some deal that involves them leaving."

"I will never surrender. We'll all be killed."

"Aren't we dying either way?" Tedbalt crossed his arms. "Might as well be with your mother. Sir Gid," he turned to the knight, "you agree with me, don't you? You've known Rila de'Tro longer than anyone, even her own son."

Gid cleared his throat. His golden cloak danced around his feet. "I do whatever His Grace wishes."

"You don't sound very convincing," Tedbalt rolled his eyes. "Guess we'll have rioting in the streets once more, and you'll get your wish since I'm the only one out here. I'll be dead."

Ultiir's nostrils flared. "Death would be too good for you. You committed treason for the last time. Sir Gid," Ultiir motioned to the knight, his chief consultant, "arrest the traitor."

Old Gid didn't hesitate, and Tedbalt didn't resist. *He's*

lucky Gid didn't cut his head off right here, Ultiir thought as he wandered into the street. Gid held Tedbalt's hands behind his back and pushed the old man forward. Crashes and booms in the distance reminded Ultiir of the siege. He had been so busy with the court and Sophie and Tedbalt's treachery that he almost forgot that his city would starve. And the palace would run out of food eventually. *I don't need more problems. I don't need the peasants turning to cannibalism and banditry.*

"I need to end this," Ultiir said.

Bertin

Ansehar was dark and damp. Not at all what Bertin had imagined. He thought it would look like Suktir, with great red towers and shops made of bricks. The border town was instead made of wood, no doubt from the Sruhq Forest that overshadowed its gates. The wood cracked, and mold grew from the crevices. Roofs caved in or slid off houses. Not even the ancient elven city looked so bad.

Gray clouds hung in the sky as they had wandered into the village. The rain started soon after. The people glared and spat at him, which disappeared in the rain. He knew he looked different from everyone in this town, but he also knew Torlem and Barhi would keep him safe.

The whorehouse wasn't much better than the rest of the town. People with half-torn clothes draped from their side exposing one or the other breast. Their skin sweaty and their hair messy from the customer before. With every step came a creak that sounded like a moan. The ale too dark and water too yellow for Bertin to drink. If only Thatar were here to find a nice stream; instead he was dead, his wife dead atop him.

Torlem and Barhi fucked the whores with their eyes as

they sat at a crooked table. Bertin had to keep hold of his tankard of poison so it wouldn't end up on the floor. Though, the ale would probably clean the place better than the owners.

Torlem must've been watching Bertin after peeling his eyes from a half-naked woman. "Not enjoying yourself? Houses of whores are meant to be pleasing."

"The ones north of the Ters-Veck are nicer, it would seem." Bertin tried to sound kind, but his disgust was all there.

Torlem downed his tankard. "You've never seen the whores in Bardekan. First, the woman joins you in a bath, kisses you all over. Then they massage you in the finest oils the world ever saw before mounting you as if you were a stallion. Truly the best girls. Perhaps they'll give you a good fuck before you go north." Torlem laughed. "I suspect you'll never want to leave."

Barhi said a few words and disappeared into a crowd of girls. Bertin took small sips of his ale to combat the taste. He studied every person in the building. The men were mainly fat and drunk, though a few were lean or muscle. Most of the women were pretty, but they were also mites. "The Southerners are called that because they can infect you." Aveline used to tell him when he was young. "Of course, the people who say that are infected with shit themselves," she would add. The women were always scratching every bit of their bodies, clothed and unclothed. Bertin finished his tankard to get the thoughts out of his head.

Barhi emerged from the group with multiple people. Laughing, they made their way back to the rooms. "They're popular." Bertin said.

"Barhi doesn't partake, only watches." Torlem said. "The whores pleasure each other, and Barhi does nothing. But they tell me they enjoy it."

"Are you sure that's true?"

"Barhi does not lie. Never has." Torlem smiled as a girl sat on his lap, her large breasts in his face. "I think I'm going to be a while. You should find yourself a whore." He found Barhi's ale and shared it with the woman.

Bertin looked around and saw only one person. She played with her hair and strutted over. She found herself on Bertin's lap, gyrating her hips, and whispered in his ear. "*Bin emteku zu sin git gorsé.*" Bertin didn't need a translation as she dragged him behind her by his trousers. Torlem cheered in the background.

Making their way through the pleasure house, they stopped at a room with a broken door. The girl had to kick for it to close. She pushed Bertin onto the bed and undressed. His palms sweated, and his stomach churned. He didn't know whether he was still capable of this.

She slid off her blouse and pulled down her skirt. "Wait," Bertin told her, and she stood naked. "I'd rather no—" then he saw her ears. He went closer and brushed a finger over the points. "You're an elf. Isn't that dangerous?"

"*Nitt.*" The elf slowly lower Bertin's pants, but he stopped her.

"Why are you here? Shouldn't you be with your people?"

She sighed with annoyance. "Do you not want this?" She motioned to her body. "You only wish to talk? Either way is fine, but you must still pay."

Bertin nodded, and the elf cleared her throat as she slipped back into her clothes. "I was curious, is all," he said. "I've heard … stories."

"If you must know, yes, it is dangerous. I do not pull my hair back often. Why so interested in a she-elf? Do not see many?" She sat beside him on the bed.

"I've been around elves for months now. We traveled over the Jorbstah in secret. If only they knew it was safer to play whore."

The elf took offense at that and pushed him aside. "I am not playing whore. I am one. Elves must earn coin as any other people. Even if it has the ugly twisted god on it."

Bertin padded his pockets. "Well, actually, I don't have any money."

"No money in brothel?" She cocked her head and pursed her lips. "Did you plan this? I don't work for free."

Bertin chuckled as she leaned away and said, "I was away for months. I'm trying to get home now, but the elves had captured me in Telemaw."

"Captured?" The elf leaned back toward him. "Did they treat you well? I haven't been around my own kind in a very long time, but I know humans go into the forest and never come back."

He rubbed the stump of his finger. "It wasn't all that bad. I found nice elves to call friends. But every friend I make seems to die."

She gripped Bertin's hand, not worrying about the stump. "I am sorry. Sometimes *Raig* puts heavy burdens on us. I hope he lets you find peace."

"Did he put burdens on you?" Bertin didn't know this *Raig* but figured he'd add him to his list of gods to pray to who wouldn't listen.

"My children are my burden. I must be here to earn coin

for food. They must hide in the kingdom. There are people who would want their heads."

"I'm familiar." Bertin looked into the never-ending soul of the elf's eyes. "The two I came here with would gladly take your children, and yourself too." He could see another piece of her soul break away. "Don't worry, I'm not like them. I wish I could stop them, but I'm too weak, and they're much stronger than I am. I wouldn't want to cross paths with them, at least not until I get home."

"Why must they be that way? What good is killing those not bothering you?" Her hand slipped away, tucked under her thigh.

"They have something to prove, but also nothing they love in this world. They've already lost it all. Why not kill a few before they die?"

Now it was her turn to see Bertin's soul. He felt her seeing his broken and beaten-down spirit. The two of them, shattered shells of what they once were. "I think you are stronger than them. It takes a weak man to kill, and you do not kill."

The sound of Kelltar's screams filled his ears. "I think you should go." Her head cocked again. "Before they find out what you are. I don't trust them to do the right thing."

"And where would I go? I cannot leave my children or my home."

"You could escape to *Mi'rallen*. The elves I spoke to seemed to love it there. There are fewer hunters there than in the Sruhq. I'm certain you would be safer."

The elf shook her head. "My people left for the forest; the others stayed on their island. They would not welcome me back with hugs and kisses. They would sooner see me taken by the dark ones."

"The dark ones?"

"A legend," she waved her hand, "we call them *Liaden*. They are not of this world, but they are our ancestors. A few traveled here when the Dragon first came here. I've heard stories from travelers and refugees that there is some darkness to the north."

"Refugees?" Bertin asked. "Where are they fleeing from?"

"There is a war in Viguran; uncle and nephew fight one another for the crown. Many ramoryr who were north of the ropfryn have left or moved back home."

"Uncle and nephew?" Bertin said as he let out a breath. *Not Devro, surely not Devro.* But that was the only thing that made sense. *Does that mean Hurvir is dead? And my father? What is the world turning to?*

"You seem upset?" The elf said. "Shall we lie down?" Bertin nodded, and she fluffed the goose down pillows. "I hope the war is not where your home is. I'd rather stay here than deal with battles and knights and death."

"Me too," Bertin said as he gripped the wool blanket. "What's your name? I never asked. I'm Bertin."

She snuggled close to him; her body was warm, and Bertin had forgotten what it was like to be comfortable. The elf whispered, "They call me Ioela," and Bertin shivered. That night he dreamt of Ioelena. Her blood-soaked body lay alone in the empty desert.

Tundavik

Horses ran as fast as the wind as the camp buzzed by, kicking up dust behind. Pollard rode in front, Tundavik behind. A few soldiers followed the trail.

This couldn't happen. Not now. Not while a siege was taking place. He had more important things to attend to. Yvanne needed help with the plans. He had to train the young boys and those who'd never held a sword. Now he had to deal with these fools.

Tundavik's horse slowed; his mind wandered. Tundavik couldn't stay focused. The huts and tents went black. Everything turned into a forest. Ritaeum was in the distance; he ran to it. His family. All his family, every uncle and aunt, sister and brother, cousin, and his wife and kids, blood smeared and they were gone. Ritaeum burst into flames.

"Lord Vandes?" Pollard snapped Tundavik back. They had stopped near a tent full of sleeping men; snoring escaped. "Are you alright?"

Tundavik waved Pollard away. "Yes. I got a little confused, is all."

Pollard's eyes narrowed. "We must continue. I can hear

the shouts." So they did. They rode for a short bit until they came across the group of people. Men encircled other men, one holding a woman with a knife to her throat.

Tundavik broke through the circle with Bera. "Put your weapons down." He shouted at the men in the middle.

One spat and pulled the woman closer. She wept as blood dribbled from her neck. "We don't take no fucking orders from you. You're not our leader. You lead the Flewthmen vermin."

Shouts of protest escaped the crowd. Pollard silenced them with a quick yell. Tundavik kept an eye on each man. There had to be over twenty, every one of them betraying their king. "What is the meaning of this?"

"We want to go home." The man licked his lips. "We want to be done fighting for asslicking lords who don't care if we live or die." Now, shouts of support escaped the crowd. Maybe this was bigger than Tundavik thought. "And this whore is going with me." He patted the girl's face. "She's to be my wife. You'd like that?" The girl only shuddered.

Tundavik wanted to drop from his mare and kill the traitor himself, but there were too many. Finally, Lord Toware and the men from Riverend cascaded behind him like a wave. Another lord, Gyro of Newbrook, brought his men as well. *At least I have some support.*

"I know this siege has gone on longer than expected," Tundavik shouted over their heads, "but you mustn't quit just yet. The usurper is close to suing for peace, I can feel it."

"Fuck you," someone shouted in the crowd.

Lord Toware's face was full of rage; his ears steamed. "I hear one more word from any of you and I'll have my men run through you like a stampede." Toware came closer to Tundavik atop his horse. "Unleash me on them, would ya? This can be over in minutes, and no one else will think to mutiny again."

"Wait," Tundavik whispered. "We can't kill our own men when we've a battle to win."

"If I may," the stout lord named Gyro said from the ground, "but these are not *our* men. They are Asaramen. They follow the queen and the mountainfolk. Our men are of the Flewthlands, of the Eastlands. Letting Toware have his way is far too generous in my opinion. Mutineers deserve torture first, but I digress."

"Enough," Tundavik clamped his jaw. "What is it you want?" He said to the crowd. "How can I keep you happy?"

"Food!" someone shouted. "Shelter!" Another. "More women!" "Better clothes!" "Shoes without holes!"

"Alright." Tundavik held up his hand, and he was glad even the would-be-deserters listened to him. "

The man with the woman and a knife glared at the men on horseback. "Us out here haven't had a good meal in weeks. You've forgotten us! You eat cheese and wine with that whore of a queen and leave nothing for the rest."

Pollard clutched his sword pommel. Tundavik had to give a calming look before things turned worse. "I'm not sure what stories you've been told," Tundavik said, "but the only delicacy we find is the flies." There was some laughter. *Maybe I can get through to them.*

The man tugged on the woman's hair. "You let us go home. You let us all go home. That's what we want."

Pollard laughed as he clenched a fist. "You'll be hanged for desertion. Left as a traitor. The Four will never allow you to feast with them."

Tundavik bit his lip. "I'm certain once Ultiir comes to his senses then we can find you some better food. Food for everyone. We have to make hard decisions right now to save our king."

Shouts rang out from the crows. "Bastard king!" "Coward!"

"That's all I can give you," Tundavik said.

"Let's butcher your mare and feast on her!" A boy yelled, and Tundavik wanted to throw his hands up and let them leave.

"Traitors!" Now a shout from behind. One of Lord Toware's men. The lord nodded with a hard face. "Kill them!" Another said. Then of the Newbrook men said, "Why treat these traitors better than us?" And another. "Their bodies should be cut up and tossed into the Ritae." More cries rang out. The crowd moved. The mutineers held up their weapons and prepared for a fight. Toware licked his chops.

Tundavik was over it. The crowd was too far gone. They started moving as one, growing relentless. Insults flying. "Fine," was all he said to Lord Toware.

The lord of Riverend gave a devilish smile and shouted. "Kill the traitors!" And the men of Riverend did. Tundavik twisted Bera and escaped the riot before he too was taken.

Tundavik and Pollard watched as the frenzied crowd attacked one another. They used whatever they could find as weapons; rocks and rakes, others had their swords. Blood splattered as people screamed. Toware seemed gleeful as he hacked at bodies and littered the ground with innards.

***

Tundavik could only stare as the bodies were thrown into the freshly dug mass grave. The woman he wanted to save thrown in with the others. Lord Toware clapped his hands together like they were dirty. "See what happens when you allow me to do my job? The men of Riverend are feared, and this is why."

Heads and arms and severed cocks were thrown in as well. "I just wanted them to listen. Maybe if I hadn't brought you and everyone else, they would've agreed."

"Blaming me?" Toware's lips tightened. "I only did what I was told."

Tundavik had to quickly say, "No, not you." He didn't want the lord of Riverend upset. Not after seeing the hell he unleashed. "Just that violence seems to always be quicker than speaking."

"Well," Toware gestured to the gray wall of Vigur in the distance, the camp a mess of mud from morning showers. At least the men were glad not to sweat. "And if you're worried about what the queen will think, then I'm not sure how to help. She is young, much too young if you ask me. Tell her she doesn't understand the ways of war."

"That will go over well," Tundavik said as he made sure Sir Pollard wasn't around to hear.

"Only the truth," the lord of Riverend shrugged. "It's why men fight in wars and women have the children."

"Yet she leads us," Tundavik twisted a hair on his beard.

Toware scraped mud from his boot. "For now," he said before seeing to his men. Tundavik didn't like the sound of that, but he needed as many lords and their men as he could get, especially if more decided deserting was better than staying.

Pollard brought Bera around a tent. "Shall we?" he asked as he handed Tundavik the reins.

"I'd rather walk," Tundavik said. He led Bera over the dried mud and broken wood. He wondered whether a house had stood where he was walking. Gone forever on Ultiir's orders. *The siege is almost* over; *I can feel it.* He had to tell himself that, even as his eyes sank lower and his organs trembled from hunger. "How many died?" He asked Pollard.

Pollard, who was using a cloth to clean his ever-browner white armor, said, "I didn't count, but one gravedigger said fifty. Maybe a hundred," he shrugged.

"Still too many," Tundavik cursed under his breath.

"You did the right thing letting Toware take care of the problem," Pollard said. "We need to make sure it doesn't happen again, though."

"Your outbursts certainly didn't calm them."

Pollard's head jerked back. "I was just speaking my mind."

"A good soldier knows when to keep his mouth shut. You should have stood quiet," Tundavik teeth hurt from clenching them. "I don't want to hear your voice if this happens again."

Pollard nodded, but his eyes were somewhere else. "Do you think others will follow suit?"

Tundavik didn't have an answer. Instead, he patted Pollard on the back and said, "The good thing is, if we're having problems with just a few thousand people, imagine what Ultiir is dealing with." He looked at the gate, where so many soldiers had died. He could see the red-soaked stone as if he were up close.

They made their way to Yvanne's great tent. Pollard mounted his horse. "I have patrol," he said and didn't wait for Tundavik to respond. The knight raced off.

He opened the tent flap, and then politely turned his head. Yvanne was vomiting in a bucket, Jacka held her hair. The queen looked up and wiped her mouth. "Tell me what happened. We're not losing control, are we?"

"Never," Tundavik insisted. "Just a few men who thought they could do whatever. They were killed, and order was restored." Mar stood in the corner with a cloth and handed it to the young queen. He nodded a hello to Tundavik.

Yvanne breathed heavily as she sat on a cushioned chair, rubbing her forehead. "I'm worried. I'm always worried. The daken say it's not good for the baby. But neither is leading an army." Yvanne placed her hands on her stomach. "What if we don't take the city in time? The baby is getting closer with every passing moon. Ultiir should be at my feet begging for forgiveness. Instead, he waits as his mother gets older and older. Is he trying to make sure she dies on us?"

"Anything's possible." Tundavik said.

Yvanne tensed, and Jacka raced over with a wet cloth. She dampened her queen's head until Yvanne pushed her away. "I need this to be over."

"I can take command if you'd like." Tundavik broadened his chest. "You can spend the rest of your time getting ready for the baby." Yvanne shook her head. "I'm a capable commander, and I don't like how much stress you're putting on yourself. Devro would never forgive me if anything happened to you or the ba—"

Yvanne vomited again. "It's quite alright. And I don't doubt your ability. But it was my idea to lay siege to Vigur, so I have to see this through. The men look to me as their leader. If I give you command, they'll see me as weak. I don't want a greater number to think about deserting." Yvanne lay on her bed, Jacka propping her up with pillows. "I fear this won't be over as soon as I wish."

Tundavik left the tent to give Yvanne her privacy. *Asking to take command,* he laughed at himself, *at your age? With your dreams and headaches and sores and pains. Idiot. I came back to see my home, not to lead a war. What would Adile think of me?*

He had a young soldier fill a wash bucket from the river. Tundavik stripped, poured the bucket, and scrubbed himself clean. Glem had just finished bathing in the river when he came over. "Is everything alright?" Glem asked. "I heard of a fight on the western edge of camp."

Tundavik washed his bug-infested beard. "I brought it under control … well, not me." He couldn't lie to the young boy. "Lord Toware finally got his wish. All the ruffians dead. Some woman too. I was trying to protect her."

"I'm sure you did all you could. Fights broke out all the time in my village. We tried to stop them, but sometimes men just want to brawl and kill."

"That's why we have war." Tundavik chuckled. "What have the lords been putting you up to?"

"I was watching the animals to make sure no one stole them. It was Sir Pollard who sent me out there. It was a good fit. I didn't have to do much though; no one wanted the horses or mules." Glem scratched his head. "You'd think someone would have eaten them by now."

"Don't give them any ideas." Tundavik looked at the skinny squire. "What have you eaten? No horses, I presume?"

"Not much, some old bread. What I really want is salted pork, or even a stew. My mother used to make the best stew." Glem started drooling.

"Have you gone fishing with anyone?"

"A bit. The river seems to be filled only with fingerlings. You should fish. Isn't that what you did in the West?"

"I have other things to worry about." Tundavik watched as Glem smiled understandably. His childish face could have been who Guis grew up to be. "I have nothing to do now. We can fish if you'd like. Show you how to do it properly."

"That'd be great. I think there are poles by the Montla."

Tundavik dressed and tossed the pail aside. The two began walking when Gordo, one of Yvanne's brothers, came racing over to him. He could barely speak as he wiped sweat and coughed. "You must come with me. We've a problem."

Tundavik quickly followed, not wanting his mind to wander. He saw Yvanne in the distance, so he knew she was fine, Sir Mar as well. Pollard was off riding near the Ritae. Lord Toware's blue flag was to the east. The only thing that made sense was Ultiir had killed Devro. Sent his body to them.

But it wasn't Devro's body he saw. It was Rila de'Tro. She was dead.

"What happened?" Yvanne asked with a green face.

The old woman was slumped in the barred wagon. Her eyes stared at them all, but saw nothing. "Old age," Aimora Dore, lord of the Lodean, said as if he couldn't believe it.

Diero unlocked the wagon and said, "Sir Robern came running and shouting." The knight held his head in shame. "He heard a gasp and looked inside, and she was dead."

"And she isn't faking?" The old Lord Cul asked, his beady eyes never moving from the body. Diero grabbed and dropped an arm. Nothing. Then trumpets blared.

"Oh, what now?" Gordo panted.

They all turned toward the city gates to see the commotion.

Riders came through the gate with flags of the four-pointed star. The flag of peace. Tundavik's eyes grew. "Hide the body," he said. He ran forward, Glem and the lords following. When he was far enough away from the dead Rila de'Tro, he stopped, holding his chest as he took in breaths. A white horse and a rider stopped in front of him. Lord Aimora and Diero didn't take their hands from their swords, but the flag meant it wasn't an attack. *As long as it isn't a trick.*

"I come with a message," the rider, who looked about Rila's age, said. "I, Sir Gid, as chief consultant to His Grace, Ultiir, give you this letter." He gave a letter to Tundavik. The wax seal an owl with wheat in its talons. "You have until tomorrow to respond," and the old rider raced back to the city.

"What is it?" Yvanne asked as she reached them.

Tundavik had read the letter a dozen times before she arrived. "Ultiir wants the siege to end. He wishes to have a meeting with you," he looked to Yvanne. "To discuss the terms of trading Devro with ... Rila de'Tro."

It was as if the entire world went silent.

Yvanne

I figured I'd be back under different circumstances," Lord Urses de'Marisco said as the portcullis rose to enter Vigur. "I thought we'd be marching in triumphantly."

"Is this not?" Yvanne asked as she climbed atop a litter. She knew she wouldn't be able to make the entire walk to the palace; her ankles bulged, and her feet were tender. "Ultiir has decided to make peace. I see that as a win."

"Yes, of course, but the queen mother …" Urses let that hang.

"Don't let the whole city know," Yvanne said as her litter was lifted and she was carried into Vigur. She had never been to the capital before, never seen the domaton or the palace or the streets. Stories of the grandeur and wealth and of all the food and banquets filled her childhood. But Vigur was nothing like she expected. The homes and shops near the wall were destroyed. Glares followed her. Enormous boulders had smashed the area into pieces. Her men walked over debris and heirlooms and didn't think twice about it. The people peeked out from their shutters. Hid behind intact walls. The boulders had stopped flying, but now the streets of Vigur were filling with Asaramen.

Yvanne made sure Diero and Gordo came along since it was their idea to take Rila de'Tro captive anyhow. Sir Mar walked near her litter. Urses next to him. He was the only one who knew Ultiir and how best to handle him. Pollard cried and stomped when he was told to stay out of the city. "But I don't trust that anyone else can protect you," he had said.

"Your temper sometimes gets the better of you," Yvanne had told him as she held her belly after a round of vomiting. "Remember how you reacted to Rila? Besides, you and Tundavik seem to get along, and I need someone strong out here in case Ultiir pulls any tricks."

Her brother still didn't like it. But he did as he was told and stayed near Tundavik. Lord Vandes was gleeful Ultiir wanted peace; he was the only one who wasn't worried now that Rila de'Tro was dead. "You must lie," he had told her hours before in her tent. "You mustn't let Ultiir know his mother is dead."

"Maybe we can come to another deal," Yvanne suggested as Jacka slipped shoes on her feet. "He doesn't even like his mother. He might want the siege lifted, and that's it. We leave, and he releases Devro."

"No." Tundavik's face was hard. "Make him believe his mother is alive, no matter what. That's the only way he'll release Devro. If I've learned anything from Ultiir's actions, is that he is too proud. He doesn't want to do anything he deems beneath him. Trading Devro for nothing at all would put a stain on his legacy."

"So what am I to do?" Yvanne stretched out her pants that felt constricting. "How am I supposed to lie to him? I'm not sure I'm good at it. And what of the others? What if

Gordo lets it slip? What if that old knight saw and reports back?"

"Meet him alone. Just you two. Then you've nothing to worry about."

"And when he finds out we lied? What will happen when he brings us Devro and I bring him the corpse of his mother?" Yvanne was getting tired of her pants; they were choking her belly. She ripped the top and pulled even more to stretch them, Jacka gasping.

"I don't know," Tundavik said as he looked away as Yvanne stripped to find new pants. "Maybe tell him once we have Devro we will leave and Rila will sit here waiting."

"But it will be a dead woman."

"What else is there to do?" Tundavik raised his voice. "Sorry, Your … Grace. It's the only thing I can think of." Once Yvanne was in new pants, he turned and walked over to her. "I want Devro back as much as you, and this is the only way. But you must lie."

Yvanne stared at the palace in the distance as they passed through charred homes that reminded her of Fielding. "What happened here?" She asked Urses as if he knew.

"I believe," Urses rubbed his chin, "that the Rat's Nest burned." It was a gaping hole in the middle of the city. Wooden houses on either side, the four points of the domaton to the west, but in between was nothing but rubble and pockets of ash. Commoners walked the streets. Feather-filled sacks used as beds. Every so often, a stray mutt tugged on a dead person's bone. "Could've been the people or Ultiir," Urses said. "The peasants around here are an unsavory lot, to say the least."

"I always enjoyed the Rat's Nest," Mar added with a shrug.

"But maybe that tells you all you need to know."

"That doesn't mean they deserve to live like this," Yvanne said as she saw a babe feeding at her mother's breast. Dirt and dust covered the mother. She wore almost nothing. Her face was empty.

"No need to worry about it." Urses waved it away. "They chose to move here, did they not?"

Yvanne sighed and said, "I'm sure that babe did," as she held her stomach.

They continued down the cobbled street and the houses and shops came back, though they too looked abandoned. The city was quiet. Empty. Even though hundreds of thousands of people still lived in Vigur. *Surely I didn't kill them all,* she thought. Then she saw a gathering of people at the domaton as they moved to the south of it. The statue of Meret looked over her. Eyes watching. People were praying and crying, and the doma were all scattered about, relieving people's fears, praying with them, telling them it will be alright. The high doma stood at the door above the steps. "The traitors have come to end the siege. Our suffering is almost over. Thanks be to the Four and the Many. Let Vigura judge them harshly for what they subjected us to."

"He's a drunk," Urses said, "don't listen to rubbish."

"I wasn't going to," Yvanne said. Red blotches stained parts of the cobbled streets, and Yvanne wondered if there had been some sort of fight. "It must be odd," she said to Lord de'Marisco, "for you to be back after these few months away."

"I see now what a blessing it was that I was the one to bring Gofrei's head to Whitehall." He said as he looked around the city as if it stank. "Things here have changed for the worse. I'm not sure I'm ready to see the palace."

"How will Ultiir react when he sees you?" Sir Mar asked.

"He'll wish to hang me as a traitor," Urses rubbed his throat. "My queen, I ask that you don't offer me up in your exchange."

"I'll think about it," Yvanne giggled, but the lord bit his cheek.

"What about you?" Urses eventually turned to Mar. "You've not been in the city since leaving with Devro all those years ago. Does it feel the same?"

"More or less," Mar said. "A little more crowded, but that's to be expected. Definitely drier than Gereduss, and for that I'm grateful. We'll see how much Ultiir has changed the palace though."

The men who carried her litter were all breathing heavily as they made their way through white manses to reach the wall of the palace. It was made of stone, but behind it, taller than any peak in the Asara, the white, marble palace built by the elves towered above all. Clouds wisped around the towers. Birds nested in the high arches. Eyes from the windows stared at the entourage.

"Thank you for coming," the old man, Sir Gid, said in his golden cloak. "Ultiir awaits you inside the palace. He wishes you to leave your men behind."

"Absolutely not," Diero said. "For all we know, Ultiir has an army behind his walls and will sic them on the queen when she is alone."

"It's alright," Yvanne said as she was helped off the litter. The palace guards seemed surprised at the sight of her belly. Eyes widened, and whispers followed. "I am trusting Ultiir. I will take a few men with me, and that will be all." She looked to the old man. "But I have many runners who we'll be back to Fielding before you can blink. If anything is to happen to me, the siege will restart, and it will never end."

Sir Gid nodded. "Come with me."

Yvanne, Mar, Urses, and Gordo followed the old knight under the wooden gatehouse of the palace. Diero stayed outside to command the two dozen men-at-arms she brought for protection. As they passed under the portcullis, she held her belly and prayed Ultiir was a man of his word. *But what will happen if he finds out about his mother?*

As they made their way across the barren fields, Urses said, "Looks like the false king couldn't keep the slaves under control."

"Is this a mistake?" Yvanne asked as she saw a burnt barn. "Was Ultiir already losing? The city is half burned, the slaves have revolted, there is blood in the streets. Maybe I made the wrong decision."

"No," Urses said, the word only a breath. "You heard what Tundavik and your brother dealt with. If the siege had continued for weeks and weeks, the men might've mutinied. Then we all would've lost. This is the best way."

"I agree," Gordo said. "The few men I brought were getting tired. Itching to go home."

The large door to the palace swung open; it groaned like a huge beast. Inside was dark like a cave. "Then let's end this," Yvanne said.

Once they entered the mouth of the palace and the doors slammed, it was as if the air was sucked away. It was as quiet as the city. There were no servants or slaves running around. No cooks with trays of food. Not even mice scurrying across the cold floor. The old knight led them through a corridor of arches and statues. Yvanne had never seen as much detail on statues before, not even statues of the Four were as complete. The gray stone eyes were watching her. Judging her every step. *Do they resent me for starving their city as well?*

Then some guards bowed at another door and opened it to reveal the throne room. At the far end was the velvet throne of red where Ultiir sat. His wife at his side. A long table beneath him where some lords sat, probably his councilors. Windows lined the walls, and columns and arches divided the room. Lords and ladies, all in their finest silk for the heat, stood in silence as they watched her move through the chamber.

"Your Grace," Sir Gid bowed and his gold cloak fluttered, "I bring to you the besiegers."

"Thank you," Ultiir said. "Take a seat." Gid found a seat at the council table. Yvanne and her men stood in the center of the room. "Welcome, my lady of Whitehall." Ultiir said with a smirk. Yvanne could tell that he was Devro's uncle. They shared the same blond hair, though Ultiir's was getting lighter. His skin was paler to remind everyone his father was from Rowan. His lips were thin, and his eyes were distant. It was almost the same look Devro had after his father and Gofrei and Raimund were all killed.

"Thank you for having me," Yvanne said. She had to fight the urge to bow her head. *He is not my king,* she repeated to herself. "I wasn't expecting to see all the court here, and the Prince of Goldfield sitting on the throne."

"He is king," Gid said with a growl.

"And I am queen as well as duchess of the Lands of Asara," Yvanne said. "But I have yet to be referred to as such."

"No need to bicker," Ultiir said. His words were dripping with cockiness.

He sees himself as better than I, even though I'm the one who led a siege. "My lord," Yvanne said, "are we going to dictate terms in front of the court and your council? Or are we going to go somewhere private?"

"Private?" Mar's brow raised.

"You don't think the lords of the court should hear?" Ultiir rubbed his chin. "Interesting." He fluffed his red cloak, and his wife quivered for a moment. Sophie sat where Yvanne would sit once the war was won. She wondered whether she would have any influence on Devro. Maybe she would just be raising their heir. Yvanne rubbed her stomach as Ultiir motioned to a corridor behind the throne. Yvanne followed, even with Gordo and Mar telling her not to.

"You do what you want," Urses smiled as he came along. "You trust Ultiir that much?"

"He won't hurt me," she said and prayed it was true. "We will starve them out if he does."

As they entered the corridor, Urses stopped and bowed to Yvanne. "If you don't mind, Your Grace, I saw an old … friend of mine. If you don't need my help to negotiate, I would love to talk to her."

"Friend?" Mar chuckled. "I think Urses was in love."

Urses blushed. Yvanne saw Ultiir disappear into a room and nodded. "Very well. See you outside?" Urses bowed away. "I expect the two of you to stay outside the door."

"Of course," Mar and Gordo said.

Yvanne walked into a room with a stained-glass window on the far side. The colors lit a long, cracked table.

Parchments and scrolls and dust and spiders covered the room. "Not much use?"

Ultiir was sitting at the head of the table, and motioned for her to sit opposite him. "The council doesn't meet much anymore. I've no use for most of them, and some have come to be traitors. Do you have traitors in your midst?" His eyes were flashing all about her. She could feel his stare on even her soul.

"Not that I'm aware of." Yvanne rested her arms on the table. She could imagine the council chamber full of shouting and arguing. "You don't take that as a sign? You have to deal with traitors and deceit. All I have are people too loyal. Some of them want to go above and beyond, and I have to pull in their reins. If I hadn't, I think this war would've ended months ago."

"Well, I can tell you're lying about that," he gave a breathy laugh. "You don't take me as someone who wants this war. What were you doing the day Devro rode into Whitehall? Playing with dolls? Fixing your hair? Then your father sold you to some bastard, and he isn't even be alive to see if his daughter wins the throne or not."

"It's not my throne to win," she said as she pushed her red hair from her eyes.

Ultiir let out a full laugh at that. It echoed in the empty room. "I see you're just like my wife. Yes, even Sophie has betrayed me. More times than I can count if I'm being honest. Devro will have to be on the lookout when you're around."

"You're wrong," Yvanne smiled. "I have never once thought of usurping his crown. I'm not your wife, nor you."

His nostrils flared for a moment as the smile disappeared. "I did what was right." He cleared his throat. "I sav—" he went silent. He blinked a few times before saying, "I stepped in when my brother unfortunately choked on his drink. But others saw a chance for power. Some of my councilors, some lords and dukes, the little bastard I have beneath the palace. They all want to be king. But I am *king*."

Yvanne rubbed dirt from a nail. "I don't want to argue about inheritance and all that. I'm here for Devro, and you're here for your mother."

Ultiir stood and tapped his fingers on the wall as he looked out the window. A bird whistled from a birch tree. "How is she? Was she kind to you?"

"What do you think?" Yvanne said, avoiding the first question. The less she had to lie, the better. "She was wretched, horrid. How she's grown so old with that much hate I'll never know."

He turned with his hands behind his back, his face rigid. "Being the last de'Tro to die would make her happy. Then she would get to gloat at the feast with the gods." He popped his knuckles. Each one echoing. "Were you kind to her?"

"As kind as I could be," Yvanne said as she wiped sweat from her upper lip. "She didn't make it easy, and my brother hated her. I had to keep them away from each other." The world went still for a moment as they actually laughed together. That didn't help Yvanne's sweating.

"Not to alarm you," Ultiir's lips curled, "but I heard what a monster she was to you."

"Funny," Yvanne said. "Trying to make me just as paranoid as you? That someone in my midst is feeding you information? It won't work. So, are you going to take the

355

deal? I think the queen mother for my husband is a fine exchange."

"I don't have much of a choice," he whispered. "Fine. Devro for my mother. We'll trade on the morrow."

Yvanne nodded but chewed her lip. "We have a problem. The wagon and the stress, I guess, have caused your mother to ache even worse. She ... can't walk very well."

"Then carry her."

"You know just as much as I that she would never let that happen."

Ultiir chuckled. "Then what do you have in mind?"

"You give us Devro, and I will turn my army to the east. We'll leave the city like you want and leave your mother behind. I'll give her ample food, water, and shade before we go. That way, there isn't any temptation for our armies to fight."

"And I'm supposed to trust you?"

"I give you my word ..." Yvanne took a deep breath. Lying to a man about his mother, pretending she were still alive. It all felt wrong. "... on the Four and the Many."

Ultiir, "Fine again. Destroy your siege engines and back your entire host beyond Fielding. Then I will release Devro and watch you leave. I want my mother unharmed."

Yvanne prayed they would be long gone by the time Ultiir found his dead mother. *What would he do to me if he found out?* She thought with a shiver. But she needed Devro back.

So she said, "You have a deal."

The Prince Below the Palace

His body ached from sleeping on the cold stone floor. At first, Devro was tied up like an animal, like the rats that scurried across the ground, but eventually, the jailer stopped caring, and let him loose. Devro prayed all the time, hoping it was a different day. There was neither moon nor sun in the depths of the castle. No torches to light his cell.

This darkness must be what it's like to be dead. Eyes shut forever to the world. Total black.

Devro stretched his legs across the floor. The smell of dried blood permeated his nose. Usually it was masked by the smell of his own shit, but Olier decided to be nice and take the bucket. The problem was now he had nowhere to release what little waste he had.

The ache of hunger stopped long ago. Days, weeks, months, hopefully not years. He had no sense of time, no idea what was happening. Adedor could have sunk into the world's ocean, and he would only know when the waves came to take him.

Devro hoped for the waves. *That would be better than a dungeon.* He tried to remember where it had all gone wrong. How he let some backwoods lord capture him and steal him down the mountains. How no one came to rescue him. *Have they even realized I'm* gone?

He spent his hours doing nothing. Sometimes he watched the stairs hoping for rescue; other times he caught spiders so he could eat for the day. He prayed to Mother Meret that they weren't deadly. Then he prayed to Vigura that they were. He could be with his father, feasting with the gods.

His dreams were filled with his father. Everything from the teachings of reading and writing to the slaps and beatings. Why he endured his father, he would never know. He was just a child. What could he have done?

"You're *still* a child," a voice said.

"I know," Devro replied, but he sounded different. He hadn't heard his voice in so long. It was sadder than he remembered, and deeper. Maybe one day he would sound like his father. Maybe he would be cruel like his father, perhaps harsher.

"Don't believe those lies," the voice said to Devro. "Don't let your mind play tricks."

Devro rubbed his eyes and looked at Lord Gofrei Geary. He sat opposite Devro in the cell. "I like the tricks my mind plays. Keeps me busy," he said as he played with some dirt at his feet.

"And what about me?" Gofrei laughed. "I've been by your side for months. You're lucky I didn't leave you and run back to some tavern. Vigur has some of the best drinks in the entire world."

"Then go," Devro rolled his eyes as playfully as he could, "but bring me something back. I can barely talk with how dry my throat is."

"Maybe your uncle will bring you some," Gofrei and

Devro laughed together. "Or maybe the Four will. You'll have better luck that way."

"I miss the streams of the mountains. Never thought I'd say that." Devro took in a deep breath as he thought of Whitehall. His heir. Of Yvanne. That made him smile. He still remembered her face. The red locks that fell onto her pale face, the mountain air blowing through her hair. He barely knew her, but he yearned for her. For her embrace.

He would have liked anyone to be with him. Mar or Raimund especially. They would have protected him as they had for years while he grew. Even the old lord, Tundavik, could've kept Ultiir and his goons away. He curled in the corner, tears in his eyes and memories that wouldn't go away.

Gofrei stood over him. The lord was getting older, his dark skin beginning to wrinkle. "Sweet dreams, Devro. Hopefully, I'm still here in the morn."

But Devro didn't go to sleep. Instead, the door to the dungeon opened, and chains rattled. Olier and a guard brought in an old man, lit only by a small torch that burned Devro's eyes.

"Company," Gofrei said.

"I guess," Devro agreed, and Olier rolled his eyes.

"The bastard is deranged," the jailer told the old man. "Hopefully, you don't catch whatever he has. Talking to ghosts or whatnot."

The cell across from Devro opened, and Olier threw the old man inside. He huffed after he hit the wall. "You're very kind," he told the guard. "Though I'd rather be in here with the bastard than outside with your crazed king." Olier punched the man in the face, and he collapsed to the ground.

The jailer and guard laughed as they left them in darkness.

"I know this man." Gofrei rubbed his chin. "But I can't remember his name."

Devro rubbed his burning eyes, which were getting better with the lack of light. "I don't know who he is."

"My name is Tedbalt Masson," the man said with a groan. "You may not remember me, but I was around when you were a child, Devro. Your birth was a scandal. You being sent away less so, but then you returned and brought a war." Tedbalt chuckled. His voice was slow and scratchy. "So, how have you been enjoying the dungeon?"

Devro said nothing. Gofrei stood over him and shook his head. "This lord must've helped kill your father. I'd not trust him."

"Never," Devro agreed. Then finally he rocked himself to sleep as the old lord groaned in pain.

***

A cold, metal hand shook him awake. Normally, he would jump with fear, but not today. He could barely move. Bugs had not been enough; he had only a few drips of water. Devro was not ready for another day of torture. His eyes opened to find many men and many torches. The dim light was like the sun; it blinded him to everything.

"It smells bloody awful in here." A man yanked him to his feet. Devro squinted at the man's face. It was just Olier again. "How's your companion?" They both looked at Tedbalt, who huddled in a corner. He shivered and kept his head down. Olier laughed and whisked Devro from the cell and prodded him forward.

The jailer didn't help as Devro stumbled over to the stairs, falling so many times he lost count. The other guards' laughter echoed in the small chamber. They pushed and poked him up the stairs, scared Devro with fire like he was a Kruheshian beast. He had just enough strength to focus on walking. He couldn't fight off multiple men.

"What's happening?" Devro took a large breath. The stairs and corridor grew brighter as they ascended. "Where am I going?"

"To be hanged." Olier said without any hesitation. Devro wanted to fall back and roll down the steps. He wanted to die right there, not admonished in front of hundreds of people. He was finally defeated, and Ultiir wanted to make a spectacle. Then he heard snickering. Olier hit Devro's back, making him fall. "I'm joking, bastard. Your uncle wants to see you." Olier tossed Devro up the stairs and through the open door.

Gofrei stood next to Ultiir. A small golden crown on his uncle's head, with his red cloak hanging to his feet. "Finally free," Gofrei said, "let's hope my head doesn't get chopped off this time."

Ultiir pulled Devro up and fixed the boy's hair. "Can't have you looking like that."

Devro tried to stand on his own but couldn't. Olier had to keep him from falling. "I don't understand."

"Nor should you." Ultiir brushed off his shoulder. "You've been locked away for so long. How could you know the going ons of the outside world?"

"Your slut wife wanted to see you." Olier squeezed Devro's arm.

"Olier," his uncle began, "maybe you should go clean the

cell, and pay a visit to our dear friend Lord Masson." Olier didn't protest but sulked away. Ultiir grabbed Devro and walked with him. Devro had seen this hall many times. The paintings and busts of past kings and queens.

"All these remarkable people reaching the highest form of power. Now," Ultiir scoffed, "we squabble over it. Did you know the first siege Vigur ever endured as a human city was by her own people?"

Devro nodded and Gofrei said, "Do we really have to listen to this? Now I need a drink."

Ultiir continued. "Thimoy was successful as King of the Lodean. The same people who march behind your wife. They saw the city walls fall hundreds of years ago. Not this time." Ultiir smiled. They stopped at a portrait of a stoic king with a falcon on his arm and a longsword in the other hand. Valor the Iron. "Even though the Lodean took the city, it was Valor who ultimately became king. The losers do not get a portrait on this wall."

They turned to see the newest paintings. Devro's father stood tall while holding a red sword. Next to him was a portrait of Sophie. Devro had heard stories that the painter never did too well on the queen's portrait in fear the king would find a new wife. The newest portrait—it even looked like the paint still hadn't dried—was of Ultiir. An owl soared behind him through the castle and clouds.

"Only one of us has a kingly portrait on this wall," Ultiir said. "Remember that when you march to Whitehall."

Devro barely heard what Ultiir said. "Whitehall?"

"Don't you want to go back there?" Ultiir pulled Devro along as they made their way to the great doors. "You're lucky you have a wife who thinks about your well-being. I haven't been so fortunate." He said while looking at Sophie across the hall. Devro had forgotten what she looked like, but he hardly knew her.

"I hope my husband was treating you well," she said as she brushed a finger along a bruise on his face. She gave him a cup of water, which he didn't hesitate to drink. "I was assured you weren't beaten."

"Save your posturing," Ultiir said as he rolled his eyes. "You never once cared for him while he was rotting away in the dungeons, and I don't want to hear it." Ultiir took the mug even as water spilled from Devro's lips.

Castle guards bowed as they pushed open the doors. Devro didn't exhale until the sun bathed him in heat and life. He wanted to break into tears as if he were a toddler once more. He had forgotten how light felt on his skin, the colors that bounced back, the white marble of the palace blinding him. It was better than he remembered.

With squinted eyes, they made their way past the defensive wall and stuffed into a carriage. Ultiir, his old knight, Devro, and Gofrei. Lord Geary yawned as the carriage departed. "Remind me to never come back to this city, even if you are king."

"Noted," Devro said. Ultiir and the knight squinted their brows but said nothing.

The carriage went by old memories. He saw the best butcher shop near the castle. His servants and slaves would take him there for pork slabs, the best meal for a boy of seven. They whisked through the streets of noble houses. Crests and sigils lined the cobblestone. He had to search through almost-lost memories. De'Orro, Vastes, Arral—all the family names came sweeping over him.

Further down the road was the domaton, the great star shining to the heavens. Nothing had changed since he had been there last. The same stone and color. He could make out the piss marks that all the children left when they grew bored. He wanted to laugh and tell Mar about the red-faced doma.

The eyes of the old man never left his back. Devro could see the white-haired knight in his periphery. He would cut Devro down if he tried to escape. The knight wouldn't hesitate.

There were shouts and a sound Devro was familiar with. The rising of the portcullis, the opening of the gates. Devro rested his head on the cushion behind him. His stomach churned, and his eyesight blurred. What if everything had changed? Mar and Tundavik could be dead like Raimund. Yvanne could hate him. His people could think of him as a weak boy.

He glanced at Ultiir. Why would the false king lose his bargaining chip? Devro couldn't understand. He would've had Ultiir executed the moment he was captured. He knew the usurper was not lame; he was smart enough to steal a kingdom. Devro's stomach twisted with the thought of a plot.

"Don't concern yourself with him," Gofrei whispered. "I worked with him for years, and even then he was as slimy as a fish." Devro nodded in agreement.

He laid his eyes on the field outside the carriage before reeling his head back. Blood and carnage sprawled outward from the wall. Stone had turned red and splattered with matter. Animals and insects picked and prodded at the carcasses that lay across the field. He closed his eyes to the horror, but his own thoughts weren't much better. Images of men dying to rescue him, swords and spears impaling and cutting, boulders crashing and boiling water dumping.

His eyes opened when the carriage came to a halt. The false king and the old knight emptied, but Devro stayed. He clutched the chair, his heart pounding. The old man came over to the door and rested his hand on his sword. Devro knew what that meant and disembarked.

The grass crunched under his feet. It looked black for miles. They began their walk, stepping through the charred landscape. Every so often his step would be soggy, blood or shit he didn't want to know. They neared the town on the outskirts, where the grass greened, and buildings and tents rose from the ground. If he didn't know about the war, he would guess it was a normal day. Instead, it was his people who made this town their home.

The train of people that followed Ultiir stopped in unison. He glanced back at the wall, where hundreds of men with bows stood ready. In front was more of the same. Men and boys with weapons in hand. He gulped.

The men parted, and out they came. Tears would've swelled if he had water. Tundavik, even more rugged; and Sir Mar, his friend, but still no Raimund. Soldiers followed behind them until they stopped across from Ultiir.

Devro felt like a young child. The adults would talk, and he would stay silent. He wanted to go hug Mar, ask him about Raimund. Wanted to cry thankful tears to Tundavik. He wanted to sob like a baby, like the child he was. But he kept it all in. He wore a stoic, tired, and beaten face. A face that hoped everything would go well.

"Finally made it," Gofrei said and elbowed Devro. "Ready

to go home?"

"Thank you for bringing him." Tundavik broke the silence. "As was part of the deal, Rila de'Tro will be left just over there," he pointed to a small tent. "A dutiful knight'll protect her to make sure our men don't bring her harm, and she will have food and water to last until nightfall. We should be gone by then."

Ultiir stretched his neck. "Very well." He nodded to the old knight, who pushed Devro forward. Devro walked one foot in front of the other. He couldn't believe it was happening, and so quickly. He was free, finally free. Sir Mar grabbed hold of him and kept him close. Devro could see tears filling his eyes. "I expect you to hold your end of the bargain. If not, I will unleash my men on you, and this time the Eastlands will assist me."

"Don't worry. We would never break a vow," Tundavik said. "We'll be on our way back to Whitehall soon enough."

"I hope you don't feel too bad," Ultiir sighed. "The walls of Vigur have not fallen in two hundred years. They've withstood the test of both strong and weak armies. Armies from great powers and rivals and armies like yours. If you ever attack again, I expect the same result will befall you. But next time, I will not be so hesitant to kill each and every one of you."

Tundavik laughed, and the men behind followed suit. Even Gofrei laughed, though Devro stood silent. He gripped Mar's arms, not wanting to be taken. "*When* we do attack again," Tundavik said, "our army will be even stronger than last time. The walls won't stand, and the crown on your head will be ripped from the ruins. I hope you take this time to prepare your defenses."

"It will be a good battle." Ultiir smirked. His company turned and began back to the wagons.

Mar quickly brought Devro to a table. He brought him well water and sighed with relief. "Time for a whore or two," Mar chuckled as he wiped his eyes. Devro laughed with the friend who raised him. He hadn't heard his own laughter in so long. "I hope you feel alright. It's a long journey ahead."

Tundavik stalked over and hugged Devro with a beaming smile. "He's our king; of course he's ready for the journey." Tundavik found some tack and fed Devro. Even though it tasted like nothing, it was the best thing Devro had ever eaten. His eyes lit up for the first time in months. "Here she is," Tundavik said and motioned to Yvanne, who was walking with men who shared her features. Her belly had gotten so large it was ready to burst. Her hair was still redder than flames, and she looked soft to the touch. Devro just wanted to sleep in the same bed as her again.

"No, Your Grace," some lord said to Yvanne, "Urses still hasn't returned from the city."

"Then I guess we leave without him." Yvanne's eyes stared into the distance, looking at nothing. Tundavik cleared his throat and got her attention. Her empty face turned to a smile, though it seemed forced. "I can't believe it worked." She hugged Devro as best she could with her belly and the chair. "It's too bad we have to leave so soon, but we'll have to catch up on the road."

"Not like you've much to talk about," Gofrei said to Devro, no one else hearing him.

"To Whitehall?" Devro coughed.

"Actually," Tundavik began, "Yvanne and the council have

decided to go to Ritaeum. There's no time for breaks in war."

Mar squinted. "The Woodlands have yet to attack. Why should we provoke them?"

"Ritaeum is the last major city not to be attacked," Tundavik said. "If we can take it, then we show Ultiir that we're not weak."

"But the men *are* weak." Mar waved a hand at them. "They've just been through a siege. They watched their friends die." He looked at Yvanne. "Their brothers."

Yvanne straightened her back. "The decision has already been made. Cada is doing a fine job in Whitehall. We can worry about the fighting." Mar scoffed and shook his head. Yvanne bent down and grabbed Devro's hand, her skin so smooth. "We'll celebrate when we get somewhere safe. Right now, we need to ready to leave." Yvanne, along with her handmaid, wandered back to a large tent.

Tundavik sighed. His eyes drooped as the bags under them grew larger. "Mar will keep you company while I rally the troops."

And he did. Mar kept Devro eating and drinking and talking. But the whole time while the camp was readying for departure, he felt eyes on him. Not eyes of envy or graciousness, but eyes of mocking and loathing.

"I'm worried about Ritaeum," Gofrei said.

Devro nodded to the ghost and said, "So am I."

The Twisting Trees

Flora

Flora wrapped herself in a tight blue cloak before leaving Vanette to sleep. She snuck past the drunken men snoring and the naked women sleeping.

The rains had stopped in recent weeks. The Flit no longer flooded the town, leaving her boots dry. Lord Poden's castle had a long shadow from the moon that covered the sleeping town in darkness. It was almost time for the sun to rise, with a hint of pink in the east. Midnight meant the day was her godly Mother's, and she needed any help she could get.

A small, crooked four-pointed domaton sat nearest the water. The wood was rotten and splintered from the floods. The inside was no better. She had to watch her step using the light of a candle. *Mother, forgive me.* She thought as she found the Book of the Four. Next to the damp pages was a painting of the Four. *The doma outlawed that centuries ago. What could it be doing here?* She pushed aside the false idol so as not to offend the gods before touching four fingers to her heart.

"I hope you hear me," she said to Mother Meret. "Tonight I pray for the safety of all those who went south, even Tundavik." Flora sighed, wishing she could forget the old lord. "Forgive me for my mistakes. Lord Vandes and I will not meet again. Will not sin again." Lightning lit the sky for the first time in days. "And I will not sin with anyone else. Lord Poden might have information I need. I must stop him from committing to his terrible plan of war. This I pray."

Lightning flashed and thunder cracked as she made her way to Lord Poden's stone castle. Only a single servant was awake, getting the stew ready for early morning. It wouldn't be much, but the thought still made Flora drool. She'd been eating scraps in the brothel. The servant gave her some bread from yesternight and led her to a small table near a hearth. The fire was the only thing lighting the chamber.

"Why have you come?" Sir Len asked as he rubbed sleepy eyes. "My lord hasn't yet called you." The castle was dark. Wood creaked and groaned as the knight's weight moved across the boards.

"Business," was all Flora said.

While she sat at the table, she could hear the creaking steps as Poden Bruce made his way down. "You're here early." He said in his gruff voice.

Flora smiled as meekly as she could. "We've already wasted much time."

"You may leave us." He told the servant, who complied. Sir Len stood in the corner. He was still rubbing his eyes as the fire lit his face. "You want to speak of war?" Poden asked. "Maybe other things?" He brushed a finger across her shoulder.

Why must he do this? Flora wiped crumbs from her lips as she shrugged her shoulder of his touch. The flames were hot on her back. To Poden she would be just a dark figure. He was lit to her. She could see his devious smile and his curling fingers. "Do you have any news?"

Poden gave a laugh. "Yes, why I do have news of the war. It seems the bastard king has been rescued from Vigur."

"Tundavik took the city?" Flora wanted to jump up. It would surely mean the end of the war. "You must tell me everything."

"No, no." Poden waved a hand. "The letter said Ultiir released him to end the siege. Now, the bastard king and his troop march east with your lover at the head. I've no idea what Ultiir is planning now."

Flora didn't know how to react to *your lover*. She wanted to pretend the words had never escaped Poden's mouth, because she didn't know how he would know. Unless…She shook her head and remembered Tundavik talking of his family. That's where he would be going. "The Woodlands," she nodded. "The whole wood will be on fire soon."

"Just as we run out of water," Poden said as he looked to the sky out a window. "I dreamt last night of all the Ritae being routed from their land. It was a good dream."

"You think it an omen?"

Poden's lips twisted in a smile. "Why wouldn't I?" The hearth cast dark shadows over his face. The glint in his eyes made Flora shiver. "You may not believe me, but the Four and the Many have given me signs. I plan to ride out in the coming days for Storyah."

"Attack?" Flora's heart banged against her chest as she thought of Florance. Her daughter would be defenseless. Thunder cracked. "I'm here to broker peace, and you've yet to hear me out."

A sweaty hand from Poden found her palm on the table. His scratchy fingers wrapped around hers. "There is one way to get me to listen. If you so decide." When Flora pulled her hand away, he said, "Your father would be disappointed. I'm sure he wants you to do everything in your power to make a deal."

"Perhaps," Flora said as she stared at the fire, not looking at the lord of River Watch. "But I am married, and so were you. It would be a sin, and I wouldn't want your dreams to stop because you let desire take over."

"Now you care about my dreams?"

Flora cleared her throat and found a jug of water to wash the dry bread down. "I guess we can go upstairs."

Poden held out his hand, and she took it. His fingers were almost all bone, sweat dripping. Flora's brow was low as she watched the lord walk up the stairs. She didn't want to be with him, but if that's what it took to get the information. *Mother Meret would never forgive me.*

"Are you alright?" She asked Poden as they entered his bedchamber. The sheets were a mess, with pillows thrown about. "You look a little pale."

"Fine," the lord brushed it away. "The dreams keep me tossing all night," he said as he straightened a pillow. Poden took off his tunic to reveal a hairy chest. He had liver spots on his cheeks. Wrinkles on his skin. Graying hair and beard. *He's as old as my father,* she thought. She prayed there was a different way to get the lord to talk. She didn't want to be unfaithful to her husband. Not again.

"Do you know Tundavik?" Flora asked to stall for time.

"I've only heard of him," Poden shrugged. "Some banished duke from the Woodlands, ruling over the Ritae people," he spat. "A raper, a pillager. What's more to know?"

"You called him my lover?" Silent air fell over them. Only the fire in the hearth could be heard. Crackling. Roaring. Then there was a thud above Poden's bedchamber. A *knock, knock, knock.* "What is that?"

"Rats." Poden's eyes never left her. "I've people in Storyah who tell me all, my sweet. Servants and peasants and guards and whatnot. I pay them handsomely to bring me reports of the duke and his family. Even if that report is about who his daughter is fucking."

Flora wanted to scream, to curse him, and his spies, but she needed answers. *Knock.* "You spy on my father so you can strike like a snake when he is weak. These spies believe in independence as well? Believe my father is failing? A traitor?"

"Of course. An independent Flewthlands, free from Viguran and your father." Poden reached out to grab her, but she took a step back, keeping a smile on her face not to offend. *Thud.* Poden stretched his fingers. "It might come true if I hold my end of the de—" he went quiet.

Deal, Flora thought as she took another small step back. *Who have you made a deal with Poden Bruce? And please don't tell me what I already suspect.* Barnet was on her mind. *Thud.* Her husband sent her away and kept her busy while he plotted. *But my husband would never betray me.* Thud. *Betray his daughter. Hurt my father.* Knock. *He wouldn't.*

"Sometimes," she took a large breath, "sometimes my lord husband wishes for freedom. He likes to read stories of the Flewthlands after the Nowexerts left. Though he would never go against my father."

Flora saw Poden's eyes dart from hers for the first time

since entering his chamber. *Thud.* "I wish to go back to that time … without Lord Pyre Blume as ruler."

"And how would you be free of him?"

Poden glanced at her before standing, but she knew what he would've said. *Murder him.* Poden looked out the window as the townsfolk woke. Flora had everything she needed, though she didn't want it. "Am I free to go?" She didn't want him to turn around and take advantage of her. She didn't want to be that close to him, not with a man who dreamed of murdering her father.

Thud. "We'll talk more later," Poden said without turning around, and Flora sighed with relief.

Flora raced to the brothel. She needed to find Sirs Edmond and Marbert before Poden decided to march. She couldn't bear to have her father die.

She lifted her dress and crossed the dried mud. In the windows of the castle stood Poden, overlooking the town. Watching her. She set her sights on the brothel. The first person she found in the whorehouse was Sir Marbert. He was walking out of a room with a naked woman on his arm. "Find something to drink." He told the girl. "Where did you run off to, my lady?" He asked Flora.

"Where is Sir Edmond?"

He looked around the warped building. "Perhaps in the back where the men sleep."

Flora took deep breaths as they made their way down the hall. There was a back room with the door open only a crack. She peered through and saw her knight lying naked on a bed. "Edmond," she bellowed as she pushed open the door. Another man wearing nothing fled the room, his cock bouncing as he shuffled away. The knight shot awake and found a blanket to cover himself. "Marbert, close the door."

Once Edmond dressed, Flora peered out the window. Poden was still in his castle. His eyes burned into her. "Who are you looking for, my lady?" Edmond asked.

"We need to do something," Flora said as she backed away from the window. "Poden wants to see my father dead. He told me he is marching on Storyah in the coming days. We have to stop him."

"Is that not why he started a rebellion?" Marbert asked. "I guess peace isn't an option."

"We must bring our men together and confront him."

"In River Watch?" Edmond scoffed. "We'll be outnumbered. It will be like Floodpan again. The only thing we can do is escape, maybe tonight. Ride as fast as we can to Storyah and warn your father."

"You've a better chance floating down the river in your dress than racing away," Marbert said to Flora. "We don't have many good options, my lady."

"Then we do as I said." Flora flared her nostrils as she took in a deep breath for courage. "We confront Lord Poden and threaten him into submission."

Sophie

Angry lords had been bogging her down for weeks. But she still enjoyed it. Her plans had come together perfectly. Now, the entirety of the royal court was beside themselves with Ultiir and his power-hungry ways. *Just a little extra push,* Sophie thought as she made her way down the grand staircase. What was once a lifeless shell of itself, the palace had gotten livelier, louder. Lords and their ladies wandered the halls. Some took over empty chambers to sleep. Servants scurried to help them. What food could be found was flowing from the kitchens. Ultiir's idea to turn this place into a morgue had failed. He not only had to deal with the aftermath of the siege by the bastard's army, but also a siege of his home.

"Your Grace," Lord Tyler bowed as she walked by with Sir Achen in tow. "I've been meaning to talk with you." Sophie nodded for him to go ahead, her diadem peeking from her hair. "I've heard Lord Mer is rallying men to your side. He's calling for a complete overhaul of the succession laws."

"It took some convincing," Sophie said, trying to hide her smile. "But I'm glad to hear it. I hope you're doing the same? I've been talking to many a lord and lady."

"Well, the wives are the easiest to convince," Tylar laughed.

"They all want a share of their husband's wealth and power." When Sophie didn't laugh, the young lord cleared his throat. "Since many of the lords are upset at Ultiir and his handling of the war, I think they might be even easier."

Sophie nodded in agreement as a few conversing lords moved out of her way and bowed. The grand corridor from the throne room to the door was full as men and women and guards and servants made their way for court. Ultiir would surely not come. He was angrier now with his mother dead. She hadn't seen him for a few days. Somewhere off with Lord de'Marisco, or talking with his sister, or crying over his mother. She didn't care. The more he hid, the more the lords saw he wasn't the best to lead them. That maybe they needed a queen to fill the role.

"I also heard some other news," Tylar whispered as Lady Yura entered the throne room. "I'm sure you know Lord Masson was arrested." Sophie nodded to that too. One of her oldest allies in this process was rotting in the dungeons where Devro had been. "Well, I heard the council is going to push for Ultiir to execute him."

Sophie whipped around at that. Her dress flying and creating a dance of blues and reds. "Excuse me? Why would the council want that?"

"They wish to punish him for treason." Tylar said with a shrug. "I thought you should know so that you can speak with him."

"He won't die," Sophie said with a shaking head. "He cannot. The council would be fools to let one of their own die, even if Lord Masson betrayed them. Who's to say Ultiir wouldn't call them all traitors?"

"I must be going," Tylar said. "We've much to discuss in

court today."

Sophie coughed as her head swiveled about the corridor. She saw no members of the king's council. *Whose idea would that be? Stupid Lord de'Viere probably.*

"Did you hear that?" She asked Sir Achen, who nodded. "I cannot believe they would be so shortsighted."

"Well, Your Grace, if your wish comes true, then maybe you can stop Lord Masson's death."

Analere came down the hall in a white smock, her white shoes freshly clean and reflecting the sunlight that arched through the windows. "One minute," Sophie told her knight. She stepped in front of Analere with a smile, even though inside she was burning. "How goes it being the chief daken?"

"Very well," Analere said. "I never imagined I would be on the council. I actually never imagined I would be back in Viguran, but when the king calls."

"Walk with me?" Sophie asked and held out her arm, which Analere took. "We're sisters after all. Oddly enough, I've been a sister to you through two brothers."

Analere laughed, though the smile didn't reach her eyes. "Every family is strange in its own way. Ours is a little stranger because of all the royal blood and matchmaking."

"Of course," Sophie smirked. They didn't turn into the throne room like they usually did; instead, Sophie took Analere down another long corridor where blues and yellows and reds shone on their faces from the stained glass. One of the glass artworks was Maller's Trial, depicting the fire that killed both Maller and Margo Vandes in Udello. "Do you think Ultiir and I will be so unfortunate?"

Analere followed Sophie's gaze and snickered. "Well,

one story says Maller purposely burnt the room and killed everyone, including Margo. I don't think my brother would burn you alive just for having the thought that women should be able to lead. He did push for me to be the chief daken after all."

"Then you don't know him," Sophie said. She wanted to tell Analere that Ultiir was the reason Hurvir was dead. That he was a murderer. But that implicated Sophie as well, even though she didn't pour the poison. "Well," Sophie began, "he has thrown a member of his king's council into the dungeon. I'm not sure Ultiir can be trusted with anything."

Analere nodded as a door opened, and they turned a corner. The stairs to the lower levels were just in front of them. "So you wish to talk to me about Lord Masson?" Analere asked. "I honestly know nothing about him, just that he is a traitor."

"According to Ultiir."

"According to the council." Analere said. "You think Ultiir just makes things up, but he was never like that as a child. He only told true. I was always thankful to him for that."

"He's changed," Sophie said, then bit her lip. "I'm not here to talk about your brother. I heard the council wishes to see Tedbalt dead. Is that true?"

Analere slipped out of Sophie's grasp and stopped walking. "I've only been in a few meetings, the siege and all," she waved her hand. "I know they were talking about what to do with traitors, and they all settled on death. Now, as daken, I see that as a little … harsh, but who am I to stop them? They've all been at it longer than me."

The staircase below was dark; the scent of leeks from the

kitchen wafted up; eventually the smells of shit and piss from the dungeon would fill the air. "I shall see what Lord Masson says," Sophie said, "and if I must, I will present my case to the council and the lords, and he will live."

Analere nodded as she backed away. "Don't get caught up in this, Your Grace. I don't want to see you hanging from the gate as well."

"You won't," Sophie said, getting the last word in before she set off down the stairs.

She passed the kitchens with Achen, and her stomach growled for the stew, but it was even more imperative now that she talk with Tedbalt. *He wanted me to escape during the siege; perhaps I can do the same for him.* Olier was waiting at the steel door to the dungeon, a torch lighting the folds in his chin. Sir Achen came from behind, his hulking shadow engulfing the room.

"I would like to see the prisoner," Sophie said.

"No can do," Olier laughed. "His Grace don't want nobody in unless he's here." Sir Achen sighed and cracked his knuckles. Olier only shook his head. "Why'd you think that will scare me? I've been at this post for some twenty years. Saw mite war prisoners. I've seen far worse than you."

Sophie stepped in front of her knight. "I don't want this to come to violence. I just want to speak with him for five minutes at the most. You can keep watch if you must."

"No," Olier said. "I'll let you in, but this man stays out 'ere with me."

"Very well," Sophie said as the jailer unlocked the door. The many bolts and locks would keep her from busting through and taking Lord Masson to safety. And if Olier was really as hardened as he said, then it would be even harder.

She was holding a small taper that lit her hands and nothing else. She stumbled a few times, but eventually made it to the cells where Tedbalt was. The deepest he could be. *Ultiir hates him, so Tedbalt must suffer in squalor.*

The old lord squinted as he saw her. Sophie brought the taper to the bars to see his face. His cheeks were sunken; what was left of his hair had fallen out; his wrinkles caught dirt and grime and turned his face brown. Tedbalt had always been old, and had been getting older, but now he looked ancient. Only Rila de'Tro herself would've rivaled him in looks.

"How are you?" He said in a raspy voice, like he was holding in a cough.

"Does it matter?" Sophie said. She shook her head and kept a sneeze from the dust at bay. "You're rotting in here."

Tedbalt chuckled, which turned to a cough. He spat phlegm before saying, "I look that bad, huh? Guess that's what happens when you live in the dark with almost no food or water. You know I had to lick some condensation off the walls?" The old man laughed again. "Ultiir doesn't want me around much longer, I reckon."

"No, he doesn't. Lord Tylar told me that the council wants you dead. Of course, Ultiir will agree." Sophie took a breath as the taper was getting smaller in her hand. "I need to figure out how to keep you safe."

"Nonsense," he waved his hand. "I've been praying some to Meret. I think it's my time to feast with my ancestors, or rot in Veltoora," he said with a shrug.

"How can you say that? You're needed here. The lords

respect you, the dakenry look up to you, the people know you. You're my … my closest ally in all this mess." Her voice broke at the dark circles under the lord's eyes. "Without you, I wouldn't be here. Ultiir would surely've sent me away to Terrop or even killed me. Sufar would've told him all I was planning. I would still be like the young girl I was when I married Hurvir."

"Why do you think I had anything to do with it?" Tedbalt shook his head with a cough, spittle leaving his mouth. "All I did was support you from afar, take care of some issues that arose—nothing much. Sure, I sat in on council meetings and reported to you, but it was you who went after the lords. You who decided we needed a spy for Ultiir. If not for your work, you wouldn't have Lord Tylar telling you secrets, would you?" Tedbalt wiped the spit from his lips. "No, without you we would be doomed to live in Ultiir's world."

Now, Sophie's eyes had tears forming. "So I'm supposed to let you die?"

"If that's what Ultiir decides. But you must live. Be sure to oust Ultiir and keep the bastard from the throne and end the dreaded reign of the de'Tros. They've brought nothing but misery to this kingdom."

"I'm not sure I can do that."

Tedbalt scoffed and sat on the hard stone. "My only regret is not being able to see you wield power of your own as queen. No need for a king by your side. It would've been nice."

Sophie had nothing left to say. She turned from the cell and made her way back up the jagged steps as the flame died and tears stained her cheeks.

Tundavik

A weak king is all I see." A man with missing front teeth said over a fire. "Maybe we should've let him rot in that dungeon. We wouldn't have to fight a war in this dragon's heat."

"Keep your mouth quiet, Ide," said another with a missing ear. "You want the king's men to throw you in the fire? I assure you it's much hotter than anything Sendo could send us."

Tundavik kept his hood up as he inspected the camp. The night was dark, and the trees in front of them made it ominous. Whispers called him to the Woodlands. *Old memories. Nothing more.* He had to focus on the army. His tired army.

He and a few knights he trusted, such as Mar and Pollard, walked the camp every night. There would be no talk of mutiny or desertion any longer. He had to keep the men fed and clothed. They raided any home or hamlet they came across for wool and oats and boots. The men were happy so far.

Except those who think Devro weak.

Tundavik couldn't blame them. Had he found out someone imprisoned Hurvir, he would have laughed with his men about the weak king. But his duty was to protect Devro. *Ide and one with no ear. His left ear.* He had to make a note of anyone who might hurt the king.

After he made his rounds, he went to his tent, but not inside. Instead, he watched the woods. *Swallowood.* They had passed Vigurawood two moons ago. The last forest in the Kinglands. It had lighter trees than the forests of the Woodlands. His home had dark sentinels that masked the day and blended with the night. *At least the men shouldn't complain about the heat.*

"Excited to be back?" Pollard unclipped his white cloak and handed it off to a squire. "When was the last time you were in Ritaeum?"

When I held their bloodied and broken bodies, Tundavik thought. "A long time ago. I'm sure a lot has changed."

"I expect you'll be the first to wake tomorrow. To lead us into the Woodlands."

"It hasn't been my home for many years. I'll be lucky to know my way around the paths and twisted trees."

"Well, you should be happy," Pollard said as he brushed a hand through his sweaty curls. "I know I'll be happy when we return to Whitehall. I hope this place brings you peace, or anger if that's what you need." He ducked into his tent.

Tundavik hoped for nothing before turning to his tent. Glem had polished his armor and oiled his blade, even made his bed. "In case of battle." He said as Tundavik entered.

"I would hope the neutral Woodlands would let us through." Tundavik said, though the duchy couldn't stay neutral any longer, not with Devro's army marching. He just hoped the duke joined their side. If not, then they would have to take it from Lord Valles.

"I prayed for no more fighting for a while," Glem said. "The siege was already enough for me, but leaving would make my father right, and we don't want that. Though my prayers may go unanswered. Sometimes I think the Four don't hear me. I prayed Vigur would be easy and …" he pulled up his loose shirt revealing a long scar, "… look how the gods rewarded me."

Tundavik stretched his aching neck and said, "Men make war, not gods. No wonder they didn't listen."

Glem lowered his shirt. "Would you like me to stay here for the night?"

"I'm sure there's some girl following who wants you in her bed. Who doesn't want to fuck a hardened warrior?" He laughed. "I got rid of all the whores in Sayer's River just to find out Yvanne has allowed her men to fuck their way south." He just shrugged. "Hope you have enough coin."

"Only a silver."

Tundavik chuckled. "That will be enough, especially during a war." Once Glem left Tundavik stripped off the day's clothes. They stank of sweat and smoke and horseshit. Tomorrow he would have them washed with lemon water, if Glem could find some.

Lying on his hard mat, he stroked his graying beard, pieces of dried skin falling out. *What will tomorrow bring? More war or peaceful passage? Grief.* It wasn't a question. He knew what would happen. He stopped with his beard as he thought of his family. *All dead. Killed by the man I swore my allegiance to.* Tundavik didn't sleep that night. He couldn't risk the dreams that frequented him. The death and destruction. The stains on the walls and floors. Wood soggy with blood. His two children.

He stood once the morning horn woke the army.

The camp was being disassembled at a slow pace. *The men are tired. Another battle won't go well for us.* They were granted safe passage through the Kinglands from Vigur as part of Ultiir's deal. Tundavik didn't think it would actually happen, especially once Ultiir found Rila de'Tro's corpse, but it had to be done.

He saw Yvanne with her brothers, guards, and her handmaid. They helped her into a wagon and fed her only the best, which was bread made from barley. *Better than most of the men.* Tundavik also saw Devro emerge from a greater tent than Yvanne's white. It was packed away all this time until the king joined. Adorned with owls on the brown cloth, gold-like stitching lined the folds, the inside covered with rugs and tapestries as far away as Somertin; a gift from the wealthy of Storyah.

Devro laughed a little with Gordo, though it looked forced. Pollard rode on his horse, making sure the weapons were stored properly. Mar was in the rear, packing the food. Far back were the followers. *Whores and merchants, no one of use. Let us hope they disappear in the trees.*

Glem brought Tundavik's horse, Bera. Tundavik gave Glem yesterday's clothes before shuffling onto the saddle. He wore mail today over leather garments. His plate would be kept safely in the queen's wagon. *There will be no battle today.* He couldn't have another. He couldn't risk driving the army away and surrendering to Lord Valles and then Ultiir. Not after getting away from Vigur safely.

Mar rode on Brun's back to Tundavik's side. "Everything is ready as far as I can tell." He turned back. "Will you ride with the king today?"

Tundavik looked at Devro, who mounted a bay stallion. "If he wants, but he hasn't left his wife and her brothers since coming back. He needs to be out in front, though. He needs the men to see him as a commander."

"I try to talk to him every chance I get, even though you keep me busy."

Tundavik leaned over and patted Mar's back with a laugh. "It's because I trust you."

"Are there people here you don't trust?" Mar asked.

Tundavik couldn't tell if Mar actually cared or not. He looked through the trees at the lords and soldiers they had amassed on their marches. The Asaramen and the Flewthmen kept separate. Lord Aimora Dore and Lord Cul joked about the peaks. Lord Toware and Lord Furrow spoke with Commander Wright about Lady Ceala. Yvanne's brothers inspected sacks and tightened ropes. There were hundreds. At least one of them had to wish ill on Devro, and it was Tundavik's job to figure out who.

"Have you heard the men talking?" Tundavik asked.

Mar shook his head with a raised lip. "Nothing important. Yes, some think Toware's handling of the deserters was a little much, but you can't please everyone." The knight shrugged. "Now that we're actually moving again and finding supplies in these little towns, it helps too. More food to eat."

"That won't last though. We may find a thousand pounds of salted pork in Ritaeum, but sooner rather than later the men will eat it all and starve again. I don't want to sic Lord Toware on anymore of them."

"Do you regret that?" Mar asked as they kicked their horses and moved to the front of the company. "I heard it was a bloody mess. Almost sorry I didn't get to see it with Toware always talking up his men and all."

"You didn't want to," Tundavik said with a frown. "But at least everyone is under control."

"So what's the plan? Ritaeum then what?"

Tundavik twirled hair from his beard. The plan he and Yvanne had come up with was barely a plan at all. "We get Lord Valles on our side, or his lords at least. We seem to have the Awarites' help, and the Rowai took back Redington. If we all come together, we can march back on the Kinglands and end this."

"If?" Mar paused. "And if they don't all come to our aid?"

Tundavik tossed his hands up. "I'm not sure."

Mar bounced atop Brun as they rode over dried creek beds and pebbles. "Good to know you're leading us at the moment. Always have an idea," he said with a snicker. "And when Lord Valles stays neutral? Or worse, joins Ultiir?"

"He won't," Tundavik said as he looked over the hordes of men behind him. "At the moment we have the advantage. The Asaramen, the Flewthmen. The Eastlands are at war within themselves. Ultiir's fleet was decimated in Storyah. Lord Valles has to join us, or he risks death."

"Would you raze Ritaeum?"

Tundavik looked at the trees that surrounded him. Visions of them aflame popped into his head, and he knew the woman from his dreams would be waiting. "If I have to."

Horns blared, and they were off. Thousands of armed men, cooking wenches and whores, and lords and ladies descended on the tree gates of the Woodlands.

Raimund

Nostara looked through the trees. Yellow eyes stared back at them. The dragon was watching, his breath ruffling leaves. "If you do not ride on the back of Nardal, then you cannot save your world. It is the only way. The Elders have searched for centuries for another way to no avail. If Ryobas of old did it, then so shall you."

Raimund rubbed his eyes. They wanted to fall out of their sockets. "So I have to forgive a monster?"

"You can forgive or you can hold your grudge. As long as you join as one, it makes no difference." The yellow eyes of the dragon slowly blinked. A puff of smoke filled the air and made the pools hazy. "Now," Nostara said, "I will wait here while. Go."

"Killed Sile though," Raimund said out loud toward the direction of this *Nardal*. He'd rather find Bera and ride with her to stop the end of the world. *If only I had more say in this prophecy.* Raimund scratched his palms. He wanted to see the fire escape them like they did when he rescued Potter. Maybe if he had been thinking clearly. then Sile would be alive. But then he wouldn't be Ryobas.

Maybe everything was happening like it was supposed to

be. Perhaps his parents had to die to push him to the pits and to Sir Mar. All of that to send him south to become a knight and protect Devro, the war and his failure in Riverton causing his capture. Maybe all the death in his life was for a bigger purpose. If a few deaths weighed on his conscience for the rest of his life, then it was a small price to pay to keep millions alive. "Wonder if the old Ryobas thought like this?"

The dragon hummed. A low rumble shook the ground, and Raimund sighed. "I'm supposed to forgive you or something." He told the dragon as he pushed through the trees. The purple light was like a sunrise in the darkness of night. "If you could talk, that would make it so much easier." The dragon's throat shook in the light, and he let out a small groan or roar or something. "You should've burned me on the mountaintop," Raimund said. "You should've killed me like Sile. Things would be easier. My friends wouldn't be wondering where I am. I just know Mar is already plotting how he's going to look for me." Raimund chuckled. "And when he finds me, he'll call me a 'dumb cunt' and we'll laugh about all our misadventures. That is, if he's alive." Raimund kicked the ground. In the night, the grass was blacker than the dragon. "Why couldn't you've taken me to Viguran? Why is this my destiny? I'd much prefer my destiny to be sitting at some tavern hearing about Devro jousting and Mar drinking."

Raimund clasped his hands together. His fingers were warm, but he couldn't make a flame. "But I am Ryobas. You are Nardal. Somehow I'm supposed to ride upon your back and destroy … whatever she said. I'd rather chop your head off and throw it in one of these pools." The dragon blinked, and when his eyelids closed, it grew even darker. The monster's eyes were as bright as faraway stars. They stared at Raimund. *Is this what Sile saw before she died? Was it your eyes or your fire?*

"And no matter how many times you save me, or try to protect me, or carry me on your back, I won't be able to forget what happened. Sile was a good person. She was strong. She had been alone for so long, and I wanted to send her back to her family. You took that from her. You took it from Yvanne." Raimund took a step back, surprised to feel tears in his eyes. "I couldn't save her. And now that I'm so far away, I can't save Devro. I can't save Mar. Yvanne and Tundavik and everyone else on my side could die. But I'm supposed to be okay with that. I'm supposed to let them all die so I can save the world."

You are Ryobas reborn, echoed in his head.

"Am I wrong to believe her?" Raimund asked the dragon. The beast curled on the ground, sinking into the dirt. "Nostara isn't even human. Isn't an elf. I've never seen … things like this before." The dragon's eyes drifted to sleep like this was the most boring thing he's heard. Raimund walked over the dark beast and stopped in front of his nostrils. Warm smoke escaped them. Raimund's hair and beard blew back. He didn't think, though. He kicked the dragon on the snout.

The dragon roared and lifted his head. It was as if a house were floating above Raimund, waiting to crash on him. Red flames escaped the dragon's teeth as he bared them. His four legs brought him back as his wings flapped. Raimund fell to the ground from the force. Trees toppled and dirt flew. "Finally," Raimund said to himself. He wanted nothing more than to be done with this nonsense. If no one could take him back to Viguran, then what was the point of living any longer?

But the dragon didn't kill him. The beast's shadowed face fell, but didn't crush Raimund. They stared into each other's eyes. Raimund didn't feel like he was in shadows any longer. The monster's yellow eyes shone on him. Raimund felt like the dragon was looking into his soul. But Raimund was doing the same. For some reason, the dragon looked sad. It might've been his imagination, but the beast had low eyes. They weren't as menacing up close. Just like back on the mountain, Raimund couldn't stop himself. His bare hand found the dragon's face. The scales were both prickling and soft. Hard and smooth. Underneath them was a warmth that Raimund had never felt before. All the time he spent on the back of the dragon, never did he really *feel* him.

Raimund couldn't stop his tears from flowing now, the ground around him wet. "Why did you kill Sile? There was no reason. She was good. Good. And you killed her."

The dragon lifted his head and breathed fire into the night sky. Reds and oranges and blues all swirled toward the stars. Raimund wanted to crawl into the fire. Collect the heat. But he didn't need to. His face burned red, but it didn't hurt. He could feel the sadness he saw in the dragon's eyes as well. A life of misery. Hiding and being hunted. Deceived and betrayed. Then something else blossomed from Raimund's chest. When the dragon finished breathing fire, Raimund felt acceptance. Understanding. Friendship.

He felt they were one.

The dragon backed farther away. His tail flicked behind

him as he lay back down. Raimund stood and brushed dirt and drool from his clothes. "I ..." Just a few moments ago he didn't want to say it, but now he understood. At least, he thought he did. "I forgive you now."

The beast did nothing. He didn't even acknowledge the words. But Raimund could feel a shift in his mood, inside himself. He could feel that the dragon was happy. Unburdened. He nodded at the dragon and went toward the pools.

"Are you one?" Nostara asked when he found her.

Raimund shrugged his head, not answering her, but more because he understood nothing. "I think so."

Nostara walked to a pool before standing still as it rippled. A thousand images of destruction and blood and death filled Raimund's eyes. He leaned closer to the blue light, as if in a trance. He couldn't stop himself as a voice said, *"Abhai senn,"* over and over again.

That's when he fell into the pool.

Yvanne

Urses had lied to her. Led her on. Betrayed her. Yvanne had been dumbfounded since she and the hundreds at her back marched out of Vigur and across the Kinglands. *I was a fool to trust him,* she thought as Jacka gathered her things around her. *Some cunning lord from Vigur who brings a head in a sack—and I trust him. Fool. Stupid. Stupid girl.* Jacka carefully handed a warm bowl of stew to Yvanne. It was venison. Lord Cul and his remaining warriors were lucky on the hunt yesterday.

"What a fool," Yvanne muttered about herself as she chewed a bit of meat.

"Pardon me, Your Grace?" Jacka said.

"How is anyone to trust my judgment now? Why would any lord respect me when I let a spy into my inner circle?" She found a stump to sit on while her tent was being taken down. They would begin their march anew that day. Tundavik would lead. Yvanne would follow with Devro close by. *Even he shouldn't trust me anymore.*

"We all make mistakes; you mustn't dwell on them," Jacka said. "Too much stress is bad for the baby anyhow."

Yvanne nodded while she rubbed her eyes. The small fires that gave the dark forest eyes were being culled. As the sun rose in the east, the moon was still in the sky. When her mother left, Yvanne would look at the night sky, finding comfort in the fact that they saw the same moon.

They were far from Vigur now, even farther from Whitehall. *Has Cada taken well to leadership?* Then she thought of Helge. *Has the old doma cried herself to sleep? To death?* She would pray for Helge to still be alive by the time Yvanne returned, but the Four would not answer. *They never have.*

She was so angry with herself for her mistrust that she blamed the gods, Helge, her father. Anyone who could've told her no. Who could've taught her how to lead. Who to trust and who to jail.

"I've never been this far south before." Jacka said. "I never imagined a land without snow and mountains." She picked at her nails. "And you, Your Grace?"

Yvanne glanced around the deep forest. At the dark pines that swallowed you, and the great canopies that made day almost night. She knew Jacka was trying to clear her mind, but Yvanne didn't want to speak. She wanted to march back to Vigur and take Urses' head from his shoulders. But that wasn't an option. "My mother liked to visit Ealna. She would take Pollard and me when we were young. The Woodlands always frightened me." So far, they haven't scared her. *Will that change as I go deeper?*

Her handmaid smiled. "I hope it brings good memories," then noticed something. "It seems His Grace is on the move."

Yvanne followed her handmaid's eyes and saw Devro emerging from his tent just to the side of Yvanne's own. She had given Gordo and Diero the job of protecting him, along with Sir Rickart. Some squires and helpers moved toward the tent and began breaking it down.

"How has His Grace been since returning?" Jacka asked. Sweat had bound her long black hair together. And it was merely morning.

"Distant." Yvanne didn't want to lie to her handmaid, one of the few people she could trust … maybe. "I am giving him time to feel like himself again. Months in a dungeon cannot've been good." Devro was alone, her brothers behind him, as a squire handed him some stew. He was muttering to himself. Always muttering. "I do wonder what he whispers about."

"If I may, why don't you ask him?"

Yvanne laughed but agreed. If Devro was having trouble adjusting back to his role as king, then maybe she should help. "Will you find Lady Lolly and ask her to find some fans for the wagon? This heat will only get worse."

Jacka nodded before helping Yvanne to her feet. She hated walking now. She hated most things about life now. The babe took all her energy, made her sore and achy and tired. Any day now he would be out of her, and she could return to normal. *Unless Devro wants another right away.* The thought was terrifying, but it was her duty as his wife and queen. Her body used only to give birth. *Maybe I should've left him in the dungeon,* she thought for a moment before cursing at herself for thinking such a thing.

"Your Grace," Jacka said before leaving. "I should tell you I've heard horrid things in camp. I don't want you to be caught by surprise if you catch wind."

"What is it?"

Her handmaid took a breath. "Some say you have fallen out of love with the king. They say you're all dried out and won't … won't *fuck* the king until you get a strong man in bed. Some men are hoping to court you."

"I am happily married." She said dryly, not wanting to hear gossip among soldiers. "If you hear words like this, tell Gordo or Diero or Lord Aimora. They will handle the men."

Jacka nodded but continued. "Others say the baby is not his. That you went to bed with Pollard while the king was imprisoned. They say—"

"I do not care what they say," Yvanne said. "Don't let these rumors upset you, because they certainly won't upset me." She placed a hand on Jacka's cheek, her eyes low. "Go find Lady Lolly."

"Yes, Your Grace."

Yvanne wobbled on sore feet and swollen ankles to Devro and her brothers. Devro was wearing a new iron crown with an owl as the head ornament, and a bear on the back. "The crown looks better than I thought," she said to Devro as she kissed Gordo and Diero's cheeks.

He took it off. "I think it's cutting me," he said with no emotion in his voice. His face was blank. Nothing was on it. Yvanne had no idea what he was thinking. Devro picked at his fingers. "Gordo is nice. Diero as well. They make good company," he said without a smile. "Lady Lolly waved at me once before disappearing into your tent. I didn't even know your siblings had come."

"A lot has changed in the months you were gone." She took his hand and smiled as best she could. She wanted him to be back to the way he was the day he rode into Whitehall. Before all the warring and death.

He placed a hand on her belly after a slight hesitation,

and their baby kicked. "I know," he said. "You led an army south. Tundavik from the east. I thought Ultiir was going to parade me around the capital before executing me. Taking my head like Gofrei." Devro looked past Yvanne and said, "Yes, you did." He turned back to her before saying, "I'm excited for my heir to come. The dungeon gave me a lot of time to think."

"And I cannot wait for you to raise him. You'll be a wonderful father, Devro." She touched his cheek. "You've seen all the things not to do."

"Then the next will come, then more, and the castle will be overrun." He laughed, but his eyes were low, his blinking slow. "Eventually the castle will be overrun ..."

Yvanne didn't want to think about other children while one was still inside her. "And I will love every minute. Better to have multiple heirs to keep luck on our side. I'm sure the de'Tro dynasty will last for thousands of more years. The history books will talk about how you vanquished the man who stole your throne. Won't that be exciting?"

"Yes," Devro said before his eyes seemed to glaze over. "Happy?" He didn't say to her.

Yvanne looked around, but there was no one but her. He was speaking to no one. Nothing. Not even a tree. "Devro," she clasped his hand on her belly, "are you feeling alright? It must be so confusing coming back to an army."

Devro's eyes came back to her, and a smile came to his lips. "I'm fine. But it is a lot. I forgot how it felt to have so many people following you, looking to you for guidance. How did you do it?"

A blue jay sang in the trees above, jumping from limb

to limb. "It wasn't easy, but I had help." She tightened her grip on his fingers. "As do you. I don't want you to think you cannot talk to me or Lord Vandes or Aimora Dore or anyone else. We're all here to serve you."

He took his hand back and stretched his fingers. "I listened to Urses once," he said. The blue jay went silent as if it were listening to them. "Now I wonder how much he led me astray." Devro looked over his shoulder as if someone were speaking from behind. But there was no one. "We'll see," he said.

Yvanne gave a silent sigh. "Sometimes we make mistakes. But now we can learn from them and not trust everyone we see. It will make us stronger in the long term." Lord Vandes and Pollard and Mar rode by on their horses as they made their way to the front of the train of people. "We'll be leaving soon. Are you ready to take Ritaeum?"

"We'll see," Devro said, but Yvanne didn't know if he was talking to her or something else. "I don't want you or anyone else I care about to get hurt. Your brothers told me of Ed the Loon. I don't want you to lose anyone else."

"It is the price we pay for war." Yvanne said. "Ed knew the risks, and he died valiantly, fighting to free his king. Any of the other fighters would relish in that sort of death."

Devro shrugged as he said, "Death is worse than any realize."

"And how would you know that, my king?"

"I should get ready to leave," Devro said, then stood. "I'll see you when Tundavik allows our first stop."

Devro didn't wait for Yvanne to say anything or kiss him goodbye. He disappeared with Sir Rickart to get his new horse ready to ride.

"I've brought the fans," Lady Lolly appeared with two squires who held fronds, "and the special gift I've been telling you about." She motioned to a woman bringing up the rear. She had a small babe at her large breasts. "It was easier than I suspected with the train following us."

Yvanne brushed off her dress as she walked away from where she and Devro had been talking. "And who might this be?"

"Your wet nurse. Like I've been saying, a queen cannot feed her baby and rule with her husband at the same time." Lolly touched the woman's breasts. "Full as a well after a rain."

Yvanne had forgotten she had asked her sister to find a wet nurse. "How are you, my lady?"

"Very well." The woman did a haphazard curtsy while trying not to drop the babe.

"Not a lady." Lolly said. "She came from the followers' camp. Maliz is her name. I believe some knights were passing her around the other day. And I don't believe in the dakens' silly suspicions about a mother's milk deciding whether a child will become a whore or ruler." She felt Yvanne's stomach. "Is the baby alright?"

"Yes, he's fine."

Lady Lolly and Maliz climbed into the wagon after Lolly insisted Yvanne feel the woman's breasts. They were fuller than her own. *At least you'll be well fed,* she told her child.

Yvanne looked forward and found Pollard's white helm over the hundreds and hundreds of men and women and squires and servants. The van was so dangerous, but her brother wished to fight once more. When she fell into the seat in the wagon, taking up more room than normal with her pregnancy, she rubbed her belly and thought, *Once you're out of me, I will send you to Whitehall with Maliz. Cada will keep you safe. You will learn of your ancestors and how to rule.* But it was Devro the child had to impress.

Bertin

The city and the brothel were days behind them as they made their way into the forest. Bertin didn't know what to expect in Sruhq. Would enormous bats swoop down and draw blood? Perhaps a dragon would appear and burn the forest in a rampage, like the elves believed happened before. The moment he stepped into the dark wood, he imagined the most dangerous creatures and horrifying deaths. His eyes pecked out, skin peeled off, head pulled apart, so far none of it had come true.

Instead, the woods were peaceful. The dark, towering trees that reigned over the land scattered the sunlight into dancing glimmers. Wildflowers of every color and more marched across the bright green grass. Nothing could beat the beauty of the forest. Bertin hadn't felt so much peace in so long, maybe never. The world seemed to stop the deeper they went.

But Torlem and Barhi abhorred the wood. They didn't see beauty or peace; they saw a grotesque wood inhabited by vile creatures. The forest was stolen and changed into something it was not. "The Rainvealandians ruled this land for a thousand years, ever since the landing," Torlem had told him, "and the maggots crawled from the depths of the dirt to take it from us." Bertin had heard all the stories as the day dragged on. Some long-dead emperor named Ami Maka who first traversed the forest. The rush of mites to chop the timber. The great shipbuilding campaign of Emperor Yemi Miçi to counter the naval might of Delerous. Bertin tuned out most of the details to focus on the world around him.

He watched every bird in great detail, wondering if they were normal or some sort of monster. The screams of beasts and animals didn't scare him but made him curious. He wanted to know what they were, what color skin, eye shape, number of teeth. If they would attack him. Hurt him like all the ghosts from before. Torlem made sure Bertin wouldn't get that chance. If so much as an insect moved the wrong way, the mites would kill it. "How do you know what will hurt us?" Bertin asked after they caught a boar.

"We don't." Torlem shrugged. "Anything that moves here deserves to die."

Bertin didn't ask another question about the creatures. He kept his curiosity to himself, making up any answer he wished. The robin that nested near wasn't actually a robin; instead, it was a spy for a woodland king. The king sent birds to get reports of any danger in his kingdom, and the three had come to kill the creatures. He hoped that none of his stories were true. He needed Torlem and Barhi to take him to Bardekan. *As long as the elves don't find us first, we should make it just fine,* he told himself.

He went to sleep dreaming of elves.

The night ended quicker than normal. Rain sprinkled through the canopy and soaked into his clothes. The water felt as if someone were touching him, rubbing his torn and scarred back.

He darted up and swung his dagger, slicing through a thick skin. As his eyes adjusted, he saw what had been cut. One of the sentinels of the wood. A majestic tree that made castles seem small. No one was there. Torlem and Barhi slept on the other side of the fire. Bertin dropped his dagger and scratched his stump. "So much for peace," he told himself. He'd rather be back in Ansehar for the night and wait for the sun to come back. The trees sang songs of horror with howls and screeches as the chorus. He didn't sleep as darkness held its grip. He poked and prodded at the fire to keep it going as small droplets of rain fell.

Torlem seemed surprised to see Bertin awake. He tossed a leg of lamb sold to him by a merchant in Ansehar. "Cooler here than elsewhere in the south. Once I was down in the Jorbstah Steppe during the summer. It was horrid and humid and painful. I'm still not sure how anyone can live there, much less with millions of others."

"It was dreadful even in spring," Bertin said as he remembered the elves that took him across the steppe, and how they all died. "The mountains were nice, though." Bertin drooled over the lamb. "Much nicer than the Delerous."

Torlem ripped at the meat and took a swig of water before passing the flagon to Bertin. "Why were the elves taking you to Anha Jorbstah? Why go through all that trouble of carrying you over mountains and through deserts? You seem unimportant to me." Torlem scanned Bertin from head to toe. "Maybe you're a better liar than I thought."

"Not me." Bertin croaked. He took a drink to pass the time. How would he answer this? At first Torlem didn't care, but Bertin knew eventually he would ask. "I told you

I was their prisoner. There weren't many cells in Lisan Biresdea."

"Why not kill you?" Torlem picked his teeth. "Why remove a finger and not your head?"

Bertin gulped as he thought of any lie. He just needed one—a good one. "We all have our gods. I have the Four, you the Ancient One, the northmen have their vatya, even the elves have a god. But their god is a dragon, and the beast demands a sacrifice." He stared at his stump of a finger, feeling a tingle that could never be scratched. "They just wanted to teach me a lessen."

"And did they?"

Bertin didn't answer as there was a movement behind them, but it was just Barhi. "Shouldn't you two be sleeping?" they asked. "If we run into any elves out here, you better not be tired. I won't save you both."

"I guess you're right," Torlem said before he slipped back to sleep. Bertin dropped his shoulders, relieved that he believed the story and didn't take out his hooked blade.

***

Barhi ate very little as Bertin and Torlem took down their small camp. They all left just as the horror turned back to peace. Torlem led them through the dark day as the trees blocked the sun. He carried his sword always, Barhi too. Bertin kept his dagger away, afraid of stabbing himself or another tree. As they went on, a beautiful voice rang out. It sang a sweet-sounding song in a different tongue. It reminded Bertin of the elven language but had a different rhythm. "Shall we go see?" Bertin had asked.

Barhi laughed and looked back. "They're trying to lure us in; don't fall for it."

Torlem agreed. "If we go, whatever the monster is will melt our faces."

"I thought you hunted these things?" Bertin asked.

"We do not hunt anything that gambles with dark magic," Barhi said as they scratched their chin. "It is a forbidden art and not one we wish to be canvases of."

So they went on, ignoring any beautiful song or note. The forest grew brighter as noon arrived. They fed themselves on bread and finished whatever was left from Ansehar. Now they would have to hunt their own food. Bertin was first. He knew it was a test of his strength. They sent him off into the depths of the woods to bring back meat. "We will all meet here as the light fades." Torlem said. "Do not die fighting a squirrel." Bertin prayed to the Ancient One to drop a boar out of the sky, but the god didn't listen.

In Rowan, a group of knights would set out once a year with his father. They would roam the northern reaches of the kingdom, where the red-leafed trees grew, until coming back with boar and deer aplenty. The hunts would feed the entire palace for months. But Bertin never went along. He would sneak away to Gereduss to accompany his cousin. He never liked the smell and sight of the hunt, something his father scorned him for.

Bertin was taught neither tracking skills nor how to skin an animal. No one showed him how to drain blood or where to cut. "It's important you learn this," Blis would explain. "Someday you will be in charge of the royal hunt. It's best for your father to teach you when he's young and spry." Now his father was dead.

Perhaps the Ancient One did answer Bertin's prayers, either that or he was lucky. A well-defined pig rut caught his eye near a lowly creek. He relieved himself, drank some water, and looked for more prints. He counted four but no more. It wasn't until squeals pierced the tranquil place that he knew where the wild boar would be.

Crossing the creek bed, he saw tufts of fur along the great oaks. Even though he didn't know how to hunt, he took the fur as a sign to follow. He kicked through brush and leaped over fallen trees, wondering what had knocked the lords of the wood down. The squealing had stopped after he cracked branches with his steps. He rubbed his eyes trying to figure out what to do.

Bending over, he picked up the many sticks and threw them around the forest. He threw one at a tree, another into a thick bed of shrubs, then one into the leaves. There was no sound. He wanted to curse and be done. A king needed huntsmen and dogs to find food, not sticks, though Kelltar was able to find game in the middle of nowhere. *I won't let that elf beat me.* He grabbed a broken branch and hurled in anger. It flew into the air, bounced around branches and leaves, and fell with a thump.

Squeals rang out near a hollow trunk. Bertin wasn't prepared for the rush of black fur. Large boars bearing tusks raced past him. He dodged them and turned back to the trunk. High-pitched squeals let loose. He saw small boars running through the thicket that made the floor. He didn't think. This would be his only chance.

He jumped for one but missed and slid across the ground. Green stained his tunic as he lunged for another, again missing. The piglets were confused as they ran in giant circles, or they were taunting him. It would be even more embarrassing if he weren't able to catch a baby pig. He wondered what his father would say, what Blis would advise, how his sister would laugh. Aveline would be able to do it. She could do everything Bertin couldn't.

He grabbed his dagger and waited. The baby raced near his legs. He positioned himself with a wide stance. The boars ran under trees and leaped over branches. The dagger almost slipped from his sweaty hand, but he held steady. Finally, a piglet charged directly at him. As it crossed under his legs, Bertin grabbed it and wrangled it as it squirmed. He gripped his dagger and slid the blade across the boar's throat. It lurched and gave one last squeal.

Bertin dropped it and spat vomit. The blood had mixed with the grass on his tunic, staining it a dark brown like the trees. He used a leaf to clean his dagger and picked up the boar. The mother had fled as well as the other piglets. He could hear faraway squeals.

He held his nose with one hand and the boar with the other. The stench of iron oozed from the baby. Hopefully, Torlem and Barhi would clean it for him. Bertin passed over the creek once more, washing his hands of the blood, before moving to the meeting spot. No one was waiting for him; he was alone with a dead boar.

Then he heard more singing. The sweetest song he had ever heard. And his mind entered a trance as he moved through the trees.

Flora

What is the meaning of this?" Lord Poden Bruce shouted from atop his steps.

Flora stood with Edmond and Marbert at her side, behind her the dozen men who came along, all ready in their armor. "Peace has failed," Flora said, "so I have taken a drastic option. I will not let you kill my father and bring ruin to Storyah."

Poden laughed, grabbing his belly as it shook. "I'm not sure if you know this, my dear lady, but you are in enemy territory. You are outnumbered." The ground rumbled, and just outside the city, a dozen horses were riding forth. "Ahh, look who it is," Poden smiled. "Luk has returned from his raid in Lonydd. I'm sure he'll be happy to see his father surrounded by men from the capital."

"Father," Luk jumped from his black gelding and slipped off riding gloves as he walked to the castle. His eyes scanned the crowd of men-at-arms, and his mouth twisted in disgust. "What's happening? Some rabble-rousers?"

"Just some girl who thinks herself strong," Poden laughed again. "I'm glad you made it back." Poden and Luk embraced. Flora tapped her foot as she waited for the reunion to be over. But they were ignoring her and the armed guards. "How was Lonydd? Any trouble from the people?"

"Not with Lord Tipper gone." Luk brushed his black hair from his eyes. "The people let me do whatever I wanted to them. A few of the men might even have bastards coming along."

"Lord Poden," Flora said.

"Well, hopefully the bastards don't cause any problems for them. We've seen now how dangerous a bastard can be."

"Poden," Flora said again. She bit her lip as her face reddened.

Luk waved that away. "The difference being we won't let a bastard claim what isn't his. We'll drown them in the river before they get old enough to do that." Father and son laughed together. Ignored together. Make her look like a fool together.

"Lord Poden Bruce, I will not ask again." This time she shouted. Luk slowly turned with smugness on his face. His eyes wide and a frown forming. Poden only smirked. "Listen to me, surrender to me, or face my men."

Poden flung his head around. "We don't have time for this. Now that Luk is back, we are going to ride to Storyah and demand the same of your father. If he doesn't listen, then I hope you already said goodbye to him."

Luk came closer to Flora, looking like he had just smelled a dead cat. "I commend you, but I could single-handedly stop your men and not even break a sweat." He turned to face his father, his back to Flora and her guards. "What happened while I was away? Weren't you leading the fight to Floodp—"

Luk's arm was twisted and Marbert brought him to the ground with a dagger at his throat. Poden and the men of River Watch gasped. Any commoners outside were scurrying away. "Lord Poden," Marbert said as he held Luk, "you will listen to the lady of Woodrun."

"Please," Luk cried, "let me go."

"Tell your men to stop advancing," Edmond added as the men on horseback were slowly making their way with weapons drawn.

"Stop," Luk said in a shrill voice. He sounded like a scared boy even though he was older than Flora. "Don't come any closer." His men froze. "Father, listen to her. Do whatever. Don't let me die like this."

Poden put his hands up to calm the situation. "Sir Marbert, you are making a grave mistake. Remember, I have scores more men than you."

"If they fight anything like Luk here, then I'll be fine," Marbert chuckled as he tightened his grip on the heir to River Watch.

"How about," Flora said, "we go into your castle and talk some more. This doesn't have to end in violence. But with Luk in my grasp, I hope you are more receptive to my offers."

Poden's eyes were low, his skin was pale, his brow wrinkled in frustration. "Come inside."

Flora started walking, but a hand found hers. Sir Edmond said, "Let me come with you, my lady. This lord cannot be trusted."

"I'll be fine, thank you for your concern. Marbert," Flora looked at the knight, who wasn't even sweating as he constrained the lord's son, "keep little Luk here until I return. If I'm not back by noon, then kill him." Marbert nodded while Luk whimpered.

Flora went inside the castle again, Sir Len's eyes on her as she walked with Poden up the stairs once more. "We do this often," she said.

"And yet it always ends the same," Poden said in a low voice. "Perhaps this time will be different?" Flora did nothing but look forward. She knew what Poden Bruce wanted. She had always known. Even as a child, his eyes always found themselves on her. Flora took a large gulp as she ascended the stairs.

Thud. Thud.

"The mice are worse, it seems." Flora said.

Poden wiped the corner of his mouth. "The rains have pushed them in. Eventually I'll get my ratcatcher on it." *Knock, knock, knock.*

They turned a corner, a Flora bumped into a young serving lady. "Excuse me," the serving girl said as her face turned red. "I must be careful."

"Get," Poden spat.

The girl fluttered down the stairs. She had come from a dark hallway with steps leading to a lonely door. Poden pushed Flora past it.

When Flora entered Poden's room, she went to the window. It was her turn to overlook River Watch. Luk still wrangled below, but Sir Marbert was too strong for him. Lord Poden's men were spitting and cursing as they watched Flora's guards. *I don't want a fight,* she told the Four and the Many, *but I will do what I must.*

"My husband is involved, isn't he?" Flora said without turning away from the window. The glass was sweating from the heat outside. *Thud.*

"You think little of your husband, do you?" Poden said as he took a sip from a goblet. "Others tell me Lord Barnet is an honorable man. Besides, why would he want to kill your father? His child's grandfather?"

"He sent me away to deal with your attacks, but he was involved in the planning. He had you attack Floodpan so he could send me away from Storyah." Flora's eyes were filling with tears. Even if she didn't love Barnet, hadn't loved him in a decade, he was betraying her. Betraying their daughter. "Does he want to split the Flewthlands with you? Does he want it all to himself? He might just be using you," Flora finally turned. The tears fell down her face, dropping onto her shoes. "Did you think of that?"

Thud.

Poden cleared his throat and drank more. "Would you like some?" Flora said nothing, instead, just letting the tears fall. "If it helps, Barnet never told me to kill you. He didn't say what to do with you. So I figured I would relieve some of the stress by being with you." He went closer, setting down his drink, the red liquid sloshing. There was a splatter on the other side of the room. Flora couldn't tell what it was, but it came with a *thud* above them. "I know the best way to end this fighting, though." Sticky fingers brushed against her cheek, wiping the tears away. "Be with me, and I can sic my men of River Watch on your husband. We can save your father."

Flora cried on his shoulder. He smelled of death. Like the rotting corpses after Ultiir's men attacked the beach in Storyah. "I should freshen up. I don't want to get tears all over you."

"I like tears," Poden said with a wicked smile.

Flora didn't stay, though. She walked over the splatter and tried to make out what it was. All she saw was a mix of black and red. Once she was outside the room, she wiped her eyes and tiptoed over to the steps that led up. She wouldn't be able to leave with Sir Len downstairs, but she could see what Poden was hiding. See what was making the *thud thud* sound.

To her surprise, the door was unlocked. Though her sweaty hands had a hard time gripping the metal knob. She said a silent prayer and pushed the door open as quietly as she could. Afraid she would see a horde of rats or a ghost or something worse.

But what she saw was straight out of a nightmare.

She saw a foot tapping against the ground. *Thud, thud, knock, thud.* Blood was dripping down a toe and leaking through the ceiling. As her eyes followed the leg up to the torso, she realized who she was looking at. It was Poden's wife. Her body was a mess of pipes going in and out of her skin, red blood trickling through to vials. Chalices and goblets sitting near.

Flora wanted to vomit, to scream and hide, to run to her guards or her father or even her husband. Poden's wife was mostly bone, her skin so translucent Flora could see her inner organs. She was so frail and skinny that her tapping foot seemed to hold a mountain. *Thud thud.* Flora took a step closer, the smell attacking her nose. It was as if she had dug up a mass grave. Flies and maggots swirled and crawled all over the wife's body.

She took a breath and decided she had to help. There was nothing else on her mind but helping the dying woman.

"Stop," a scared voice came from behind. It was the serving girl. She had come back with another vial. "Please do not touch the Lady Willa. You might kill her."

"What is this?" Flora said. The tears had come and gone. Now her eyes were fire. *If only I had a sword to cut them all down,* she thought.

"Lord Poden …" the girl hesitated before continuing. "He wishes for the visions. He speaks with the gods, but he can only do that if he … if he drinks her blood."

Knock, knock.

Flora kept her vomit down as she remembered Poden drinking a red liquid. "Why? Why would you help him? Why would he do this to his wife?" Flora wished she could yell, but if Poden found out, then he might never let her leave.

"The Four came to him one night, he told me. They wished to speak with him, but they needed a sacrifice. He said the gods were green," the serving girl giggled. "I wish I could see the gods."

"This is awful," Flora said. "This is an affront to the gods. They would never allow this."

"But they would." The serving girl dropped the vial and clasped her hands together. *Thud.* "Please don't speak ill of the gods. They have set Lord Poden here to cleanse the earth of sin and restore purity. You mustn't tell anyone you've seen this. If you tell his lord you understand, then he won't do anything to do, I promise."

"Does Luk know?" Flora couldn't imagine a son letting something happen to his mother. "Or Poden's son in Caiag Rock? His daughter?"

"They would not understand," the serving girl said. "Poden swore us all to secrecy, and if I were to go against him, the Four would forsake me."

Thud.

"I have to go," Flora said. The serving girl wouldn't let her save Lady Willa, so she had to think of something, and Luk was right outside.

"Please say nothing."

Flora took the girl's hands and said, "Of course."

She clambered down the stairs, not caring whether she was being too loud. Poden's door was ajar. She could either confront him herself or get help. Tears fell from her eyes. *I've no other choice.*

As she entered Lord Poden's bedchamber, she smiled with downcast eyes. "Ready?" She asked Poden, who had already stripped off his shirt. Flora walked over to the bed where he sat. A butter knife lay on the bedside table. *Thud.*

"I've been waiting for this day for a long time." Poden opened his arms to her, and she straddled his lap. "You were always a beautiful girl."

Flora tensed, but she allowed Poden to kiss her neck and rub his hands on her breasts. *The Four will forgive* me. *I am stopping a monster*, she thought as her fingers stretched alongside the bed and reached for the table. *Thud.* She could feel Poden's hardness under her skirt as he ground into her. It was taking everything not to vomit on his face as a splash of blood fell behind her.

Her fingers wrapped around the handle of her knife as Poden started undressing her. *Knock.* Flora's whole body ached from fighting against him the best she could. Once she had the knife in hand, she brought it to his neck, and with all her might slammed it into his skin.

The lord screamed and pushed her onto the floor as blood spurted from his neck, his hand trying to stop the bleeding. Flora didn't wait to see what happened. She ran out of the door; screams and curses escaped the room, and she tumbled down the stairs. Sir Len didn't stop her since he was racing to his lord's room. Flora shoved the doors open and sprinted to Sirs Edmond and Marbert.

"What is this?" Luk asked, still captured.

"We need to leave," Flora said. "And Luk, before you decide to follow and attack us, please," she took Marbert's hand from Luk, "please go to the top room in the castle and see your mother."

"My mother is dead," Luk said as he stretched his twisted arm.

"I wish that were true. I'm sorry." Flora turned and ran with her guards to their horses and wagons. She heard screams behind her, from inside the castle. Luk didn't follow, at least not yet. He stalked into the castle instead. Flora climbed atop Marbert's horse, and they raced away. She didn't want to see anymore of River Watch. She didn't want to see what happened next.

Flora had her own problems now. She had to confront her traitor husband.

Aveline

The road was long and dry. There was not a tree in sight for shade. Aveline rolled her pants to her shins, tied her hair in a bun, and fanned herself with her hands. Nothing was working. *At least we have horses this time,* she thought from the wagon. Zoell and Ivlin were driving the horses. Joking and talking like they did. All of her guards were shirtless as the sun beat down on them, their backs and chests sticky and shiny. If she weren't a princess, she might even join them, but she had to keep some of her modesty.

They had set up and broken down camp many times on the road, their eyes always searching for Bertin, but never finding him. She couldn't fail, so they pushed on in the hot Southern summer. With the lack of cities and villages in this barren part of the world, Ivlin snuck onto farms to get food. They feasted on green, unripened fruit. If they were lucky, he would find eggs and chickens. That made the nights better as they prepared to sweat through their sleep.

"I believe this is Ansehar," Ivlin said as he looked at the map.

Ansehar was the nicest thing they had seen since leaving

Jorbstah, but it wasn't anything beautiful. Some houses had caved in. The roads were all dirt. The people were too skinny for living right next to a forest full of game to hunt and fruit to pick. No one wanted to live near the monsters that took over the woods. She kept her eyes low as they came under the gate. She didn't want problems. As they passed under the gate, Aveline looked at a hanging post near it, a person swinging in the slow breeze. Then she saw the pointed ears.

Badyn's sweet smile but terrified eyes filled Aveline's head.

"Wait," she said to Ivlin and Zoell. Before they could bring the cart to a halt, she had already dropped to the ground. The elf was a woman, blonde, tall. Her body was bulging and red. Villagers watched from their homes and shops at the newcomers. Aveline hoped they saw what she planned to do. Dern had followed close behind her, so she whipped around and unsheathed his heavy blade.

"Your Grace," Dern said. That's how she knew he was serious. "Don't make them angry with you when we've just got here."

Aveline didn't say a word; she merely drug the sword through the dry ground to the hanging post, the elf's feet lifeless as they swung. Aveline took a breath and summoned all her strength as she lifted the sword and brought the blade to the rope tied to the wooden beam. The dead elf went crashing to the ground in a cloud of dust.

"Bert," she called to her guard. "Find us some shovels. I don't care how much they cost."

"I'm not sure that's a good idea." Bert said as he looked to the village.

Aveline, still dragging the sword, went not even an inch from Bert's face. "It was a command. Remember, I am your princess, and it is your sole duty to do as I say."

Bert nodded and then went into town. Her other guards also said nothing. The villagers didn't seem to care, but they still watched her as they went about their day. Aveline handed Dern his sword back. "Sorry," she said.

"Your Grace," Dern said, "we cannot save everyone, and this is an elf. We might be royal guards, but even we can't take on an entire village if they decide to get revenge."

"I say she did the right thing," Ivlin said. "Shows everyone that we're serious. Could make it easier to get some information."

Bert brought back three shovels and passed them out to Tomas, Ivlin, and Dern. "No," Aveline said. *I didn't do it to show the village I am strong.* She looked to the elf. Her dead eyes gave nothing back. "Give me one." She took the shovel from Ivlin and found a soft patch of ground. "Here."

Dern was the first to make a hole, then Aveline and Tomas got to digging with him. The ground was still hard, but altogether they would be done quickly. The sun blazed upon them. Aveline could feel her neck turning red and burning, the sweat catching in her shirt and beading down her nose. Bert had gone back into town and found a well with water. But she couldn't drink it. Not while the elf was still lying on the ground, dead and desecrated.

"They're watching," Zoell said with her sword at her hip. Aveline wiped sweat from her burning eyes and saw the village. Children were sitting on the ground playing with dirt. Adults were eyeing them as they beat their rugs or led their goats or baked their flatbread.

"We won't let them get close," Ivlin said. "We've come too far to die in some backwater."

Die like her, Aveline thought of the elf.

As the sun continued to bake them, and the hole seemingly not getting any deeper, Bert was busy. He had gone into town and asked some questions. When he came back he said, "What few words they could say to me weren't very kind. But they said no horses in the forest, so I sold them."

"Don't have to steal anymore." Ivlin said as he took the pouches of coin. "I can find us some food and rooms."

"Don't bother," Bert said. Aveline was in the hole now, the dirt cooling her as she dug deeper. "There's only one place to stay, and it's a brothel. We somehow always find our way to those."

"Even better," Ivlin said with a laugh.

"Done," Dern the Third said as he and Tomas helped Aveline out of the hole.

"I'll get her," Aveline said. She brushed the dirt off her pants and grabbed the elf by her shoulders. Tomas grabbed her feet. They lifted the dead and shimmied over to the grave. "Gently," she reminded her guard. Tomas nodded, and they lowered the elf as best they could into the ground. She fell the rest of the way with a thump. "Maybe we can teach these people some decency." Aveline said of the village. She grabbed her shovel again and went to work throwing the dirt atop the elf woman. She looked so young too. Elves aged slower than humans, but the elf looked almost Aveline's age.

The moon rose, and the night brought chills, and she was happy to be freezing. *At least I can feel something. This poor elf's last moments must've been awful.*

"You're done," Bert said. The grave filled. Instead of a hole, there was a patch of fresh dirt. "Will you drink now?"

Aveline didn't realize how dry her throat was until she went to speak and only a scratchy sound escaped. She took a cup and let the water quench her thirst. "Yes ... sleep." Her guards gathered their belongings and began walking toward the brothel. Aveline stayed near the grave. The moonlight was shining straight onto her. "What do you think she did?"

Bert, the only knight still with her, shrugged. "Does it matter?"

"No," Aveline said. "I guess we've done the same in Rowan. An elf walks into the city and never makes it out."

"Been that way for a long time."

Aveline bit her lip. "Do you think we can change that? Baldewin or Bertin or whoever sits the throne? Or do you think it will always be like this?"

"Maybe," Bert said. "You weren't alive during the flames, but I was young then. During that time, I saw a lot of things. Queens killed, the domaton sacked, royal chancellors afraid of peasants. Do you know what really surprised me?" Aveline shook her head. "On the day the peasants forced the chancellery to approve equal protections for all people, I saw elves celebrating in the streets. Even more shocking, I saw humans celebrating with them. So yes," Bert said with a shy smile, "I think it can change. Now, let's get some rest."

The whorehouse was teeming with men and women and others. Aveline wished she could hold her breath as she walked through. As her guards ate their fill, she went to the owner, who stood behind a table wearing a glistening black tunic.

"Wish for me to find you a whore?" They asked. "They're all the same price and will make you feel better than any northern flesh."

"You speak the common tongue?" Aveline asked.

"Yes, good for business. Now, would you like one or two?" They looked at her head to toe. "I would even allow you three if you paid."

She set down a silver piece. "I'm not here for pleasure, but I would like to know if you've seen another … *northerner* around here recently. Looks similar to me with brown hair."

"Ansehar does not see many people from across the Ters-Veck. I remember his face well, though," the owner nodded. "But you just missed him. He seemed a child but made love to my exquisite creature." They dabbed their eyes in mock tears.

"How did she die?" Aveline asked, even though deep down she didn't want to know.

The owner shrugged. "Oh, the secret got out. It wasn't a very good one, I must say. But some men found out she was an elf and ended a very lucrative deal I had with her."

"That's it?"

"What's more to know?" They asked. "Happens all the time since we're so close to the forest. In fact, your northerner went with two Rainvealandians into the woods only a few days past, the reason I do not know. The monsters are aplenty there, especially with the elves attacking outside our small gates. Much safer in my brothel." The owner slipped the silver into their pocket. "Anything else?"

She shook her head and went back outside. The forest loomed over the city like a black cloud. The shadows of

trees danced on the dirt roads. Aveline didn't have any weapons, but she had to go into the dark nest of monsters.
    She had to find her brother.

Tundavik

The trees were smaller than he remembered. When Tundavik was young, they seemed as tall as the giants of myth, or the palace in Vigur. Now they looked smaller than the walls in the capital. *How life changes everything.*

Making their way through the forest was harder than he thought. The wagons and carts had to form a line or break apart depending on the density of the trees. Horses would get caught on upended roots. But most of all, it was difficult to keep a watchful eye. *Deserters, assassins, anything could sneak through these woods.* Tundavik would never know whether men left or others joined. The trees cast shadows that blocked his view. He lost sight of Devro's bay colored horse and Yvanne's wagon. Even Pollard pulled off to the side. Mar was with him though. *At least I can trust him.*

The train stopped when they reached a small hamlet by a creek. The townspeople peered out of their shutters while an alderman with gray skin and a white beard came forward. "We don't want no trouble from your lot. What is it you need?"

Tundavik recognized the man, Embalt Velkes. "You used to teach me poems of the heroes of old," he said. "How were you granted a town to watch over?"

Embalt studied his face. "Little Tundavik Vandes." His eyes went wide. "I heard reports you were warring against the king. I chose not to believe them." He motioned to his people and the wooden town. "Corville became mine because I left Ritaeum before the gods cast down their wrath." Tundavik grimaced at that. "What is it you're here for?"

"We only wish to water our horses and men. We've been traveling since sunrise and need a rest. Better Corville than any other."

Embalt did not smile; the gray hairs growing out of his nose danced. "Make sure none o'your men take my girls. I don't need a raping to occur."

"You have my honor."

He spat. "That's how us Ritae feel about your honor. The whole of Woodlands would rather put a pox on you than let you through." He motioned to the stream. "Hurry and get on with it."

The stream barely had enough water for their lot. The entirety of Devro's troop needed their fill. And whores and merchants came from the back. *Shame they didn't get lost.* Horses and men and some women drank. Others pissed and shit downstream; Tundavik had Pollard make sure.

"Shit is what it is," the familiar voice of Lord Toware said to a few of his men from Riverend. "Who knows what we're doing?" The lord's voice was almost a whisper, but still loud enough to carry, and Tundavik didn't like what he was hearing.

"My lord," Tundavik called out as he made his way to Toware. He was clad in river-blue tunic and trousers, his armor lying with a squire who was taking a nap in the daylight. "What seems to be the problem?"

"No problem," Toware smiled, his teeth gritted. "Just chatting with my men. How is His Grace?"

"I have spoken little with him." Tundavik leaned his arm against a storage wagon. "I should find him, give him your salutations."

"I would like that," Toware picked at a loose fingernail. "Would you mind asking His Grace, if he's ready to talk about it of course, why we march into the Woodlands?" Tundavik pushed off the wagon and took heavy steps to Toware. "I just don't think invading the one neutral duchy is a very good idea, is all."

"I will talk to His Grace, but I must tell you, it was I who chose the Woodlands."

Toware nodded, and Tundavik could see the lord's brain working. "Homesick?" He chuckled. "I, for one, think going to Riverton and taking down the largest army is more important, especially for the Flewthlands' sake, but if you insist."

"Sounds like you're homesick too," Tundavik said.

The lord shrugged, and his eyes were dark. "First, we abandon Vigur, and now we fight trees. I'm worried for the future of our campaign, is all. The Flewthlands and the Lands of Asara," he added after a moment, "are vulnerable to attacks from Ultiir now. Hiding in the woods won't change that."

"We're not hiding, my lord." Tundavik patted Toware's shoulder like he was a dog that needed praise. "Just licking our wounds. Don't worry, you'll be back in the fight soon enough."

Toware bowed before turning back with his men and muttering under his breath.

Tundavik went to the small creek to collect water when he finally saw Devro smiling on the left bank with Yvanne's brothers. Tundavik looked into the water. Guis stared back at him with bloody tears. *Just like my dreams.*

"He was a good man. I only wish we had given Ed a proper burial." Gordo said to Devro and his brother Diero as Tundavik approached. "My lord," Gordo slightly bowed.

"I'm not a lord," Tundavik reminded them, "but I am here to talk to the king."

Devro looked at nothing beside him and then said to Diero. "Will you find someone to feed my horse?"

"Of course," Diero said, and the two brothers left.

"Are we to talk battle plans?" Devro asked. "You know Ritaeum better than anyone and surely know how to easily take the keep."

Tundavik looked to the east. "The alderman said this village was Corville. I've been here." He pointed through the trees to a patch of sunlight. "My father hunted with me there. Shall we?" Devro didn't object.

Through the trees and brush, they saw deer and squirrels and boars among other beasts. They gathered around a small pond, taking their fill. "Was it easy hunting?" The boy asked.

"It was, and I was bad at it my first time. My father did most of the work. He would injure a buck and corner it for me to do the rest."

"And now you lead an army. Hopefully, the same happens to me."

Tundavik smiled. "I think living a life where you can say

you didn't kill anyone would be far more enjoyable. How many kings can say that?"

"Gobert the Timid. I don't want to be known as timid." Devro chuckled, then his face staled. Tundavik could see pain on his face. "Though I also don't feel like killing anyone." Devro studied his hands. "I don't know how others do, some without even thinking, Ultiir sending Gofrei's head to us. I know," Devro said to the air. Tundavik shook his head at that. Devro enjoyed speaking to no one and nothing. It certainly didn't endear him to the men.

"Some do it for fun; I'm sure Ultiir is that way. They like to watch others in pain."

"Like my father." Devro looked over the clearing. "Hopefully, I haven't that in my genes, but with my father and uncle both causing mass destruction, I have little hope."

"When we get to Ritaeum, you can read about some kings who decided peace was better than war. Learn from them. You don't inherit everything from your family. You can pick and choose what to take and what to leave behind."

"Are you sure Ritaeum was the right place? Maybe even killing those you know?"

Tundavik shrugged. He had been trying not to think about that. Bathing his home in blood for the second time filled him with dread, but at least his children weren't there to see it. "Everyone I knew died all those years ago. The keep is filled with strangers and rats. I will be fine."

Devro nodded as his fingers played with the pond water. Commander Wright and the men from the Fall entered the clearing as well, happy to see water as they held long hunting bows. "Your Grace," Wright bowed to Devro. "It pains me to say that we have spoken little; I know Lady

Ceala would've been delighted to see you. She has always been fond of the de'Tro dynasty."

The boy looked up from his crouched position by the pond, blond hair falling into his eyes. "I've never heard of this Lady Ceala, but I will thank her for the help rescuing me. I didn't think any from the Kinglands were on my side."

Commander Wright twirled his bushy mustache. "It was Tundavik here who convinced her. Lord Leur marched on the Fall with a vast army, but Tundavik and my lady came to some agreement, so he sicced his hounds on the men of Saltcreek and sent them running home crying. That's when I knew Commander Tundavik was one to fear." Wright wiped his bald head of sweat. It had gotten redder under the heat of the day. "You picked a good man to put your trust in."

"I know," Devro said as he stood.

Wright bowed away and joined his men in bathing in the pond. Sun broke through the trees to bathe them in light as well. Shadows went deeper into the woods. Tundavik was finally home. His entire journey east was to get back to Ritaeum and see it one last time. He scratched his head as it ached, and he thought of the dreams that would find him when he slept. *At least the woman should be happy. I'm finally doing what I was told, even if that could put Devro and everyone else in more danger.*

"I never said thank you for rescuing me from Vigur," Devro said, cutting through Tundavik's thoughts. "I'm not sure how long Ultiir would've kept me alive."

Tundavik rested a hand on the boy's shoulder. "I couldn't lose more of my family. Ritaeum was enough." *Family ... my family.* "Truth is, I missed you. Not only as my liege lord and because of duty, but I had to find you again. To keep you from death." Tundavik thought of his children, his wife, all lying dead. "You're the reason I stayed in the east. Without your cause, I would have gone back to Attrima. I didn't think after what happened I would stay, but you convinced me. I guess this is what I was looking for." Tundavik patted Devro's back and found a spear from one of Wright's men. "We should get a deer before more men discover this place."

Devro nodded, and they went deeper into the woods, trying not to make a sound. Of course, Devro stepped on a fallen branch and sent squirrels running and birds flying. Tundavik only laughed. "Be sure to watch your feet, but also keep your eyes and ears ready."

"It would be easier with a bow," Devro whispered.

"You don't always have one, like now," Tundavik replied. They stalked through the birch trees and tall grass. Some wildflowers had bloomed, mixing reds and pinks and blues with the green carpet of the earth.

They saw a herd of deer enjoying the grass as the sun lit them. Tundavik had Devro bend behind a rock and hold the spear. "Now you have to remember it arcs when you throw it," Tundavik told him and pointed to a buck, "hit the bigger one."

Devro's head was dripping sweat. "I'm not sure I can," the boy said. "I've never thrown one."

"Just a little higher." Tundavik helped Devro aim the spear. "Now pull back and throw. Just enough to reach the deer."

"I really don't think I can."

"You can do anything, Gu—" he cleared his throat, "—Devro. You are the king. Some deer are no match for you."

Devro popped his neck and shook his head. His arm went back before he flung the spear across the meadow and through the trees. The deer ran before the spear even hit. But then there was a scream.

Tundavik was laughing as he brought Devro through the trees. On the other side was a dead deer, not the buck, but a younger one. It had stopped moving. The spear sticking out of its neck. "I did it …" Devro's mouth dropped. His skin turned pale as his eyes were wide. "I killed something."

"Might as well have your first time be a deer," Tundavik laughed and hit Devro's back with joy. "Let's bring this thing to the butchers so they can see their king provides for them."

They carried the carcass back to the cooks, who congratulated Devro on his first kill. "I'll find you later," Devro told Tundavik as he was climbing onto his bay horse. "Maybe there's more to hunt in Ritaeum."

"I hope so," Tundavik beamed with pride. He found Glem and Bera and said, "Shall we go deeper into the forest?"

"I'm ready for anything." Glem patted the sword at his hip. "Ghosts or men."

The trees swayed, and Corville looked on with joy as the train departed from the creek. Tundavik rode with Mar and Pollard at his side. Glem was right behind, and Devro was farther back with his brothers-by-law, who had become close guards to him. Yvanne was with her sister and handmaid in the wagon, surely getting ready to birth the babe.

Tundavik smiled at his family.

Blis

The old innkeep, scrubbing a glass and picking specks of dirt from it, said, "Pleasure having you here. Few of the Southerners are as nice."

Blis nodded as he leaned against the counter. "Sorry to say, but we haven't found many hospitable Northerners here."

The woman shrugged. "Calling us Northerners is one way to get us angry. We are from the Glybelm. We're islanders." She swatted toward a window. Somewhere across the sea was Adedor. "Those out there are mainlanders. Icky. Sticky. They don't know what it's like to weather a storm that destroys your home and more. Ya know, the winds were so icy one year we lost twenty sheep. We've no wolves out here, mister. All killed by the gods. They were angry that year."

Blis gave another nod, even though he was tired of listening to her ramblings. They had been staying at the only inn in Cahlun for a few days, ever since the *Sea Glider* burnt to a crisp in the harbor, the black, smoldering remains slowly sinking. "I know about storms," he said. "I captained ships in the Western Ocean. Hard business out there, though the water wasn't nearly as cold as up here."

"A seaman? So you understand." The old lady batted her eyelashes. "We get hundreds if not thousands of sailors come through here looking for adventure only to tuck their tails and run back to the mainland. But you know the hard life living near the sea can bring. I like that."

Blis' cheeks blushed as the lady looked him up and down. He couldn't have looked good. His tunic was stained with salt and sea. His trousers were loose-fitting, with his belly hanging over the belt. All of his belongings were at the bottom of the sea now. *Along with Baldewin's crown.* Baldewin rarely came out of his room as of late. He was back to isolating himself. The burning of the ship made him sad and angry. Except he was angry with the islanders, while Blis was mad at the councilors. Blis suspected— no—knew that Caxton and Wycleaf and Jac were behind the fire. Maybe they hired some of the Glybelm to do it, but the councilors ordered it. Why? He didn't know. But Blis was going to find out.

"I should be going." Blis knocked on the counter. The innkeep sighed before going back to her duties. Washing and cleaning and collecting payment.

"Where are you off to?" Mari asked as he made his way outside. The handmaid was wrapped in a small woolen coat. "Won't the king be looking for you?"

Waves crashed along the rocky shore at the bottom of the hills. Blis scratched his eye and said, "You and Delmar will keep him company. I need to speak with the councilors. Maybe a few sailors and Captain Pitor."

"To find out what happened?"

"Yes," he nodded. There were other Rowai ships in the port, but Blis didn't trust anyone who wasn't close to him.

He barely trusted Sir Delmar and Mari, but sometimes there wasn't a choice. He needed to be back in Rowan so he could watch over Baldewin and not have to worry about some poor Glybelm man taking coin from Caxton and murdering the boy in his sleep.

"I agree, you know," Mari said. Her dark hair whipped around her face as the wind rushed over the island. Chimes and barking dogs filled the air. Clouds covered the sun. It looked like winter in Rowan, but it was summer in the Glybelm. "But I worry you're going to get hurt," she looked at his aching knee, "again."

"I've been around long enough, don't worry. I know how to keep myself safe."

"Yes, but Baldewin … His Grace. I cannot protect him like you can, no matter how much Aveline wishes I could. I'm just a handmaid. You at least have friends and influence."

Blis looked over the island. Rocks jutted out from the green hillsides. Smoke rose from stone chimneys. Birds tried to fly but the wind kept them in place. "I don't have many friends here."

"I'm here." Mari gave a curt nod. "And if there's anything you need, just ask. I know I'm only a handmaid …"

"You keep saying that, but you should give yourself more credit. Without you, we wouldn't have a king right now. Honestly, I'm not sure what would've happened had Baldewin fallen off that ship, but the councilors certainly would've tried to take more power. Because of you, we at least have a chance to keep control."

Mari took a step closer. She was shivering as the wind hit. "Does Baldewin want to keep control?" She asked, as if saying it could get her in trouble. "I mean, Aveline told me she would run away with me, and I've been looking forward to it since the day she left. What has Baldewin said?"

"It's different for women. Someone long ago decided they cannot rule, so Aveline would never be queen, anyway. Baldewin and Bertin, on the other hand, were expected to rule. At least as a powerful lord in Baldewin's case. He cannot give up the crown so easily, though. Yes, he is young, but that means he will have a long reign. We just need to get these unruly councilors to see that."

Mari opened her mouth, then shut it before nodding. "I'll go inside. You stay out of trouble."

Blis gave a mock salute. Down the hill was the tavern that the councilors had taken over. The place they got drunk and hatched plans. The same place Blis had heard Wycleaf say, "I just wanted the girls to know the future. They will be queens!"

"They'll never be queens as you won't be kings," Blis said in a huff as he started his way down the hill.

After Blis kept himself from tumbling downhill, he reached the tavern. He heard snores escaping from inside. It was still early morning. Fog was settling in the many bays and inlets of Stadvik. There was at least a lack of wind farther down the hill. Inside the tavern would be sailors and guards and the councilors. Blis would have to tread carefully if he wanted to glean information from the men.

As he neared a window, he heard voices. Wycleaf was speaking. "... and now we have to figure out what to do."

"Well," Jac said, "our best course of action is to go home. Leave the crybaby and get to William."

"I'm not so sure. You don't think *he'll* want to stop us?"

Jac sighed. "Not now, I don't think. We've all the power,

and we've shown how destructive we can be. He'll have no choice but to listen to our demands."

Blis took a step back when the tavern door opened. A sailor with dark circles for eyes waved and pissed in the wind. Then he heard Caxton say, "How are you?" and thought he was talking to him, but the councilor was inside as well, speaking to Wycleaf and Jac. "We still need to figure out what happened …"

Blis took a few steps away. He didn't need the sailor to report back to the council that he had been spying. He kicked some dirt and watched the wind take it. The royal ships were docked below in the harbor. The large mass of blackened wood marked where the *Sea Glider* once stood. He wasn't one to be scared. He had braved storms and war and seen much worse. But accusing the council of treason made him tremble. *But I know I'm right,* he thought. *It's just a matter of whether or not they will lie.*

He turned to follow the sailor back into the tavern, but a fat boy, barely older than Bertin had been, called out. "Hi," he said. "Do you speak the common language?" He had a Western accent, but he wrapped himself in a black cloak, ripping and dripping with water.

"I do," Blis answered.

"Oh, thank the gods," the boy said. "I've been wandering this island for hours and no one will so much as glance at me. I've just been wanting to ask where I am exactly."

"Stadvik," Blis said. "You look a mess. Rough seas?"

"Rough life." The boy said. He had a welt on his cheek. Not only was his cloak tattered, but so were his trousers, and a toe was sticking out of a boot. "I haven't been having the best of times lately. You see, I was on a ship out west, but we was captured, and I've spent a lot of time in a prison." He shuddered. "I saw horrid things after that. My friend … well, he may be dead." The boy cried. His cheeks turned red, and his large fingers wiped the tears.

Blis walked over and put a hand on the boy's shoulder. "Everything's alright. What's your name, son?"

"Potter," he sniffled.

"I am an adviser to the king of Rowan," Blis said. "I'll gladly help you get back home. You arrived here this morning?" The boy nodded. "On a boat?" The boy nodded again. "Would you show it to me?"

Potter waved a hand, and Blis followed. He didn't need the councilors to leave Baldewin on this island. If they could find a boat and start sailing before Caxton made his move, then they would be one step ahead.

Ultiir

When Ultiir entered the domaton, he prayed the peasants wouldn't rise up and kill him in the place of worship. It was full of the poor and starving from the burnt Rat's Nest. He left his crown at the palace. He had to see to his mother's corpse.

Rila de'Tro was dead. His mother. Gone. The bitch wife of the bastard had lied to him. When the armies had marched away from Vigur, Ultiir and his men journeyed from the walls. There, his mother was alone in a tattered tent, her body already decaying with flies and crows and field mice biting at her. Her eyes were open. *They didn't even bother to close them.*

Ultiir had sent his men away and cried and cried until his face hurt. He hated his mother. He loved his mother. Now she was gone. No more yelling, no more cursing, no more judging. She was already old when he was born, and she had grown ancient, but still Ultiir didn't want her to die. He didn't want anyone in his family to die. *But I killed Hurvir.* He spent that day in the tent with the corpse of his mother, the smell of the body under the hot summer sun attacking his nose.

"Now you know," he had told his mother. "You know

what I did to Hurvir. How I betrayed our family and murdered him. What does he think? What does everyone else think? Do they laugh at my suffering? Curse me? Will you join in or defend me?"

It was night when Sir Gid entered the tent. His cheeks were stained with tears as well, but Ultiir was sitting in a puddle of his own making. Gid helped him up and said, "You must be strong, Your Grace. Think of what your mother would do to the people who lied to her. What will you do?"

Ultiir had no idea.

Once he was stripped and gowned in brown, he found the High Doma. Maller hiccuped once Ultiir entered the small office. When Albon was His Holiness, the office would be a mess of scrolls and letters from parishioners the world over, but Maller was a drunk, and he didn't seem to care for the religious fortitude of his people.

"How have you been?" Maller asked. A liquor bottle was empty below his desk.

"Well, my mother was murdered," Ultiir said as he kicked a rat away from his boot. "So I've had better days. Is everything in place to send her to Goldfield?"

Maller nodded, though he had little control of his neck. "Reports say that Goldfield isn't being held by the traitors, and with a few of your knights and guards and my warriors of the Four, I'm sure there will be no issues."

Ultiir nodded. His mother would be entombed beneath the ancestral seat of the de'Tro family. She would rest forever next to her husband and all of her children who had died before her. *Including Hurvir,* thought Ultiir as he bit his cheek. "How are the doma? A lot of people are filling your home."

"Well, that is the purpose of the domaton, is it not?" Maller smiled, and Ultiir rolled his eyes. He didn't want a drunk to lecture him on the teachings of the Four and the Many. "My doma are happy there are people who need helping. Makes them practice instead of just preaching about helping the poor. Vigura's Feast is also coming up, with that usually comes pilgrims, though the war has certainly stopped many from traveling."

"We don't need anymore coming to the gates." Ultiir said. "I've a question." Maybe he did need a drunk to quote passages to him. "The feast with the gods that my family is having … do you think they judge me?"

"The eternal banquet?" Maller stroked his chin, stubble forming. "Is that not what Swallow told us? Your ancestors all feast and look down at this world with the Four and the Many. They take a close look at whoever still lives and who is born. They try their best to guide you from the afterlife, but sometimes must look on with disappointment if you are sinning." Maller stood, though wobbly, and found the tome that was the Book of the Swallow. It was written in the old tongue, and Ultiir was embarrassed to say he couldn't read it. "Yes, yes," Maller nodded as he read. *"Fianna sen mi chydon, for weer ewfaths edan imbri we. Fianna ..."*

Ultiir's ears seemed to close as Maller read in the old tongue. Usually a prince's mother would teach him to read the original words of the Four, but Rila de'Tro was too busy being hateful and sending her children to get beat to teach anything. *"... weth Vikcura ..."* Now she was dead. Ultiir had to fight the feeling of happiness. He was bitter. Sad. But joyful. He would never have to hear her yell at him again.

"... top dryhom ..." Tell him how awful he was and how his father and brothers were always better. About how difficult her life of opulence and riches was. He would never hear her speak again.

"… which means," Maller continued, "Do not sin, my children, for your forefathers look upon you. Do not upset them, my children, for they speak with Vigura, for they help pass judgment, for they see all." Maller closed the large book, and dust flew into the sunlight as he hiccuped one more time. "Are you afraid of judgment from them? Shall we pray for forgiveness? Absolve any sins?"

Ultiir wanted to say *yes*, but it caught in his throat. But he wasn't afraid because he already knew how his dead family members felt. They would judge him harshly for murdering his brother, for the hint of glee he felt that his mother was dead, for being a warmonger, for executing Albon who was once the High Doma. Ultiir knew he would never feast with his family and the gods in the afterlife. Veltoora, the home of evil, of flames, of demons, would become his home.

So he said, "No."

***

Water crashed down on the lord below. Lord Urses de'Marisco was soaked, his clothes dark with stain, his hair dripping. He spat out the water and took a few deep breaths before another douse of water fell on him.

Ultiir stood over the lord … the traitor lord. Knights carried the large tubs of water; Gid watched over all. Urses put his hand up, but it did nothing to stop the waves from hitting him. "We've a whole river to empty," Ultiir said with crossed arms.

"Please," Urses spat and wiped his face, "I promise, Your Grace, I had no knowledge of their evil deed. I merely pretended so I could make it back to Vigur in one piece. Back to you." Splash. *"Ptuh ... ptuh ...* I have been sending you messages since I reached the lowlands months ago. I would've told you about your mother if I'd known, but they kept it from me, kept it from all."

Ultiir nodded to the guards, and more water dumped on the lord. *We're going to have to take a break to refill the tubs,* he thought. They were in a small cellar below the palace made entirely of stone. Wooden tubs and barrels filled the corners. Guards with large muscles had carried them all the way from the Ritae. The river of death.

So Ultiir questioned Lord de'Marisco, though he was hard to break. Ultiir bent down to the soaked lord, who was sputtering. "The water is only the first part." He looked at Urses' nails and grabbed his fingers. "Should Gid get some pliers?"

"It won't help," Urses protested, "because I know nothing. I told you of the army's movements. How we were marching on Goldfield and then Vigur. I wanted you prepared." Ultiir had never seen Urses so upset. There was a hint of a tear in the corner of his eye as his voice strained. "I stayed close to Yvanne so I could gain her secrets. If I wanted to betray you, I would've told them about Vigur's weaknesses, but I stayed silent."

Ultiir stood from bending over the lord and popped his back a few times. "Sir Gid, I wish to find out all Urses knows. Do not let him leave this room without telling you exactly what happened since he arrived in Whitehall."

"More torture?" Urses' head fell back.

"You call this torture?" Ultiir laughed. "You haven't even been through half of what I have these past few months. My own wife has betrayed me countless times, not to mention the many lords, you included. My men killed. The city riots. The lords of the royal court have invaded my home and hold me as a hostage to their whims. My brother died. Now, my mother." Ultiir's jaw was sore. "I want you to feel half that pain."

Ultiir turned to leave, but when his hand touched the door, Urses yelled out, "Wait!"

"What now? Remember your betrayal?" Ultiir said as he turned.

"I can help you take revenge on Yvanne and all the others loyal to the bastard. I know many lords who aren't happy with her. See her as weak. As a usurper of Devro's power. A power-hungry whore. Let me write to them. Let me show you my loyalty."

"And after receiving your many letters while you were with the enemy, I'm supposed to trust that you won't tell my secrets to the bastard's army."

"You can read them." Urses had gotten to his knees. Ultiir couldn't help but smirk at the lord who was reduced to begging. "I promise you I can get lords to go against her. Kill her and the bastard if that's what you desire."

"Big promises," Gid said with crossed arms.

"But I always follow through." Urses' brow lowered. "Just give me some parchment and a little time. Before long, you'll have the entirety of the bastard's army at war within itself."

Ultiir sighed and settled his eyes on Gid. "Fine. Forget the pliers; instead, get some ink and quills and read everything he writes to the last word. I want no surprises. I just want that bitch dead."

He flung his cloak and found the stairs, a knight accompanying him. It wasn't anyone he knew. He had forgotten his knights' names save for Gid and Ard and Lovis … another who died. "And that's why I burnt the Rat's Nest," he said.

The unknown knight said, "Your Grace?"

"Nothing," Ultiir said. If Urses was truly on his side, then he had a powerful friend once more. But he still had Tedbalt in the dungeons, and he had to figure out what to do with him. And with his wife.

Yvanne

We should've discussed it is all I'm saying,"it, Lord Cul said from his small wooden chair. His eyelids were drooping; what was left of his hair frayed. "I think we had the advantage; in fact, I know we had it."

Yvanne itched her nose as the baby moved inside her. Her head craned to see Lord Cul speak. She was so used to sitting in the high seat with all the lords of the council looking to her that her neck began to ache. Devro sat at the front of the room instead. Yvanne was on the right side of the table, close enough to hear her husband's mumbling. Tundavik sat across from her. The rest of the council a hodgepodge along the table. Lord Aimora blew his hair from his face. Diero and Gordo shook their heads at Cul. Pollard and Rickart guarded the tent entrance, though they looked half asleep. Sir Mar pulled on his tunic to stretch out the neck. "I haven't worn anything other than armor in so long," Mar had told her. "Bloody different."

"The goal was to rescue Devro," Gordo said, "which we did."

"But Vigur was close to falling," Cul added with a point of his finger to the sky.

They had been discussing Vigur for so long that the candles were all half-burned. Yvanne had to stifle many yawns throughout the night. She couldn't leave, even if Devro wanted her to. They were talking about her decision to abandon the siege. *I will not let them put me in the wrong,* she thought.

Tundavik cleared his throat as he played with a loose piece of wood on the table. "While I agree Vigur was weakened, we already tried to break through the gates once. It didn't turn out so well, if you remember."

Pollard stepped forward and said. "We should've rushed the gates when they opened them to release Devro." No one said anything. The men outside the tent snoring were the only thing filling the silence. "His Grace," Pollard added.

Cul's brow raised. "See? Even your brother agrees." He looked at Yvanne.

"I am the king," Devro whispered to a corner before he said, in a louder voice for all to hear, "I am the king, not Yvanne, so look at me."

Lord Cul slowly blinked as he turned his head. "Your brother-by-law speaks true, Your Grace."

"And his other brothers-by-law?" Diero said as he rested his elbows on the table. "We disagree with Pollard. And I'm sorry to say," he glanced at Pollard, "he is a bit more rash than we are." Pollard scoffed but kept quiet. "He'd've had us keep attacking the day we started instead of turning to a siege. Most knights would."

Mar's head fell to the side in sarcasm. "I'm sorry, Diero, but not all of us share your sense of honor."

"I forgot." Diero said dryly as his eyes bore into Mar.

"All I want to know," said Aimora finally, "is why Ritaeum?" There were a few murmurs of agreement around the table. "Not that getting the Woodlands wouldn't be in our best interest, but so far they've avoided the war. Ultiir hadn't even tried to court them as far as I know. So why?"

The table looked to Tundavik. Everyone knew he was once duke of the Woodlands, lord of Ritaeum. And it was he who pushed Yvanne to agree. *But it was my final say,* she thought. "I decided," she said, and the heads swiveled to her in surprise, "that we needed more men, and the only other place not in the war was Ritaeum. Tundavik agreed with me, as did my husband, His Grace. The Flewthmen and Asaramen are already stretched thin protecting the borders and sending some to march with us. If Lord Valles and his lords join us, then we will match Ultiir and the Eastlands in strength. Then we march on Vigur once more, and that time we won't have to worry if Lord Gallient is going to surprise us because we'll be ready."

"That's a lot of hope you've put into Lord Valles," Cul said.

"Do we know anything about him?" Aimora asked.

Once again, the room was quiet until Tundavik spoke up. "I know of the Valles family. They used to be lords of Baeum. Arnoll was the first and I believe Arnoll the Twelfth was lord when I served as duke. They were a small family. Kept to themselves. To me blunt, I never heard if Arnoll had any children, so I guess this Lord Valles was one."

"Onnu," Devro said to everyone's shock, "that's his name. I read a book," he shrugged before nodding a smile to the corner where no one was.

Yvanne bit her cheek. *Why must he do this? Why must he talk to ghosts? If anything makes the lords turn against us, it will be that.*

"Very well," Aimora said. "So Lord Onnu Valles, the heir of a quiet family, is our only hope to get the Woodlands on our side. And if he says no?"

"There will not be a no," Yvanne said, her eyes ice. "I know there are many who think me weak or stupid for leaving Vigur—"

"—Your Grace," Lord Cul said, "I didn't—"

"—But Onnu Valles will say yes because if he doesn't then we will march our armies on Ritaeum and burn it to the ground." Yvanne finished. Tundavik's mouth moved like he wanted to speak, but he said nothing. "Now, I would like my tent back," she said.

As squires and servants came in to take the table and chairs, the lords left. Only Yvanne, Pollard, and Mar stayed behind. "She only needs one knight," quipped Pollard.

"I just wanted to ask Her Grace how she thinks Devro is doing." Mar said. "I couldn't help but notice her face while His Grace spoke."

She touched her face to make sure it wasn't moving. "Did I have a face?"

Mar laughed. "You seemed a little confused, worried, maybe scared. I don't know." He found a cracker and munched on it. "I've seen it too. He's changed a bit since coming back."

"A dungeon will do that." Yvanne said.

"Sure," Mar nodded. "If you see anything out of the ordinary, let me know." The knight left Yvanne and her brother alone. Not even Jacka had come back from wherever she was.

"It used to be Tiro who guarded me," she said as she slipped gloves off her arms, sweat making them sticky.

"Now it's you. Not that I'm complaining."

Pollard rubbed the bridge of his nose. "Can I say, something is wrong with that boy."

"Tiro?" Yvanne's face twisted. "He's dead."

"No, not Tiro, Devro." Pollard looked to the tent flaps, but they were only moving in the soft breeze of night. He pushed wet red curls from his brow. "He talks to himself all day long. Treats you and the council as if you weren't the ones governing in his absence. We risked everything to save him, and he's never said thank you."

Yvanne shook her head and made her way to her brother. "Don't let anyone hear you. He is king, so why should he thank us?"

"It would be nice," her brother shrugged. "And what about Diero? He acted as if he was better than me. Me?" Pollard scoffed as he whipped around the tent. "I should show him what type of knight I am."

"Do you hear yourself? Diero is our brother. He meant nothing by it." Yvanne tapped her foot when she saw Pollard's face was redder than his hair. "This is what happened in Goldfield. You let others get to you, let them upset you. Yes, Rila de'Tro was one of the worst people I've ever met, but Diero? Devro? They're on your side."

Pollard sighed. "I know. I'll forget what Diero said by tomorrow, but Devro? That *child* is not who should lead us."

Yvanne threw her hands up. "Treason now," she said as she shook her head. "I cannot win with you. How do you feel about Ritaeum?"

"I think it's a mistake, is what I think. When I saw Ultiir's face with Devro, I wanted to run up and kill him, end the war for good. But no. We have to drag it on. Make Devro feel powerful again or something. Did you ever think maybe this kingdom would be better off without the de'Tros? There's only two left, and we lost an easy chance to do it."

Yvanne touched her belly. "There's about to be another."

"Yvanne," Pollard said, "I didn't mean …"

"Why don't you leave? Send Sir Loc to guard me for the night."

Pollard cursed under his breath as he opened the tent flap, but he wasn't able to find Sir Loc.

There was shouting. Pollard found his sword and backed toward Yvanne. But there was no metal on metal ringing. "Let's go find out," Yvanne said as she lowered Pollard's sword for him before wobbling through the flaps.

Outside, men stood armed, facing a dozen bushes. Only they weren't shrubbery. Sticks and vines and straw-thin grass wrapped around them like a dress. Their arms were seemingly made of wood, as thick as a tree branch. Their grassy hair was pulled back, and wooden bows in their hands. Others rose from the ground behind the tree-like women. What looked like normal bushes spun and revealed upright women with arrows at their sides.

"Do not attack." Tundavik shouted at the men. "These are Miena's Hunters," he said as he ran toward the bushes.

Cul grunted. "They are pointing arrows at us. One slip and we're dead."

"Let me speak with them," Tundavik said, "then I'll tell you if they're still friend or foe."

One of the bushes—hunters—lowered her bow and took a few steps forward. The wood and grass on her were turning gray and brown, as if she were aging. She walked slowly, with her gaze fixed on Tundavik.

When she reached him, she put her hand on Tundavik's face. "Lord Vandes?"

Bertin

He dropped the piglet as he went deeper into the woods. No thoughts entered his mind except to find the singing. He couldn't make out the words, and it wasn't a melody he had heard before. The dark trees grew closer together as his feet drug through the grass and flowers. Then they parted. On the other side was another clearing, this one with a pond. The water so blue it looked like a painting. Lily pads floated over the smooth pond. On the far side was a figure serenading the whole of Sruhq with their words.

"Bekyt mudos en mende ende." The song went. Bertin was so lost in the words that he almost didn't notice his boot hitting the water, ripples spreading over the whole pond. He shook his head, and the singing stopped.

I almost forgot where I was, Bertin thought. The figure in the distance was cloaked in shadow. The trees rising behind it like mountains, towering over the pond. "Who are you?" He shouted over the water as he dried his pant leg. But there was no answer. Bertin gripped his dagger and went forward, wanting to see who was singing, who had him in a trance. *Is it just a ghost like before? This time my mother?* He wasn't sure if he would be okay seeing his mother again.

His only memory of her now was rocks embedded in her skin.

As Bertin got closer, the world turned warmer. The sun bathed him in yellow and red. Green grass was brighter, brown trees were darker. The figure was wearing a green robe wrapped around its body, its face covered by a hood.

"Come here, child." A shrill voice said from the shadow.

He didn't move his legs, but he walked closer anyhow. The pond reflected the light into his eyes as he got a better look at the dark figure. It was an old woman. She held a wooden staff, curved at the top. Her skin was pale, her green robe made of leaves, twigs in her gray hair, wrinkles on her face, and a smile. "What are you singing?" He asked.

"Just a sweet song," the old woman said. "I sing to the heavens above and the hells below. To the land we stand on and the water we swim in. I sing for our protection. To spare us from the wrath that will be unleashed. The evil."

"What evil?" Bertin asked like a scared child.

"Oh, you've much to learn," she said. The old woman opened her robe with her arm and ushered him closer. He stepped into her embrace like a fool, but it was almost comforting. Like the grandmother he never knew. "I sense so much loss in your heart. So much pain. Are you alright?"

Bertin couldn't stop his tears from falling. Everyone he had met wound up dead. Before long, Torlem and Barhi would follow suit; he knew it. "I'm afraid. Lonely. I don't think I'll ever get home."

"There, there," the old woman patted his back. "Nothing to cry about. You see, I can see the future. I can see all that is to come. But it isn't a very bright one, though I see you in my visions."

"Me?" Bertin wiped his tears. "Who are you?"

"The mother of this forest. See all the trees and animals and bugs?" She waved a hand all around. "Those are all my children, and you have entered my domain, so I must care for you. But those two with you have evil intentions, do they not?" Bertin nodded to the woman. "They mustn't be allowed to kill my children."

"I'll try," Bertin said, then remembered he had killed the boar. A piglet.

"Do not fear." She waved her hand, and the dead piglet was at their feet. "You do this to survive; I know that. But you must ask for forgiveness."

"I'm sorry. I shouldn't've done it, but I was hungry, and the pig was the only thing I could catch."

The woman twisted her fingers together, and an apple fell from the sky. She polished it and handed to Bertin. "In my domain, you merely need to ask for help. I am a kind soul. I allow you all to traverse here, even those with dark moods. I wish for safety for you all."

Bertin held the apple close to his heart. For a moment, he thought the apple had a beating heart as well. "I will try my best to keep it safe. I just want to make it home."

"Of course you do," her shrill voice said. "But you will come to a crossroads. Which you will choose, I do not yet know. The future is so hazy nowadays. Bleak."

"Why?"

The Mother of the Forest took a deep breath. "I will show you," she said as she lifted and slammed her staff into the ground. Blackness blanketed them. Then, a purple haze descended on them. Bertin and the woman were floating in the sky. Down below was a war. Millions against millions. Fires raged, consuming entire cities. The earth shook, breaking apart. The sun and moon falling out of the heavens and crashing into the land. Everything dying.

Then the blackness was gone, and they were back in the forests of Sruhq, the pond in front of them, a frog going *ribbit ribbit.* "You see?" The mother asked. "That is what your world is coming to. It is so sad. But I know there are ways to stop it; it has been done before."

Bertin's head hurt. He understood nothing. "What was that? How do you stop it?"

"You've been amongst the *doesan,* the elves. You know their words. Nhamcaryn, you've heard it?" Bertin nodded. The old woman continued, "That is what is coming. It is the merging of worlds, and some wish to stop it, but it is inevitable. The only way to stop it is to allow it to happen. Allow the hardships to bring about a better day. But if it is stopped, if the worlds cannot merge, then a newer evil will descend on this world as they have many others."

"I do not understand," Bertin said.

"You will," the woman smiled, "but first you must find the source. It is in the woods, far from here. I have seen many die trying to close it, but only one may close it, and you must stop them."

"Where should I go?" Bertin shook a disappointed head at himself. He only wanted to go home, but something, perhaps this old woman, was making him want to find this source. To help the world.

"It is back east. You will find a cousin there."

"Viguran?" Bertin asked, but he was alone. Only the dead piglet in front of him to keep him company.

"Where have you been?" Barhi asked as they found the

pond. "I was beginning to think you had died or been captured." Barhi looked at the piglet. They were carrying a deer carcass across their back. "An *omuz*? Good enough." They bent down and tossed the pig back to Bertin. "This should be enough meat to last us," Barhi said. "Let's go back to the clearing and wait for Torlem." Bertin just stared at the pond, barely noticing the piglet in his hands. His mind lost with images of war and burning and crumbling cities. "Are you alright? Have you seen a *şytan*?"

"No," Bertin said as he remembered Barhi was in front of him. "Let's go find Torlem."

Barhi nodded, and they both walked back to the clearing they were to meet at. Barhi started a fire, and Bertin imagined the sticks screaming and the Mother of the Forest shaking her head. "Was the deer easy to fell?" Bertin asked as Barhi skinned the dead animal. "I'm not much of a hunter, so this piglet was hard enough for me."

"Not much of a hunter?" Barhi scoffed as they slid the knife under the deer's skin and cut and pulled, blood staining their clothes. "How were you ever going to survive out here? Would you have if the *adér* didn't find you?"

"I … I don't know."

"I am still confused on how you wound up here? A traveler captured by elves, but not a hunter. It's all very confusing to me. And what were you doing by the pond? I swear *içkoll* came down and spooked you."

"It was nothing. Just a daydream," Bertin lied, though it could have been. The mother had vanished, and it wouldn't be the first time his mind had played tricks on him. "I've had those lately."

Barhi set the knife down and sighed. "I'm sorry to say,

but I always feel like you're lying." Bertin gulped but said nothing. He could only ear a bug buzzing around his head. "Torlem seems to like you, and I go along with him because we are brothers in arms, *rikte,* but sometimes he makes bad decisions."

"And you think I'm a bad decision?" Bertin asked.

"I'm not sure yet, but you must tell me the truth. Who are you? And what were you doing with the *adér*?"

"I …" Bertin stopped himself from speaking. He couldn't reveal his true self, no matter what Barhi thought. They might capture him, kill him. He couldn't have that. He had to get home—no—he had to find the source, and telling Barhi he was a prince would get him nowhere.

Fortunately for Bertin, that's when he heard screaming.

Barhi and Bertin both jumped to their feet and left the carcasses behind. The scream sounded like a woman. Could it be the monsters trying to lure them again? Maybe an actual person who wandered too far from home. Bertin didn't want to think about that. He just wanted to follow Barhi and not have to mention who he really was.

Barhi was too quick for Bertin, and they were able to get away from him, but Bertin continued all the same. He ran through the woodland, dodging the trees that towered above, hoping he was going in the right direction. He unsheathed his dagger and prepared himself for anything. A fanged beast, a beautiful but deadly succubus, or even an elf. He heard voices and languages he knew all too well; the ancient tongue of the Rainvealandians, and the even older elvish tongue. He could make out nothing.

Hiding behind trees and brush, he saw what was happening. A small female elf, no older than his brother Baldewin, was on the ground. She was a dark-skinned elf with flowing black hair and a torn dress stitched with leaves. Torlem stood over her with his blade out. Barhi was nearby, their hand on the hilt of their sword. They spoke to each other in their language. Torlem pointed and laughed at the elf.

Bertin twisted his hand around his dagger and watched as Torlem sulked closer to the elf. He gave a laugh that matched the forested nights of horror. And gave Bertin no choice. As the mite was nearing the elves, Bertin leaped from the thicket and brought his dagger up. "No!"

Torlem whipped around, and his eyes grew big and his face red at the sight of Bertin. "What are you doing? Don't you want me to finish my hunt?"

"Please," Bertin said as he lowered his dagger. "You don't need to hurt her. She hasn't done anything wrong."

"I told you," Barhi said to both Torlem and Bertin. "He was lying the whole time. I knew it." Barhi unsheathed their blade and pointed it at Bertin. "Now tell us why you were really with the elves."

"It's not what you think," Bertin said. He locked eyes with the elf, who was crying. So fearful. Afraid this day would be her last. "Fine, but put down your swords." Torlem and Barhi looked at one another and did as they were told. They both sheathed their weapons, and Bertin heard the elf's breath shudder. "I was sent to Telemaw by my father, but I was captured, tortured, kept for ransom. The elves, they ..." he took a breath. It was time, and he would face whatever consequences it brought. "My father was the king of Rowan. I am the heir to the throne, the prince of Rowan. The elves wished to ransom me to my father for coin and weapons and anything else they could get. They brought me to Anha Jorbstah to meet with their elders. I was to be a prisoner there until my father changed his mind. But that never happened."

Torlem and Barhi stared at him. Both of their brows were low. Then they started laughing. "You could've come up with a better story," Torlem said.

"Are you still not going to tell us the truth?" Barhi laughed.

Torlem whipped out his sword again and started toward the elf. She cried out in her tongue, but it didn't matter. Torlem had his eyes set, and he was too far away for Bertin to reach. *I can't do a thing to him anyway,* he thought. But Barhi was closer. Their back was turned to him.

Bertin took a deep breath and gripped his dagger. He had already killed before. What's another? He ran and jumped onto Barhi's back, bringing his dagger to their back. Barhi screamed and threw him off, but it was enough commotion to distract Torlem, who ran over to his friend and away from the elf. Bertin didn't know what to do, so he followed the elf's lead as she raced away.

He ran. And ran. And ran.

Shadows danced over him as he raced through the trees. He worried for ghosts, monsters, elves, and Torlem and Barhi. The mites would surely kill Bertin if he were found. Shivers went down his spine with every caw of a raven and crow, every croak of a frog and toad. His dagger was out and ready as he disappeared into the forest. Alone.

Raimund

The world was dying.

Dark clouds cast shadows that covered the ground, making everything gray and dreary. Small raindrops littered the stone path. Dead animals lined the paths. Homes in the valley below were dark and falling apart. There was a great tree off in the distance. His eyes got lost in it. It grew out of jagged mountains. A million branches but no leaves hung on the branches, almost no branches attached to the trunk, whatever was still on the tree sagged into the mountain. Raimund imagined his world, the one from before. *When was that? Where was that?* But images of colors, the singing of birds, the sounds of laughter all filled his head.

A purple light. He had fallen. Was pushed … no … jumped. He wanted to go. But now he regretted it. "Where am I?" he asked, and no one answered. "Who am I?" he asked, and no one answered.

He looked at his hands, his pale skin. Dark hair on his head. Dirt covered clothes. "Devro? Are you here? Mar?" Still nothing. "I am Raimund." He felt his head nod. It was heavy. Like he was swimming under the ocean and the water was keeping him down. He was supposed to be in

Redington. "No," he said. "That was long ago. Things have changed."

Raimund looked to the sky. Black and gray with streaks of slow-moving lightning. A dim sun couldn't light the world. It all felt like a dream. But his feet were on the ground, and he could take steps. He was breathing in the air, small bits of dirt and dust filling his lungs with every inhale. He looked to the tree again, and his eyes filled with tears. Nothing could stop it. He wanted to race across valleys and mountains to fix the tree. To bring it back, but it was dying. Just like everything else.

The world shook. Birds shot into the sky. Raimund fell to his knees as he saw the earth cracking and splitting, new valleys forming below, lava leaking out and creating rivers of death. The only colors in the entire land were the reds and yellows of the burning liquid, and Raimund had to make sure he didn't get too close.

He went into the town below. It looked safe enough. It reminded him of the towns he had seen in his past life. The place where Devro and … and … he had forgotten the name. His friends had traveled through wooden towns before. But they were full of fruits and vegetables; lords and ladies; workers and vagrants. Life. This town had nothing.

The stone path was covered in moss and grass. Raimund had to find his balance a few times, almost slipping. He didn't want to die here. Though he didn't know how he would get out. How he would get back to safety. The buildings he passed were all abandoned. Broken glass strewn about. It looked long empty. Like no one had set foot in the town in many years.

"How did they live like this?" he asked the great tree in

the distance. He imagined a world full of life. Birds singing. People cheering. The tree covered in a million leaves all shaking in the wind. But there was no noise now, only his footsteps. Raimund set his sights on one home that had a flame lighting a window, as if someone were still there. He had no weapon, but hoped whoever it was wouldn't want to fight. He pushed the door open—a white door made of wood. It hadn't cracked like all the other homes. Inside he saw a table set with plates and silverware, a hearth with fleeting embers, and portraits. They were of a family. Four. A father, mother, son, and daughter.

They had pointed ears.

Raimund thought back to his past life, of the place he came from, to find the word. He had seen pointed ears before. He had known their name. "I can't remember," he told himself.

The lone candle was melting near the glass window. It had burned for so long that the wax had melted onto the floor. That reminded him of something. Of somewhere. A woman, candle wax making a mess of her home, books all together. Raimund rubbed his head and thought of the red-haired woman. Flames devouring her.

A door to a bedchamber was ajar. He pushed it open and saw a body. Bloody tears stained the cheeks. It was the mother. Her hair was thin, with clumps all around the room. Dried black blood running down her shirt, a knife sticking out. Her hands near it like she killed herself. Her ears weren't pointed, though. There were only scabs where the points should be. "Cut off," Raimund said.

Once Raimund was back outside, he saw freshly dug graves. A stick above them with writing he couldn't read.

Rain fell on his head. Small, piercing droplets. He ran under an awning as the tree pulled his focus. Lightning flashed slowly across the sky. The sun was getting ever darker behind the noble tree. His world was different. The sun burned brightly and lit everything. That he remembered.

A branch broke off the tree. The boom echoed throughout the world. Then another. Raimund put his hands over his ears to keep them from hurting; the booming so loud his skull vibrated.

Then another crash shook the world, the town moaning from the force. The trunk of the colossal tree had snapped in the lower half. What was left of the tree rolled down the mountain, crashing along the rocky cliffs, the last of the birds panicking to get away. It rolled and bounced and smashed until it broke into a thousand pieces in the valley, the world shaking, the sky darker than it already was.

The world stopped moving. The world was still alive, holding on by a string. Raimund hoped for a quick death, though he felt he had more to do, more to see, a world to save.

But nothing happened.

He was still alive. Breathing. Crying. He hadn't felt the tears come on, but he couldn't stop. Seeing this world dying was too much for him. His head ached. His body shook. Then he vomited. He wished he were dead. He wanted to die with the world, with the tree, with the sun that was going black. The town was harder to see. His hands were harder to see. There was no light as a black cloud ate at the sun. Raimund reached a hand out as the last sliver of light was taken.

He stood in nothingness. Crying.

Then there was a roar, and he looked to the sky. Fire bathed the darkness, lighting the snout and wings in shadow as the dragon descended upon him. His tears turned to happiness. There was a thud, and the dragon huffed flames again. Raimund could see the town as it was set on fire. The fire lit his way. This time he didn't hesitate. He climbed atop the dragon's back and smiled as he lifted off the ground and soared through the black.

Raimund had no idea how long he was on the dragon, though it felt like months, but he woke in a forest. His memories flooded back. But the coldness of the other world made him shiver in fear. Made him cry as he opened his eyes. Purple light cascaded over him. As Raimund stood, he remembered who he was. "I am Ryobas reborn."

Tundavik

I hold much shock that you have returned." Ainmel said as they walked through the woods. "After everything that happened." Her brown eyes looked into his. "I do feel sorrow for you, and how I could do nothing to stop the killings."

Tundavik was leading Bera as they made their way to Ritaeum. The men and followers were behind. Miena's Hunters huddled to the side, always glancing at Tundavik and Ainmel. When they first appeared, the hunters had taken on the appearance of the trees and brush, but seeing an old friend they had transformed into a more human-like appearance. That calmed the nerves of the rest of the troop. Tundavik didn't care one way or another. He was once the duke of the Woodlands, and Miena's Hunters were his to control. He had sent them to Ealna to fight off the Riorsken all those years ago.

"There was nothing you could have done. I surprised myself when I decided to help Devro win the crown," Tundavik said. "The longest I had been away from Attrima before this was when a ship captain got lost and we stepped foot on Okros. Much too cold for my liking."

Ainmel's bow was slung over her shoulder, her arrows in

a quiver at her hip. When she looked human, she reminded Tundavik of all the people he ruled over as duke. Her skin was brown, her eyes as well, and her hair black. Some of the other hunters followed along; others turned more brown and green to remind everyone of the trees. "But Ritaeum, of all places?" Ainmel asked. "Why not back to the mountains of Asara? Surely it would be safer than the woods."

"I have to do something here," he said as flashes of a burning world filled his head. "But enough about me. I haven't seen you in over a decade. I saw you were graying like me," he laughed.

"Yet I'll still outlive you." She smiled. "Gemar was killed in a terrible fire brought on by the Rainvealandians at the end of the war. The hunters chose me as leader and steward of Miena's cause. I was thrilled to be at your service, but you disappeared."

"Hurvir forced me," Tundavik said as he stepped over a stream, moss floating down the water, algae sticking to rocks. "Your hunters made the right decision. I'm sure you've been a great leader. What've you been protecting this new lord from?"

"Anything that means him harm. Bandits from the west, Maermen from Ealna, even pirates from Eotros. It has been a busy decade." Ainmel watched her bare feet so as not to step on any sticks or fallen branches. "You hold much luck that I was here. When the hunters heard an army was marching through our land, they wanted nothing more than to slice your throats."

"You're also lucky. The army would've fought back, and not even you can take on a thousand." Tundavik and Ainmel turned their heads to watch the army march. They weren't as organized as they had been when marching through the Kinglands. The trees had spread them out. Banners got lost in the leaves. The sun tried its hardest to reach them, but sometimes the canopy was so thick it turned to night. "But you scared me. At first I thought Ultiir had attacked, or this new duke of the Woodlands."

"Not so new anymore. Lord Valles has been here since you were driven away. He has been a good lord to all, as much as it may pain you to hear. It is the truth." Ainmel found a dead leaf and clasped her hands around it. The brown turned green, and she put it in her hair. "He had to rebuild after the war. He gave the people their lives back."

Tundavik mustered a smile. "The people of the Woodlands deserve a good lord after the wars. One that will fight for them instead of running."

Ainmel lowered her voice. "Though the trees tell me the Ritae are not happy. They wish one of their own as liege and whisper in the night air. You may ignite the Woodlands if you take the castle."

He saw the Woodlands burning a bright orange. *My home.* But it wasn't the Ritae who were burning it; it was an army of shadows. "Not if I can help it. There hasn't been a Ritae as lord since the Veck'kop pushed them from the river."

"Things change," Ainmel shrugged. "A thousand years ago my kind thought the humans would kill us all, but now we work in the duke's service."

Tundavik patted Bera's soft snout. She huffed and nudged him. "Do you think we can take Ritaeum?"

Ainmel glanced back once more at the army. "Lord Valles hasn't called his banners. You'd be fighting women and children and blacksmiths and bakers. The one thing that could stop you is the weariness of your men. The trees have told me their secrets."

"I already stopped a possible mutiny. I don't need another."

"Then Ritaeum needs to fall quickly, especially after your failure at Vigur."

"We didn't fail at Vigur. We went to rescue Devro, and that's what we did. Though the city falling would have been better. The war would be over, but I made the decision with the queen. I'm not sure how many men we would've lost if we'd stayed."

"That is not how your men see it. They want to end the fighting. Go home. Now they march through thickets and trees and over streams and swamps. And they are more tired than you know."

"Only a few more battles, I'm sure of it." Tundavik said, and Ainmel rested her hands on her hips. "Okay," he relented. "I hope."

"Ainmel," a hunter called from behind. *"Vrimatá kon Ritamaih. Erhseis mazá rinla."*

"They wish to disappear into the woods," Ainmel translated.

"Not helping at Ritaeum? It would be much quicker with your bows."

"Miena would curse us for attacking our lord," Ainmel whispered. "But we will not fight unless our lord calls us into battle, and so far he hasn't. So, we will wait in the trees. I do hope I will not have to fight you." She went off with her hunters and disappeared into the trees as they all morphed into sticks and limbs and leaves.

Tundavik mounted his horse and found Mar riding

behind. "Tell the men to stop here. Ritaeum is upon us."

***

It was easy to see they were nearing the seat of the Woodlands. The trees went from rough growth and misshapen limbs to lines and columns. Orchards of all kinds were nearby, mostly apples and lemons. Large tree nuts grew on trees, and abandoned baskets lay at trunks. "Does this mean they knew?" Glem asked as he watered the horses. "This won't be a surprise."

"Only a precaution," Tundavik said. "That's what I'm telling myself, anyway. Perhaps Ultiir saw we were marching to the Woodlands and sent a rider. But Ritaeum is hard to defend; that's something I know well. The lack of men and walls makes it a prime target."

Glem found an apple on the ground and gave it to his horse. "How will the people react to seeing you, my lord?"

"I am no lord." *Not anymore and never again.* "They probably won't recognize me. Most were killed when Hurvir attacked."

Glem kicked some sticks and said, "I had forgotten that. I am not learned, but I remember the stories of my childhood. The lord who rebelled and took Suktir back from his own people." Tundavik winced at the lie. "Of course, few believed it. Especially those who chose to follow you."

"So what do you think happened?"

"Hurvir was angry." The squire shrugged. "That's all it takes for a king to kill."

For men to kill. He left the squire with the horses and found a large tent. Inside were the usual confidants of

471

Devro and Yvanne. Lord Aimora Dore of Lodeanhold, the angry Lord Cul, Pollard, Diero, Gordo, even Lady Lolly all stood for Yvanne. As he settled at the head of the table, he watched her fire hair and Lolly taking care of her. Devro stood with Mar, and somehow Lord Furrow of Nye talked his way in.

"Shall we talk plans?" Lord Aimora stood. "I've been discussing some ideas with the queen's brothers." Tundavik tapped his foot before giving a nod. "Good, and you know Ritaeum better than others. What say you?"

Tundavik cleared his throat. "The town and castle will be utterly defenseless, but that doesn't mean the men won't put up a fight. I'm sure they've been preparing for a few days. There won't be a siege this time. Instead, we will assault them from all sides. I will lead the men from the northern road. Another group will branch and hit the southern road." The thoughts of his old home flooded his mind. The people he would share laughs with. His parents and brothers and sister. The old barber. The bloodied corpses of his wife and children. "Lord Aimora, you are able to go through mountains quite well?"

"Of course. I am a Lodean, and so are my men."

"Trees are easier. You will go to the east and stretch the length of the forest."

"The sun could set. We'll be blind."

"Then, the west with the sun at your backs," Tundavik said. "Take all your men and any other archers you can find. Fire from the trees until we wave Devro's banner. Then you will join the attack."

Gordo leaned forward. "Are we to follow you?"

"You can lead from the south, my lord," Tundavik said.

"Diero, you will join him. Pollard will be with me."

Pollard shot up. "I need to protect my sister."

"Sir Mar will protect Yvanne as he has done before. I need your expertise on the battlefield. You did well in Vigur," Tundavik told Pollard as Mar rolled his eyes.

"You can fight with me on the battlefield." Devro piped up. Tundavik had forgotten he was there.

"You won't be fighting." Tundavik told his king. "It's much too dangerous."

Devro was taken aback. "Not fighting? The men will think I'm scared. I have to fight. I need to lead."

"The last time you fought, you were captured," Tundavik said softly. "We cannot have that happen again. I'll tell the men you are awaiting word from the rearguard. We should be done with no need to call you."

"Kings are in the van, not the rear," Devro whined. "My father always led his armies." His small fist hit the table.

Tundavik clenched his teeth. "Every moment we spend on this means more time we lose to night. This battle will take time, and I need it over before the sun sets."

"I have an idea." Yvanne stood with Lady Lolly's help. "If you'll hear me."

"Of course." Lord Aimora spoke.

"If we want this battle to end quickly. Why not set it alight? The town I mean. It would be easy, and few of our men will die."

Diero nodded. "The wood will burn fast."

All eyes were on Tundavik, not the king nor queen. He had to decide what would happen to his old home. "My lord?" Gordo asked.

The thought of Ritaeum burning made him wince. "No."

The air was sucked from the room like these people wanted innocents to die. "There will be no fire."

"And why not?" Lord Cul asked. "Surely you do not care for our enemies. For your old castle?"

Tundavik's head whipped to the ancient man. "I will not have the forest burn while I lead the armies. What will we eat when the fruit trees turn to ash? How will we warm ourselves with charred wood? Game from the woods will flee, and we will starve."

"Is it possible to burn only the castle?" Gordo pondered.

"It meets the trees," Tundavik said. "The entirety of the Woodlands will burn if we set it alight."

Aimora nodded. "You were born here and don't want to destroy it, but sometimes we must make hard choices."

"Would you destroy your own home?" Mar asked. Tundavik wanted to give him a smile.

"Lodeanhold is made of the finest stone carved from the mountains," Aimora smirked. "It would not burn so easily."

"And we've tried," Pollard quipped.

Tundavik rolled his eyes at the stupid argument. "Who knows how many will die if we set the place aflame. I will not risk it."

Cul turned to Devro. "You are the leader here, my king, not Tundavik. It is your decision and no one else's. We either burn Ritaeum or risk our men's lives."

Devro's eyes darted between them. *Do not choose that angry lord,* Tundavik thought as he glared at Lord Cul.

"Burning the town will make them yield," Devro said, and Tundavik held his breath. "But it is too dangerous. I can lead our army into battle, and we will win before nightfall." He said with an enormous smile, his neck stretched and his chest puffed as much as he could get it.

"You will not." Tundavik jumped in. "Stay in the rear—"

Yvanne groaned and clutched her stomach. Lolly was on her as were her brothers. Lady Lolly looked at Yvanne's lower region. "The baby is close, but isn't ready yet."

Tundavik took the chance. "Your Grace, stay with your wife in case she has the baby and needs more protection. The rest of us will ready for battle." Tundavik did not listen to anymore objections. He rushed from the tent and found Glem with his helm and spear and sword.

"I heard a ruckus," Glem said. "Is everything alright?"

"We are going to take Ritaeum. Ready my horse, then find the rear."

"But I want to fight." Glem gripped a sword.

Must everyone object? "You will be in the rear. Once the battle is over, you will tell the other men how the king was ready to fight gallantly, but his wife needed him, and we took the castle before he could join us."

Glem nodded and fetched Bera, who wore leather and a few plates on her chest stolen from a small village outside Vigur. *Time to take back my home.*

The vanguard moved about with Tundavik at the front. Lord Aimora slipped into the trees with the Lodean, and the rearguard stayed at the ready. The groves of trees passed them by, all empty of people. Small huts abandoned and animals left to fend for themselves. Tundavik made sure to notify the cooks of the animals.

Through the dark sentinels, he saw the towers of his old home. They were nothing great nor magnificent like Vigur. The towers were much smaller than the walls of Riverton or the castle in Storyah. But it was home. Screams filled his ears. *They're not real. Those are the screams of children, women, old men.* He closed his eyes to forget the massacre. *Is this how my family saw Hurvir's army?*

But he was not Hurvir. He would not massacre the people of Ritaeum. He needed only the castle. There were battle cries and chants, and Tundavik knew Lord Onnu Valles would not yield.

Sir Pollard rode up from behind. "Do you see that?"

Tundavik nodded as he closed the visor of his helm. Coming from Ritaeum was a charging array of farmers, planters, merchants, and old men … all armed.

Yvanne

Sounds of fighting sang through the trees. "My men are fighting without me," Devro said with a red face. Yvanne held her stomach as they walked through the mostly empty camp to her tent. The only people not fighting were the injured, a few daken, the cooks, and the camp followers.

"I mean no offense," Mar said to Devro, "but these men have fought all their battles without you. There were many on the march to Vigur. They do not need a king to lead them, just a good commander and some spirit."

"That makes it worse," Devro whined. He tilted his head to listen to no one, then nodded. "What if they decide Ultiir is a better king than me? A king should lead."

"Based on what?" Mar laughed. "I never once saw Ultiir ride into battle. He hid away in his palace far from the field, which is much worse than you standing in the camp."

Lady Lolly was standing close to Yvanne, making sure she didn't fall. "How are you feeling?"

"Fine," Yvanne said, though her insides were heavy and tight. "Your Grace," she turned to Devro, "you are the king. You can do whatever you want. I know Lord Vandes just wants to keep you safe, but if you feel strongly about it, then it's your decision to make."

The young king nodded. "Let's go see the rearguard."

"I don't think that's a good idea," Mar said with wide eyes.

"But I am king." Devro smiled.

Lolly grabbed Yvanne's hand. "It is imperative you come with me and we lie you down just in case the babe is ready to come. We don't want the heir born on a battlefield. He would be destined to bring war."

Yvanne shook her sister off. *I am not having this child right now. He can wait.* "I will inspect the rear with His Grace, and then we can go to my tent."

They changed course and made their way through the camp and out a little way through disturbed trees. Yvanne was panting by the time they saw gray and brown leather armor poking through the leaves. The forest smelled like a mix of sweat, piss, and wet wood. The amount of ankle-deep water was increasing as they pushed farther into the woods. Small, biting insects devoured everyone. Yvanne swatted a bug away as she saw soldiers doing the same.

They reached the men who stood with their weapons, some steel, others wood, whatever they could find or steal before they reached Ritaeum. Murmurs defeated the silence of the rear. Yvanne couldn't hear what they were talking about, but Devro said, "They speak of me."

"I don't think that's true," Mar said.

As more and more of the soldiers saw Devro and his small crown, they bowed, some lower than others. A young man came over in leather armor. He took off his helm and bowed his head. A mess of brown hair spilled out, and he reminded Yvanne a little of Tiro. If the boy had been allowed to grow up. "Your Grace," his teeth chattered, "Tundavik told me you were staying in camp."

Devro looked him up and down. "You are Tundavik's squire?"

"Glem," the young man said. "Would you like … like me to show you the horses?" Glem nervously picked at his brown-covered nails.

"That will work," Devro said with a nod.

"We want to keep His Grace safe," Mar said. "War is a dangerous place, even for kings."

"Of course," Glem nodded. "This way."

They followed the young man to the front of the rear. Soldiers murmured as they went by. Now, Yvanne heard talk of Devro and how he was king and how he should lead the van and not be hiding away. She also heard whispers about herself. About her pregnant body. Snickers of how men would like to impregnate her next. "She needs a real man," some stupid soldier said.

"Is this truly safe?" Lolly whispered. Her face was in a constant state of looking offended. Like being at the battle lines was an affront to nature. "The heir is so close to being born, if anything were to happen now …"

"It won't," Yvanne shook her head. "The trees and soldiers protect me."

Glem easily led them to the horses at the rear. Through the lined orchards, Yvanne could just make out glints of metal and steel. The screams from the van filled the air. There was no Ritaeum though, no large castle in sight. She had never seen the town before and wondered if it was worse off than Whitehall.

Some children were brushing or feeding the horses; women and old men were placing what leather they had over their chests and heads. Glem went off to talk to the horsemaster. "This one is called Herb." The horsemaster named Fon patted a light green mare as he brought her over to Devro. "I'm sure she'll be to your liking. Fast and agile, yet sturdy when needed. But His Grace may pick another."

"She'll do," Devro said. He looked at Yvanne, and his eyes were glassy and upper lip sweaty.

Yvanne got close to her husband and said, "Hide the nerves." She wiped his lip. "Show these men that you are a better king than the rest. That you will actually fight alongside your men."

"I should be fighting in the van," Devro whispered.

"The rear is just as important. And if you wish, you don't have to wait for any signal from the van. Lead the army yourself. Make decisions yourself. This war is almost over, and if we're going to rule in Vigur, you need to—ugh …" a pain hit her like a wave. Her lower back tensed, and her pelvic muscles tightened so hard Mar had to catch her from falling.

"Your Grace," the knight said, "you should listen to your sister. Go to your tent to lie down and rest."

"I … am … fine," she stomped a foot as tears filled her eyes. Sounds of fighting sang through the trees. "A king must find his glory, and where better than the Woodlands? It will be easier to fight now than when we march back on the Kinglands."

"Here is some armor for His Grace," Glem said as some soldiers were stripping off their armor to give to Devro. "And a spear if you'd like." The squire swayed as he bit some nails.

Devro nodded, and Mar, shaking his head, helped him

into an array of leather and mail. The spear was much taller than Devro, and it wobbled in his hand. But he looked like a fighter all the same. "This is still a bad idea," Mar said, "but I will fight with you."

Devro said, "No, you must watch after Yvanne. My heir is important." Mar didn't argue, only sighed.

Yvanne kissed Devro's cheek. "You will come back to us. Back with glory and Lord Valles bowing at your feet. I will be right here wa—ahhhh—" She grabbed her belly. She didn't want to have the child now; she couldn't. Not without a bedchamber and clean water and Helge and … *Why didn't I bring Helge with me? She would've known what to do … Gods, I miss her so much.*

"Sir Loc," Lolly called to the knight, "we've no time. Go find Jacka and Maliz and bring them here." The knight raced away. Mar and Lolly grabbed Yvanne's arms and dragged her into a small tent meant for maybe two people. Devro's words to the soldiers were muffled outside.

Mar held her head as they laid her down on a blanket over the ground, the lumps digging into her back. Her body shuddered as it was hit with another wave. Mar's hand was in hers, and her nails dug into his skin as she screamed out. When it was over, she let go, and Mar pulled his hand back in pain. A burn mark on his palm. His eyes grew wide at the sight, but he said nothing.

"I need linen," Lolly said as she fled from the tent.

"Where is it?" Mar asked, and Yvanne shook her head. She had no idea what he was talking about, but could barely speak as more waves hit her, over and over, beating at her body. "Your hand," Mar said, "where is it?"

She looked at her hand, thinking it was lost. Instead,

she saw flames licking her fingers. If she wasn't careful, she would burn down the entire forest and out herself as an éithrio. That would mean certain death. *And possibly my child's too,* she thought. "My ... neck .... neck ... lace ... gggguuuhhhh."

Mar nodded and ripped her necklace off her. The flames vanished, and so did all the energy flows of the world as well. It was as if she were blind. No longer could she see where fires were, or bodies, or where death was. She was normal.

Lolly burst into the tent with towels. Jacka and Maliz and Loc followed. "Not enough room," Lolly cried. Mar and Loc left the tent, Mar with her stone in a pocket.

Maliz was carrying herbs and the Book of the Four. "I've prayed for Vigura's blessing and that he send word to Mother Meret for a quick and painless birth," the nursemaid said. "Now chew on this." She gave Yvanne a white flower.

"I don't ... don't ... want ... uugggghhh ... this ..." Yvanne said as tears spilled down her cheeks.

"We rarely do," Lolly said as she brushed Yvanne's hair back. "But you must be strong."

Men were shouting outside, all excited and chanting for Devro. Yvanne's body shuddered. It was as if the entire weight of the world was between her hips. She gritted her teeth as her face strained. "Ahhhhh"

"It will be alright," Jacka soothed her. "I have delivered countless children, all healthy, their mothers too."

Yvanne shook her head in defiance. It was stupid of her to get pregnant. Stupid to lead an army. Stupid to marry a king. She wanted to curl up in her bed and listen to Helge's prayers and her father's laugh. She missed the cold of the mountains. She missed it all.

A rumble shook the ground as Yvanne heard Devro shout, "Charge!"

Yvanne lay on her back ... screaming.

Aveline

This place is hell," Tomas said of the forest as they walked deeper into the trees. "Not even the elf city was as bad as this." The trees glowered down at them as they rose far into the sky. Gnats wisped across their faces, spiders hung from webs, ants crawled up their pants. Aveline shivered, and it wasn't even cold. There was an air of darkness in this forest. She couldn't put her finger on why, but it reminded her of her father's burial. The way the peasants looked at her. Wanting to beat her, or rape her, or kill her. Except there were no peasants in the forest. Only the six of them. And silence.

"Are you afraid?" Ivlin said.

Tomas chuckled, then gulped. "You know, I just might be. Giant spiders could eat us, or a horde of gnomes attack our ankles."

"We'll be fine," Dern said as he puffed his chest. "No creature is strong enough to fight royal guards."

"Let's not find out." Zoell said with a glance into the forest.

Aveline's eyes glazed over from staring into the wood. The towers of trees made her feel like a scared child again, which meant Bertin would be terrified. But they were getting closer to him. She could feel it.

"Why haven't we seen any elves?" Zoell asked. "Ansehar hanged one, so I'd thought they'd be more of a problem."

Dern laughed. "Perhaps we frighten them."

"Or they're stalking us," Aveline said. Out of the corner of her eye, Tomas clenched. "Hopefully, they don't want to avenge the dead elf and send us back as a message."

"We're not mites … hrm … Rainvealandians," Dern said.

"Not sure they care about the difference," Ivlin said.

"Shall we make camp?" Zoell asked. "Get our bearings and settle in for the day."

"We've barely explored," Bert said. "Can we at least find a creek?"

Zoell relented, so the group continued through the vast forest. Aveline didn't know how large it was, and Ivlin's map just had a few hand-drawn trees to mark a forest so dense she couldn't see a hundred feet in front of her. Her feet ached without the horses. It was a nice respite from walking hundreds of miles to ride in a wagon. *Wonder why the horses don't like coming here?* She thought.

So far, the forest wasn't anything horrifying. There weren't dead humans littered and decomposed. Elves didn't show their faces. Nymphs or dryads or anything else never came at them either. As a child, her mother would often tell her stories of the horrors that befell any human dumb enough to waltz into the Sruhq. For hundreds of years, the Rainvealandians controlled the woods, but somehow they lost it to the ancient creatures in a rebellion. Her mother would tell her, "Your father would never let something like that happen. He is a powerful man and a great king. I hope you grow up and learn from that strength. Make sure no one ever rises against you or your brothers. That you keep them safe." Then she would tickle Aveline, and they would giggle away.

And now she journeyed deep into an unknown world just to find Bertin. She wished she could be in two places at once. One of her would be here, searching for her brother. The other would be with Baldewin, keeping him safe from the parasitic councilors. *And be with Mari too,* she thought, and could feel her cheeks blush. *I'll see her again. She and I will live a long life together, away from the mess of politics. I wonder where she'll want to travel first?* So she spent the rest of the day thinking about Mari and how great their lives would be.

They made camp near a thicket under the ancient trees, hundreds of years old. A brook babbled close by for them to relieve themselves and find fresh water upstream. Supper was some strips of pork and apples they had bought in Ansehar. Aveline was just happy not to have to eat figs. Zoell boiled water so they could drink. Tomas hummed a song about a horse mating with a bear. "Northerners love it," he said after strange looks.

No one seemed afraid as darkness came over the forest like a blanket. Dern the Third told about the time he bested a knight in a tourney. "… my destrier, Bow, named after the river, was a magnificent chestnut with sturdy legs and chest. I donned my armor with diamonds, and Bow was armored in black plate with a jewel on his head. We charged the old man. I kept my eye on the beautiful maid, Lucia, then I lowered my lance and never looked. That's when I heard the old man fly off his horse. To no one's surprise, I had won. The Horse Knight sheepishly left Gereduss and was never heard from again. And Lucia fucked me for a week straight." Dern laughed and laughed as he remembered the story. Her other guards did too. Aveline let a few chuckles, but she had heard the story a million times already, usually with a different woman at the end. She only hoped anything they ran into in the forest would fall as easily as the Horse Knight.

Zoell always prayed to the moon, but tonight it was hidden behind the canopy of dark green leaves, so instead she sulked. It was an odd sight, but Aveline knew how much she hated going without prayer. The rest prayed to the Four, except Bert. Bert had guarded Aveline since she was a child. He never prayed and spoke about gods only in jest. The horrors of the world must have changed him. That was her only explanation. She didn't pray either, but not because of the horrors, but because the gods never answered her when she asked about her brothers. Any gods she would worship wouldn't bring so much trouble to her family. She would still have a mother and father and would be traveling with Mari. Not stuck in a damp forest.

Aveline couldn't sleep, not for lack of trying. Her mother told her to save her brothers every time she shut her eyes. She poked at the fire to keep it going, tossing in more wood as the forest grew ever darker. The fire danced with images of home. Blis had taught her about the Bruthaki Flames when she was young. The revolt that killed thousands and deposed a queen. Caxton would surely bring about strife in the kingdom if he turned on the royal family. She could not let that happen, but first she needed Bertin. *Let me find him.*

"Are you ready for what we will find?" Bert rose from

his snoring and found his way to Aveline. He brushed dirt from his face.

"You mean Bertin?" Aveline shrugged. "Surely he's alive. I mean, he can't be dead. We'll find him in the middle of the forest, just begging to go home with us." She hoped, at least.

Bert nodded. "What's the plan after that? We're a long way from any city."

"Bardekan or Çakiz. I'm not sure which is better. At least Bardekan is only across the bay from Rowan."

"And Baldewin?"

"We'll send word to Redington that he can come home. As long as Caxton and the rest let him. Bertin will be king, and this will all be behind us."

"And if the council resists?" Bert traced a finger in the grass. Dern's snoring shook the ground.

"We'll see," Aveline said. There wasn't much more she could say. If the council tried to take control from Bertin or Baldewin, then it would be war. She didn't see any other way around that.

Bert was about to say something when they heard a noise. It differed from the cries of animals or the flapping of wings or the buzzing of insects. It was a plop in some water. Then a twig snapped.

"He was traveling with people," Aveline told Bert as she stood.

"But we're not sur—" Bert tried to say, but she had already found a dagger. She motioned for Bert to follow, and so he did. He drew his sword and kicked the others before leaving them to wake.

Orange sun peaked through the slivers in the trees. It

helped them find their way to the water, a clearing on either side of the brook. Aveline dropped behind a thicket with Bert next to her. Her breathing labored as she watched. There were two people. One was holding a wounded neck while the other was using a wet cloth to clean it.

"Don't worry, we'll find that fucker." The one with the cloth said in the ancient tongue.

"I told you he was a liar," the other said. "But you don't listen to me."

"Calm down," he said as he wrapped the other's neck. "Even if that boy is a prince or whatever … we'll kill him."

Aveline couldn't keep the tears from welling in her eyes. She could feel Bert's eyes on her. Her guards rustled behind them but said nothing. "Ready to go hunting?" She asked Bert.

Flora

Storyah was in their sights.

The last few weeks on foot had been miserable. Flora had prayed atop the horses for food to appear, but it never did. "It is against my knightly vow to steal." Edmond would say when they reached a town. "It will draw us more attention." Marbert echoed.

"At least carry me." Vanette would say, but the knights refused. Flora hadn't seen Vanette run away from River Watch as Spider sprinted across the land, but one night a guard had found her in nearby bushes. "I want to see the world," Vanette had told Flora.

"Very well," Flora said. There was nothing good in River Watch anyhow. Luk would find his mother near death and hopefully kill his father if he hadn't died already. *Bleeding to death,* Flora thought as she again felt the skin and tendons tear beneath her knife when she stabbed the lord's neck. *Father would never believe me, and what would mother think?* "I'm capable of great violence," she had whispered to herself at camp.

They had traversed the levels, crossed rivers and streams, found any shelter they could in towns, and were now at the gates of Storyah along with the thousands of refugees from the war-torn Eastlands and beyond.

"Is this what large cities are like?" Vanette said in disgust as a man coughed on her. "This has more filth than a man with a diseased cock."

"You get used to it," Edmond said with his hand on his hilt. Flora stayed near the dozen guards who had made it back from River Watch.

Vanette pushed a dirt-covered woman away. "Never get used to the cock."

"Come with me," Flora motioned. "I'll get us into the city faster." She walked to a guardhouse, but Marbert pulled her back.

"My lady, do you want your husband to know you're here? Especially if your suspicions are true?" Flora shook her head at the knight. "I have some friends here. I'll get us inside."

They made their way through the crowded outer streets. A sickness had ravaged the people. Dead bodies were being carried out to mass graves. The tents and dirt had blocked wagons and merchants from getting to the city. Guards robbed the poor and threatened them with spears. Flora kept her head down as fighting broke out around her. *I hope Meret helps you all. If only I could.*

Marbert laughed away with some guards while Vanette, Edmond, and Flora sat on an overturned wain. The other guards stood around, joking and keeping refugees from them. "I didn't know the war was so bad," Vanette said. "River Watch hadn't been touched."

"Lord Poden tried." Edmond explained. "I sense it's far from over. Maybe Kruhesh is the safest place."

The woman smiled. "Would you go with me? I could use

a skilled knight for protection, though your pay would be awful."

"I took a vow."

"Vows mean nothing in times of war." Flora added. *My husband taught me this.* "Life is too short to spend it in a castle. Kruhesh may be fun, though I've never been. Where would you go?" She asked Vanette.

"I was dreaming of Teeraj. The rich lands have always called me."

"To Teeraj than." Edmond said. "If Poden Bruce's son doesn't find us."

"I pray he won't attack us," Flora said. "I pray he sees his father for the monster he is."

"Are you going to speak of foreign lands all day or come with me?" Marbert came from behind. "I found the key."

His friend snuck them through the Eotros Gate in the eastern part of the city. They followed the roads to the castle. Vanette had to be pulled along from distracting shops as she was trying to buy necklaces that matched her coal-like eyes. The city was silent to Flora. She couldn't hear the horses trotting, or the bakers kneading, or the peasants conversing. Only one thing was on her mind ... her husband. *Please be wrong.* Flora told herself as they neared the castle walls. She didn't want Barnet to take over, but he was capable.

The castle was where she left it. The salt of the ocean filled her nostrils, and the golden sun reflected off the roof. "This is it."

"We do not have to go in, my lady." Marbert told her as they walked toward the gate. Flora stopped to overlook the beach below. Fallen armor rusted as the waves crashed.

Marbert cleared his throat. "You can run north or south or wherever. We will go with you and keep you safe."

"My daughter is here, and my father still. I must find them."

Vanette came from behind. "I wish you luck, but I'm only a whore. I'm going to the harbor so I can get away from the streets of shit before blood flows. Maybe find a way to Teeraj."

Flora nodded and then Edmond spoke. "I'll go with her, at least to find a ship. She'll need protection in the harbor. But I will be back by nightfall, my lady."

"You both can go." Flora said, and they did. A dozen ships were being unloaded across the small bay. She wondered if they would all leave if Barnet followed through with his plan. Flora sighed before turning to Marbert. "If you wish to go to the Brothel Square, then do."

"I joined your troop. I'm not leaving now."

Good. At least I have someone on my side.

"Welcome back to the safety of the castle walls." A guard at the gatehouse said to Flora. "It can be dangerous out there. Those refugees have grown larger with every passing day. The men who stayed behind have to keep any riots at bay, but they haven't reached the castle. At least your father can keep you safe."

But can I keep him safe? Flora wanted to say.

Marbert whispered as they walked through the baileys. "Barnet will know you have returned."

"Good," Flora said. "Maybe he will rethink whatever plan he has concocted."

"What will you say to him?" Marbert's hand rested on the dirk at his hip.

"Hopefully, he sees me and remembers the happy moments we shared. That I am his bride and the mother of his only daughter. It's the only thing that might work."

She would soon find out. Barnet stood at the castle doors with a retinue of his men who had stayed behind from Vigur. The stone of the castle looked like gray clouds. Storyah was overcast with gloom. Nowhere did she see her father. "It's too late." She whispered to Marbert. The tears welled in her eyes, but then the doors opened, and Lord Pyre Blume boomed out.

"I knew the old Poden Bruce wouldn't hurt you." He embraced her. She dug her nails into his back, remembering when she was a child, smelling his freshly shaven face. "You'll have to report to us all on the happenings of the Flit Levels, but first we feast." Her father put a hand on her back and led her up the steps.

"If I may," Barnet started when they reached the door, "I would like to speak with my wife. We need to find little Flora so that she can see her mother. She's been missing her."

"Of course." Lord Blume said. "I think Nama has taken her to the library."

But they didn't go to the library. Barnet led her through the twisting halls of limestone until they were out of view. He smiled as he pushed open the door to their bedchamber. It was the same smile as before she left. The room was sterile. The hearth empty, the floor cleared, her belongings gone. Sheets tucked in tightly. *Florance must not be sleeping here, nor Barnet. They've been busy ... him more than her.* Flora went toward the bed; her husband stayed by the door, his hand resting on the gilded handle. Outside, a light rain fell.

The terror she felt when Ultiir's forces bombarded the city was nothing compared to what she felt now.

"I received a letter from River Watch a few days back." Barnet picked at his fingers. "Lord Poden is dead. Luk, his heir, has taken over. You have put this entire land in jeopardy. Did you even try for peace?"

"Poden is a monster; he did not deserve peace." Flora said as she sat on the bed, all the weight she had been carrying pulled her down. "You should've seen Lady Willa, his wife. The horror he caused." Flora didn't want to cry yet. She needed to save her tears for her father. "He claimed the Four wanted him to purify this land. I'm glad Luk ended his father's reign of terror. I just hope he is a good lord."

"Luk?" Barnet reached his hand into a pocket and for a moment Flora thought he was going to bring out a knife. End her life. But it was only a slip of parchment that he unrolled. "Luk tells me you were the one who killed Poden Bruce," he said as he threw the paper toward the bed. "And you're sure you tried? Did he tell you any of his plans before you killed him?" She said nothing. The room was quiet. Raindrops hit the window. Barnet sighed and sat on the bed next to her, but she kept her eyes forward. A painting above the hearth showed two lovers embracing; the canvas blackened from the fire below.

"He wanted independence, is all," she said in a monotone voice. *Barnet knows. So why lie anymore?* She took a deep breath. *Meret, please watch over my daughter.* But she knew the prayer wouldn't be answered. Today was the day of Vigura. He punished, not protected. "How will he die? My father?"

Barnet didn't look at her. He rose and stared into a mirror, fixing loose hairs. "You do not need to know."

Flora shot to her feet. She wanted to slap him. To yell. Cry. Shout about how he was ruining the life of their daughter. But he wouldn't care. He never did. "How could you do this? How could you kill my father, your wife's father? He has been kind to you, kind to little Flora, kind to this land. He has done all he needed to keep us from being massacred by Hurvir. You must know this." He said nothing. "Is this for power? You want to be lord of the Flewthlands? King? My father is not getting younger. He will die eventually, so let him. You do not have to murder him."

"I am saving this kingdom from him." Barnet seethed, veins popping around his throat as he turned to her. "He *saved* our people? He has condemned us to death by agreeing to join wars we do not wish to fight."

"If you didn't want to fight for the bastard king, then why did you vote to send the army south?" She was afraid of the answer.

"Your lover had a way with words," Barnet said as his eye twitched. "He convinced me to vote with him. Of course, I had just one stipulation. For my men and the men of other lords to go south to Vigur, he had to turn a blind eye to Storyah."

All she could say in complete defeat was, "He knew."

"Yes, he knew it all. He knew I would strip your father of power and how I meant to do it."

"You would murder him? What would the Four think?"

"I do not fear the Four. They hide away in their halls, feasting while we men must fight and die in this world. They are cowards. At least I take the initiative."

"Florance. What of her? How will you explain what you've done?"

She thought his eyes filled with tears for a moment. "I will tell her nothing. That is for you to do."

Without thinking, Flora burst through the door and ran. Ran through the maze, over the tile, through doors and arches. The palace had turned into a blur. Her eyes dripped tears as she passed the men and women. *Florance. I have to get to her.*

Marbert was slurping done soup in the mess lined with long wooden tables when she found him. Flora yanked him to his feet and brought him over to the wall. Others watched in silence as they ate. The limestone was cold to the touch as Flora leaned against it and panted. "You must help me find my daughter. She should be in the library, but I need protection." She hoped Marbert understood.

"Of course," was all she heard.

They raced through the twists and turns of the palace to the library. She was exhausted as she opened the gilded door. It was empty. Silent. The quiet was so overbearing that she didn't hear the knight behind her latch the door. Then everything went dark.

Soon, she woke with a small hand on her face. "Mother." Flora recognized the voice. "My sweet child." She said before turning to see Barnet and Marbert in the door of a room. *He lied to me. Marbert has been lying this whole time.* She clutched Florance's hand.

"You should stay here." Barnet said through a strained voice as he and the knight left her alone with her daughter.

The door latched from the outside. Just a few moments before, Flora would've run to the door and banged until her fists were bloody. But now, she was defeated. Done. There was nothing she could do to stop her husband, her own husband, from killing her father. *At least I got one more hug.*

"Father said this was our new room," Florance said with a look of wonder at the candles and stone walls. Enjoying the new sights.

Flora looked around and noticed the window too high to reach. *A cell.* There was a dead fire in the corner with a small cookpot above it. Only one bed in the center of the gray room. *I can't believe he did it,* she thought before thinking, *am I?* Ever since her marriage to Barnet, she knew how secretive he was. How cunning he could be. His dealings with the people of Woodrun should've told her to run. The way he would turn a blind eye to thefts if it was a powerful friend. Give harsh punishments to the most helpless. Hang those he saw as traitors. *But killing my father?* Flora shook her head as she sat on the bed. She didn't want to cry over him, not anymore. She had spent countless days and nights crying, wishing Barnet were better to her. "What am I going to do?" She whispered to herself.

Florance peeked through the keyhole of the door, laughing as she explored. They would be below the castle. Upstairs was where the blood would pour. "Do you th—"

Screaming erupted. Florance jerked to the bed and clutched Flora's chest. Flora clenched her jaw and held her eyes steady. One movement and she would burst into tears. Her father would be dead; she couldn't let Florance be next. "Shall we pray?"

Blis

I 've never stolen no boat before," Potter said. Delmar, Blis, and Potter were all carrying sacks of goods and clothes down the rocky hills. Mari kept Baldewin close. And if anything were to happen, Sir Delmar would whip out his sword and send the councilors to Veltoora.

"It's been a long while for me," Blis told the fat boy. "But those were mite ships back then. Boarded and captured everyone." He smiled at the fond memory, wondering where most of his sailors were now. Back then it was hard enough to put together a good crew with the flames and all, but Blis had scoured the coast from Dunniage to Coastburg, and found those he deemed strong enough. Little did he know his ship would become the champion of Seler Bay. He did well back then. Now he was running away.

It was dark when they set out on their plan. They were to take the *Kutski,* the ship that Potter came on, and sail it to the mainland. The Drewogh shores would be all mountains and cliffs, so Blis decided to sail to the Flewth-Vet. At least they could find allies there.

"I haven't commanded a ship in decades," Blis had told Baldewin earlier in the day. "I may get lost in the sea or crash against the land or—"

"—I trust you, Blis," Baldewin said. "Trust you more than the councilors, I guess."

Blis had straightened his shirt and nodded to the boy king. Sir Delmar had been packing with Mari, and Potter sat in the corner of the small hut they called home. It was a tight fit for them all, and the ceiling was leaking as it rained outside. The only light they had was candles, as clouds had hidden the sun. "Thank you. I'm sorry we're in this mess, but the sooner we get back to Adedor, the better."

"It's my fault anyhow," Baldewin said. He touched his blonde hair. The crown gone. "If I had just listened to Aveline, we'd be back home. Away from all this. Maybe even saving Bertin."

"You can't change the past. Now, let's get going."

So Baldewin straightened his back and followed. They walked as light as possible. Difficult for Blis with his bad knee, and the terrain didn't help. Every few steps, pebbles slid down the road. Rocks fell as they took switchbacks from Cahlun down the steep hills of Stadvik.

"There it is," Potter whispered. He pointed to the dark sea at the bottom of the island. Behind them was the candlelight of the town. In front of them, there was nothing. A single torchbearer walked the rocky beach near the *Kutski*. Blis' eyes had adjusted to the darkness, and the sliver of moonlight helped as well. The ship wasn't as large as any of the ships from the Rowai fleet, but it was still a ship all the same. The sails were folded as it sat near a wooden dock. They had landed on the other side of Stadvik, so there was no port to call home. The sound of waves muffled their footsteps as they kept on down the hillside.

"Everyone knows what to do?" Blis asked.

Huffs of agreement escaped them all. Potter and Blis would first try to plea with the sailors, though they didn't know a lick of Heller. Mari would keep Baldewin back in case things went wrong. Delmar had the sword. He was to be ready for anything. Either the sailors to fight back, or Caxton to bring an army.

As they neared the ship, Blis could make out the hull. The wood was all black, even when the moonlight hit it. The tucked-away masts were even black. "Are you sure this wasn't a pirate ship?"

Potter shrugged. "I'm not sure of anything. All I know is that they picked me up off the coast and led me here. I didn't ask no questions."

"Very well," Blis said. "Let's do this."

But they never got a chance to go through with their plan. Captain Pitor was talking to a sailor. They were conversing in Heller. When the captain saw them, he almost spat out whatever he was drinking. "Didn't think I'd see you here," the captain said. "Isn't it late?"

"We feel the same about you," Blis said for the lot of them. "Since when could you speak Heller?"

The captain rubbed his face. "Hmm, many decades, I reckon. A sailor should know at least one other language. Don't you?"

Blis' face flushed. He was glad it was too dark for anyone else to see. "I used to speak a smattering of the mite tongue, but ..." he trailed off. Language wasn't important at the moment. "Why are you out here? Shouldn't you be at the harbor?"

"Getting a drink with this here ..." the captain turned to the sailor. *Tol nava ak?*" he asked in Heller with what Blis would say was an awful accent.

"Arnyz." The Northerner said.

"Arnyz here was giving me a taste of his special liquor. Odd fermentation process." Pitor waved a hand. "It would take too long to explain. What about you? With His Grace as well?"

"The king wished to go on a walk," Sir Delmar said.

"At this hour?" Pitor looked to the night sky. Clouds blew in from the west, dark and gray. "I believe they call this the *zerzine za*. The hour of monsters."

"His Grace isn't afraid of anything," Mari added. Blis rubbed his head. He didn't need everyone speaking. Blis was supposed to do the talking, even if Pitor was here.

Then, torches dotted the hillside, and shouts filled the darkness. "The king is gone." "Where is His Grace?" "Kidnapped." "Find him!" The last was Caxton. His voice carried over the rocks and water.

Captain Pitor lowered his brow. "I guess no one else was told."

"Captain," Blis began. He didn't want to tell anyone else his suspicions. *What if Pitor knows? What if he is with Caxton and the others and this is their plan?*

"I think it's okay," Baldewin said.

Blis hated that the boy king could read his mind so well. He took a deep breath. "Captain Pitor, we strongly believe the king's council is planning on usurping the throne." More shouts rang from the town above. The Northern sailor looked lost to it all. "We need this ship. We're to get to the mainland and keep His Grace safe. Now, I ask you to please move aside."

Pitor lowered his drink. His feet stumbled on the rocky

shore. Waves beat against the beach. Night owls hooted from trees. "Move aside?" He spat near his boot. "These councilors have anything to do with the *Sea Glider*?"

"I think they did."

"Very well," the captain said. He looked to the Northerner and spoke to him. It seemed to never stop as torches glowed from the hill and the town came alive. Blis was sweating even as the cool breeze from the sea hit him. "Okay," Pitor finally said. "Arnyz here says we can come aboard. His captain might not like it, but leave that to me."

"Us?" Blis asked.

"Well, I won't let the fuckers who burned my baby get my king as well. Let's go."

Blis stood still for a moment as Pitor waved them forward. Everyone else followed the captain and the Northerner to the ship, but Blis was in shock. He didn't have to do some grand plan. Delmar didn't have to swing his sword. *Guess my plan was no good after all.* He snapped back to the moment when the clouds broke and moonlight came over him. There was shouting from the hills. "Down there!" "I see the king!"

He had no more time to think. Blis wobbled on his aching knee as fast as he could. Baldewin and Mari were following Pitor up the gangplank. Potter was saying, "Thank you, thank you," to the Northern sailor who didn't acknowledge him.

Delmar was waiting for Blis. "No time to dally," the knight said.

"Of course," Blis agreed. Delmar slowed his pace and fell in behind Blis. He hated that. He didn't want his old age and his slow leg to cause Delmar harm. The councilors at any time could loose their men like hounds. Blis would be responsible if anything happened to the knight. Luckily, they reached the gangplank, and Blis only had a few more steps. Pitor was shouting in Heller, probably at the ship's captain.

Baldewin reached out his hand and grabbed Blis' fingers. *I don't need your help;* he thought as the boy king led Blis onto the ship. *Maybe I do.*

"How's the captain?" Blis asked.

"Which one?" Mari crossed her arms as if she were hugging herself. "If the Northerners don't let us leave, then we'll be prime for the taking."

"Yes," Blis nodded so hard his jowls shook.

"They're taking the king!" A voice shouted. Blis had forgotten they were being chased. Torches were snaking down the hillside. Men much younger and fitter than Blis could easily climb down the steep rocks. They didn't have much time.

"Captain Pitor?" Blis called out.

Pitor was shouting at an old man. He took a break to say, "Things are going fine." Then went back to yelling.

"Loose! Don't let the king be taken." That was Jac yelling at the men of Rowan. Blis barely had time to process what was said before an arrow whizzed past his ear.

"Down," Delmar called out and crashed into Baldewin. Mari and Potter fell to the deck as well. The Northern sailors all dropped too, even the captain. Blis followed suit. He wouldn't let the councilors take him.

Pitor was laughing as he made his way up to the helm. "Captain Druz here says to take the wheel." He kept laughing as he grabbed the ship's wheel and barked out orders in

Heller. This Captain Druz called out to his men as well, and they all started racing about the ship. Sailors grabbed a long, thick pole and pushed off from the shore. There was little wind, Blis could tell, but hopefully they'd be able to row far enough from the arrows.

"Is it safe?" Baldewin asked as he lay on the black deck.

"I'll check," Mari said. It was stupid of her, but she did all the same. She crawled over to the gunwale and lifted her head up. Blis closed his eyes. He didn't want to see any horror. He'd have to explain to Aveline if Mari got an arrow through the skull. So he held his breath and waited for the scream. But it never came. "They're still running." She said as she crawled back over. An arrow flew overhead. "And loosing arrows."

The ship lurched as someone below shouted, *"Nosić! Nosić! Nosić!"* Men heaved and Blis could feel the movement of oars below. He wanted to cry with happiness. He had saved Baldewin from the council. The hardest part was over.

"Keep an eye on that ship!" Caxton's voice rang out over the water. "We'll follow. We must save His Grace!"

Blis lifted himself up and saw a hundred torches lighting the beach. It reminded him of the *Sea Glider's* burning. This time Caxton didn't look to be smirking or smiling. He didn't look smug. He looked angry. Full of rage.

Yvanne

Her child lay on her bare chest. Yvanne rubbed her cool hand over the baby's back. "That was tougher than war." Lady Lolly japed with shadows under her eyes. Jacka slumped in the velvet chair near the door. "I hope all is going well with you."

"Of course." *All is well. Why wouldn't it be? The gods ... I have had a child.* Yvanne glanced at the sleeping child. She watched with tears in her eyes as her parents would never see their grandchild. "Have you sent for Maliz?"

"Just like you wished. I can take the child to her if you do not want to wait."

Please, Yvanne thought. "No. I can watch over her."

Her. The child was a girl. "I don't need a princess." That was what Devro had said the last time he saw the child. Tundavik had led her people to victory in Ritaeum, Devro successful in bringing up the rear, and now she lay in a wooden bedchamber that reminded her of Whitehall, though warmer. Her chest was sticky with sweat as the babe lay on it.

"How did your husband react to your children?" She asked her sister.

"He loved them all. The girl and both boys. Our daughter

will be the perfect lady to a handsome lord one day, and my boys are both training to be fighters." Lady Lolly could do nothing but smile. Yvanne hadn't smiled in days.

"Your husband didn't get upset about having a girl?"

Lolly lost her smile and sat on the bed. She took the sleeping child and cradled her head. Yvanne felt relieved she didn't have to hold the baby anymore. "Devro will be happy about her," Lolly said. "I don't know when, but it will happen. You can try again and again until you have a male."

That might have left Lolly with a feeling of happiness, but the thought of another birth made Yvanne want to die. She would rather run into a fire than experience that pain again. "Of course," she lied with a smile.

Her sister left with the baby, leaving Yvanne in bed with a sleeping Jacka across the room. She studied the room. The reddish wood that matched the trees outside, the tapestries that hung from the walls with only one god, but the one thing that caught her attention was a portrait of a small girl. *Will Devro ever allow our child to have a portrait? No, you idiot, he hates her; he hates me. Why did I do this? Why?*

Tears fell from her eyes like they had for the last few days, which felt like years. The days drug on, and the heat of summer didn't help. She would throw the blankets off in a fit of rage as sweat clung to her, then clamber to find them again as a chill took her. The bedside table was covered with bowls of food. She hadn't eaten since the birth. She couldn't bring herself to do it. To do anything. Sleep was the only thing Yvanne liked to do now. *I never want to see the baby again. Please, Lolly, just take her away forever.*

"Why do I feel like this?" she cried to herself as Jacka snored. Yvanne closed her eyes to sleep, but it never came.

Her heart was racing too fast. The pounding filled her ears. She covered them to stop the noise, but it didn't work. *Thump thump thump.* Now all she wanted was to rip her heart out to stop the beating forever. "It's what I deserve. I failed. I didn't give the kingdom an heir. Why would anyone fight for us now?" She let the tears and snot run down her face. If it were up to her, she would drown in it.

Jacka stirred awake in the corner and squinted her eyes at Yvanne. She brought a towel, and Yvanne welcomed being smothered, but Jacka only wiped her face clean. "What is it, Your Grace? Are you alright?"

"Of course," Yvanne forced a smile. "Just a little sad is all."

"Did Lady Lolly take the baby?" Jacka looked around the room as if Yvanne had hidden the child. "Do you want me to bring her back?"

"No," Yvanne didn't hesitate. "I … I just want to be alone for a little while."

"I'll go find some food."

"You can stay," Yvanne said as she patted her bed for Jacka to sit. The handmaid sat next to her while stifling a yawn. "I just want to be away …" she didn't want to say it, but Jacka would understand. She had to understand. "… from the baby."

Jacka grabbed Yvanne's hands and kissed them. "You've been through so much recently. It's perfectly fine. I've seen mothers who wanted to throw their children into a river—"

I do.

"—but then grow to love them."

Not me.

"Have you tried eating?" Jacka picked up some bread from yestermorn. "It will help you get your strength back.

It's very important."

Yvanne pushed the bread away and rubbed her head. "I would like to sleep is all."

"You've been sleeping for days," Jacka said while putting the bread down. Her voice was gentle. Almost motherly. But Yvanne was the one who was a mother. "Maybe we should take a walk. We're in a castle. There is much to explore here. I'm sure the men would love to see their queen is safe after the birth."

"I doubt it. They all hate me for birthing a girl instead of an heir."

"I'm sorry, Your Grace, but that is nonsense." Jacka stood and looked out a leaded window into the forested village below. "They will celebrate her. Young princesses are beloved."

"Not mine," Yvanne rolled on her side away from Jacka. Tears stained her pillow. "I cannot even remember her name. Why would the men?"

Jacka came back and pulled the blanket over Yvanne. "Her name is Seine, remember? You named her after your mother."

"Of course," Yvanne cried as she drifted to sleep.

She dreamt of her mother emerging from the flames as if she were a goddess herself. She held the child and whispered while tapping her foot, "You will be a great queen someday." Yvanne thought her mother was speaking to her, but she was talking to the baby. Telling the baby she'll be queen. Yvanne wished to speak with her mother, but her words got caught in her throat.

"I will be here to love you," her mother told her grand-daughter, "no matter where your mother or father have gone." Yvanne dropped to her knees, her hand clutching her mother's dress, watching as she tapped her foot. She wanted to sob to her, tell her what she was feeling. *I need guidance.* But she still could make no sound. "Do not forget your claim."

Her mother turned to Yvanne. "Leave this child for another. You are not fit to be a mother." Yvanne burst into tears. Then she was in a dark room. Her eyes were dry once more. Her baby lay on the ground across the chamber. Yvanne walked … and walked … her legs would take her nowhere. "Leave this child." Her mother tapped her foot. "She is better without you." Yvanne clasped her hands over her ears as the tapping grew louder. "Leave her." Louder. Louder.

The tapping morphed into a knock when she woke and opened her eyes. Jacka fetched the door, and in walked Maliz with Seine at her breast, Lolly coming in with a plate of sliced apples and some white cream to dip them in. "It's the best I could find at the moment," she said as she handed the plate to Yvanne. She took it, but it felt heavier than a stone.

"We thought you'd want to see sweet little Seine again." Maliz said as she fed the child.

"I love seeing her," Yvanne lied. She felt her face getting hot. *Why must these people come to me? Disturb my sleep. Don't they know I just want to be left alone?* Her hands were squeezing the plate so hard they turned white. She blinked and set the plate down on the table. "I appreciate it."

Maliz sat on the bed. The baby was suckling on her nipple, milk dripping down her mouth. The nursemaid was smiling with bright teeth at the child. Yvanne's eyes glazed over. "You were lucky with this one," Maliz said. "She latched soon and with ease. I was very surprised. She'll grow into a strong and healthy girl. I'm sure you're excited to see the lady she becomes."

Tears filled her eyes once more. *I have to raise this thing until adulthood. That's so far away, so many years wasted on her. My life wasted. Why? I should've fought back against father when he sold me into marriage. I should've fought. Why, oh why?*

Lolly wiped her own tears. Tears of happiness. Yvanne's were only of sadness. "I cried many times when my children were just suckling babes," Lolly said. "They were so sweet and innocent then."

Jacka looked on while resting her head in her hands. "Perhaps Her Grace should get more sleep," her handmaid said to the others, a smile to Yvanne as if she understood. "This has been a long, hard journey, and a well-rested queen and mother will do wonders for her health."

"Would you like to hold the babe first?" Maliz asked.

Yvanne hesitated, her hands frozen. If she took the child, she would drop it, then what would everyone think? The women would be hysterical. The soldiers would gossip that she had murdered her babe. Devro would be the only one happy. Happy his daughter was dead and that they could try again so soon for a boy.

Lolly took the baby from Maliz, who covered herself. "Well?" Lolly turned to Yvanne. "Would you like to hold her? It's very important Seine knows who her mother is."

"Hold her." Maliz said.

Lolly then said, "Would you like to hold her?"

"Hold your baby," Maliz said again. "Hold your daughter."

"Hold Seine."

"Hold me," the baby said. "Please, Mother, please hold me." The baby stretched her arms to reach for Yvanne, to smother Yvanne. "Hold me, Mommy."

"Get out!" Yvanne shouted. "Get out, all of you!"

The child cried, and the ladies looked on in shock. Jacka ushered the women out the door and followed behind. Yvanne was left alone. Only her tears to accompany her.

Ultiir

Ultiir rubbed his head and stifled a yawn as the councilors spoke over one another. He missed the days when the palace was empty and he could be alone. "Ritaeum has fallen," Lord Dovi Lyons said. "Unfortunately, that means taxes from the Woodlands won't be coming." As chief collector, Dovi dealt with the funds, but the war was costly. Ultiir couldn't do much to bring in more coin.

"That will certainty help our severe lack of funds." Lord Serle Verrier stated the obvious as sarcasm fell from his lips.

Dovi nodded. "I don't need to be reminded. Your Grace," he turned to Ultiir, "I'm not sure what more we can do. The men won't be getting as much pay."

Ultiir's eyes were heavy; it took all his power to keep them open. But even still, they had glazed over from the talk of taxes and war. He wanted his nephew's wife dead. It seemed the only person who was going to help was Lord de'Marisco. Then there was the problem that Olier had mentioned. Sophie and her knight spoke with the traitor in the dungeons. *I wonder how she'll betray me next?* He thought of his wife.

"His Grace has told me to increase the price of goods entering from sea," Gid said. "Isn't that right?" Ultiir nodded, but he barely heard what Gid had said. He could feel Analere's eyes on him from her side of the table, but he paid his sister no mind.

"One issue," Dovi said, "our trade numbers have dropped drastically. There's a war."

"The war is almost over," Lord Edel de'Viere said. "His Grace has plans in the works to take revenge on the bastard's army. It won't be long until they break."

Serle shook his head and shrugged. "And if it doesn't work? Then what? The Awaran ships are still blocking river trade. If the bastard besieges the city again, then we'll lose. What is that plan?"

Ultiir waved his hand as he yawned. Outside, the sun was setting, which meant it was almost time for bed. For nightmares.

"You'll find out in time," Gid told the chief ambassador.

"Alan would've told me," Serle whispered.

At the sound of the dead chief commander's name, Ultiir's ears perked up. He straightened his back and rose in his chair. "Do you not trust me, Lord Verrier? Do you think me dumb? Or that I'm not fit to rule?"

The lord hiccuped and then chuckled. "I said nothing of the like."

"I think we're tired," Analere finally said to calm the situation, her white robes flowing over the table. "Your Grace, why don't we come back to this tomorrow? Maybe we can all think of solutions to the coin problem while we sleep."

"Why do I doubt that?" Ultiir said.

"I agree with the chief daken," Lord Lyons said. Lord Verrier rolled his eyes but nodded. The lords on the council, save for Gid and Edel, weren't too fond of Analere occupying such a high seat. But Ultiir didn't care.

"My lord," Ultiir said to Serle Verrier before he stood, "you seem to not be enjoying your time on the council any longer."

"I'm not sure what you mean," the lord said.

"If the chief daken here didn't stop you from answering my questions, you'd've surely made a fool of yourself. Yet you still disrespect her."

The lord shook his head. "I did no—"

"My lord," Ultiir smirked, "no use in interrupting me. I'm sorry, but I think it's time you handed in your cloak, much like Tedbalt did. I don't need anyone on my council who doesn't fully follow my decisions and respect the other councilors."

Serle was taken aback, his jaw low. It was as if he had just seen a murder. "Your Grace, I meant no disrespect. I didn't …" The lord grew quiet when he looked to the other councilors and none came to his defense. Ultiir interlocked his fingers and waited. Lord Verrier stood, bowed his head, and took off his cloak. "I hope you find it within you to allow me to come back. I've only ever served you as king."

"I won't." Ultiir smiled as the lord sulked out of the chamber. "The rest of you," Ultiir said, and Dovi clenched his fist, "let us take a break." He waved his hand in dismissal, and the remaining lords all left the chamber. Analere stayed behind, though.

"You still haven't filled the chief commander's seat." Analere said as she brushed blonde hair from her eyes. "And the chief watcher is still empty. Do you think it's a good idea to leave the chief ambassador empty too? You don't have anymore siblings to fill them with."

Ultiir gave a sarcastic *ha ha*. "Funny. Honestly, the more I think about it, the more I want to disband the council entirely. What have they done for me? Tedbalt was a traitor, and Alan couldn't win me the war. Lord Verrier was only useful with foreign dignitaries and, if you haven't noticed, we don't have any with the war going on. Gid is my knight and will stay by me all the time, though it would help if I didn't have to listen to his 'advice' any longer. Edel de'Viere is young, but he has helped the most. After sending Lord de'Marisco to the mountains, I didn't think I'd find anyone to replace, but Lord de'Viere does the job well."

"And your chief daken?"

"She's fine, doesn't have a lot of news to report, but with the dakenry in disarray with all the wounded, that's to be expected."

"But I do have news." Analere said as a magpie squawked from the window behind Ultiir. "It involves the queen, and I'm sure you want to hear it." It was as if she wanted Ultiir to pull it out of her, but he didn't have time for games, so he sat in silence as he waited. Finally, she relented and said, "I saw Her Grace a few days ago before a meeting of the royal court. She was heading toward the dungeon. I know you've said that she and Tedbalt Masson had an odd relationship. She seemed distraught. Convinced that the council was going to have his head."

"Where would she get such an idea?" Ultiir asked. "No one's mentioned that treacherous old fuck since I took him away." He shook his head and stared at the black and white bird outside as it pecked at insects. "Do you think she wants to free him?"

"I know it, just don't know how. I don't see her as being violent, but afterward when I spoke with the jailer he told me how her knight threatened him."

"Olier? Sir Achen would cut him down in a heartbeat. That man killed a guard stationed at the wall weeks ago. He's a dangerous man, which means Sophie is dangerous." Ultiir stood and rubbed his chin; a layer of stubble had formed; he would have to shave it. "She's even more dangerous with her parents in Terrop. King Anvrin was supposed to send troops as soon as the mountain passes melted, but as you can see, there are no Terropians here."

"I wonder why," Analere said. It wasn't a question.

"So I separate Sophie from Tedbalt and that knight of hers, of all her guards. Make her vulnerable. Maybe, just maybe, she'll finally relent and stop pushing her nonsense with the lords of the court."

"What will you do first?"

"I have a lord to hang," Ultiir said.

***

"What do you think you're doing?" Sophie asked. She was out of breath from chasing after Ultiir, who was strolling over the palace grounds. In the distance, just below the palace walls, was where the noose and platform were located. Lou was getting everything ready. Guards and lords and ladies were already finding the best places to watch. Lord Masson would die today. *Finally.*

"What I should've done when I saw how close you two

were getting."

"You're a madman." Sophie shook her head. "What did Tedbalt ever do to you? What did I do to you?"

"You lied to me," Ultiir spat, "spied on me, betrayed me … lied to me," he said again as tears started bubbling to the surface. *No reason whatsoever to cry.* He was tired of being treated as lesser by lords and ladies and his own wife. He was the king, the most powerful man in the kingdom. "You said you loved me." Ultiir finally said. "But you lied to me about that. All you do is lie and deceive me and go behind my back. Well," he wiped his tears and let the anger take hold. "Now I'm fighting back. Getting rid of your closest ally or lover or whatever he is will surely slow you down."

"I won't let you do this."

"And how will you stop me?" Ultiir smiled as Sophie's shoulders dropped. "My sister is very close to me. Next time, don't antagonize her." Sophie turned her head as tears fell down her cheeks. Ultiir stifled a laugh, even though he didn't want to. Sir Achen, Sophie's large knight, stood behind her. His eyes were clouded, and Ultiir had seen that cloud before; it was the same one that shrouded his eyes when he was full of anger. That knight was dangerous. *But Tedbalt first,* Ultiir thought as he turned away from his deceitful wife and worked his way down the gentle slopes of the palace grounds.

Among the lords and ladies were all of Sophie's 'Queen's Council'. There had been whispers they were pushing for inheritance changes too. *Who hasn't she recruited?* Ultiir thought of his wife. Lords Tylar and Ompter and a whole slew who had turned against him were also outside. They all wore glares. Very few looked happy to finally see the treacherous old bastard hang. *I'll keep all the joy to myself, I guess.*

Behind the hanging post were Lou and a few guards. They all surrounded Tedbalt Masson. The old, decrepit man was chained at wrists and ankles. He was grayer than the overcast sky; his head was bald, his bones poking through his skin. "I see the dungeon did wonders for you." Ultiir said.

The once great lord looked up; his eyes were dark and sunken. "It was a pleasant time."

"And now you're ready for the noose?" Ultiir already knew the answer. Tedbalt was just like any other person who lived far past their prime. Ready for death.

"Of course," he said. "I've been looking forward to it for many years."

"I assume you didn't picture me as your executioner?"

Tedbalt let out a dry cough as he smiled. "On the contrary, I knew you'd bring about the fall of this kingdom. I didn't see you kicking the bucket out from under me, but I guess you still aren't, that's Lou's job. You see, when you first came to Vigur as chief consultant, I was greatly worried. I had been on the king's council since the days of your father. Helped him and Hurvir through the war with the mites. Once that war was over and poor Lord Balt was dead, and Hurvir chose you to consult him, I knew you would never compare. Lord Balt was older than I. You are so much younger. You didn't have the experience needed to help govern a kingdom. Goldfield is one of the easiest places to rule with all the money pouring from Vigur. You were green. You still are."

"I didn't come to get a talking to, old man."

Tedbalt nodded, and Ultiir thought he heard bones creaking. "Very well. But just know that it didn't need to come to this. We were friends once, long ago. Remember how we dealt with that uprising in Red Rock? That was the last time I held a sword. A daken," he laughed, "holding a sword? I'm sure it was quite a sight."

Ultiir bit his lip to keep from smiling at the thought. "I didn't hold a sword much either, still haven't, but we did good commanding those soldiers."

"I lived a long life," Tedbalt said as his wrists clanked together. "A good life. I'm ready. But you must promise me one thing: do not hurt Sophie. She hasn't done half the things I have. She doesn't deserve your wrath."

"You are both traitors. That's enough for me."

"Yes," the old man coughed. "But I killed that slave of yours. Sophie had no part in that, so I say I deserve worse than her."

"Sufar?" Ultiir didn't even want to say his name. Sufar had been his slave for over a decade before he found him dead. "We hanged the other slaves for that."

"Yes, well," Tedbalt shrugged, "I made it look like it was their fault, didn't I? You were so enraged you didn't even listen to their pleas of innocence."

"The riot happened after that hanging." Ultiir's face burned red. "Sir Lovis died that day, as well as many lords and ladies. You're saying I could've hanged you and been done with it?" His voice was rising, but he couldn't let all the lords behind him see how upset he was. "I was being merciful today." Ultiir went to Lou and patted the sword that was at the executioner's hip. "Use this, not the noose. Use this and make it slow."

Lou nodded as Ultiir handed him a gold piece. Ultiir could barely breathe as he walked to the gallows. His heart wanted to beat out of his chest; his face was redder than any fire. Tedbalt had been more than a traitor. He was a murderer. The murderer of an innocent man.

When the crowd grew louder, that's when Ultiir knew Tedbalt was being dragged out. He watched as the old man was forced to kneel over a stump. Murmurs flowed from the crowd. "There has been a change of plans," Lou started. "His Grace, Ultiir de'Tro, has judged Tedbalt Masson guilty of heinous crimes that befit a sword instead of a noose. Do you've any last words?" He asked Tedbalt.

The old lord said nothing; instead, he looked toward the palace at Sophie. The queen had wiped her tears and was staring back. "Very well." Lou unsheathed his longsword, raised it above Tedbalt's head, and swung … slowly.

The first hit of the sword cracked his neck, but Lou didn't go clean through even though he had done it a thousand times before. Lords and ladies looked away in disgust; others gasped at the sight; Ultiir only smiled. Lou raised the sword again and brought it back down. Again, just the crack of bone and muscle and tendon. Tedbalt's eyes were open, but he was dead. Though it didn't matter. Lou would take his time getting the head to roll away.

The executioner brought the sword down again and again, purposely not cutting all the way through. Then, with one last hit of the sword against Tedbalt's neck, his head fell to the ground below, rolling in blood as it spilled and stained the stump. Lord Tedbalt Masson was dead, and he would never betray Ultiir again.

Tundavik

Tundavik Vandes stood on a hill overlooking the town of Ritaeum. What was once a stronghold for the Ritae people was taken by the Veck'kop hundreds of years ago. His ancestors given the seat of the Woodlands after Valor the Betrayer was deposed as king. Then the Valles family took over, but now it was Tundavik's again.

A three-legged cat limped over to Tundavik, rubbing its head on his leg. Tundavik laughed and bent down to pet the tabby behind the ears. It purred and smiled. "I guess I'm home," Tundavik said.

"*Meeeooowwww,*" the cat sang in response.

"Mr. P!" a girl called out. "There you are." She scooped the cat up, and Tundavik stood, his knees popping and aching. "Hi there, mister. Thanks for finding my cat. He likes to run."

"How long have you lived in Ritaeum?"

The young girl tapped her chin while Mr. P meowed. "Umm, my whole life. Are you the one my parents told me to hide from? You attacked the town?"

Tundavik nodded. "Sorry about that, but I'm glad you and the cat are safe."

"Me too," the girl said and skipped down the hill while the cat meowed in her arms.

The forests of the Woodlands grew all around the town. Small huts for peasants with stone chimneys in their wooden houses blended in with the trees. Now, tents and cots were littered about as well. Homes taken over for soldiers. As were food and tools and weapons. The army needed provisions, and the people of Ritaeum were going to give them.

The shops and bakeries and tanneries and cobblers were also made of wood. It would've been easy to burn the whole town like Yvanne had said, but then he would bring about the same destruction that had caused him to leave all those years ago. Instead, they fought peasants and farmers and the occasional slave; the slave revolt not yet reaching Ritaeum, it seemed. But they were no match for the battle-hardened troops Tundavik commanded.

Then Devro rode on a mare and commanded the rear. *Stupid boy,* Tundavik thought, *could've gotten yourself killed.* But Devro was still alive. It certainly helped that Tundavik's men had already reached the castle when the rearguard arrived.

Tundavik made his way down the hill, the trees that once grew here had been cut down, probably to build the castle and town. Lord Valles' castle wasn't large, but it was imposing. It was made of dark wood and stone, looking almost black. The town of Ritaeum didn't have a wall, but the castle did. It was a perfect square with the house in the center. Each corner of the wall had a watchtower that lifted over the canopy of the forest. The courtyard was small, but full of flowers, like Lord Valles never thought an attack would come. When Tundavik was lord, the gate was always closed, and soldiers never moved from their positions. The Rainvealandians were at war, though. Lord Valles had known peace. Too bad Tundavik had to break that.

As he made his way over the beaten-down grass that made paths, he smiled and waved at a few troops. Lord Tylo and his men from Heavensfield set up camp near the bakery. Fresh bread mixed with onion and garlic filled the air, and he knew his men wouldn't be able to behave themselves. Tundavik had sent out a directive that no man was to rob, kill, or rape the people of Ritaeum. But how many would listen?

"I've castrated three men already." Lord Toware had told Tundavik just days ago. "If we stay here too long, we might lose more men to their wants and needs. I've also heard some complain of the heat far too much for my liking."

"You think they'll leave because of the weather?" Tundavik had laughed.

"Men have deserted for less." Toware said as he let an ominous note hang.

Tundavik sighed. "Make sure the lords know they will be held responsible for their people deserting, and if their men get out of control, for the rapes too. I don't want to punish anyone else."

"You've punished no one," Toware had smirked before walking away.

Glares followed Tundavik as he walked through the town. Peasants and farmers who weren't happy being dragged into the war. He scanned their faces, but none looked familiar. *Everyone I knew died long ago.* When he neared the castle, the portcullis raised. Smiths were working on blades and spears, groomsmen were tidying the horses, guards were walking with swords. The courtyard was buzzing. Too many people and not enough space. Atop the wall stood Devro and Mar. They looked into town as they spoke. For a moment he thought about joining them, but something was telling him he needed to go deeper into the castle. So he went inside. Black wood and stone swallowing him. He didn't need a tour of the place, didn't need to think about where he was going. His mind held onto a map of his former home for almost two decades. It was as if he had never left.

Tundavik turned down a small hall with a single torch as light. His shoulders brushed against the walls on either side of him. He was in the slave quarters. Lord Furrow was given the job of making them work since he owned slaves in Nye. As he passed a closed door, he heard shouting and whips, but he wasn't going to see some slaves. He continued to a small staircase that went into the earth. He followed it down to a dungeon with two cells.

Lord Valles lay in one of them.

Onnu had been stripped of his clothes, silks and linens and gold rings. Now he was wearing brown and gray rags. He didn't look like a lord any longer; in fact, he looked more like Tundavik. An older man, Onnu Valles had tight skin around his dark face. The hint of wrinkles pulling on his brow. A small beard formed haphazardly on his chin.

"Lord Valles," Tundavik said as he pulled up a wobbly chair made of wood, "His Grace wishes to execute you for treason."

The lord stretched like he had just woken from a good nap. "How is my wife? My children?" Onnu said in a raspy voice.

"Fine, they are locked in a room in the castle but given enough food and drink."

"Good," Lord Valles pulled his knees close. "When's the execution?"

Tundavik laughed until he realized Onnu was resigned to his fate. "You're not going to try to get out of it?"

"Is it possible?"

"I don't know; some have been able to sway His Grace, though."

Lord Valles waved a hand. "Save it. I will not grovel to a traitor bastard and his traitor followers."

"So you're on the side of Ultiir?"

"Did he attack my home and put my family under arrest?" Onnu squinted as his eyes watched Tundavik. "How does it feel to be a traitor to two kings?"

"Hurvir and Ultiir?" Tundavik scoffed and scratched at his beard, the hairs curling around his fingers. "Hurvir betrayed me and my family. I'm sure you heard what happened, but you took this duchy anyway."

"I was not afraid of Hurvir, may the Four watch over him, because I would never betray him."

Tundavik rocked in the chair, the leg squeaking, "And I did?"

"I know what happened in Panscar. I know what you did."

"I did nothing but take the city," Tundavik said as his face got hot. "I didn't mean for his sister to be killed in the process, and Hurvir took out his anger on my family, not me. He killed innocent children. He massacred all of my people. You're lucky it didn't happen to you."

"Yet here you are to kill me." Lord Valles stood, his body was loose as if he didn't have a care in the world. Like he wasn't about to have his head chopped off or a noose around his neck. "You've already killed some of my men, and I've heard the cries of rape from my cell. I assume my family is next."

"They aren't." Tundavik looked up at Onnu as he gripped the bars of his cell. "And your men ran at us with weapons. It's not the same."

"You're just trying to justify it, but you know it's the same. You support my death because I swore a vow before the gods to a different king and to follow the laws of this land. Yet you would be wild with anger if I captured Whitehall and put Lady Rely to the rope. You're a pretender. You act as if you have honor, so these men follow you to their deaths. If they knew who you really were, they would spit in your eye. If the bastard knew what you did. That the great Tundavik Vandes sat by while his men threw the Princess Analla de'Tro from the highest tower in Panscar ... Perhaps those will be my last words." Onnu nodded to himself; spit had stained his lips. "Yes, that will do good."

Tundavik stood as he swallowed and then pulled the chair across the room, it scraping and leaving black marks on the stone. "I will talk to His Grace," Tundavik said. Onnu squinted his eyes. "I will ask that he stay your execution, and I promise that your wife and children will not be harmed."

Lord Valles scoffed as he rolled his eyes. "Sorry to say, but I don't much trust your word."

Tundavik nodded since he knew Lord Valles would say something like that, but he didn't care; he knew his word was good enough. *I'm not a monster,* he thought as he left the dungeon and moved through the slave quarters.

As he made his way outside, his head screamed in pain. Devro and Mar were still talking atop the walls, but Tundavik could barely see them as his vision clouded. He knew why this time. The woman from his dreams. She had told him for months to go to Ritaeum. Now it was time to find out why, at least he hoped. *I can find Devro later.* So Tundavik made his way back inside and hobbled up some steps, holding his eyelids as he did, his head pounding. In one motion, he opened the door to his chamber and fell onto the bed to sleep.

Sophie

She didn't know what to do anymore. Lord Masson was gone. Sophie had watched in horror as the executioner gave him a slow, painful death. *Will he do the same to me?* she thought. In her dreams, it was Ultiir wielding the sword though, not some lackey. The good thing about that is she'd never seen Ultiir use a sword once, so he'd probably miss.

Sophie took a deep breath as Renna slipped her into a blue dress. Amalla was mixing some roses with water to put on her wrists. They all crowded into the handmaid's bedchamber. No matter how powerful Sophie felt, when she saw her own chamber all she saw was blood and guts from Atrice. It had been months since she had slept in that room. At least the handmaids kept her company, them and all of her guards outside in the hall. If Ultiir were to attack and try to imprison her, she would be ready.

In the mirror opposite her, she saw her hair braided down her back. Fresh makeup covered her face. She was tired of always dressing up, but the only way to get the lords on her side was to play the part of a good queen and woman. They couldn't know what she was really after. That she wanted the throne to herself. *For* herself. "Do you think I'd be a better ruler than Ultiir?" She asked Amalla, who dabbed the rosewater on Sophie's bare wrists.

"Of course, Your Grace," her handmaid said. "In all honesty, I think a wild dog would be a better fit for the crown than that man."

"Would you actually want to rule, Your Grace?" Renna asked as she stepped aside to look at the dress and make sure it fitted properly. "I mean, it seems like too hard of a job."

"I'd rather run away and spend my time in Masa Naq. You could show me around," Sophie said to Renna. "But I was born into this life, so I have to play the game. Being the ruler of my own kingdom would surely make my parents happy, or jealous—I'm not sure which."

"Have you spoken to them lately?" Amalla asked.

"Not since my father wrote me. It's for the best. I can deal with the lords of the court myself and show the world that I am even more powerful than Ultiir."

"I doubt the world cares," Baroness Mara said as the door opened. "They'd say something about Valor the Iron and how you can't match up to him." The baroness strolled over and fixed a necklace around Sophie's neck that had moved to one side. "So why do anything for them at all? It's better to move on your own accord."

"Of course," Sophie agreed. "I'm just not sure what to do now that Tedbalt is gone. It seems all of my allies are disappearing, and I'm going to have to fight alone."

"I'm still here," the baroness said. "I don't plan on leaving like Lady Volles."

"Have you any word on Abre? I'd like to know how her campaign is going."

Mara shrugged before she spoke. "No letters, no matter how many times Filra has written. But I heard some traders talking the other day. They were selling cattails from the Woodlands. Something about disappearing people, but more importantly they said that Oceantree was doing fine with its new ruler. Could be good. Could be bad."

Sophie nodded her thanks to her handmaids as they finished dressing her. "Well, let's pray for the best. Why are you here? Did something happen?"

"I can't see my friend?" Mara chuckled. "Yes, actually. I came to get you for a session of court. Ultiir called a meeting."

"He did? That would be the first time in months. Why the sudden change? All he's done is complain about the court trying to sabotage him and take over."

"Guess we'll find out."

The baroness led Sophie out of the chamber and past her guards and knights. They had made the corridor outside her room their new home. Sleeping mats and dressers and clothes had been brought from their quarters in the low part of the palace. Sir Achen continued to tell her it was their duty and that they were happy to sleep on the floor. But some blinked their way awake. Others stared at the candles burning. Someone had scraped a drawing onto the wall. They were bored, and bored guards weren't as quick to defend their queen.

"Remind me to send them back to their rooms when we return," Sophie told Mara. "I want them well rested." Sir Achen fell in behind them as they continued to the stairs. Sophie sighed after taking the first step. It was a long way down, and she had done it so many times. She was tired. It would be much easier if Ultiir just left the city and never came back. She wouldn't have to work so hard to undermine him. Not that his paranoia was helping his cause anyhow. Lord Verrier stewed outside the palace walls. Lord Lyons had been whispering to Lord Tylar about Ultiir's state of mind. Perhaps she could sleep all day and let Ultiir do all the work for her.

As they turned a flight of stairs, Lord Mer Lasie stood at the bottom. He was out of breath. "I … had just climbed … I was coming … to you."

Sir Achen went in between the lord and Sophie; Mara gripped her arm. "What is it?" Sophie said.

"Ultiir …" Lord Mer inhaled and slowed his breathing. "You know how I am usually late to meetings of the court? I try my best, but we're not all perfect. Anyway, not the point. When I went to open the doors, some of the king's men pushed me back. I heard shouting and banging from inside the throne room. I'm not sure what it is exactly, but it cannot be good."

Sophie turned to the baroness, who shook her head in disbelief. Sophie cleared her throat and said, "You think he's trapped them inside?"

The lord shrugged and wiped sweat from his brow. "It appears that way. I'm not sure what he's doing next, but it could be a massacre of the lords for all I know. I came to stop you from going downstairs. Your Grace, you need to get back to your chambers and bar the door."

Metal clanged below them. Footsteps climbed the stairs. The lord's eyes widened. Sir Achen whipped around to Sophie. "We go. Now."

"I will get you more time." Lord Mer said. He raced down

the stairs while Achen pulled Sophie and Mara up.

She had to hold her dress to keep from tripping as they ran. Sir Achen was skipping two stairs in one bound. Sophie tried her best to follow. Somewhere below Lord Mer Lasie was shouting, then screaming, then only metal boots echoed.

Sophie's heart was racing as she climbed and climbed. The stairs seemed to go on forever; there were many more than she remembered. The metal grew louder in her ears. She barely noticed they reached the queen's chambers and Achen was shouting and all the bored guards were grabbing their weapons. Mara went through the door to the bedchamber, but Sophie stayed behind. "Come on," the baroness pleaded.

"One moment," Sophie said. She found Sir Achen, who held his blade high. "My good sir. This is it, isn't it?"

"You will not die today, nor will I nor any of the men," Achen said out of breath. "Now, Your Grace, board yourself in your room."

"No," Sophie said. "I need you to do something for me. Something you'll hate." The knight lowered his shoulders to listen. "Remember the secret passage out of Lord Geary's office? Take the slave stairs. No one should be waiting for you there. Get to the passage and get to my parents."

"No," Sir Achen didn't hesitate to say. "I will not leave you. If you want me to do that, then you must come with me." The sound of metal boots filled the corridor as they echoed up the stairs. Any moment and her men would have to fight if that was what Ultiir wanted.

"Do not argue with me," Sophie said with pursed lips. "I am your queen, and you will do as I say. Get to my parents and tell them what's happened here."

"Hurry," Mara called out from the bedchamber.

"Will you do it?" Sophie asked her knight.

Achen's eyes were watery, his jaw clenched. He whispered, "Fuck," then sheathed his sword. "Do not let that man kill you."

"Go," Sophie said.

Sir Achen called for Sir Velle. "You're in charge again, my good sir. I'm going to get reinforcements." Velle nodded, and Achen ran in the opposite direction of the clambering of boots. He took one last look at the corridor before disappearing into the slave's section of the wing.

I pray this works, was Sophie's thought as the corridor filled with knights wearing golden owl surcoats. The monster, Sir Gid, led over a dozen men. Their swords were all drawn.

"Give us the queen and no one gets hurt," the old man said.

Sir Velle stepped forward, as did the rest of her men. She never should've doubted them. "You know the rules of the palace. No king's men are to step foot in the queen's wing. Get out, or you will regret it."

Gid laughed. "His Grace has suspended the rule on account of the bitch queen being a traitor."

"Well then," Sir Velle said as he gripped his sword, "looks like we're at an impasse."

Mara grabbed Sophie's arm and dragged her into the chamber. "Are we?" was the last thing Sophie heard Gid say.

"Come on," Mara said as she and the handmaids pushed a dresser in front of the door. "Did you want to die?"

"Either I die here or out there," Sophie said. "You must all stay safe, though."

"Why do I doubt Ultiir has our safety in mind?"

Shouting filled the silence. Then, there were clashes of metal and groans and screams and yells. Renna wiped tears away as she sat in the corner. Amalla paced in front of the door. Mara chewed her lip. Sophie could do nothing but listen, but her ears couldn't tell who was winning and who was dying. Metal on metal was what she heard the most. She prayed her men remembered how to fight. They'd been out of practice for far too long.

There was one last scream before the palace was silent. Not even the birds outside were singing. "We're alright," Mara whispered.

Then a door burst open and footsteps filled the bedchamber Sophie used to sleep in. At any moment they would turn their attention to the handmaid's room. And that moment came quicker than she had been expecting.

The door kicked in, wood pieces splintering and flying into the room. Renna screamed, and Mara ran over to Sophie. Some young knight came in. His helm had fallen, and his face was bloody, and over his armor he wore a surcoat with an owl on it. Her men had lost. *Dead, all dead.*

Amalla ran like a crazed fool, screaming and gripping a small knife. She plunged it into the young man's throat, and blood spurted onto her face and clothes. Other knights, with shocked eyes, ran into the room. Men pushed Amalla off the dying man and kicked her in the stomach as she cried and yelled. Sophie wanted to look away, but what kind of queen would she be if she couldn't watch the repercussions of her actions?

After enough kicking, Amalla lay still. Her eyes opened, and tears spilled out. Blood leaked from her mouth. Mara's stomach lurched, but she kept her vomit in. Sir Gid followed his men into the room. "See what happens when you go against the king?" He grabbed at Sophie, but Mara hit his hand away.

"Get back," Mara said. "Get out of here and leave us all alone."

Gid shook his head and slapped the baroness' face with his metal gauntlet. The force was so hard Mara's cheek concaved and teeth clattered across the floor. She fell in a lifeless heap. "Anyone else like to play the hero?" The monster looked at Renna, who shook her head as she sobbed.

Sophie didn't fight back when the old man grabbed her arm, his metal fingers digging and breaking into her skin. "Let's go see what His Grace wants with you." As the knight pulled Sophie out of the room, she finally saw what had happened to her men. Blood bathed the tiled floor. Metal helms had been kicked around, swords had fallen. Her men all lay lifeless across the corridor. Sir Velle's face was a mess of blood with a knife lodged in the side of his head.

Sophie had shed enough tears. She didn't want to cry anymore, especially in front of the monster. She would wait to see what her fate was before crying. Whether that was in the dungeon or at the gallows. As they walked down the hall, she heard one last scream. It was Renna. She was being killed. Sophie couldn't hold back the tears any longer as much as she wanted to. She sobbed as Gid dragged her away.

Tundavik

He woke in a dark world.

Off in the distance were purple lights illuminating leaves and limbs of trees. It reminded Tundavik of spending dark days in the Woodlands as a child, hunting with his father away from the town. But there was no moon nor stars to help guide him. The ground was black. The sky was black. It was so dark the lights in the distance hurt his eyes as he strained to see them.

But they moved closer. He didn't take one step forward, but the purple lights were in front of him in an instant, and it was like the sun rose. He shielded his eyes from the light, but still his pupils burned. "What is this?" he asked the nothingness as the pools bubbled near him. Hundreds if not thousands surrounded him. His eyes were drawn to the one below him, and he had to tense his neck to keep himself from diving headfirst. He saw Ritaeum, but it was on fire, like most of his dreams. He was used to it by now. The bakeries and the tailors all burning. The tanneries and the smithies going up in flames. His army's skin all melting. It was a horrid sight. *But it doesn't scare me like it once did.*

"It shouldn't scare you," the voice of a woman said. *The* woman. He hadn't heard her in so long, but her voice still haunted him. A deep accent, her tongue sounding too big for her mouth. She moved the pool with one hand, and it skirted away. Bumps snaked up and down her body, creating spiral shapes. "That is good."

"Am I dreaming?" Tundavik asked as he looked at his hand. He couldn't feel it or any other part of his body, like he was a wisp, a ghost. *Dead.*

"You are not dead," the woman giggled. That was the most emotion he had ever seen from her that wasn't despair. "And yes, you are dreaming. This is *tor aistìr*. The dreamworld, you would call it. This is the only realm I can speak with you."

"Usually there's no speaking, just yelling."

"Yes," the woman nodded, purple light casting shadows on her pointed chin, her skin not the color of a human's, but Tundavik couldn't tell what it was. "That is because I set my *tagrah* on your town of Ritaeum. Before you reached here, all I could do was give you flashes, glimpses. Now we can finally speak."

Tundavik was staring at the fingers that didn't feel attached to his body. They were slightly transparent, with every twist of his hand, the light from the pools shone through. "Why? Why have you invaded my dreams? Made me ache the farther I was from the Woodlands. What did I do to you?"

"You've done nothing. You are merely a *tachaire,* a sort of messenger. If not for my claim over you, spirits of the otherworld would come visit you and cloud your mind."

"I don't understand a thing you're saying," Tundavik said as specks of light floated into the air from the pools. "This is only a dream. None of this is real."

"It is very real." The woman's face tightened. "As are the flashes I've been showing you. Nhamcaryn is coming, and you must join in the fight to stop it."

"None of these words mean anything to me." He was glad he could still feel annoyed. He was tired of secrets and the paranoia. The war caused enough of that already.

"I will explain all." The woman motioned to a pool. "These are the portals to other worlds, thousands of them. I cannot journey through the light, only dreams. You see, I have been restricted; my entire kind has been. There was a war long ago. The binding. Every few thousand years, the worlds come together. That is how your world is populated with humans and dwarves and elves and all other beings. My kind wished to conquer worlds, but I betrayed them. If the binding is stopped, then conquering a world is easier. Destroying a world is easier. That is what feeds us. But if the binding is allowed to occur, then it becomes harder. The last time my kind were defeated and banished and locked away from the portals. My … species have been, how did you put it? invading the minds of humans and other creatures throughout the worlds. Poisoning them. The last world, *Sahnal*, was conquered. Every living being on that planet killed. When I saw that, I knew I couldn't take part in that any longer, so I have been showing you glimpses of what would happen to your world in an effort for you to stop it."

"And how would I do that?" Tundavik asked.

"You must not allow the portal to close. You must let those from *Eile* come into this world and help you fight off my kind."

"What portal? Am I supposed to look for these pools and

fill them with dirt?"

"No, you must find the way." The woman rubbed the bumps on her skin, then her head jerked like she heard something, even though Tundavik could only hear his breathing. "I have been branded a traitor," she said as she continued to map the bumps with her fingers. "I must go, but you must stop Nhamcaryn from occurring. The end of your world. You must." There was a flash of light, and the woman was gone, her skin looking green in the light. The world went black again, and the earth fell out from under Tundavik. He fell into the abyss.

****

Tundavik's bed was a wet mess of sweat. It stank, and he sank into the wet mattress. When he raised his arms, they were shaking. "The end of the world," he laughed at himself. "What did I do to deserve this?" He rubbed his wet beard. "Only a dream ... right?"

He didn't trust his own mind anymore. He had been seeing visions and dreaming for months now, but this time it all felt real. And all he wanted to do was go back to sleep to see if it would happen again, but the woman left in a hurry. *Nhamcaryn,* he thought. *I've never heard such a word. Maybe a doma read something in their books.* He rubbed his eyes. His body felt as if he had gotten no sleep in days.

A knock. "Lord Vandes," Glem's voice cracked as it carried through the door. "The men need ... there's an incident in the courtyard ... Lord Toware ... they need you."

Tundavik sighed as he flung the blankets off and gathered

himself. *I needn't concern myself with dreams and visions right now. I have an army to lead. A war to win.* He found his clothes and followed Glem out the door. The castle was bright with sun shining through the windows. Knights and guards were usually walking the halls, protecting Devro and Yvanne and the new baby, but it was empty. Tundavik's footsteps echoed. "What is it?" He asked Glem.

"Toware …" the boy's words caught in his throat. As they descended the wooden stairs, the air filled with hollers and chanting. Tundavik didn't like that one bit. He pushed the doors open, dark carvings of Vigura's face on either side, an angry face. Outside was a horde of men. Tundavik wished he could turn around and go back to sleep. He'd rather dream of a dying world than deal with more mutineers.

"My lord," Tylo came running. He and his few men were clad in armor. "We'll escort you." The men from Heavensfield used spears to part the crowd as they fought their way in. Glem's eyes were wide, and he gripped Tundavik's shirt like a scared child as men frothed around them.

Then they pushed past the last of the men and came to Lord Toware kicking a woman in her belly. Blood and tears stained her face. Her clothes were ripped, but it didn't look like a rape had occurred, and that at least made Tundavik give a sigh of relief. "Enough," Tundavik said, but the men were shouting, and Lord Toware paid him no mind. "My lord! Enough!" The woman clutched her stomach as a metal boot rammed into it. *Another kick like that and she would be dead.* Tundavik ran as fast as he could and slammed his hands into Toware's blue armor. The lord stumbled and whipped around, his gauntlet colliding with Tundavik's chest, sending him to the ground.

The chanting men quieted. Toware's blue armored knights took a step forward, grabbing their sword hilts. Tylo's men gripped their swords and spears as well. Tundavik tried to take a deep breath, but his chest was so sore every little inhale felt like another punch. "Enough," he said, pushing himself up with a wheeze. "What ... what is the ..." he didn't want to look weak in front of the men, but he was dizzy from the lack of air. He could feel his chest puffing into a bruise. "... meaning of this?"

"This whore is a murderer." Toware shouted, spittle caking his lips. "One of my men, poor Cavi, was found dead with her this morn." The lord stepped toward the woman and drew his leg back to kick, but Tundavik quickly pounced over and pulled the lord back. "Unhand me," Toware shouted and shook Tundavik off. "How dare you touch me! I am lord of Riverend! You are a lord of nothing! You are nothing more than a peasant, and I should cut off your hands for attacking me."

Tundavik brushed dirt from his tunic as he took a deep breath, fighting through the pain in his chest that made him want to fall to the ground. "Do you want to change what you just said?"

"No," Toware said. He spat at Tundavik's foot. "I was charged with keeping the peace in Vigur when we were dealing with deserters and a mutiny. Ever since then, my men and I have done the tough work of keeping your army," he stabbed a finger at the crowd, "in check. Now you come to me and demand I stop? For a whore?"

Tundavik looked at the woman. She shuddered in a pool of sweat and blood. He turned to Tylo and said, "Find a daken," before turning back to Toware. "I didn't know whores could mutiny."

Toware let out a dry laugh. "Very funny. She has committed murder, and I was handing out a just punishment, and I was given free rein to do as I will." The Riverend knights glared at Tundavik, their swords at the ready to come out of their sheaths. Tylo returned with an old daken who tended to the woman's wounds. Following behind him were Miena's Hunters, Ainmel at the lead. They all looked like walking trees. Men couldn't hide the fear on their faces as the hunters came through.

"My lord," Ainmel said, her bow in hand. "We've come to restore peace."

"I can handle it," Tundavik said, but he was thankful to have more help in case things took a turn for the worst.

How many would join my side? Tundavik thought. He had Glem and could count on Mar wherever he was, and it seemed Tylo and his men would back him. The hunters followed Ainmel, and they were the best archers to ever walk the earth. But it was risky. Going against Lord Toware could fracture the Flewthmen from everyone else. He didn't need a war among his own troops.

"I'm sorry about Cavi. I'm sure he was a good fighter, but," Tundavik sighed, "this woman is not part of the army, so you have no authority over her. And I know you are angry, but she deserves a trial, not barbarism." Tundavik's chest throbbed and burned as he saw Lord Furrow of Nye and Commander Wright in the distance. He would have them too, and being a commander meant making hard choices.

Lord Valles' words rang in his ears. *You act as if you have honor, so these men follow you to their deaths. If they knew who you really were, they would spit in your eye.*

"My lord of Riverend," Tundavik said to Toware, "I'm sorry to say this, but I must place you under arrest for the assault of this woman." He tensed. His jaw ached. Toware's men glanced at one another. Murmurs rose through the crowd. Tylo shifted his stance, his armor jangling.

Lord Toware took a few steps forward, his breath hitting Tundavik's face. "Very well," he said.

Flora

It was night when the door opened, and Marbert appeared with a small child. Florance knew the girl, they were given wooden dolls, and they played while a doma from the domaton in the city watched. Marbert kept his hand tight on Flora's arm.

"I don't understand why you would work with him." Flora said as they walked the maze to the stairs. Sir Marbert would not answer her. "What do you gain? Why go to all this trouble? Is independence really that important that you would kill your liege lord?" Silence. *He is more a coward than I thought.* "Did you think of Sir Edmond and how he would react?" *Unless he is part of this too.* "You're able to look at me, to touch me, to stare into my child's eyes and not feel guilty for what you've done. You are more a monster than those sea spiders that live at your village. I hope Vigura sends a pox on your home. On you. On your family."

Marbert had enough. A stiff hand slapped her face. She felt a slight cut and puffy flesh. "Enough."

"Such a strong knight to hit a defenseless daughter of a now-dead lord." It took everything for her not to cry at the smack. *Strength. It's what Father would have wanted.* She wasn't certain her father was actually dead, but Marbert did not keep her suspicions at bay.

"I was hired for a job, and I did that job. Anyone who was against your husband was dealt with, and now the palace is at peace. It would be best if you followed along."

"I would follow them to the grave if I must. I am not afraid to die and meet the Four and be welcomed by my father and mother and their ancestors."

"Does your daughter feel the same? Is her time in this world to come to an abrupt end?"

"Now you threaten a small child who doesn't even know how to use a knife to cut her bread. Would Lord Barnet be fine with you killing his one true daughter?"

"No one else has to die if you follow along like I said. You are to see your husband and wait for him to send you on your way. Is that too much to ask?"

They continued up the steps and turned a few corners. "Tell me," Flora said, "who did it? Who killed my father?"

"Ask him." Marbert pushed open the door. Flora doubted her husband would tell her.

But it wasn't her husband in the room. It was the body of her father. As lifeless as any other dead man. He looked neither wealthy nor poor. Just another body to add to the war. Sir Marbert shut the door and left her to her father.

Flora circled the table. His skin had grown grayer. His eyes shut. She reached out her fingers and interlaced them with his rigid bones. He was clean, and lilac masked the smell of rot. Under his purple coat, there was an area of concave. *I shouldn't.* She did. Flora lifted the cloak and revealed the blow to his chest. She could see where the bones had broken and caved in. The area wasn't cleaned as well as his face. There were still marks of red.

First mother and now you. Why weren't you prepared? Why didn't we see this happening sooner? You distrusted Barnet at first, but came to love him. "That was a mistake." She said, hoping Lord Blume could hear. "What am I to tell little Flora?"

"Tell her the truth." Barnet said as he latched the door. "We should not shield children from the truth." He had brought in a flagon of ale and two cups, handing her one.

She didn't hesitate to drink it. *Let it be poison, I do not care.* He poured her more. "Am I to tell her the whole truth? That her grandfather was slain at the hands of her father."

"I did not kill him. Some lowly guard did."

"But you gave the order." She drank as he nodded. "You locked us away, Florance and I. We couldn't say goodbye." She clenched her jaw. "*Our* daughter could hear all. The prayers were not loud enough." Flora burst into tears. No longer could the dam she built hold them back. "You vowed to protect me and our family. You failed."

"But I did protect you. I kept you in the cell with Florance so you two wouldn't be raped and killed."

Flora wiped her eyes and shook her head. "Do not play the savior. What you did was monstrous. You turned people against me, held me without consent, killed my father. He was your lord."

"And now my lord is feasting with the gods you love. Is that so bad?" His words were like venom. She winced with every word.

"What made you this way?" That's all she could say. *I need to know. My own husband, also my enemy. How could the Four allow this?*

"I only want what's best for our fellow people, I told you

that. Nothing less, nothing more. Once this is all sorted and Tundavik wins the war to grant us independence, then the people can have a new lord. My work will be done."

"You despise Tundavik, and he you. Why would he do what you asked?"

"We're helping the bastard take the throne, dying and looting for him. All for some decree granting us freedom. I say it was a good deal."

"And if Ultiir wins and the bastard dies?"

Barnet shrugged. "I can say I was the one who overthrew Lord Blume. Surely I would be granted a pardon for ending the life of a traitor."

"My father."

"And a traitor to the crown. Just because he felt it was right doesn't make it legal."

"If the Flewthlands were to become independent, we would be invaded, most likely by Plajul. You know this. You know it is not safe."

"The Plajulish are weak. There's a reason they fell to the Nowexerts and are ancestors had to push them back to the frigid shit of a continent. The people of the Flewthlands will fight anyone who encroaches on our sovereignty."

"Sovereignty?" Flora shook her head. "We are not Awaran. We are not united as one like they are. Those in the west hate those in the east. The people of Storyah spit on the farmers, while the farmers fling shit at the city dwellers. This is more difficult for you to understand, and you do not wish to learn."

"Enough."

"Why did you bring me here?" *Was it to show off your trophy? To chide me?* She wished she could say it, but Barnet might kill her too.

"I thought I would give you time to say a final prayer for your father."

"I have." Flora wiped her face clean of tears and snot and spittle. "May the Four protect my father and show no mercy to my husband. That is my wish."

Barnet took a sip of ale, not reacting to her words. "I want you to know that I am truly sorry. I wish it didn't have to come to this."

Flora wiped tears welling up and stood by the door. "May I leave?"

"Marbert." Her husband cleared his throat.

"My lord." The knight came in.

"Take her back." Barnet closed his eyes. "And send for bed linens my daughter."

"You have no daughter." Those were her last words to Barnet that day.

Marbert didn't have to grab her arm. She was too exhausted to run and feared it would be the end. *Florance cannot grow old without a mother and father. She needs me. She needs me.*

"Did you say all you wished to say?" Now it was her turn to stay silent.

I won't tell you anything, you coward, she thought.

"I'm sure Barnet said all he wanted. He can be tough but makes sense when you listen to him."

You disgusting filth. Barnet calls my father a traitor. He should be speaking about you.

"It reminds me of a story in the Book of Meret. When she was on this world disguised as a whore. She saw the world differently and was better able to help her people.

She was tough on those who disobeyed the gods, but held so much wisdom that her words were as normal as rain and poured into the hearts of those who listened. Did you read the story of her travels to the Well of Men?"

Flora didn't answer. *Why the gods? Why describe devotion when you've shown none?*

"She preached as a doma instead of a god, and everyone listened except the king. All his material wealth had clogged his ears and heart. He reviled his people until one day he was cast aside for a newer, much nicer, young man. But Our Mother still showed great wisdom. She vowed to help the king, no matter how far he had fallen. Eventually, that king was put back on the throne. His bloodline reinstated. She always helped those when they were at their lowest." They came to her door. "She still does."

"Was that to comfort me?" Flora asked with dead eyes. Marbert shrugged.

The knight ushered the doma and child away from the cell. "Someone will come by later with new bedclothes. I hope they are what you desire."

Flora was shut in. Behind her, Florance dangled her feet from the bed with tears on her cheeks. *She needs me.*

"All will be well." Flora said as she bent to her daughter's face and wiped the tears.

"What's happened? Why can't we leave? Where's father and grandfather?"

"They're all right." *I should tell the truth. Lord Blume is dead, and Lord Barnet is the cause. Your father is a regicide, a murderer.* She knew it would be too much. "The city had come under attack again, like when the ships sailed into the harbor. It's safer here than up there."

"Will the castle be okay?"

"I am sure the castle will have a few broken pieces like last time, but nothing some masons cannot fix." They sat on the bed together the rest of the day. The light from the barred window grew fainter as little Flora yawned. That whole day she didn't let go of her daughter. She couldn't. *She needs me.* They prayed more than usual. They sang a few songs. Then they cried silently together as the cell grew cold. Flora's hands always wrapped around Florance in a hug.

There was a knock on the door as the moon rose. Florance was curled on her bed while the door unbolted and a washerwoman came in. "These are for the lady." She said with a veil on her head, pulled down so the shadows concealed her eyes. "Freshly cleaned and packed full of comfort." Flora smiled as she took the bedclothes. "Use them tonight. With the moon comes the cold." She lifted her eyes to reveal a deep black, almost like ocean cliffs.

"Vanette?" Flora whispered as the woman left. *Why would she be here?* She turned to her bedclothes and unfolded them. Her head was spinning. *She and Sir Edmond should be gone. What if Marbert saw her?*

A book fell out of the clothes. It was leather bond with a four-pointed star engraved on the front. *A Book of the Four?* Something took over, and she turned to the Book of Meret and flipped to her journey to the Well of Men. Beside the chapter title was a crown on a woman's head. *This is not right. Meret is not a queen. She helped a king.* A king pushed out by a younger man, who in turn was reinstalled by Meret. Flora pushed the book under the bed, looking at Florance. *I don't care what happens. She needs me.*

Aveline

They were stalking their prey through the dense leaves of the forest. The Rainvealandians were cursing with each other as they hunted. Aveline was just glad they hadn't seen her and her guards yet. Bert was by her side, Zoell and Dern off to the right a bit, Ivlin brought up the rear. Tomas stayed back at the camp in case Bertin stumbled through.

Aveline gripped the dagger, and no matter how many times Bert protested, she wouldn't give it up. *I'm the one who needs to save Bertin. If these people have hurt him ...* she let her thoughts trail. She had never killed. Couldn't imagine herself killing. *But if I had to?* She gulped as she stayed low, beneath the brush and behind leaves. A smattering of sunlight hit her face. Even as the day grew brighter, she still couldn't see Bertin. The forest was large. Her brother was small.

The Rainvealandians ducked under a branch and searched. Aveline and her guards paused; she couldn't even hear breathing. A robin flew overhead and startled the Rainvealandians. "We'll never find him at this rate," the one with the bandage said.

"You worry too much, Barhi. You saw how weak he was

when he traveled with us. We'll find him."

The one named Barhi kicked the grass. "Does this look weak?" They pointed to their neck, the cloth red with blood. "He did it to save an elf, of all things. I want to rip him limb from limb."

"In time," the other said. He looked through some branches and tapped Barhi. "This way."

Before Aveline set off, she grabbed Bert's sleeve and whispered. "Do you really think Bertin could've stabbed someone? And for an elf or whatever?"

"Maybe your brother is stronger than we all thought," Bert whispered.

Aveline's knuckles were white around the dagger. "Maybe I am too."

She motioned, and her guards were off again. It was harder to see their prey as they went farther into the forest. Eventually, all they could see were shadows. "This isn't good," Zoell whispered.

"No," Aveline said, not wanting to relent. "I still see them." But when she peeked around a tree, the shadows were hopping rabbits.

Now, the Rainvealandians were nowhere to be seen. "They couldn't just disappear." Dern said as he watched his step.

"Vanished like ghosts," Bert said. "I say we go back to Tomas, eat some food, and think things through."

The sun was already at noon, and she didn't feel any closer to finding her brother. "If we go back now," she said, "there's a chance we lose them forever. They can't've gotten far. We have to keep going."

Zoell bit her cheek. "I'm not sure."

"My brother is out there," Aveline said. "I must find him, and you must help me. Please. We've come all this way. If we go back to camp and set out tomorrow, then Bertin could be out of the forest and heading to Bardekan or some other city. He's lost, and he'd be even more lost."

Ivlin stepped forward, letting out a warm breath. "I agree with Aveline. I say we split up." The other guards all shook their heads, but Aveline nodded. Ivlin nodded back. "We know they went this way," he pointed in a direction. Aveline was so lost it could've been north or south or east or west. She had no idea. "I'll go off alone," Ivlin continued.

"Don't go too far off," Zoell said. "We want to find each other again. The tent is that way," she pointed behind her, "so let's meet back there in an hour or so." Aveline was glad her guards seemed to know their way around.

Bert said, "I'll take you back."

He was talking about Aveline, and she made a fist. "How many times do I have to tell you no? I'm finding my brother."

Bert shook his head but said, "Okay," anyway.

So Aveline went with Dern the Third, leaving Bert to Zoell. Ivlin went whichever way he said. Alone. She didn't like that, but Ivlin was stubborn and Tomas was back at camp.

"I'm glad you chose me," Dern said as they jumped a creek. Frogs croaked as they neared. "Between you and me, Bert's only getting older. I'm afraid he won't be able to protect you like I can."

Aveline wiped sweat from her brow, her hair sticky. "He won't have to worry about protecting me once we reach Rowan again. Maybe he'll actually retire this time, or become a sentry."

"He would rather die in battle."

"Hopefully not yet," Aveline said. The dagger was still in her hand; she couldn't bear to be apart from it. The silver reflected the sun into her eyes. "How do you do it? Kill? So easily, I mean."

Dern wrinkled his nose as he pulled a branch out of the way for Aveline. "I'm not sure," he said with a shrug. "Guess I'm used to it."

"That's all? What about the first time?"

"I don't remember," Dern said. "It was long ago; I was a boy. I didn't think there would be so much blood, I guess. Nor did I expect the pissing and shitting." Dern laughed as he washed his face with some water. "What can you do? I wouldn't let you kill, though," he said and pointed to her dagger. "That feeling, or whatever it is, that's not for you to find out."

"And why not?"

"Well, I don't remember most of my kills. I feel nothing. Don't you see the problem in that?" Aveline nodded and Dern, a smile with hints of sadness on his face, waved her forward. They passed a blue and green twinkling in the leaves above.

"Fairies?" Aveline asked like she was a child seeing the stars for the first time.

"I would say so," Dern said as the lights glittered away. "Strange seeing all this and still no elves."

"But the Rainvealandians said something about an elf. About Bertin."

Dern nodded. "You think he's helping them? The elves?"

"He was captured by elves, though." Aveline shrugged. "It

doesn't seem like Bertin to help them or to hurt anyone. All he did was whine when father wanted him to do any sort of training."

"Perhaps the desert and the ancient city changed him."

"Perhaps." Aveline nodded as her fingers twitched around the dagger.

There was a scream. It came from a man. Aveline didn't wait for Dern; she raced through the leaves, jumped over limbs and sticks, and barreled out of the bushes. She was in a small clearing, birds flying overhead, crows cawing. On the grass was Ivlin, his sword flinging and bracing against metal. One of the Rainvealandians was fighting with him.

Dern pulled up the rear, panting for breath. "I'll help him," he said, but before he could take a step, the hilt of a sword flew down and hit the back of his neck. Dern collapsed onto the grass.

"No," Aveline said. It was the one named Barhi. The cloth had peeled from their neck, dried blood falling onto their shoulder.

"Why are you following us?" Barhi asked. They grabbed Aveline's arms and tried to wrestle the dagger away from her.

"No," she said again, her teeth gritted. "Leave me alone." She found her footing and kicked Barhi's shin. They dropped to the ground in a huff. Aveline gripped her dagger and placed it in front of their chest. "Where is my brother?" She asked in the ancient tongue. "Where is Bertin?" Barhi spat as they held their leg. "Fine," Aveline said. But before she could bring the dagger to their chest, she was pulled behind and slammed to the grass, the dagger flying into the leaves.

"Torlem," Barhi said to the other Rainvealandian. "They want Bertin too."

"I don't care," Torlem said as he positioned his sword just above Aveline's head and went to pierce through her brain. As Aveline closed her eyes, she saw her mother. She saw her father. They were smiling at her, welcoming her. Bertin and Baldewin came behind her, hugging her. But then they vanished, and she saw Mari. The last thought Aveline would have before she died. The sweet sound of Mari laughing and kissing her. She would never hear it again.

But Torlem's sword never found her. Ivlin had surprised him this time and pushed the man to the ground. Barhi stood, grabbing their sword, but limping still. Ivlin and Barhi sparred, the metal deafening to Aveline, who lay on the grass with tears streaming down her cheeks.

There was movement in the forest, and she watched as her remaining guards all emerged from the darkness. Barhi stood no chance. Bert's blade found them and cut their bowels out. The slop and plop of innards that fell next to Aveline made her want to vomit, but as Zoell helped her to her feet, they watched as Torlem screamed for Barhi and rammed his sword into Ivlin's neck. The blade covered in red as he wretched it free from her dead guard.

Zoell nearly dropped Aveline as she whipped out her sword and stalked over to Torlem. Aveline could barely breathe. Bert was running to Torlem as well. Dern was stirring awake. Everything was happening slowly. She could see Zoell's moves with ease. She whacked away Torlem's sword with her own like it was a bug. Then she pierced his torso with her blade.

Then a familiar voice rang out. "Wait." When Aveline turned, she finally saw who she was looking for. The reason she crossed the Ters-Veck at Ealna, why she wandered Rainvealand for weeks. For pushing through a mess of leaves and thickets and limbs.

Bertin stood disheveled across from them all.

Aveline couldn't keep her emotions in any longer. Her jaw trembled, and tears poured from her eyes. She ran, not caring if Bertin wanted it or not, and wrapped her arms around him. They nearly fell, but she found her balance. Bertin moved little, but the hug was everything for Aveline. So much had happened since he had left. For weeks she thought he was dead. She spent months thinking they'd never find one another. But her brother was standing. Her arms wrapped around him. She could feel his breath.

Aveline pulled back and wiped her tears. Bertin had overshadowed Ivlin's death, or maybe her tears were for them both. "I …" she could hardly speak. "I … can't believe … it." She hugged her brother again. She could tell he needed one. Her brother didn't look like he did on the last day they saw each other. His face was sunken, a cheekbone was poking his skin, his eyes were dark, his hair a mop of sweat and grass and bugs. His body had very little fat. Bertin reminded her of the abandoned children she would see in Rowan. The last thing she noticed after seeing his torn clothes was a missing finger. Just his small one, but it was gone. "What happened to you?" Aveline said as she grabbed his shoulder. "I'm so sorry."

"You didn't have to do that." Bertin said. His voice was dry and scratchy.

Aveline followed his gaze to the dead and bloodied

Torlem and Barhi. Ivlin lay near them as well. Her guards were sulking around their fallen ally. "They killed Ivlin," Bert called out to Bertin.

"I know," her brother said, "but they … they didn't need to die. Everyone always dies."

"We're here now." Aveline pushed a piece of sweaty hair from Bertin's face. "You're safe. You don't have to worry about Rainvealandians or elves or anything else."

"Always dies." Bertin repeated. Then he chuckled to himself. "What am I saying? Who am I talking to? This is just like the flood. You're not real."

"What?" Aveline asked.

"I won't go with you." Bertin said. It was as if his legs gave out as he dropped to the ground. He sat in the grass, his eyes not leaving the dead.

Zoell came over and took Aveline aside. "I think we should give him some space. This is surely a lot for him to take in all at once."

"We need to bury Ivlin anyhow," Bert said. "Get Tomas too. He'd want to be here."

"I'll get him," Dern said as he rubbed the welt that had formed on the back of his neck. "Ivlin always wanted a pyre. Fetch the wood?"

Zoell and Bert nodded. Aveline would get some too, but as she went into the forest, her eyes found her brother again. His fingers were playing in the grass as if he were a child. His eyes were emotionless.

"He doesn't seem okay," Aveline said to Bert as he picked up logs and handed her sticks. "I'm not sure how we're going to help him."

"In time," said Bert. "Once he realizes we're his friends

and we'll protect him, he'll go back to his former self."

"And if he doesn't?"

Bert shrugged. She could see a hint of tears in his eyes. Ivlin had been guarding Aveline for at least a decade. He was a good man. He was as honorable as one could be in this world. And he was dead. Aveline had never had a guard die on her. Die protecting her. Other princesses surely went through it. *But were they as close as we were?* Aveline's mother had always told her to treat her guards like family. And just like the rest of her family, they were dying as well.

When Tomas reached them, he cried. At first he didn't believe it, but seeing the cut throat was more than enough proof. "He died like we would all want to." Zoell said as she patted Tomas' back. "Now let us pray."

Zoell said some words to the moon. It was dim in the daylight, but above the horizon all the same. Some other prayers were said as Ivlin was placed on a mass of limbs and sticks and logs and leaves. Dern was sweating from making the fire. The torch crackled as he brought it over to the pyre.

"May we never forget you," he said. Then he threw the torch onto the wood, and Ivlin burned into the sky.

Aveline rubbed her red eyes. She was worried about how many more would die on their journey home. She didn't want to lose anyone else. *I lost Ivlin but gained Bertin. Maybe the gods are playing a cruel joke.*

Bertin was still on the ground as the fire roared into the setting sun. He was alone, shaking his head. Somehow, Aveline had to get him back to Rowan. She had to make him king.

Blis

The *Kutski* had stayed close to the shores of Adedor as it made its way south. Blis kept watch for any sign of Rowai ships. He hadn't seen any for days. The sky was a bright blue, reflected in the water. The sun beat down on them, though he knew it would get worse the farther south they went.

"And that's where I was," Potter said as he pointed to the mountains along the shore. He had told the story multiple times. Something about slavers, a prison, a dragon. If Blis had known the boy was crazy, he wouldn't have brought him along. "It was harrowing, to say the least." The boy continued. "I'm a long way from the West."

Blis nodded at that. He was still a long way from Rowan, and with the lack of wind, it would take even longer. The oarsmen did their best rowing, but Blis knew it was a tough job. Long ago, when he was first sailing, he had been an oarsman. He was strong then. His arms barely fit into his shirts. Now, his belly barely fit. "Where do you think we are?"

"Vidale, of course. I know those mountains anywhere." Potter said.

Blis nodded but looked to Pitor, who he was actually

asking. "The boy's probably right. Somewhere along the Noest. Could be Vidale or Ortan we're looking at," the captain said. He didn't have to do much work as the men rowed below. His job was to keep them from crashing onto shore. He pointed far to the south, where the mountains seemed to drop off the world. "See that? I reckon that's where the Noest becomes hills. Closer to the Flewth-Vet than we were."

Blis stifled a yawn and massaged his leg. "Not fast enough, though. I know," he said before Pitor could argue, "we're going as fast as we can. I guess the Four hate us and want Caxton and his ilk to capture us."

"Has anyone ever told you that you're not the most fun conversationalist?" Pitor laughed. "Let's talk ships or days of old. Of wars and battles. Don't worry about the council anymore. They're behind us."

Except William is in Rowan, waiting, scheming. Blis rubbed his eyes. The few days on the *Kutski* hadn't been the best. Worry kept him awake at night. Storms didn't help either. The ship had a layer of salt on it from waves crashing yestermorn. It was entirely black; even the oars below were black. He'd never seen wood so dark. But then again, he had rarely visited the North.

"Did you visit the North often?" Blis asked the captain. He was taking his advice. "I mean, enough to learn the language."

"You know how it was. Once Rowan was put back together, we went back to trading. I mostly sailed the coast of Gerot-Staller. Loads and loads of timber and wool."

"Must've been nicer than war." Blis said. "I saw a lot of men die from mite attacks. Then our queen died, and we were lost for a long time until Bartel came back."

"Much nicer," Pitor agreed. "But the Northerners can be vicious all the same."

"They don't like slaves, though," Potter said. He was leaning over the railing, watching the fish below. "That's what my captain was selling. Slaves," he scoffed. "If he didn't do that, I'd be back home with my pa and ma. We was supposed to be selling fish."

Blis scratched his balding head. He could feel that it was burning in the sun. "Was he really selling slaves?" Blis didn't know whether to believe the boy about anything he said, but he had mentioned it more times than Blis could count.

"Oh, yes," Potter said. "I didn't even know. There was some hidden room below deck. When the Hellers found it, I was shocked. I cried for days. Then they took me to that dreadful prison. I cried there too."

"And this prison was in Vidale?"

"Probably. In the mountains, at least. A massive hole in the ground. It looked like the gods had punched into the mountainside. Oh," Potter's face lit up, "I forgot to tell you all about the griffin."

"Stop lying," Pitor laughed. "Why not tell us true?"

"It is true, sir … err … captain. I swear it on my gods and your gods if you wish."

"My god is down there." Pitor pointed to the ocean.

Potter's face flushed like the captain threatened to drown him. "None of youse has to believe me, but it's true. Just wait until I find my friend." The mention of his *friend* caused Potter to rest a sad face in his hands. "You ever lost friends?"

Blis sighed. "Of course, but you'll make new ones if you don't find this one again. Where do you think he went?"

"I'm hoping down the mountains. I wished and wished he would find me on the road, but he never did, so I got on this boat. The dragon might've eaten him."

Pitor slapped Potter's back in a calming manner, though it looked a little too hard. "Nonsense," the captain's beard blew in the wind. "I'm sure your friend is out there looking for you as well. You'll find each other in the so—"

"—Captain," Blis said. "Your beard." The wind was getting stronger, and Blis could feel the wisps on his head moving. It was the first time in days he had felt any sort of breeze. The masts could finally be lowered.

Pitor touched his face, then his eyes lit up and a laugh escaped his belly. "Now we're talking. Men! Oh," he thought for a moment, then started yelling in Heller.

Blis smiled and wobbled over to Potter. "Well, we might just find your friend a little quicker now."

Blis made his way down the steps to the main deck as the masts unfurled. Pitor turned the wheel to catch the wind. Then the ship pitched, and the oars were pulled in below. Blis couldn't keep the smile from his face. He went to the captain's quarters and found Baldewin.

"You feel that?" he asked the boy. "Now we're getting somewhere."

Baldewin was playing cards with Delmar at a small table. Mari was brushing salt off her clothes in the corner. It was a much smaller room than they were used to, but after their stay in Cahlun, anything was better. The table was bumped up against the bed, fit for one person. They threw blankets down on either side of the bed to sleep. It wasn't the most comfortable, but Blis wanted them to stay together. The captain of the ship wasn't happy, but once Pitor translated how much gold he would receive from the crown of Rowan, he relented.

"How long now?" Baldewin asked as he placed a card down.

"I win," Delmar coughed. Blis was surprised at how unprofessional the knight had become since they had reached the seas, but he didn't complain. They had bigger worries. And as long as Delmar carried his sword and protected the king, Blis didn't care.

"We still don't know, but we're getting closer with every passing minute."

"I want to be home already." The king dropped his cards and leaned back in his chair. A small porthole let in the sunlight. It shone on Baldewin's face. "Do you think Aveline is back?"

Mari perked up at that, but she knew as well as Blis that they wouldn't actually know. "Let us hope." Blis said. "Your Grace, I've been meaning to tell you that you've done well since sailing without your sister. I feel like I haven't said that often enough. You've listened to your advisors, come up with plans on your own, were brave against the pirates and the council."

"Yet I let them lead me astray," Baldewin said with a shrug. "It's been you most of the time. Why didn't my father just choose you to be king and spare the kingdom?"

"Your Grace," Blis chuckled, "you were born into this role. I was just a sailor. You and Bertin were both meant to rule. The Four and the Many chose you. As you get older, you'll see this more."

"I don't know. I find it all dumb." Baldewin went to the porthole and stood on his tiptoes to see outside. "Maybe being king isn't for me. Maybe I want to do other stuff and not rule and come up with taxes or fight battles. I don't want to be stuck here. I don't want to fight off councilors and pirates. The most fun I had in a long time was sneaking away to the brothel on Liari, not for the girls, just for … being away from this all. Did my father ever think like this?"

"I'm sure all kings go through this. You've many years to master it."

Baldewin turned and shook his head. "I don't want to master it."

"We have a problem!" Potter banged at the door. Delmar opened it, and the boy almost fell in. "I saw something, well, I see something. Ships. Ships from Rowan."

Blis pushed past the boy and was hit with wind as he got to the deck. The ships weren't as big as the *Sea Glider*, but they were certainly larger than the boat they were on now. "What do we do?" He called up to Pitor.

"I'm gonna outrun them," the captain said. "Hold on tight."

The ships were coming from the east, and to the west was the mountainous shore. Pitor couldn't turn the ship around, so the only way out was to continue south. With the wind came stronger waves, and the sea foam clawed its way at the deck. The *Kutski* bounced and lurched and cut with every wave. Blis hobbled but caught himself on the deck. The Northern sailors were working as Pitor shouted orders. Delmar had his sword in hand as he tumbled from the quarters.

"I've got him," Mari told them. "We'll be in here if anything happens."

"Nothing will happen," Blis told her. But he could tell

from her eyes that she too was scared.

Pitor was grunting as he whipped the ship's wheel back and forth. The wind was picking up. Clouds started moving over them from the mainland. Blis was being sprayed with every crash of a wave. He and Delmar and Potter stood together and watched the Rowai ships. The masts with stallions getting ever closer. *Where are you, Caxton?* Not that it would help to find him. The *Kutski* didn't have any weapons. No bows, no spears, nothing to throw. Some of the Rowai ships had ballistae on board. If they shot the large bolts, then Blis and the rest of the crew would sink just like Baldewin's crown did.

"We can't outrun them," Delmar whispered. Blis could barely hear over the waves and the shouts. "They'll catch us. They have double the masts."

Blis cleared his throat and bit his cheek. "I know."

There were a dozen or more ships barreling toward them. Pitor was doing his best, but Delmar was right. Some ships had more than five masts. No matter how far they pulled away, the ships grew closer and larger and more threatening. A wave crashed against the ship, then there was a scream. The sailor, Arnyz, teetered near the edge before falling overboard. Other sailors were falling. Potter was stumbling. Blis held onto the rail until his knuckles ached.

Blis took a deep breath and climbed up the stairs. The jerking of the ship didn't help his knee at all. It felt like a hundred pounds was pressing on it. "Captain," he yelled over the darkening storm. "We need to stop. We lost a man to the sea. Stop running."

"What?" Pitor's face dropped.

"We cannot outrun them. Let them capture us. Keep

anyone else from dying."

"And what do you think will happen to me?"

Blis groaned as a wave hit and his side bounced against the rail. "Let me handle that."

So Pitor barked more orders, and the sailors stopped racing. The ship slowed, and the men threw the anchor into the depths below. They were surrendering, but if Blis did his part right, he'd be the only one in trouble.

As the ship stalled and swayed from the storm, the Rowai ships converged on it. A plank dropped between the *Kutski* and a ship called the *Mite Slayer*. Blis stood with Baldewin and the rest. They were all in a line as they waited for their captors. Blis' face dropped when it was Jac and Wycleaf who boarded their ship.

"And we thought it was a kidnapping." Jac said. "Should've known you were just running away like a boy would."

"Enough," Blis said. "You may not speak to the king that way, and you know it."

"King?" Wycleaf laughed. "All I see is a scared child."

Rowan men with weapons made a circle around them, separating them from the Northern sailors. Delmar had his sword in hand, but kept it lowered. Mari tugged at her hair. Potter and Pitor were still at the helm. No one could do anything against the council.

"It wasn't the king's idea, though," Blis said. "I talked him into it. I wanted to sail back to Rowan to consolidate my power."

"Blis," Baldewin whispered. "What are you doing?"

He winked at the boy. At the boy he had known since he was born into this world. It would probably be the last time he saw Baldewin's face. "I wished to keep the council out of this. So if you are to punish anyone, it should be me."

"Of course we would punish you," Jac said. "You've done nothing but cause us trouble. Our plan from the beginning was to show everyone how useless this boy would be as king. The council should wield the actual power. And guess what? It worked. Look at this. Rowan men at our command."

"And they would do anything we say," Wycleaf added. "Do you want to find out?"

Blis took a step forward. "Kill me here, and that'll be fine. I'm ready."

"We're not just killing you, though." Jac's smile turned devilish.

Blis' eyes widened. He thought they would fall out of his head. "You cannot. His Grace is just … just a boy … you …" he was at a loss for words. He was supposed to die as a traitor. The council was supposed to let Baldewin live. His plan failed. Again, his plan failed.

"Men," Jac said, "kill all onboard. Leave no survivors. Not one."

The men murmured to one another, some gripping their weapons harder than others. Blis heard rounds of gulps and hard breaths. But no one moved.

"What are you doing?" Wycleaf asked. "Kill them. Kill the king and all of those loyal to him."

"Do it!" Jac cried.

"They don't listen to you," Caxton said as he walked over the plank. Jac and Wycleaf looked like they had seen a monster. "Men, how about you arrest these traitors?" Blis could only watch in shock as the men did what Caxton told them. They pushed Jac and Wycleaf to their knees and bound their hands.

Caxton. The same Caxton who looked angry. Who hid things. Who shut them out. Who tried to send Blis away from Baldewin. Who was supposed to be the traitor ...

"Your Grace," Caxton bowed his head. "I'm happy to know this wasn't some islander who made off with you in the night. Why did you run?"

"We, uhh ..." Baldewin shook his head. "I don't know."

Jac and Wycleaf were taken over the plank, and the ship emptied of Rowan men. Blis couldn't keep his mouth shut. "You didn't burn the *Sea Glider?*" He asked Caxton as Pitor descended the helm.

"Why would I? The best ship in our fleet?"

"I don't understand," Blis said. Rain hit his head but he barely noticed. The storm could've been a typhoon for all he knew. "Why were you so against us? Why did you try to send me away?"

Caxton chuckled before straightening his back. "I know the royal family and the council are usually at odds, but against you? I was never against you. Princess Aveline and you all saw things your way, and I saw things mine. Just so happens others agreed with me more. And sending you away? I thought your knowledge of sailing would help our men in other parts of the Nokys. I never intended for you to take offense."

"But you hated Aveline," Mari added. "You did everything you could to undermine her. She was furious with you."

Caxton shrugged. "Pardon what I'm going to say, but she is young. We're all hotheaded at that age, are we not? King Bartel and I regularly argued, but it didn't mean we hated each other."

"So we're just supposed to trust you?" Blis asked. "What if this is all a ploy?"

"I can't answer that for you," Caxton said as he started over the plank. "But I was thinking of going back to Redington. You can come if you want."

Blis turned to the king, to everyone. He was flabbergasted. They all looked shocked as well. "I was wrong," Blis said. "So very wrong."

"It's alright" Baldewin put a calm hand on Blis' arm. "You were just trying to protect me. My father would be proud." Baldewin cleared his throat and brushed off his clothes. "Let's go to Redington."

Yvanne

Yvanne jerked her head to keep herself awake. If she fell asleep, she would have terrible nightmares of her mother and the baby, so she had to stay awake. She could feel the bags under her eyes getting heavier and heavier with every passing minute, but she had to do it. Last night she dreamt she had drowned her babe in the ocean. With glee. The night before, she dreamt she was with her child and her mother and father in Whitehall. All sitting happily around the fire. Pollard off in the corner, Devro finding wooden toys to play with his daughter. But the night before that, she dreamt of the baby abandoning her.

"Just like I am," she said to herself.

A shrill cry broke through the silence in her room. Elsewhere in the castle, someone else was taking care of her baby. *Someone else.* She wiped tears before they could fall. Her blankets were stained enough. *What if my mother hadn't taken care of me? How would I have turned out? Why am I trying to make the baby's life worse for her?* But no matter how hard she wanted to, she couldn't bring herself to even look at her own child anymore. One look at her child and Yvanne's heart would race so much she would shake.

Lolly and Maliz took care of the baby most of all. Jacka would tell Yvanne how her baby was doing. Though she didn't truly care. She didn't care about anything right now. There was a ruckus in the courtyard, and all Yvanne did was cover her ears to shut out the world. It could've been an invading army and she wouldn't have cared. *At least they would put me out of my misery. Or maybe they would make me feel something again, even if it were just fear.*

Yvanne sighed as she pulled the blankets tighter around her. It wasn't cold at all in the Woodlands, but she wanted nothing more than to burn. She reached for her necklace, but it wasn't there. Mar had taken it. Stolen it. Who knew how many people he'd told already? Tomorrow, Yvanne could be brought outside and hanged as a mage. *At least my daughter won't have to deal with me as a mother anymore.*

Sir Loc slowly opened the door and peeked inside. "Your Grace," the knight said, "you've visitors." Yvanne's head felt like a rock on her neck, but she nodded all the same.

It wasn't Jacka, or the other women like she was expecting. It was Sir Mar and Lord Vandes. *No Devro.* Yvanne straightened her back as best she could in the bed, but she didn't care how awful and undignified she looked.

"I hope we're not disturbing your sleep," Tundavik said. Mar found a corner to lie in wait. He and Yvanne made eye contact several times, and she wondered if tomorrow came early. "I wished to speak with you."

"Whatever you want," Yvanne said.

Tundavik sat at the foot of her bed, completely inappropriate to be so close to a queen's bed, but Yvanne had no energy to tell him off. "It's about the babe. Your sister has told some of us how distant you are from her. Is there a reason?"

"Sometimes," Yvanne clenched her jaw, "I like to be alone."

Tundavik glanced at Mar and tapped a finger. "Is it Devro?" Yvanne didn't answer. "He'll come around. Sometimes boys aren't the best with their emotions. He's upset right now, but eventually he'll see your daughter as his own."

But will I?

"Plus," Mar said from the corner, "Devro is young. I've been talking to him. He's afraid of losing the war and losing support because he doesn't have an heir." The knight shifted while his hands found pockets. "I've tried to change his mind, but he's stubborn and likes to talk to himself. Eventually though."

"I think," Tundavik said, "once we win the war, Devro will be happy again. The stress of it all, coupled with his time in a dungeon, has caused him to act out. No matter what he said about the babe, his mind will change."

"Well," Yvanne forced a smile, "I thank you for the kind words. But you put too much stock in Devro's words if you think that's why I'm not focused on the baby."

Tundavik nodded and looked at the portrait of the small girl on the wall. It was at that moment Yvanne realized Tundavik and the girl on the wall had the same nose. "My wife, Adile, was also distant after our first child. It was a boy, though, so there was no arguing over a successor. She wanted nothing to do with Guis, but the servants and I took good care of him. A few months later, she was fine and wanted nothing more than to be with her child."

Yvanne again said nothing. She didn't want Tundavik to think his words had any effect on her. She didn't need anyone at the moment. All she wanted was to be alone.

"It happened again when Ertha was born," Tundavik said as he stood and walked over to study the portrait. "But again, a few months went by and Adile was her happy self again. I'm not sure what's going on with you exactly, but this will pass. At least I hope so—"

—*for the baby's sake.*

"—for your sake," Tundavik finished.

She dabbed her eyes. Holding back tears hadn't been working lately. "And she was a good mother?"

Tundavik's face lit up. "The best."

"So I should just wallow," Yvanne said. "Are the men worried? I don't want Devro to have to deal with anymore nonsense. I heard things outside the other day, worried they were about me."

"Never you," Mar said.

"No," Tundavik nodded in agreement with the knight. "Lord Toware was acting out. He sits in the dungeon right now with Lord Valles and awaits Devro's judgment."

She rubbed her eyes and saw the men with blurry vision for a moment. They didn't look happy. All she saw was pity. "Well, I'm glad Toware is being dealt with. Will you leave me now?"

"Can I have a word?" Mar said before Tundavik left. "I just want to talk about Devro some more." Yvanne nodded, and Tundavik left them alone. Mar dug into his pocket and pulled out her necklace. "I thought you'd want this back."

The sunstone glistened in the light. Yvanne could sense the energy that radiated from it. *Maybe my lack of power is what's causing me to feel so bad,* she thought with a glimmer in her eye. Mar dropped the necklace into her hand, and it felt like she stepped into a hearth. All the heat from the castle danced around her.

"Don't burn anything." Mar said.

Yvanne gave an actual smile for the first time in days. "I'm surprised you didn't go telling everyone."

Mar shrugged. "Then I'd've had to tell them how I knew. Not a conversation I wish to have."

Yvanne rubbed the stone with her index finger. The ridges. The heat. All of it was too overwhelming. Her body was shaking with tears. "Did Raimund tell you?"

"No," the knight shook his head. "Is that why you two were close?" Yvanne nodded. "Well, that's a relief," Mar sighed. "There were a lot of rumors flying about. Some that you two had been fucking. I chose not to believe that one."

"Thank you for taking care of it for me." Yvanne said. *Just like Lolly and Maliz is taking care of my own child.* The thought of the baby made her smile drop. Any heat that had been twirling toward her went cold. She rubbed her eyes and gave a forced smile to Mar. "I should get some sleep."

Mar bowed his head and went to the door. "Everything will be fine," he said before opening it. "Devro will come around."

Once the knight was gone, she set her necklace on the side table where uneaten food usually sat. Even with the sunstone in hand, she still felt like her child was a burden. That Yvanne herself was a burden. She cried herself to sleep wishing the necklace had fixed all. Wishing for her death.

***

"Jacka told me you'd be out here," Pollard said as he stood next to Yvanne. "I almost didn't believe it. Does this mean you're feeling better?"

"I didn't want to get bedsores." Yvanne said as she leaned on a wooden railing. She didn't look at her brother, instead watching the courtyard below and Ritaeum beyond. Slaves worked the land in the far reaches of the domain. Small fields being rotated, trees being picked or planted; the occasional whip cracking through the air. Her father had always been too poor to own slaves. The beatings were unusual to her. The people of Ritaeum didn't seem to mind that they were being occupied. They walked along the dirt and paved paths, through trees and over streams. Some kept their heads down when a knight walked past, but most paid them no mind.

What were once soldiers were lounging around, except for the contingent of blue-armored men from Riverend. They were clad in mail and plate, and their weapons were nearby. *I don't like that,* she thought. "Were you there when Toware was arrested?"

Pollard sighed. "I was actually in the trees scouting, making sure no one was marching on us. I'm not sure what Tundavik was thinking, but let's hope it doesn't get us into trouble with Lord Pyre or the Flewthmen."

"I'm sure we'll be fine," Yvanne said before she heard a babble. Once she finally turned her head toward her brother, she saw he was holding her baby. Her face went white, and her legs shivered under the weight of her beating heart. "What are you doing?" She asked as her eyes blinked back tears. "Why do you have her?"

"I thought she could use some air too," Pollard smiled as

he cradled the baby's head.

Yvanne pushed herself back from Pollard and her child. "So you did this on purpose? Did Lolly tell you to? Did she tell you to force this … this baby on me?"

"Your baby?" Pollard's voice was soft. "No. No one sent be out here, and it was just a coincidence I ran into you, is all. You don't need to be paranoid."

She rubbed the bridge of her nose; a headache was coming on, and she wanted to lie down again. "I'm sorry." Yvanne said as her baby looked at her. She was so tiny. Her head was slightly pointed with wisps of hair on her scalp. And her eyes matched Yvanne's. Green but fiery. She quickly lurched her head away from the baby. "I'm glad you're taking her out, and bonding. Doing more than I am."

"Do you want to hold her?"

"No," Yvanne said. "I'm afraid I'll drop her."

"Nonsense," Pollard said and leaned forward with the child. The alien to Yvanne. "It's simple, and I've seen you old newborns in Whitehall before."

"No." Yvanne stepped back. Pollard scoffed but nodded. "I don't …" she didn't know if Pollard was the right person to talk to. What she needed was Helge; at least the doma could see into her future. Whether she grew to love her baby or continued hating her. "I don't like her."

Pollard's eyes went wide for a second before he turned his head away from his sister. "Did Devro cause this?" His voice was low. "I heard how he reacted—instead of love, with hate. He's just like his father in a way. But you can't concern yourself with the opinions of bastards. Don't let his feelings hurt you."

"It wasn't—"

"—I fucking hate him," Pollard whispered. Yvanne followed his eyes and saw the blond boy in the courtyard, Sir Mar by his side, probably talking about her. "Why Father made us follow a bastard into war, I'll never know. And now he upsets you. He's lucky I'm holding Seine right now."

"This is treason," Yvanne said. "I don't want to hear anymore; you could be killed."

"At least he'd be dead too, and you'd be free of his chains."

"Well, that isn't going to happen," Yvanne said. The baby cooed at Pollard and gripped his shirt. "And you will forget all about it."

Pollard's eyes burned just like Yvanne's could, but he nodded. "I have a question though." He looked to the world beyond the small walls of the castle. "What are you going to do if Ultiir attacks? Are you going to leave Seine to die?"

Yvanne hadn't thought about anything other than herself in weeks. The war had faded from her mind. The baby looked at her. It was like looking at a younger version of herself. "I don't know," she said.

Ryobas Reborn

He was the savior of the world. He was the one who would fend off darkness. Bring about a time of peace. Better this world and all others. Keep all people safe. Everyone, everything depended on him.

He was Ryobas.

But he was also Raimund. Though he felt almost godlike, he still remembered *his* people. They were in Viguran, and he would save them too.

And now he stood amongst the Elders. Nostara to the side, translating as the Elders and Raimund spoke. "It is a great honor to be in the presence of our savior. The one who will bring about the light." Nostara said, for an Elder. It … he … whatever was older than anything Raimund had ever laid eyes on. All the Elders were. They took the form of humans, like everyone else. Their skin green. Their hair white. They all sat on platforms that rose from the hollowed-out tree. Their arms and legs looked like trunks. Roots and vines crisscrossed their backs. They were being fed from the tree, or the tree was feeding off them.

Raimund stood in the center of the tree. A million rings to show its age. Insects crawled near on the walls of bark. It was completely hollow. It was like he shrunk to the size of an ant and went into a forest. There were no cutouts for windows like the other trees, but the bark was scratched so thin that it was as bright as day.

"Lam'a lon'te me'sum ..."

Nostara translated as the Elder spoke. "... it is very important that you do not fail. It is imperative that you banish the forces of evil back to their hell. You must close the portal and stop the binding before it is too late. Are you ready to set forth on your journey?"

Raimund didn't look at Nostara as she spoke; his eyes were stuck on the Elders. The one speaking barely moved his mouth. It was as if the words were in his head. "I am ready," Raimund said as Ryobas. "I will protect the people of our world from this threat. I will not let them be harmed."

"You will ride atop Nardal while wielding *Yllaren*," Nostara translated. "You must cast your weapon into the portal to destroy it and all who come near. And you must not fall prey to..." Nostara paused. The tree shook as another Elder, this one looking like an old woman, cleared her throat. Nostara bowed and continued, "... You must not fall prey to their deceitful ways. They will stop at nothing to destroy you and cast this world into shadow."

Raimund waited for a pause. "What is this, Yllaren? I have not heard of it before?"

"An'mi lon'te sen'u ..."

Nostara, "... It is the most powerful weapon in the world. You have already been with it. You and it are already one. Just as you and Nardal became one, so did Yllaren and you. You might know it by a different name. Valkyr."

Raimund couldn't stop his eyes from widening. He hadn't seen his sword in so long that the name almost sounded foreign. But he couldn't forget what had happened to it. He had lost it fighting the pirates who took him captive. It was somewhere near Adedor, either in Viguran or in the sea by now. "I do not have it. I've misplaced it."

"Do not be alarmed," Nostara translated, "we know where it is. We will guide you to it. It is imperative that you heed our words and go to it. Ride Nardal and find Yllaren."

"Where?"

"Redington," Nostara said, without the Elders. "You know this city, do you not?" Raimund nodded. "You must descend on Redington and scour the city for your sword. Burn everything with your dragon if you must. Without Yllaren, you are nothing."

"And if it isn't there?"

"It will be," Nostara smiled. "The Elders see all. They can see where Yllaren lies. Atop a desk in a small chamber."

"All?" Raimund asked. It wouldn't be appropriate for Ryobas to ask, but his past pulled the words out. "Can you see the ones I left behind?"

The Elders whispered once Nostara translated. Raimund counted the rings as he waited. He got lost at one hundred, and he hadn't even made it past his feet. "They say," Nostara said, "that you do not need to worry for your friends. They are safe, but you cannot see them. It would cause you to forget your new self. Cause you to throw away your life as Ryobas. It is much too dangerous. All you have now is Nardal. Is that not enough?"

Raimund gulped and tapped his foot. He stopped once he heard the echo. "You are right, of course. I cannot let my feelings get in the way. Once I stop the rav ..." he forgot the word.

"... Ravadak," Nostara said.

"Once I stop the Ravadak, then I can find them. I can make sure they are alive."

Nostara shook her head and didn't give the Elders time to respond. "Do you not see?" She asked, and Raimund thought he saw tears forming in her cat-like eyes. "The Ryobas of old did not survive. 5000 years ago, he died while closing the portal. As he plunged Yllaren into the portal, the power was too much for any one man to bear. I fear you will not survive this either."

Raimund stood still. All he could hear was the pulsing of the vines from the Elders. He would die. His destiny was to die saving everyone he cared about. It was like the stories of heroes his mother and father used to tell him. The thought made him smile. "If that is my duty ... I shall do it, no matter the consequences." He was Ryobas. His old self would've been afraid of dying, but he was born anew. Washed clean in the purple light. He couldn't let his old thoughts take over. If he had to die, then so be it.

"Good," Nostara said with a smile. "All the arym will be overjoyed that our Ryobas has returned to us. That it is you who will save us and the entire world from utter destruction. I hope tha—"

Screams echoed as the tree violently shook. Raimund fell to his knees. Nostara and the Elders came together and spoke while Raimund pushed himself up. The branches and leaves outside still shaking. "What is it?" He asked. None looked at him. The bark was thin, but not thin enough to see through. Raimund didn't wait. He was Ryobas. He was the protector of the world. If anything bad was happening, he needed to step up. He descended a staircase made of branches, trying not to fall through the gaps. At the bottom of the tree, where the roots dug into the dirt, he went through the small door. Outside, he saw fire.

At first, he thought the dragon had attacked. But he could feel the fear that Nardal felt. That's when he saw elves ravaging the place. Looting the houses made from trees. Throwing things to the ground. Ripping up the flowers and bringing shadow behind them. Raimund didn't have his sword, but surely he could fight off a few dozen elves.

"What are you doing?" Nostara appeared beside him. Her green braids flung around her face. "You cannot fight them." The elves pulled long, jagged swords. Evil grins painted their faces as they went toward the arym. "The Elders and I have agreed it is best you leave."

"Leave? No, I have to stay and protect you. Isn't that my purpose?"

"You will not survive if you fight them here. The Ravadak are powerful, and without Yllaren you do not stand a chance. You must fly to Redington and find your sword. You must close the portal so this doesn't happen to anyone else."

"Come with me. I'll need a teacher."

Nostara's eyes darkened as the Ravadak slowly pushed forward. It was like a dream ... a nightmare. The elves moved slowly and methodically through the small village. Destroying anything they saw. "I must join my people and fight this," she said." We will keep their attention while you get to the dragon." Nostara clasped her hands together and bowed. "Remember what you saw here today. The Ravadak are a violent group. This is what will happen to your home, to your friends if you do not stop them. Please. Save your world."

Raimund didn't have time to think as Nostara pushed him away. So he ran. He ran across the clearing toward the rows of trees. Behind him, there were screams. Behind him, there was darkness. The sun above was being eaten by shadow just like the one in the other world. He couldn't let his world be destroyed like this. He had to save everyone.

He emerged from the leaves and ran to the dragon, who was stretching his neck. He didn't seem worried in the slightest that the arym were being maimed and killed. "We must fly." Raimund said as he stopped below the beast's snout. "We have to get out of here."

Nardal hummed and lowered his head, the long neck resting on the ground. Raimund grabbed the scales and climbed. It was never easy. The dragon's neck itself was as tall as a house. When Raimund reached the back, he gripped onto the dragon's scales and said, "Fly. Fly!" The dragon didn't seem to need that. His wings were already flapping, the trees all rattling from the force. "To Redington!" Raimund yelled over the wind as leaves and branches hit him.

Nardal pushed off with his legs, and the violent flapping of his wings deafened Raimund, but he had to flee. The dragon soared higher and higher. The ground below became minuscule. As they neared the darkening sun, Raimund raised his head the best he could and looked over the dragon. Below, the village seemed okay. The shadow retreated from the land. *Maybe the arym won. Maybe Nostara is okay. Or perhaps once the elves take over, it goes back to normal. I can't let this happen to my home. I can't.*

Ryobas flew atop Nardal into the blinding sun.

Bertin

He had stabbed Barhi in the neck, probably killing them. *But Torlem and they were attacking an elf ... I couldn't let her die,* Bertin thought as he fell deeper into the forest. *Maybe I am a killer.* He had killed Kelltar, and who knows how many other countless souls when he let the fire fall in Anha Jorbstah. He hunted and killed a piglet. Now, he had probably killed Barhi. Torlem would either hunt Bertin or die alone as well. And Bertin had thought killing was so hard before.

His foot sank into mud as he crossed a dried creek bed. He made sure it wasn't flooding, like the last dried river he had seen. Where he had almost died. *If I died there, at least everyone would be safe. Instead, I bring destruction everywhere I go, and now, some end of the world ...*

Bertin barely had time to process what the strange woman had said. Something about Viguran. Something about a source. It was in a forest, hopefully not as thick as Sruhq. And he would come to a crossroads. None of it meant anything to him, except for the fact that the Mother of the Forest showed him the end of the world. He gripped his dagger. "I'll get through all of this just for the world to end," he said to himself as the moon rose overhead, the light piercing through the leaves. "Just my luck."

And with his luck came the feeling of being lost. Though it wasn't just a feeling to him. He had no idea where he was. How much farther until he reached a human settlement. Where elves or nymphs or man-like goats were. He had heard stories of people never coming out of the forest; he didn't want to be just a story.

Bertin was glad, at least, that nothing had attacked him. The forest was still as spooky as before in the darkness. Instead of fighting death, he fought the night. His shivers weren't fear but cold. His eyes drooped as the night went on. The canopy above him blocked his sense of direction. He couldn't get out even if he wanted to. The forest had trapped him.

That night, his dreams were filled with blood. Mostly of Ioelena. The image of her sprawled out and bleeding spooked him awake. He would never forget that. He looked at his missing finger. Sometimes it still itched. *As long as I'm alone, no one else will get hurt.* Bertin thought as he pulled his knees close. *I'll just stay alone forever. Obviously, nothing good comes from making friends or allies or anything.*

He dwelled on Torlem and the elf. Perhaps he was helping the poor girl. Maybe she had tripped and was calling out for help. But the sword and the evil look in Torlem's eyes proved to Bertin that wasn't true.

The rest of the night was full of whispers and taunts. Words in many languages he didn't understand floated through his ears. Eyes seemed to stare at him from the trees. Branches swayed unnaturally, and leaves fell on his head as if it were autumn. Every time his stomach rumbled, a frog would croak. He drooled at the thought of boiled frog legs, something he never thought would happen. That's when he remembered the boar. If he could find the clearing where Torlem and Barhi had been, perhaps he could get his food. Only if they both have left.

He held his stomach, readied his dagger, and walked into the night. Roots caught him; animals scared him. Nothing but sunlight would make this trip better. The whispers and chills followed him. The pitter-patter of a light sprinkle on his head made him shake. His legs buckled from exhaustion as he found a hollow trunk. He put his hands in to make sure nothing was there, then slipped inside. It was cozy enough. Something else he had never thought before, but it was better than sleeping in the open rain and atop the hard dirt. His eyes drifted to sleep.

The sound of his stomach woke him. Hopefully, the boar would still be there. He didn't care what it looked or smelled like. He would eat his kill.

The light rain from the night before had muddied the clearing. His shoes stuck to the ground and squished with his steps as he tried to be silent. He didn't see any Rainvealandians or elves or monsters nearby. The only sounds were mud and the occasional songbird. The boar carcass lay in the exact spot he had dropped it. It seemed to be intact. Nothing had taken it.

Bertin picked up his feet from the sinking mud and snuck over to the boar. The smell had grown worse, but his stomach ached with hunger. As he looked at the small, dead face, he had another thought: he didn't know how to start a fire, or skin a pig, or how to make sure there weren't any parasites. Luckily for his stomach, he heard clanging metal.

The forest vibrated with every clash. Bertin's ears perked, and he followed the noise, his dagger in hand. He didn't want to kill anyone, not again. *What if it's Torlem? What if he's just trying to get my attention?* He gulped at the thought. The morning sun was warm on his neck as he pushed through the brush. Yells escaped into the air. Screams and groans. If Torlem was luring him in, he didn't think he'd hear the sounds of fighting. When he finally reached the clearing, he had been expecting to see elves fighting for their lives. Instead, he saw humans.

Barhi was fighting. They were alive. Bertin hadn't killed them. His vision doubled as he couldn't believe what he was seeing. But it didn't last long. A man brought his sword down on Barhi, killing them in a flash. Torlem screamed and killed another man. Bertin was lost in the chaos. He couldn't make out any of the people except for the mites, who probably wanted him dead now. Torlem didn't last long though; a woman dressed as a knight sliced him open, and he fell to the ground, blood pooling around his body. He wanted to vomit at the sight. They both had been friends. Torlem and Barhi had been good to him for so long, only for Bertin to ruin it. And now they were dead. As dead as anyone else who grew close to him.

Bertin didn't realize the "wait" had escaped his mouth until he saw the eyes on him. He wanted to run. To hide. But the others outnumbered him. His dagger was heavy, but he could fight if need be. *I've killed before.*

Then a girl ran into him … hugged him. Bertin thought she looked familiar, almost a dream. Then he remembered the flood and how his sister had emerged from nothing to help. She was back. Aveline was here now. Her arms tight around his body, tears staining his already filthy clothes. Her mouth moved but he heard nothing. It was all in his head, per usual. Torlem and Barhi were still out there searching for him, hunting. If he didn't leave this vision quickly, then they would find him.

Aveline stepped back and took him in. Bertin wanted to tell her to "go away," but his words caught in his throat. "What happened to you?" She said. All Bertin could think about was seeing his father all those weeks ago. Then Aveline. He thought his mind had healed after Suktir, but now ghosts haunted him again. "I'm so sorry," she said.

Bertin shook his head. Barhi and Torlem hadn't done anything wrong to him. He was the one who stabbed Barhi in their neck. It was his fault they were mad. Words finally left his lips as he said, "You didn't have to do that." Torlem and Barhi were both bloodied. Viscera and gray matter had spilled out. Both of their eyes were open. Both of them stared right at Bertin.

"They killed Ivlin," another said.

"I know," Bertin said, not questioning why he was talking to the ghosts. "But they didn't need to die." His breath quickened; he couldn't stop it. "Everyone always dies."

The ghost of his sister spoke and pushed hair from his face. Bertin didn't hear anything again. His heartbeat drowned all the sounds out. "What am I saying? Who am I talking to? This is just like the flood. You're not real. I won't go with you," Bertin told his sister. He was tired of running and hiding and being chased, so he sat on the ground and played with the grass.

The ghosts all went about their day. Bertin sat alone finally and put his head in his hands. They were covered in dirt, but he didn't care. He stopped caring long ago. If his parents saw him now, or his actual sister, they would reel away in disgust. He was supposed to be the prince. He was supposed to be clean. Always proper and tidy. Bertin chuckled. "Oh, what I used to worry about." Just last year, if Bertin hadn't bathed for two days, he would've ordered his knights to find a bath. Now, all of his knights were dead. Now, the world was in danger. Then he remembered more of what the Mother of the Forest had said. "In my domain, you merely need to ask for help."

Bertin pushed himself off the ground as a fire was lit in the distance. His sister and the other ghosts all stood around. He even saw his father among them. "Wil you help me?" He asked the air. "I need you to get rid of these ghosts, to heal my mind, to help me leave this place." There was no answer. A breeze ruffled leaves, but that was it. "Please," Bertin said.

Then the leaves started singing, and Bertin's face grew large with a smile. The ghosts were too busy to notice, so Bertin walked out of the clearing and toward a tree. The dark wood thumped like his own heart. He put his hand on the trunk and closed his eyes, willing the mother to come with all his might. She never showed. Instead, the leaves spoke to him. "You have already been helped." The voices said, the Mother of the Forest's in there as well. It was like a chorus of a thousand people. "Have I not sent your sister to you?"

"She's a ghost," Bertin said as his body swayed.

"A ghost?" The Mother of the Forest's voice grew louder. "My dear child, go to her. Embrace her. See she is real and is ready to help. Your sister is the one who will take you to the source. You must know this."

The breeze stopped. The thumping quieted. Birds sat atop branches and watched, but made no sound.

Embrace her? He asked himself. Bertin went back to the clearing. The ghosts ... or people cried together over a large stack of wood. A body was burning to ash. Ivlin. Bertin dug his heels into the ground every time he took a step. His body wobbled. His balance was off. The sun was already setting. Aveline was dark. Bugs and frogs started singing in the forest. Bertin gulped.

The fire was hot as he neared, sweat trickling down his face. The others watched him. A bald one elbowed Aveline. When she turned, she reminded him of their mother. They shared the same face. It was nice to remember his mother without picturing the rocks. His lips quivered, and he couldn't hold his tears in. He wrapped his arms around Aveline and sobbed. His family had finally found him. He wasn't alone anymore. Bertin was safe.

Tundavik

The blade cut around his chin and over his throat. He forgot what it felt like to have air hitting his face. The barber stood over Tundavik, his eyes focused on the close shave, making sure not to nick Tundavik's face. "Ya know," the old barber said, "I know you."

Tundavik waited for the blade to move away from his neck and be dunked in a bowl of water before saying, "Is that so? Hopefully not because of the war."

"Other than you marching into town?" The barber wiped the blade clean and shook his head. "No. I knew you before, in your past life it seems. When you were duke."

"And what's your name?" Tundavik said as he lifted his neck for the barber to shave.

"Name's Lolan, but that won't help ya. Back then I was just some farmer in the fields." He pulled the blade down along Tundavik's neck, scratching as it tore hair from his skin. The towel over his chest was covered in gray and brown curls. He didn't realize how old he must look now. "I usually came into town during market days," Lolan continued as he grazed over the coarse hair. "The day after … well, after everyone was killed, it was supposed to be time for market. I came with my lemons and limes. Not even the buckets of citrus could hide the smell of death."

Tundavik said nothing, but he remembered the smell as well. An iron scent had formed over the town, decaying bodies burning under the scorching sun, crows flying and shitting as they picked at the corpses.

"They said the king was mad at Lord Vandes. I couldn't believe my lord duke would do anything to deserve such treatment." Lolan continued cutting, and Tundavik was worried the old man had heard terrible stories of what he did in Panscar. Worried Lolan would slice his throat open for revenge.

"But?" Tundavik said as he barely opened his mouth. Sweat formed on his brow.

"But no one, not even the most violent murderer, deserves to have their family and town put to the sword." Lolan went over Tundavik's face with a wet cloth. "I hope that bastard king is better than his father and uncle. When Lord Valles told us to prepare for a fight, I thought we'd be against the specters of the wood, but then you came charging at us, and I knew we'd be alright." Lolan carefully took the towel, his hands shaking from old age, and helped Tundavik to his feet. "Welcome home, Lord Vandes."

Tundavik bowed his head. "It's good to be back."

He found his loose shirt and slipped it on, rubbing his face every chance he got. He was so used to dandruff and dirt and grime on his face he forgot what it was like to feel clean. Now, he could see his chin again, his cheeks, his lips. *Almost a young man again,* he thought with a smile as he left the barber.

He was in the town, trees growing all around the houses and shops. People and men-at-arms going about their day.

Some shopping, some selling. Others laughed and gambled. Even Miena's Hunters, all looking more human than tree, were laughing as they drank from a well. Ritaeum was calm. Much calmer than Tundavik's dealings in Storyah, or planning a war in Whitehall, or trying to climb the walls of Vigur. He hadn't felt so much peace since Attrima. The trees provided not only shade but also protection. *No way Ultiir can pass a large army through the swamps unnoticed. I've half a mind to just stay here for the rest of the war.* But he knew that wasn't an option. Eventually, he would have to go to the fight again; Devro would make sure of it.

The boy was walking with Diero and Gordo while looking at a market stall. Apples lined boxes, and Devro was picking through them. "They're all dirty," the boy said as the merchant watched over them.

"You have to clean them." Tundavik said, making his way over. "Something people do for you before they bring you a meal." Devro nodded but moved past the apples. The seller bowed her head, but the boy paid her no mind. "Are you ready for the trials?" Tundavik asked his king.

"I guess," Devro said. He looked past Tundavik and nodded at nothing. "Though I worry about what will happen if I find Lord Toware guilty."

Tundavik shook his head. "Nothing. Even if the men of Riverend took matters into their own hands, it wouldn't matter. We've the strength."

"Unless the people join them," Diero scratched his head. "I know we beat them before, but it's still dangerous. Perhaps just giving Toware a warning and sending him on his way will suffice. Send him to Lord Plume."

Gordo shrugged. "Seems the best way to stop any

violence within our ranks."

Tundavik gave an uncomfortable smile. "Have you seen the woman? Toware beat her near death for a crime she might not've committed. We can't allow that in our army." Tundavik thought of the young whore in Sayer's River, Seena, and imagined it was her that was beat. He was even gladder he had all of those girls stay north of the river.

Diero nodded and bounced on his feet. "But sometimes things happen. And Toware is a powerful lord in the Flewthlands. What happens if the other Flewthmen feel slighted? What if they turn on us as well?"

"They will not." Tundavik stood firm.

"Besides," Devro finally said, "I led an army. I can deal with them."

Tundavik only smiled while Diero and Gordo gave their agreements. *Stupid boy,* Tundavik thought, *you're going to get yourself killed one of these days, and I won't be there to protect you.*

"Can we speak alone?" Tundavik asked Devro. Gordo and Diero looked to the boy, who nodded them away. They both pursed their lips as they left.

"I don't need convincing when it comes to Toware," Devro said as he found a stall selling wooden trinkets and toys. "I've already decided."

Tundavik picked up a wooden doll and looked to the castle. Yvanne and her baby were somewhere inside. "Well, we can forget about Toware and Onnu. I'm sure you'll make the best decision for both of them. Perhaps we should talk about your wife and daughter."

Devro froze for a moment before turning away and saying under his breath, "I know, but not now." But he wasn't talking to Tundavik, only the air, like always. "What of them?" He asked Tundavik.

"You've abandoned them."

"Abandoned?" Devro laughed, but Tundavik could tell he was nervous; the boy's leg was shaking as he stood. "The father rarely helps with the newborn; that's a woman's job. I'm sure Yvanne is doing just fine."

Tundavik put the toy down and crossed his arms. "She is deeply unwell. I worry about her, and your not speaking with her or seeing Seine is only making it worse."

"She promised it was going to be a boy," he whined. "Now I have no heir. Her brothers tell me I should try again in a couple of weeks when Yvanne's body heals. Then pray to the Four and the Many for a boy to be formed."

"I've never heard you pray," Tundavik said. "I'm not sure that's something you can control, no matter how much you wish it so. Why don't you check on Yvanne? See if she is ready for another baby. I know my Adile wanted to wait. Her mother was basically pregnant for twenty years before getting too old to give birth. Do you know how long Adile's mother lived after that?" Devro shook his head. "Two years. She spent twenty years getting pregnant and birthing over and over, and when she could finally enjoy life, she died young. Is that the kind of life Yvanne wants?"

"It's her duty to her king and kingdom. I need as many heirs as possible. Raise them all to be rulers in case anything happens."

"Then maybe you should start by getting to know this baby. Learn what it takes to raise a child, and not storm off when you don't get what you want."

Devro chewed his lip. He rustled through the crate of

toys and brought out a carved wooden horse. "Do you think Seine would like this?"

"Eventually," Tundavik laughed. "She's still a little young for it, but it will be a nice gift."

"I'll see her and Yvanne after the trial. First, I must sentence Toware and Lord Valles to death."

"Death?" Tundavik raised his brow as he left a copper piece for the merchant. "I thought Lord Valles was going to be allowed to live?"

"Only if he swears fealty to me," Devro said. He walked over the dirt streets of Ritaeum. "And if not, then I'll need to find a new duke of the Woodlands. Gof—" he paused and took a breath. "I've thought only of you. Would you be the duke again?"

A breeze sang through the trees of Ritaeum. Old oaks and birches fluttered. The castle loomed over them, looking taller than it ever had before. The gate had been covered in blood all those years ago when Tundavik raced back from the Bezir. It was the same path he walked now, and it had been flooded with guts and shit and death. Then he found his family. "I'm not sure," he told Devro. "I haven't thought much about it."

"You haven't?" Devro's mouth twisted. "Surely when you decided to go to Whitehall and ally with Lord Rely, you knew this might've happened." Devro scoffed with whatever ghost he saw. "Why wouldn't you be duke?"

Tundavik rubbed his face, forgetting his beard was gone. It was so smooth, but even with the hair shaved, he was still an old man. "There must be someone better. Someone you want to reward for following you into battle. Someone younger with children. I've nothing to offer you after we win this war."

"I guess I could move Pollard from being a knight to a duke," Devro laughed. "Is that really what you want?"

Tundavik shrugged as they came upon Diero and Gordo, both eating a frog soup. "I'm not su—" he sniffed the air. Smoke. "What is that?"

A man on top of the castle wall ran to the edge and shouted. "Fire! Fire!"

"Ultiir?" Devro asked as he looked around.

The brothers unsheathed their swords and surrounded Devro as others went racing toward the castle. "Yvanne." Diero said.

"I'm sure she's safe," Gordo gulped.

Tundavik didn't need to hear any more; he had to keep the castle from burning. Black smoke rose from the courtyard as his old legs bounded across Ritaeum. Once he passed the gate, the image of blood-soaked grass and his children's bodies filled his head. He just knew that's what he was walking into—another massacre. But it wasn't death he found. Instead, it was Lord Toware and the men of Riverend. All armed.

The smoke rose from a corner of the castle; knights were running to put it out. Through the windows, Mar was racing down the hall. Tundavik shivered as he gave a sigh of relief. *At least Mar will save Yvanne and the baby.* But that meant Tundavik had to deal with Toware.

"You broke out?" He said to the lord who had been given his armor.

"I have decided on more than that," Toware said as he clad himself in blue and found his sword. "I have decided that you are not fit to lead this army. So, I am putting it upon myself to end this right now."

"Stupid," Tundavik said. He was naked. No armor, no weapons. If Toware wanted, he could end Tundavik's life right there. Knights and guards were around at least, so Toware and his men wouldn't last long. *If they're on my side,* Tundavik thought. Commander Wright wasn't around, nor were Tylo or Furrow or anyone else he called an ally. *Maybe this is how I die. In the courtyard where my family was murdered.* "You think His Grace will forgive you if you kill his most trusted advisor?"

"What do I care?" Toware glared. "You'll be dead, and his army will be in shambles. My men and I are going to go back to Riverend and live out the rest of our days in peace. You'll be dead, and others will think twice before putting their hands on a lord."

"You were beating a woman."

"And you should've known your place. Lords do as they wish, just as your king does what he wishes. Hurvir stripped you of your duchy a decade ago. That means you became a peasant, and it's only right I treat you as one."

"Devro was going to grant you clemency," Tundavik lied. He had to say anything to get out of this. "Now you've doomed yourself to death."

Toware shrugged. "No one can defeat my men." The lord charged after him, but an arrow whizzed through the air and embedded itself in the weak spot in his armor, right under his armpit. He yelled out, and everyone in the yard looked. It was Miena's Hunters. Ainmel with the bow, nocking another arrow.

"Leave Lord Vandes," Ainmel said. "We will handle the traitor."

"Traitor?" Toware broke the shaft and pulled the arrow out of his arm, blood spilling out. "Now we have nonhumans as allies? I should've known this would happen when joining a bastard's war. Get them!" He yelled to his knights. The men of Riverend ran at the hunters with swords and spears. The hunters loosed arrow after arrow. Tundavik couldn't see how many were falling or dying as he ran out of the courtyard into town.

The army had grown lazy since arriving in Ritaeum, and nothing showed that more than hundreds of them sitting around doing nothing, just watching. *Maybe they don't know,* Tundavik thought as he ran toward Devro, *or maybe they're with Toware.*

"What's happened?" Gordo asked.

"Lord Toware," Tundavik panted as his knees cried from pain, "he wishes me dead."

Ainmel was thrown out of the castle gates, and Toware towered over her. "Traitors, you all!" He shouted at her. Her bow had fallen away, the quiver at her leg almost empty. She gripped an arrow and plunged it into Toware's leg, between the mail. He cried out and stomped on her. It was like someone was thudding against a tree stump. "Die, you bitch!"

"What is he doing?" Devro shivered as he hid behind the brothers.

Toware went back into the courtyard, disappearing from everyone. The soldiers were standing now. Some stalked to their weapons and armor. Miena's Hunters were still firing arrows as they backed away from the castle toward Ainmel, but they too were running low. Finally, Lord Toware came back with a lit torch, his men at his back. "Stop this!" he shouted at the hunters as he put the fire near Ainmel. "Or I kill your leader." The hunters lowered their bows, and Toware straddled Ainmel. "I just wanted Tundavik, but you had to be stupid and get in my way. Let me show everyone what happens when you commit treason." He dropped the lit torch on her, and Ainmel screamed as she went up in flames, her body charring like a tree on fire, the smell like that of hickory smoke.

Yvanne

The birds singing outside annoyed her. Yvanne stepped across the wooden floor and closed the windows. She had been enjoying the warm breeze, but everything she liked ended eventually. In the town below were Devro and her brothers. He was smiling. "At least he's happy," she said. "Tundavik and Mar are too naïve to think he'll ever come around."

Look how much he smiles without you and the baby, her thoughts taunted her. *Ignoring you purposely and enjoying every minute of it.* She pushed her red hair from her face and went back toward her bed; it was calling her like it did of late. But before she got there, a splinter from the floor embedded itself in her big toe. "Oww," she clutched her foot and wobbled to the bed. "Why do you hate me?" She asked the Four without a hint of a jape.

Using her nails, she removed the splinter, throwing it under her bed. She was tired of crying so much. Instead, she just sat with no expression on her face. Everything bad kept happening to her. With her luck, Ultiir will emerge from the trees with his army and a dozen dragons and burn her as she stands. "I wonder if I would cry then," she said to herself.

There was a knock, and before she could say anything, the door opened. Yvanne closed her eyes for a moment, worried she would hear the baby's cries, but it was just Jacka. "Your Grace," she bowed. "I've come to check on you."

"I'm feeling much better," Yvanne said as she crossed her legs on her bed. "Thank you, Jacka. How is my sister? And the baby?"

"They're fine as well. Maliz is feeding Seine so much. The babe is a hungry one," Jacka chuckled. "The Lady Lolly is worried about you, but she knows you'll be back to your old self soon."

Yvanne nodded. Eventually she wouldn't be so overburdened with sadness and anger and nothingness and finally feel love … or something for her child, and for everyone else. Except she couldn't imagine a world where that was possible. "What if I'm stuck like this?" she asked her handmaid. "What if I'll never be happy again? I can barely remember a time when I was. I think sometime before Devro marched into Whitehall, I enjoyed my daily prayers with Helge, gossiping about the town, but that was so long ago. Ever since then, it's been nothing but destruction and maiming and betrayal and murder and death. Death everywhere we turn. Did you smell Ritaeum when we crossed through the trees? All of those peasants killed by our army—my army—all stinking of rot and dried blood. I worry for what's to come next."

Jacka motioned to the bed, and Yvanne nodded; her handmaid joined her. "There has also been good," Jacka said with a smile. "You were named queen. You gained more respect than any other woman I've ever known, and you're younger than most. Remember how happy Lady Marla Mae was when we rescued her and the Whitefork? The smiles? Not to mention the baby you brought into this world, who I know isn't your favorite right now, but still," Jacka's eyes were lit like stars, "there's a beauty in birth. It's how we all came into this world. Doesn't that mean anything to you, my queen?"

Yvanne smiled and wiped forming tears. "You're smarter than I, that's for sure," she laughed. "Maybe if you remind me of all that, I'll get better faster."

"I hope so, Your Grace." Jacka bowed her head. Yvanne didn't know what came over her, but she grabbed Jacka and hugged her. She couldn't keep the tears from falling. She held her handmaid tight; one of the last reminders of Whitehall as everyone else grew old and died.

"Fire!" someone shouted outside the window.

Yvanne gripped her necklace, but it wasn't glowing. Bands of energy were pulled below her, she could tell the fire was inside the castle before Jacka even started coughing. "Is it below us?" Her handmaid asked.

"It must be," Yvanne said as she went to the window, slipping her shoes on as she ran. The soldiers close to the castle were running toward it; others in town looked confused or like they didn't care or hear the shouting. Tundavik left Devro with her brothers and bounded over the paths. "Maybe it's Lord Valles," Yvanne said. "Perhaps he's escaped."

Jacka coughed as a dark haze filled the room. "We need to leave then."

"I agree," Yvanne said. But when they reached the door, they heard metal on metal. "Wait," she grabbed Jacka, "it isn't safe."

"Neither is staying here."

The handle of the door jerked, and Yvanne pulled Jacka away. *I might not want to live right now, but that doesn't mean Jacka should die with me.* The door burst open, and in came Sir Mar, panting and sweating. A man in blue armor was dead behind him. "Lord Toware …" Mar said, "he's attacking us."

Yvanne didn't have time for questions. Mar pulled her and Jacka by their hands, and they ran through the corridors. His face had a streak of blood on it. The dead man must've been from Riverend since he was in blue, but Yvanne wasn't familiar with the Flewthmen. "Why is he doing this?" She asked as the smell of smoke filled the castle.

Mar halted and looked outside. The tree-like hunters descended on the courtyard, loosing arrows. Toware was hit, and Tundavik raced away. *I can't have Lord Vandes dying on me so soon. I need him for the war.*

"We must be careful," Mar said, but at the moment another blue man appeared from around the corner. His sword pointed out and facing Yvanne.

"We do not want to kill the queen," the blue man said. "We just want to hold her while we negotiate with the king."

Mar stepped forward, his sword unsheathed. "I will not let you take her."

There was a crash below somewhere in the castle, and Jacka gasped. "The baby," she whispered.

"One moment," Mar told the girls. He took a quick step and then ran at the blue man. Their swords clashed and clanged as they attacked and parried. Mar wasn't wearing his usual plate armor; he was just in leather. The attacker was in blue mail. Yvanne held her breath as Mar jumped over the sword that attacked his legs, then ducked as the sword swung over his head.

"This way," Jacka whispered again and pointed to a small side room. "There is a staircase in there." As metal clashed, Jacka opened the door, and Yvanne and her disappeared into the room. As they descended the narrow stairs, the screams outside grew louder. She prayed Mar would be alright and that the fighting wouldn't become a civil war. *But the gods seem to hate me now,* she thought as they reached another room at the bottom of the steps.

In the corridor, there was only one way to go; a burning fire of yellow blocked the other. Jacka and Yvanne both coughed as they kept their heads below the smoke that rose to the ceiling. "The baby is over there," Jacka pointed to a room where the door had been kicked in. Yvanne's heart fell. Fell. She had been so worried about herself that she forgot she had a baby, and worst of all, Lady Lolly and Maliz could be dead. *Then I'd have to take care of my child all alone.*

But Lolly and Maliz were both alive when they entered the room, though coughing as they covered their mouths with clothes. The baby cried as Maliz held her. Lolly held a cracked vase, blood at the bottom. A dead man with a bloody skull lay at her feet, his blue armor not protecting him. "I'm sorry … I'm …" Lolly said through chattering teeth.

"We must leave," Yvanne said over the sounds of fighting outside, the roaring fire, and the cries of the infant.

The ladies followed Yvanne out the door. The flames licked the ceiling above as the corridor was bright with reds and yellows. Her necklace burned at her throat. "Go without me," she told the women. "I'm going to do what I can to stop the fire from spreading."

"Your Grace," Jacka said, "that is asinine. There is no way—"

"—I'm not arguing," Yvanne shouted. "All of you, leave and get to safety. We'll meet in the courtyard when the fighting is done."

Yvanne could see on Jacka's face that she wanted to argue more, but when the baby coughed instead of cried, her face turned sad. "Don't die on us," Jacka said as she pushed the women out of the corridor.

Yvanne turned to the fire as it encroached on her. Her bedchamber above was surely gone, but she could still keep the castle from burning, and save anyone who couldn't get out in time. The only problem was that she had never stopped a fire before. Wisps of energy flowed to the fire, but when she took in power, they diverted to her. She held out her hands at the fire, hoping to take all the energy from it and store it inside herself. Her fingers went red, her skin burned, her hair smelled like it was burning.

But the fire was shrinking. The smoke was fading. She smiled at the thought of saving everyone, even her baby. The red from her fingers slowing crept up her arm like a vine, spreading, infecting. But it felt good. It was the first time in weeks she had felt any sort of power. Her heart was bursting with joy as it beat, her skin turning the color of her hair, the fire dissipating in the hall. She took a few steps forward, and more swirls of energy flowed into her from the flames. It would be over soon. Hopefully, Toware would be defeated, and they could all move on to more important matters. Hopefully, Yvanne would feel better.

The fire was gone, all of its might taken and stored in her. She was shaking as her skin itched from the burning. Her sunstone was so bright it cast a light on the wall. It was a small storage room that had been set alight, and a door to the outside had burned. She walked over the charred remains of wood and food, and reached the grass. She could feel the blades beneath her foot. The sole of her foot was flames, and below the grass turned black from the heat. There were shouts and screams from the city as Toware stalked to Tundavik and Devro. *Maybe I should help them. Show everyone I'm a mage.* She scoffed at herself. *I do that, and everyone turns their anger from Toware to me.* So she ran into the woods beyond the small town, leaving black footprints.

Yvanne tripped over tree roots and scampered through leaves and creeks. The burning in her chest and arms and legs and head grew ever hotter. It was as if she were actually on fire. She clutched her arms and groaned as she ran deeper into the woods. When she could no longer see Ritaeum or any orchards, she fell to the ground and cried. *It was a mistake to take all that energy,* she thought. *I should've let the castle burn. Let everything burn.*

Then, a fireball exploded where she lay.

Ultiir

He had won.

Sophie was in the dungeon. Tedbalt was dead. The lords of the court were trapped in the throne room. He hadn't felt this good since before he had murdered his brother. "I knew things would get better." He said to himself in his bedchamber. All the horrors that were inflicted on him were just to strengthen him. And strong he was. He slipped on his red cloak, feeling the power of the entire kingdom on his shoulders. It was finally time to end all the petty feuds and rule Viguran the way he wished.

Outside the window, far below in the city, it was quiet. Rebuilding after the siege was ongoing. The Rat's Nest still burned, and all the vermin dealt with. There were no riots. No shouts. His city was at peace. All he needed now was to be rid of the bastard, and Lord de'Marisco was supposed to be working on that. Within a month or two, he would be the sole ruler of Viguran. His kingdom united again.

The Cliffs of Iron to the north of the River Montla glowed with the sun. Beyond that were fields and rolling hills for hundreds of miles. Soon it would be full of wheat, and the kingdom would be back to prosperity. He wanted to rebuild the kingdom to the status it had centuries ago when the king of Viguran ruled from the Ters-Veck to the Sylvastist Pass. *I will do it,* he thought. Viguran would be the greatest kingdom in the world once more. All he needed now was to get the lords of the court back on his side. With Sophie imprisoned, it shouldn't be so hard, and if they resist, then they too will be thrown in the dungeon.

Ultiir took a deep breath and whipped his cloak around as he found the door. Sir Gid was waiting in his golden cloak with Lord Urses de'Marisco. The lord was skinnier than when he'd arrived. Gid was withholding food as much as he could. "Your Grace," Gid bowed. "I brought the prisoner."

"Prisoner, Gid?" Ultiir scoffed. "Not anymore," he said as he placed a hand around Urses' shoulder. "This is my new chief commander."

The lord's eyes grew large. "Your Grace," his smile was small and his eyes moved as if he were thinking, "I cannot command an army. I've never held a sword."

"But you were with the bitch during her campaign out of the mountains, were you not? You were in Goldfield when it fell. Surely you saw much and more fighting and killing. More than I have for sure." Ultiir pushed on Urses' back and led him down the corridor. "My lord," Ultiir continued, "to be honest, I have very few people I can trust in this palace. I'm remembering the fond memories we share. Hopeful that you will find it in yourself to forgive me for the torture."

They made their way downstairs. The metal clang of Gid's boots reminded him of the boots that ran through the palace searching for Sophie. When he had seen the bloodshed that had transpired, he was worried she was dead; he needed her alive to see what a king he would be without her meddling. When Sir Ard wished to clean the mess Ultiir had told him, "Leave it. Let it stain the walls and floors. I want generations from now to see what happens when you betray your king. I want them to know I was strong. That they too would've feared me." Sir Ard had nodded, and ever since then he had averted his gaze whenever Ultiir was around.

Urses cleared his throat. "Your Grace," he waited a moment in silence. "It would be dishonorable not to take your kind offering. Allowing me back onto the council would allow me to prove myself to you."

"You're doing that with your letters. Gid told me you received word from some lord in Ritaeum?"

"Yes," he nodded. "some lord who is upset at Yvanne—"

"—the bitch," Ultiir interrupted.

"Yes … the bitch. Some lord who would love to see her pay for leading his troop to slaughter."

"I can't wait to see it unfold. You can tell all the councilors in our meeting later. You've big shoes to fill with Lord Hirons dead. He guided me through the outbreak of the war, and even as he started to falter, he still had sage advice. Shall we win this war? Together?"

Urses nodded with a smile.

They made their way to the front doors of the royal court. There was jabbering inside. Some banging on walls. Ultiir's guard had surrounded the exits. All lords and ladies of the court were to be kept inside until Ultiir decided they had learned their lesson. Going against him was a fool's errand, and he needed them to know that.

"Your Grace," Sir Ard said with a nod and a look into the distance. "They're ready to see you now. We've given them some food, and the animals raged over it. But we haven't been able to clean it very well. It still smells in there a bit."

"The stench of piss and shit never killed anyone, my good sir," Ultiir said. "Open the doors."

The large wooden doors groaned open. Inside, the many lords and their ladies and servants and pages all gasped for air like they had been underwater. His ears filled with a cacophony of shouts and pleads and questions as he walked down the center of the throne room. Guards pushed back lords who dared get too close. His red cloak flowed behind him as he split the sea of people. His throne rose high at the far end of the room as it bathed in the sun's yellow light. Some manor lord rubbed his eyes awake and jumped from the chair as Ultiir's men descended on him.

Ultiir turned and sat, the lords all crying over one another. Ladies in the corner weeping. The shouts echoed and shook the rafters above. "Enough," Ultiir said. Sir Gid cleared his throat to take control of the room, but Ultiir got there first. "Enough!" He shouted over the mess. "Your king has sat the throne," Ultiir yelled. "Listen here, or face my guards." The room quieted as Gid held his sword hilt.

Lord Tylar pushed his way through the crowd, Lords Ripple and Clye followed. Count Ompter stood near a batch of Eastlander lords. Lord Mer Lasie sat with his arms crossed, his leg broken with a splint.

"My lords," Ultiir began, his voice echoing now. "It's a beautiful day outside; why are you all cooped up in here? Oh, it's because you betrayed me." Ultiir shook his head. Lord Tipe lowered his head. Lady Yura in the corner cowered. "Decided to exert any power you think you have and go against me. I'll have you know that my bitch wife's ploy didn't work. I would say it was a folly. Because while you are all in here, withering and loathing and wondering what you did to deserve this, she is in the dungeon, starving, wishing she had never called upon you to take over my throne room." There were a few gasps in the room, which Ultiir would need to make note of. He needed to remind any loyal to Sophie that they would be jailed or killed. *Nothing less,* he thought.

"That's right. Mine. You've all been deluded into thinking you make the laws of this land. That you have power. Influence. It is only tradition that I even call court to session. The king rules by absolute right. *He* has since Valor the Iron aligned this land under his vision. Somewhere deep in my family ancestry, I am descended from that mighty man. That great king. Over the years, the court has tried to take more and more power. So I ask myself, what would Valor the Iron do? What would the first king of our glorious kingdom do?

"Well, he would of course kill every single one of you for going against my directive. For being openly hostile to the king. Burn you alive. Sic hounds on you. Bring the best swordsmen to hack you all to bits." Now their faces dropped. Any anger they might have had was gone. Even the sunken eyes of the hungry looked afraid. "But that's what Valor would do. You're lucky though … I am not the Iron. I am Ultiir the Savior. And saviors help people; they allow second chances. So that is what I will do. I will allow you each to swear fealty to me once more, to denounce the wickedness of the queen. Once you have done so, I will send you on your way. Home. If the war has destroyed your manor or town, then start rebuilding. The bastard's days are numbered. It's time for a glorious rebirth of our kingdom. One ruled solely by me without the false idea that lords hold any power. So get to it. My guards are here, and they thirst for blood."

First was Lord Dally. He was from some small hamlet in the Woodlands. He bowed at Ultiir's feet and said in a deep voice, "Please forgive me, Your Grace. Accept this as my apology as I swear fealty to you and your descendants. My lands and my incomes are all allied with you forevermore. I will never go against you again."

Ultiir couldn't help but smile as more and more lords followed Dally's lead. Even Lady Ballis came forward. Ultiir rolled his eyes as the woman bowed and swore nothing to him as she owned nothing. Her husband dead sometime ago.

Lord Tylar Temps was next. He was a young, angry man. And he had been close to Sophie ever since his father had been killed in the riots. *With him swearing his allegiance, than I will know I have truly won them over.*

Tyler walked up the shallow steps. His knees never moved, though. Instead, his eyes were red with fury. "How dare you dishonor my father like this. He was a member of your court for thirty-odd years, and you trample on his legacy. You dishonor your wife too. The Book of the Four tells us to never—"

Sir Gid punched the stupid boy in the stomach with his gauntlet and let him fall to the floor. Lady Lin shook her head and gasped. Other lords and ladies followed in her footsteps. Gid yanked Tylar to his feet and pulled him to the door behind the throne, but the lord shouted. "How dare you touch me! I am a lord of the royal court! Of the greatest institution in our kingdom! Unhand me," he spat at Gid. "Unhand me!" His screams faded into the palace halls.

"Anyone else?" Ultiir asked as he leaned on the arm of the chair.

"Yes." A voice rang out near the doors. It was Lord Dovi Lyons. "I have seen how far you've fallen," the chief ambassador said as he made his way down the center of the room, much like Ultiir had done. "You have dismissed half your council and filled it with sycophants. I cannot stand here any longer and watch what you've done. I must resign my post." He unclipped his green robe and let it fall to the floor before stomping on it.

"Very well," Ultiir said. "I only wi—"

"I agree," Lord Wilt called out. "You are destroying this kingdom."

"Why should you hold all the power?" Lord Clye asked.

"This is our chamber now," Lady Yura called. "You've no power here any longer."

"Even I decide now," Lady Lin said.

Ultiir straightened his back and looked over the sea of red. Angry shouts filled the air. Shouts that questioned his authority. Some that were sympathetic to Sophie. Others that told him to step down or risk revolt.

"Enough!" he shouted again, knowing they would not risk death. But they didn't listen. Instead, they worked each other into a frenzy. Ultiir's guards huddled closer to him, Gid ran back into the room.

"Down with you!" someone called. "Down with the king!" Another. "You should fear us!"

Ultiir rubbed his temples as his head ached, but he couldn't drown out the yells. "Get me out of here," he said to Gid.

Sir Gid unsheathed his sword even though no lords were advancing on them. The lords were instead throwing anything they could at the windows. Glass shattered. Some even crawled out of their confinement. Ultiir stopped looking as he and his guards left the throne room to be overrun with savage demons.

"What are they doing?" Ultiir clenched his jaw. Sir Gid shrugged as others blocked the door.

Sir Velle came from around the corner. "Your Grace, are you alright?" He asked but never looked into Ultiir's eyes.

"No, I am not alright. I need you to end this. Sic my guards on them and show all of those fucking monsters they shouldn't've gone against me."

Velle looked to the door. The other side was shouting and banging. There was no pleading this time. It was pure anger. "No," Velle said softly.

"What?" Ultiir and Gid asked at the same time.

Velle gulped and stood tall. "I will not kill innocent lords you locked away. I will not follow your heinous rule any longer."

Old Gid, even in his ancient years, moved like a predator. He ripped Velle's helm off and pulled on the man's hair. As Velle cried out in pain, Gid dragged him to the door and opened it before throwing the knight inside. A tuft of brown hair in Gid's hands. "I will handle this," Old Gid said. Men-at-arms followed Gid's lead and, as the door shut to muffle the sounds, Ultiir heard screams of terror.

I didn't want them to rule with me anyhow, Ultiir thought. *This is a much easier way to get rid myself of them and their schemes.*

Ultiir rubbed his neck as he made his way toward the council chamber. Eventually, the chaos would die down, and the day would continue like normal. Ultiir would come together with the rest of his followers to formulate his new plans.

He sat alone in the chamber, clouds moving over the sun and casting a gray light behind him. The candles in the council room hadn't been lit, so he sat in the dark, listening to the wailing of traitor lords.

He had won.

Yvanne

Devro stood over a kneeling Lord Cul. "We thank you for your service," her husband said. The lord and his warriors from the peaks were all shrouded in blue blankets as the moon was high in the sky and candles lit the yard. While Yvanne was off in the woods dying, Lord Cul and his fighters had descended on Lord Toware and the mutineers. She didn't know exactly what had happened, having heard so many stories.

The Peakmen either attacked the men of Riverend with swords and shields like they usually did, or wrapped around them all and used their teeth to suck the men's blood. Then the bodies were either looted, spared, or raped. Lord Toware taken by Lord Cul himself. The men were then hacked to bits and fed to the pigs, or thrown in a mass grave. Yvanne believed the parts that seemed possible. She had traveled a long time with Cul and the Peakmen, and not once did they drink the blood of their enemies or rape corpses.

The council all gathered in the castle courtyard. What was left of Miena's Hunters stood in a corner, their eyes downcast as a grave for Ainmel had been dug. There were other graves too, but it was tradition for the leader of the hunters to be given a place of honor. Toware and his men didn't kill many, luckily. Cul was too quick to respond to the threat, and others Tundavik had brought were also loyal to Devro. Commander Wright and Lord Tylo both ushered their troops into battle.

And Lord de'Marisco betrayed me. I wonder what it's like to be able to trust your lords. Yvanne sighed from her place beside Devro. She had been standing outside longer than she had since giving birth. Mar was next to her. His leg bandaged, but he was still alive. Lord Vandes was rubbing his face across from them. He looked even more tired than before. With his shaved face, the wrinkles were more prominent around his mouth. His cheeks drooped. His hair graying quicker than ever.

"We should talk about what happened, Your Grace," Cul said as he stood and backed away. Lord Aimora Dore was near him. Yvanne's brothers were both listening to the council and standing guard by the castle gate.

"We survived," Devro said. "That's all that matters."

"I agree with Lord Cul," Tundavik said. "We must figure out a way to keep other lords from betraying us."

"The only way to do that is to send them home," Aimora said. "Isn't that what Toware wanted?" he spat, "to go back to his river lands? It's that or fear."

"Well, what we did to Lord Toware should be enough to cause fear in the ranks." Lord Tylo said. He was smiling, happy to be part of the council, it seemed. "If any other lords or soldiers wish to mutiny, they will think twice now lest they want to end up like Toware—bloody and bloated and, most of all, dead."

"We also have Lord Valles to deal with," Lord Aimora said.

"Toware put off his trial, but he still rots in the dungeon asking for his family. As long as he stays alive, there will always be those who wish him as lord. They might even fight us for it."

Devro rolled his eyes, the night sky swallowing him. "Lord Valles should be happy his family didn't die in the fire."

Because I saved them, Yvanne thought. She had taken the power from the flames and exploded in the forest. Never had that happened before; she thought she was dead until Mar found her. Her body was alright, her hair not burned, her skin not charred. But her clothes were gone. She lay naked in the forest. Trees and leaves and animals around her all dead and black from her flames.

"I'm lucky it was you who found me," Yvanne had told Mar when she was back in the castle and clothed. "If anyone else did … Well I don't want to think of it."

Mar groaned from the wound on his leg. His calf had been cut in two. "Very lucky," he agreed. "But I worry people will still whisper about what happened. How you disappeared." He had eyed his sword. "I'll stay close to you. You be sure you watch your back the best you can."

So Yvanne made sure her back was clear and prayed that no one would do anything to hurt her or even her baby.

"We also must consider our next move," Diero said from the closed gate. "The men have been training, but with no one to fight, they will get bored and long to return to their fields for harvest, if there is one."

"I say," Gordo said next, "that we find Onnu Valles guilty of treason, have the lords of the Woodlands declare their allegiance to us, and march back on Vigur while Ultiir is weakened. We still don't know if the Terropians will show up, and so far they haven't. We must take the capital before they arrive, Your Grace."

Aimora sighed before saying, "And going back to do the same at the capital will boost morale? My Lodean are ready of course, but others may not be happy about it. We can hold a siege for only so long."

"As we saw," Pollard added from the other side of the dimly lit courtyard.

Devro stifled a yawn. "Tundavik," he said to the old lord, "why don't you ride around the Woodlands with some men and find out which lords are traitors. Any that don't bend to me will need to be put to death." Tundavik nodded along with some other lords. Pollard in the back rolled his eyes. "I will sentence Lord Valles to death. It is the only way to show what happens to those who go against me."

Now Tundavik's eyes were wide. "My king, I again ask we show mercy."

"Mercy?" Devro laughed and looked beyond everyone in the courtyard, staring at ghosts or dreams or nothing. "He led a fight against me. I can't show the rest of the kingdom that I'm lenient toward betrayal. Onnu will die tomorrow. I will need an executioner."

"What of his family?" Cul asked. "His wife and daughter? As long as they're alive, there will be those who want his daughter to take over as duchess, as Yvanne did for her father."

"So death," Lord Tylo said. Some lords nodded, even her brothers. Tundavik shook his head, Commander Wright from the Fall pursed his lips, even angry Lord Cul scratched at his head.

How many would've killed me? Yvanne thought.

"I agree with Lord Vandes," Yvanne said to her young husband. "I would show them all leniency, especially the daughter. She has done nothing wrong."

"I knew you would say that." Devro chuckled. "But because you are a duchess means others will fight for women to take over their father's lands. It's dangerous."

"So you're going to kill the young girl?" Yvanne turned her whole body to face Devro.

"Tomorrow," Devro rubbed his eyes, "I will take Lord Valles' head. His wife and daughter will be ..." he again looked at no one but nodded, "... will be hanged."

Yvanne imagined herself hanging from a rope. Imagined her baby. It was enough to make her vomit, but she kept it down. "I will not be part of this," she told Devro, who dropped his mouth slightly. "This is monstrous, something your uncle would do."

"And he doesn't have traitors in his ranks, does he?"

Yvanne gulped to keep down what she wanted to say, all the curses that wanted to fly from her mouth. "I'll be going now," she said. Pollard was smiling as he took a few steps forward to meet her. Mar scratched his eye but followed her as well. No one spoke as she left the courtyard and went into the castle, tears bubbling in her eyes.

***

Lady Lolly made sure the baby had nothing around her as she went to sleep. Maliz was snoring in the corner. Jacka was sorting clouts for the baby. Yvanne stood in the doorway, with Pollard and Mar just outside. The bedchamber had a few candles burning as night swept over them, the light bouncing off the walls. When Jacka saw her queen, her eyes lit up. "Seine is sleeping," her handmaid said. "Please come sit."

Yvanne carefully sat on a wooden stool next to Jacka's chair. They had moved rooms since the old one had a dead man in it. Lolly had said, "That will curse Seine and our family for a hundred years. We must wash out the evil and never let her back in the room." She didn't know whether that was true. Helge never said anything about that, but Lolly had killed a man, and Yvanne could see in her eyes that she was broken.

Lolly crossed her legs on the ground in front of Yvanne and grabbed her hand. Lolly's eyes were glossy; her cheeks looked recently dry from tears. "You mustn't be too hard on yourself," Yvanne whispered as she stroked Lolly's hand. "Who knows what that man would've done if you weren't there."

Her sister nodded before quickly wiping an eye. "Yes, but Swallow tells us not to kill, that Vigura will judge us harshly. I ... killed ..."

"Vigura would be a fool to judge you harsh," Yvanne said. Lolly touched four fingers to her heart to forgive Yvanne for talking badly about the god. "I'm sure a doma would say the same. Perhaps when we take the capital, you can speak with the high doma, and he will show you that what you did is not sinful."

"That would be nice," Lolly said faintly. "Have you given it anymore thought?"

It was sending the baby away with Lolly and Maliz, far away to the West. One of Yvanne's sisters was the lady of

Meera, married to the lord. It was so far away Yvanne had never heard news from the city. It was possible her sister, Delia, was marching an army across Adedor to help Yvanne, or that she was already dead. But it was a risk Yvanne had to take. "I think it's for the best," she said. "I can get you a wagon. Pollard has already spoken to a trader in town. He'll help you to Ealna, where you can hire a ship."

"Okay," Lolly said as she bit her lip, "but I don't want to leave you. Maliz can look after Seine without me."

Yvanne was already shaking her head. "I trust you the most with my daughter, and Delia knows you; she'll be happy to see her sister again. You know you cannot stay."

"I know."

"Have you packed?"

Jacka leaned forward and said, "Yes, I've been adding whatever I can think of to the sacks and packs." She pointed to a few bags in the room's corner. "I believe they can leave whenever."

"How about tonight?" Yvanne cracked her knuckles.

Lolly's voice got louder. "Tonight?" but she quieted it when she looked to the baby. "Why tonight? I thought we'd have a few more days."

"I need you to take some people to Ealna with you. They don't have to get on the boat, but they need to get out of Ritaeum."

"And who would that be?" Lolly asked.

"I can't tell you," Yvanne said, "but know they will do you no harm. I'm helping them escape the Woodlands."

As if on cue, the door opened, and Mar peeked through. "They're next door, Your Grace."

"Get everything ready," Yvanne said to the women. "Pollard will escort you to the wagon, and I'll be by soon." She left the room without saying another word. She didn't have time to explain. In the bedchamber just next door were two cloaked figures, one tall and the other small. When the door was closed, they took their hoods off to reveal themselves as Lord Valles' wife and daughter.

"What do you want?" The wife, Femke, said in a raspy voice. "Why were we woken?"

Yvanne shut the door and whispered. "You must stay quiet and not react when I tell you."

"No promises." Femke crossed her arms.

"My husband, the king, is executing Lord Valles tomorrow." Yvanne said. Femke smacked her lips while the daughter, Filla, gulped. "He wishes for you both to be executed as well."

Femke grabbed her daughter's shoulder. "So what are we doing here? Are you trying to scare us? Help us? I see no reason you would do either."

"I'm helping you leave this castle before you are both hanged."

Filla's eyes filled with tears. Seeing how young the girl was made Yvanne even angrier at Devro for wishing to tie a noose around her neck. *How would we live with himself after that? How could he allow it?*

"And Onnu?" Femke asked.

Yvanne shook her head. "It's too dangerous to get him out, I'm sorry. And you won't be able to say goodbye either, with the guards always there. I'm afraid you'll never see him again."

Femke's nostrils flared. "And where are you taking us?"

"Ealna. It's the closest place that will get you out of harm's reach. There are ships that can take you anywhere in the world. I'll even give you some coin."

"So generous," Femke said without a hint of emotion. "When do we leave?"

"But Daddy," Filla's voice broke.

"Shush," Femke rubbed her daughter's back, "we must do as she says. I don't want you to get into trouble."

Yvanne shook her head at the thought of Devro and the lords who agreed with him. Even her own brothers. "We leave now."

Femke and Filla hooded themselves while Mar ushered them through the castle. The courtyard had gotten quiet. No more lords arguing or speaking. It was empty. A few candles burned along the walls, and a guard would walk through every now and then. The castle walls also had guards atop them. It was nothing new. Yvanne knew they'd be there, but she was the queen, and she should be able to go anywhere she liked.

Instead of making a ruckus and having the main gate opened, they slipped out the postern gate that led them away from town. There were large shadows in the distance, but they were merely trees. And before the dark forests that spread throughout were Pollard and the women with the baby and wagon. The babe was swaddled as tightly as she could be, and Lolly was holding her close.

"We must be quick," Pollard said, "before Seine wakes up."

The trader who owned the wagon was brushing his horses and checking their shoes. The wagon was loaded full of the packs. Jacka made sure one of them was tightly bound. "All's ready," she whispered.

Maliz jumped onto the wagon, her face puffy from sleep,

and reached for the baby. "Would you like to say goodbye?" Lolly asked Yvanne as she held the child.

Below Yvanne was a sleeping babe. Only her face was visible. Her eyes were closed, her nose was so small it was barely there, her cheeks red. The wisps of hair on her head just poking out from the blanket. "Goodbye, my little baby," Yvanne said. "Hopefully, when I see you again, it will be safe and I'll …" she didn't want everyone to hear, but she couldn't pull Lolly and the child away when they had to leave so soon, "… maybe I'll love you then."

No one said anything. Lolly carefully handed the child to Maliz before hugging Yvanne. "I will see you again. If you must, then come to Delia's. We'll be waiting." Yvanne nodded as she helped Lolly onto the wagon.

Femke and a crying Filla followed. "We will be alright," the mother said to her daughter as they hugged.

"I'll see them to safety," Pollard nodded to Yvanne. "Don't let the bastard do anything to you, especially while I'm away." He turned to Mar, who was stretching his leg. "I know you are close to the king, but if he hurts her—"

"—relax," Mar said. "There's a better chance Devro does nothing to her when I'm around. Now get going before the whole castle notices something is wrong."

Pollard cleared his throat and climbed atop the wagon. The trader flicked the reins, and the horses started moving over the dirt paths that eventually led to Ealna. It was incredibly dangerous, not only because of the war but also storms, or bandits, or the baby's head jerking while on a ship. Yvanne prayed the women would keep her safe. Keep Seine safe.

"Did I do the right thing?" She asked Mar when they were

the only two left in the night.

Mar looked to the stars and sighed. "Some won't see it that way, but I do, and I know Tundavik will understand as well. The people of Ritaeum have been mentioning random disappearances of others, maybe they'll think that's what happened to the women." He shrugged. "It's good to have you back."

Yvanne smiled at the knight. She was proud of herself, prouder than she had ever been. Happy that the women, the child, and even her baby would be safe. "I'm glad to be back."

List of Characters

The Coastal March:

Tundavik Vandes - once a duke in Viguran who came back after living in Baragio

Sir Mar - knight of Viguran and member of Devro's guard

Glem - a young man who squires for Tundavik

Lord Toware - lord of the Riverend

Lord Tylo - lord of Heavensfield

Lord Furrow - lord of Nye

Lady Ceala - lady of the Fall

Commander Wright - commander of Lady Ceala's forces

Lord Leur - lord of Saltcreek and a bitter rival to Lady Ceala

Gordo - father of Glem

Marya - mother of Glem

The Mountain March:

Yvanne - the young queen of Viguran, lady of Whitehall, and duchess of the Lands of Asara, also the last daughter of the late David Rely

Lord Aimora Dore - lord of Lodeanhold

Lord Cul - lord of Mount Meret

Lord Urses de'Marisco - lord of Keeland and an adviser to Yvanne

Sir Tiro - a young man in Whitehall who was knighted

by Yvanne

Sir Pollard - knight of Whitehall, David's youngest son, and Yvanne's brother

Lord Diero - lord of Weather's Edge in Maertan and a son of David Rely

Lord Gordo - lord of Haven's Field in Rowan and a son of David Rely

Lady Lolly - lady of River Tree and a daughter of David Rely

Ed the Loon - next in line to rule Gamm Lars in Plajul and a son of David Rely

Lady Marla Mae - lady of the Whitefork

Lord Oda Mae - lord of the Whitefork

Jacka - Yvanne's handmaid

Besta - a Lodean man

Orra - a Lodean man with red hair

Sir Rickart - a knight of Whitehall

Sir Loc - a knight of Whitehall

Kinglands:

King Ultiir de'Tro - King of Viguran, lord of Goldfield, and Sophie's husband

Queen Sophie Margia - Queen of Viguran, Princess of Terrop, Duchess of Aele, Hurvir's fourth wife before his death, and now Ultiir's wife

Hurvir de'Tro - previous king of Viguran, Sophie's husband, the father of Devro, and was killed during his feast

Rila de'Tro - Queen Mother of Viguran, mother of Hurvir, Ultiir, and Analere, and was married to King Ferrick of Viguran

Analere de'Tro - the last surviving sibling of Ultiir who was recalled from Pleat Isle by her brother, also a daken

Devro - the young, captured king of Viguran, bastard son of Hurvir de'Tro, and nephew of Ultiir

Lord Tedbalt Masson - chief consultant on the King's Council

Lord Edel de'Viere - chief informant on the King's Council

Lord Alan Hirons - chief commander on the King's Council

Lord Serle Verrier - chief ambassador on the King's Council

Lord Dovi Lyons - chief collector on the King's Council

Lord Henk Zazí - lord of the recaptured Redington

His Most Holy Maller - High Doma of Viguran

Countess Filra - lady of the Queen's Council

Lady Betal - lady of the Queen's Council who was recalled to Ghostfield by her husband

Baroness Mara - lady of the Queen's Council and wife to the Baron of Sheplan

Lady Ficca - lady of the Queen's Council

Lady Abre Volles - lady of the Queen's Council who went back to Oceantree

Lady Rila - former lady of the Queen's Council who was killed in the Vigur riots

Lady Alba - lady of Midriver

Lord Mer Lasie - lord of the royal court and from Sayer's River

Lord Tylar - lord in the royal court in Vigur

Count Ompter - lord in the royal court in Vigur

Lord Ripple - lord in the royal court in Vigur

Lord Clye - lord in the royal court in Vigur
Lord Wilt - lord in the royal court in Vigur
Sir Achen - chief knight of Sophie's guard
Sir Velle - member of Sophie's guard
Sir Lovis - former chief knight of Ultiir's guard who was killed in the Vigur riots
Sir Ard - member of Ultiir's guard
Sir Gid - chief knight of Ultiir's guard
Amalla - Sophie's handmaid
Renna - Sophie's handmaid from Zhepatev in Masa Naq
Olier - the palace jailer

Eastlands:
Duke Adyn Gallient - Duke of the Eastlands
Lady Annue Gallient - the Duke's elder sister and first wife of King Hurvir
Lord Delan - lord of Ruwy and the father of Reran and Mar
Lady Memi - lady of Ruwy, wife of Delan, and mother of Reran and Mar
Reran - heir to Ruwy and Mar's brother
Luxe - Reran's wife
Orson - Reran's son

Flewthlands:
Duke Pyre Blume - Duke of the Flewthlands
Lady Flora - lady of Woodrun, Pyre's daughter, Barnet's wife, and Florance's mother
Lord Barnet Lovell - lord of Woodrun, husband of Flora, and father of Florance
Florance - daughter of Flora and Barnet

Lady Lueva - wife of Lord Toware and who has an amputated leg

Nama - maid in the service of Flora and Barnet

Lila - servant in the Storyah castle

Lord Poden Bruce - lord of River Watch

Sir Edmond - chief knight to Duke Blume

Sir Marbert - knight from Grass Ridge

Sir Len - knight in River Watch

Vanette - prostitute in River Watch

Lord Olette - lord of Meadowton

Lord Rickart - lord of Uphain, known as the Crazed

Lands of Asara:

David Rely - Former Duke of the Lands of Asara

Cada - lady of Sea Snake, Sidoro's wife, one of David Rely's daughters, and Yvanne's half-sister

Sidoro - lord of Sea Snake in Terrop

Helge - local doma of Whitehall

Sir Groel - knight of Whitehall

Sir Rye - knight of Whitehall

Arold - swordmaster of Whitehall

Dera - daken from Midvalley

Lord Plantan - lord of Mount Swallow

Lord Emni - lord of Mount Samosay

Lord Aute - lord of Mount Doma

Lord Edward Tall - lord of Hightail

Woodlands:

Lord Onnu Valles - Duke of the Woodlands

Lady Femke - the wife of Lord Onnu Valles

Filla - the daughter of Femke and Onnu

Lady Abre Volles - lady of the Queen's Council who went back to Oceantree to fight for her inheritance
Lord Embalt Velkes - lord of Corville
Ainmel - a hunter for Miena
Maliz - a nursemaid
Lolan - a barber in Ritaeum

the Sea:
King Baldewin Thomas - King of Rowan and Bartel's youngest child
Blis - teacher to the royal family
Mari - Aveline's handmaid and close confidant
Caxton - leader of the king's council
Wycleaf - a member of the king's council
Jac - a member of the king's council
Sir Delmar - household guard for the king of Rowan
Captain Pitor - captain of the king's ship
Potter - a young man who escaped from a prison in Vidale

the South:
Bertin - Prince of Rowan
Torlem - an elf hunter
Barhi - an elf hunter
Faci - a healer who lives along the Bezir
Ioela - an elf in Ansehar
Aveline - Princess of Rowan, the eldest child and only daughter of Bartel
Zoell - one of Aveline's guards
Bert - one of Aveline's guards
Ivlin - one of Aveline's guards
Tomas - one of Aveline's guards

Dern the Third - one of Aveline's guards
Badyn - an elf child in Anha Jorbstah
Chel - an elf in the Pywaln Pass
Maddel - an elf in the Pywaln Pass
Sayla - a seer in Jorbstah and Filik's sister
Filik - a hunchback in Jorbstah
Mother of the Forest - an ancient being in Sruhq

Rowan:
Hecher - the High Chancellor of the Royal Chancellery in Rowan, an elected position
His Most Holy Emmett - the High Doma of Rowan
William - a member of the king's council who has no tongue

Somewhere and Nowhere:
Raimund - a knight of Viguran who was captured and taken to the North, best friends with Mar and Devro
Nostara - a mysterious woman-like creature
Nardal - a dragon